Redemption's Song

REDEMPTION'S SONG

E. L. CROSS

Redemption's Song
Book Four in The Redemption Saga

Cover Design by Erin L. Cross

Ebook ISBN: 978-1-7363603-6-1
Paperback ISBN: 978-1-7363603-7-8

Other Books by E. L. Cross

※ ※ ※

The Redemption Saga

I. Redemption's Pursuit
II. Redemption's Call
III. Redemption's Embrace
IV. Redemption's Song
V. Redemption's Grace *(Summer 2022)*
VI. Redemption Abounding *(Winter 2023)*

To learn about new releases and read exclusive content, connect with E. L. Cross at www.elcrossbooks.com

Dedication

"See, I am doing a new thing!
Now it springs up; do you not perceive it?
I am making a way in the wilderness
and streams in the wasteland."
Isaiah 43:19 NIV

※ ※ ※

To my Love.
You will never know how much your character
and sacrificial love have inspired these stories.

Contents

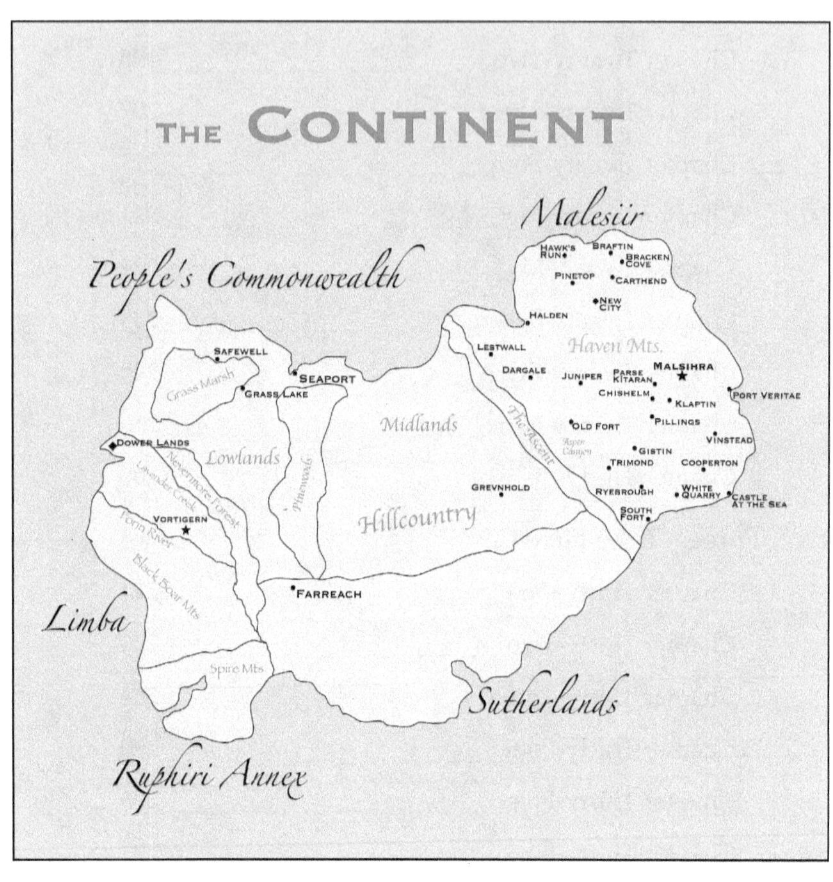
THE CONTINENT
Malesiir
People's Commonwealth
HAWK'S RUN
BRAFTIN
BRACKEN COVE
PINETOP
CARTHEND
NEW CITY
HALDEN
Haven Mts.
LESTWALL
DARGALE
JUNIPER
PARSE KITARAN
MALSIHRA
PORT VERITAE
CHISHELM
KLAPTIN
OLD FORT
PILLINGS
VINSTEAD
Aspen Canyon
GISTIN
TRIMOND
COOPERTON
RYEBROUGH
WHITE QUARRY
CASTLE AT THE SEA
SOUTH FORT
GREVNHOLD
The Ascent
Midlands
Hillcountry
SAFEWELL
SEAPORT
Grass Marsh
GRASS LAKE
DOWER LANDS
Lowlands
Pinewoods
Nevermore Forest
Lavender Creek
VORTIGERN
Forn River
Black Boar Mts
FARREACH
Limba
Spire Mts
Sutherlands
Ruphiri Annex

Part One

Streams in the Wasteland

Prologue

ERIANNA

October 20th

Strands of hair whip across my face as I stand at the foot of Leer's grave. I take my time this morning, lingering in the mists that hover over the snowy ground. I thought that today would undo me. I told Lorennt that I needed the day to myself. But as I stand over the graves, I only feel a sadness for what was lost and what could have been. I do not lay in the dirt or plead with the Almighty to reunite me with them as I did days after Leer's funeral.

I breathe deep the morning air, letting my sadness be felt to its fullest. But there is less depth to it than there once was. I feel like I have lost some of the woman that I was when I was married to Leer. I am not all of that version of myself anymore. Leer's wife has faded too.

The woman I am in this moment is tied to the land of the living. My gaze drifts away from the graveyard back to the castle. The elaborate structure with its robust walls and fanciful spires beckons me inside to greet the new day among my friends.

The chasm has grown so wide between Leer, Illyanna and I that holding on to the past no longer makes sense. I am grasping at memories that cannot be with me in the present.

It is time to let go.

I walk between their graves for the last time and make my final goodbyes. The memories that were once bright feel dull compared to the life around me. When I woke in the middle of the night, I sought the Almighty. I was completely honest and entrusted Him with all that I was thinking and feeling. After a time, my words ran out. I became still. He did not reveal all of my steps like I hoped, but He showed me the next one. With it came perfect peace.

The castle is stirring awake when I return. Servants move about the great hall, preparing it for the day. I take my breakfast in my room, leaving the courtly responsibilities to Lorennt.

The first step in letting go will be the hardest. My rooms are a shrine to Leer and Illyanna.

But I cannot live like this anymore.

I know the bedroom will be the easiest, so that is where I begin. Beyond the paintings gifted to me by Leelah's children, there is nothing much I want to bring with me. It all evokes memories of Leer. This was his room before it was ours, and despite my many playful threats to him, I never made good on redecorating it from the austere style he preferred. I toss my favorite pillow into a trunk along with the paintings. That is all.

Moving into the parlor is much more difficult. I shed a few tears over the chess board still missing some pieces. I forgot where I hid them. The chess board must stay. I refuse to recreate this space in my new room. Illyanna's empty cradle sits in a corner near the brazier. The table near the couch holds the book Leer was reading. One of my hair ribbons marks his place. I vaguely remember him reading to me those last few days. When I read the sentences on that page, I hear his voice. I lift the worn leather cover on the book once more, but force myself to close it, to let go.

The bookshelf is mine through and through. Half the volumes on it I stole from Valor's room. I stack the piles of books into the trunk and drag the shelf to the foyer. I collect an assortment of other random things from the parlor and add them to the pile.

The dressing room is the hardest.

I take my time sorting through our belongings. Leer's clothing—some which I embellished for him—provokes more memories than I can rightly keep at bay. I sit down in the middle of the room holding his red tunic, letting tears wash my face. After a time, I set aside the tunic and begin sorting my clothes.

Nev finds me seated on the floor surrounded by piles of dresses. "I came to see how you fare. Lorennt said you had trunks sent up."

"I am moving into my old room down the hall. It is time," I tell her while reminding myself for the hundredth time today.

"That seems wise. Would you like some help?"

I shake my head. "I thank you, but this is something I need to do."

Nev strokes my head, then lowers herself to the floor simply being with me so that I do not have to face this task alone.

I resume packing. It is necessary. My heart has known for awhile what it wants, though out of respect to my family and Leer, I shall still comport myself as his widow. But deep down, I have let him go and anxiously await the return of another.

CHAPTER ONE

ERIANNA

October 23rd

I raise my sword and charge my opponent. I hold nothing back. This time I will bring him to ground. He sidesteps me, deflecting the downward arc of my blade with a flick of his wrist. I correct my sword's path and step into my attack, using my body's momentum to put force behind my sword's cut. His connecting parry jars my arms, sending a line of pain through my shoulder. I ignore it, being careful not to allow our blades to lock at the cross guards where he will use his superior bulk to his advantage. Our blades sing as I slide my sword away from his, slipping away from his advance.

"Again!" He barks.

I feint twice then cut upward. His downward block looses the sword from my hands—more from the searing pain in my shoulder than from the precision of his movement. Instinct keeps the scream behind my teeth as I step out of his range, drawing a dagger with my left hand while cradling my right arm against my side.

Injured or not, a warrior must always be prepared to defend life and limb. Thankfully, my instructor does not make me prove my readiness this day as he has done in the past.

"Hold," Kragorn raises a staying hand and sheaths his sword.

My singleminded focus on battle flees the second my beautiful dagger is reunited with its scabbard. Unfortunately, without that focus, my mind turns to the next pressing matter—the throbbing pain in my shoulder. I whimper and sit on the dirt floor of the training room. Normally, we would be at the barracks in the city utilizing their large training rings, but Kragorn agreed to meet me at the castle today since my schedule is more restrictive than his.

Kneeling in the dirt with me, he braces his hands on the front and back of my shoulder and orders me to rotate it. I do so with teeth clenched tight and watering eyes, the only outward symptoms of pain I have not mastered.

"It is still in place," Kragorn determines and sits back on his heels. "I think it is time you accept the obvious."

"The obvious being that I will eventually find myself back in a sling? I have already arrived at that conclusion."

"No, the one after that."

"Which is?" I find my feet and take up my sword with my left hand.

He wisely steps back before saying, "You should abandon the sword."

"What!" I shout, brandishing the weapon in my clumsy off hand.

"Valor should have told you in Parse Kítaran."

"Nonsense. I simply need more muscle strength, more training." I place my left hand nearest the cross guard and use my right hand to steady the weapon near the pommel.

Kragorn dusts off his hands. "I am a weapons master. I have trained hundreds if not a thousand men to fight over the years. You and the sword are not suited."

"This is ridiculous! I must be able to fight with a sword. I was practically lamed without it in the city. Fighting from horseback with daggers is impractical."

"It is," he concurs. "Even so, you are not suited."

"So…" I drawl. A sometimes irritating habit of Kragorn's is his use of as few words as possible. He says what he means and little else. It is good that he was given a wife with many words to balance him. Thoughts of her present another valid argument. "Leelah can fight with swords."

"Leelah has never dislocated a shoulder. That can permanently weaken the tendons."

"Then teach me to fight left-handed."

"It will not help."

"Leelah can fight left-handed," I point out, tiring of this circular conversation. "If she can wield two swords, I can certainly manage one."

Kragorn crosses his arms and gives me his signature look—a scowl. "You are finer boned and smaller framed than Leelah. Even without an injured shoulder, you would not be able to do what she can do."

Seeming to have heard his own words after uttering them, he threatens, "If you ever repeat that to her, I will deny saying it."

Leelah would undoubtedly find insult in her husband's factual statement about her being of larger frame than most women. Since her temper tends to explode in every direction, I will not repeat his words.

"I had those swords made especially for her. Even so, I would not want her in a true battle."

"Why is that?"

"Take offense if you will," Kragorn shrugs, "but under normal circumstances, a woman can never hope to match a man for strength. Leelah can hold her own in short skirmishes with the best of fighters, but sustained fighting against men will weaken her faster than her opponents."

"I understand, but still I must be able to fight from the ground and from horseback. Would a custom sword help me?"

He considers me for a long moment, then his mouth twitches into a rare smile. "Come."

I follow him from the training room to the weapons room where he positions me in the middle.

"Assuming you master a sword, your reach is still short. You need an advantage." Kragorn selects a polearm from the racks along the wall and places it in my hands. "You are good with the quarterstaff. This will not feel much different."

Thinking he was about to give me a sword to compensate for my size and injury, I do not receive the polearm graciously. It offends.

The strong, inflexible ash pole is tipped with a two foot long curved blade. It is roughly eight feet in overall length and awkward. I have seen the cavalry practice with them before, but it is not practical to carry one with me at all times like I can carry a sword.

"You are not convinced," Kragorn notes.

I imagine myself lugging it through the castle and hand it back to him. "If I cannot use a sword, how am I supposed to use a sword on a stick? It is five times the weight of a sword."

Wearing a scowl of rebuke, he hefts the weapon and demonstrates. "This is a *glaive*. It is not the weight of the sword that is the problem for you. It is the force of your opponent against your inferior strength. This will compensate for your opponent's advantage with leverage and give you a longer reach. It can also be wielded from horseback."

"And it will fit so well on my weapons belt," I mock.

"This is a battle glaive. We will have a custom glaive made for you.

It is the ancient weapon of choice by warrior maidens of old. Especially against a man armed with a sword." He returns the weapon to the rack and strides from the room. I follow him back to the training room where he tosses me a squire's quarterstaff then draws his sword.

"Defend yourself!" Kragorn exclaims and charges me.

I dance to the side, blocking with the staff, turn, and strike for his feet. He hops over the staff and brings his sword down, nicking my arm.

"Kragorn! Stop!" I plead without effect.

I block another attack, bracing my hands wide on the staff, and catch his full strength on the wood. Astonishingly, it does not break. I pivot and knock the staff across his back. He lurches forward.

With fresh enthusiasm, I throw myself into the movements I know so well. I can block his sword without allowing him to close in on me. I am able to use leverage and agility without actually engaging him in a battle of strength. I also realize that I am not fatigued like when I fight with a sword. I have much more fight in me.

As it is, I cannot bring Kragorn to ground. He is simply too skilled. But, I see how much advantage I would have if my quarterstaff was tipped with a blade. Swallowing my pride, I concur with his assessment. In a battle or on horseback, this weapon would place me on nearly equal footing with men.

"What say you, Warrior Queen? Would you like a glaive for your own?"

I loose a feral grin. "I might."

"Good. This is the only thing of which you must be cautious." Kragorn arcs his blade. I parry, pivot, yet somehow he is upon me, advancing on my back that I left unguarded for a heartbeat. He shoves me forward. I feel a sword tip in the middle of my back.

"I yield," I say, for if I do not, Kragorn will prove that he has won the match by drawing more blood. Valor and Anders never do that. In fact, they rarely draw blood from me when I spar against them, though they have no such reserve with each other. It is only with Kragorn that I must be on my guard. He believes a little blood and pain lends authenticity to the match and increases my desire to win. He is correct, of course.

"When may we go to the armorer?"

"Immediately." Kragorn passes a cloth to me to staunch the trickle on my arm. I do not know when he cut me. "It will take him some time to complete. We may also go to the saddler to order your greaves."

My face heats. I intended to go with Valor but did not have the opportunity in the few days that he was in Malsihra after his last assignment. He set out to hunt the Ruphiri when they made a brazen attempt to raid the storehouses in Chishelm days after their attack here in the capital. They abandoned the scheme when our soldiers foiled their efforts after being alerted and thwarted by the townsfolk. It was satisfying to see our provisions pay off after the atrocity in Malsihra.

"You ought to have it done," Kragorn prods. "Valor made deposits at both shops for you, knowing he would be on assignment for a time."

"He did?" I knew about the greaves to protect my "fine legs," as he put it, but I did not know about the deposit at the armorer.

"Some excuse about you being properly armed and protected without taxing the kingdom's coffers."

"That is thoughtful, but unnecessary. I would not want him to expend so much on me, especially after buying the rest of my armor."

"And your horse and tack," Kragorn reminds me.

I shake my head. "Leer reimbursed him for those."

"I am sure the king would have, but Valor provided for you out of his own accounts while journeying across the continent. Every garment, every pastry came from him."

"How do you know that?" I demand.

"I asked," he scolds, because I did not realize his brother's generosity.

Warm tenderness spreads from my heart through my whole being. Valor looked after me in every way, even when I was not his to care for, and he has continued to do so without fail. *"It was my greatest honor,"* he told me of our time together before I wed.

Maybe, just maybe, it does not have to be the greatest honor. Maybe someday, there can be more.

※ ※ ※

November 1st

I sit in my office staring into the fire long after everyone else has gone to bed. I tap my pen on my paper to the tune of a song I heard in our chapel service this morning.

"Sing to the Creator, sing in praise of His name...Rejoice before Him—His name is Almighty.

A Father to the fatherless, a Defender of the widows is the King in His holy dwelling.

He gives the lonely into families, He leads His captive people into freedom with singing…

From His bounty, He provides for the poor."

It is good that He can provide for the poor, because Lorennt and I were called into an urgent meeting with my trade officials and advisors this afternoon informing us of more bad news.

For weeks, we have been counting on the moneys from the Commonwealth to arrive. It is a significant portion of the profits from the trade agreements Leer brokered last winter. The bulk shipments of Malesiir's goods left port bound for the Commonwealth two months ago. The profits that were supposed to be our relief fund have been eagerly anticipated.

The trade officials informed us that they received word that four of our seven ships were captured enroute to the Commonwealth before they could reach port. The Malesiirians aboard ship were killed and the ships and all their goods were taken as plunder by none other than the Ruphiri.

The ledgers drafted with this new information were disheartening. We have spread ourselves too thin with the relief efforts for our people, rebuilding after the losses from the brigands and Ruphiri, constructing a new port city in the Northern Province, improvements to the roads, my plan for activating every soldier in Malesiir, the looming winter season, and Lorennt's coronation.

It is all too much. We must pull ourselves back—in more than one area. I have already tightened the purse strings in the castle as much as I know how, including ceasing construction of the new bathing room and foregoing all personal expenditures. I have not purchased so much as a cookie in weeks. Thankfully, Valor left a deposit at the bakery to hold me over for a while.

I asked Father Boldizar to join us in the meeting today to lend his wisdom to our discussions and to provide his perspective on where we could reel in expenditures to save the kingdom from destitution without harming our people. It feels like the survival of the kingdom must come at the expense of its people. I hate that. I cannot accept it. Nothing was settled upon today. Father counseled that we take at least one night to pray and sleep on our decisions, but tomorrow, we need a plan.

From His bounty, He provides for the poor.

The song comforts my burdened soul again as I lift my pleas for wisdom and provision to the Almighty. I cannot give the kingdom what it needs. My storehouses are running dry, but our Heavenly King holds all the bounty of the earth. Surely, He can provide for His children.

I wish at the very least that I could provide for my people displaced by the fire. My heart aches for those living in tents with their children with winter settling on the mountains.

The fire stretches out its warm arms and lulls me to sleep. A few hours before dawn, I awaken certain that I have been given a gift. I still have no idea how to resolve most of what ails my kingdom, but I have been shown the next small step forward. I rush up the stairs and knock on Lorennt's door, reasoning that he is probably already awake. A minute passes, and I knock again. Finally, he comes to the door fully dressed and buckling his weapons belt.

"What has happened?" He closes the door then leads the way down the hall. I hasten to catch up with him.

"I know how to speed along the rebuilding process on the west side," I say. "I am not sure about the rest of it, but—"

Lorennt rounds on me at the top of the stairs. "There is no emergency?"

"No, I just—"

"Then why have you woken me?"

"Because I thought you would want to know."

Lorennt marches back the way we came. "Tell me at breakfast."

"But, Lorennt—"

"At. Breakfast." He growls and slams the door to his room.

Goodness, these Rodiharian men like their sleep!

I huff and cross my arms. So be it. I will go to the prison on my own.

※ ※ ※

The jailer is not pleased to see me at this time of day either. But since I have my guard with me and I assure him I have no vengeful intentions, he leads the way to the cells holding the brigands.

The jailer clangs a club across the bars, waking the brigands. The men are divided into two cells, the women in one. In all, only sixteen of the forty-odd brigands were taken captive last April, the rest were killed in the raid—by our soldiers or by their own hand.

"What do you want now? Not time for breakfast already, is it?" A lanky man grumps from the corner.

"You lot best listen," the jailer says. "Your queen has come to speak with you."

The men shift in the dark recesses of the cells. "You come to torture us?"

I push hard against the thoughts that surface, reminding myself I have been forgiven and my sins atoned. "I have come to sentence you."

"After seven months?" A woman asks from the cell further down.

Has it really been so long? "Come forward."

The brigands shuffle toward the bars of the cell. I look upon all of them, searching their faces for the obvious evil I imagine I will find there. Peering into the eyes of the Ruphiri is like looking upon hatred and every vile deed incarnate. I find that sort of look in a few of the brigands, but overwhelmingly, they look like normal folk I might come across in any Malesiirian town, albeit bitter and gaunt from months in these cells.

I begin to question how many of these men or women have actually murdered. They stole, they hid, they destroyed. But did they murder? Perhaps it was the Ruphiri all along and only some of the brigands were responsible for the deaths of fellow Malesiirians.

Spirit of Truth, grant me discernment and eyes to see.

I take time to stand opposite each man and woman. Three men I single out as being too foul for what I have in mind. Something slithers behind their eyes. The rest I would not turn my back on for a moment, but I do not believe they are murderers.

"You each know the guilt on your own hands. If you are anything like me, you have struggled under that guilt. I am not prepared to grant you clemency for what you have done. Neither am I prepared to allow you to linger down here into old age."

"It's to be the noose then?" A lanky man assumes. They have been considering their own fates far longer than I have, and it would come as no surprise to them if that is the way of things.

"It is customary for you to be tried for your actions and allowed to plead your case," I prevaricate.

"What's the point in that?" A woman asks. "You've already decided for yourself we're guilty. There'll be no swaying your opinion."

"Is that your answer?" I ask. "No one wishes to address me?"

"I will," one of the vile men says. "As the Creator is my witness, I am innocent of the worst of the crimes. It was all those Limban men. They gave us orders, and we followed them. Brogan and Gires killed some too. But what we done, we done on orders."

"So you were coerced into murdering?"

"Surely you can understand that, Warrior Queen? You wouldn't hold your soldiers accountable for the deaths you've ordered." His voice is compelling. His posture authoritative.

My skin crawls. "I do understand. But I also know that for some there is no burden in killing. Rather, they take pleasure in it, ordered or not."

A smile crawls through his scruffy beard. "Reckon you understand those people."

I shift my gaze to the others. "Would anyone else like to say something?" No one does. After so long in confinement, I believed they might be more open, but silence is still their choice.

"Very well. You leave it to me to decide." I rest my hands on my dagger hilts. "You are all guilty of theft, destruction of property, and party to murder. As such, your debt to your kingdom and fellow man is great. I sentence you to manual labor to aid in the rebuilding of the west side of the city and any additional tasks I find appropriate for making restitution for your crimes. You will begin today."

I turn to the jailer and indicate the three vile men. "I want these three to be the first out of the cells."

"Aye, Majesty."

The brigands mutter amongst themselves as I leave.

When we are well away from the brigands, the jailer says, "Majesty, with all respect, I recommend you reconsider taking the brigands out, especially those three. They are troublemakers."

"I sensed that about them. Thus, when you take them out of their cells, have the three moved to a different cell where they will await trial. My soldiers will be by to collect the others later today."

CHAPTER TWO

VALOR

November 3rd

The Northern Province is steadily being returned to the fold of Malesiir. The most foundational step, improving the roads, was begun in the spring and makes travel at this time of year easy in all but worst weather. The north cannot remain cut off any longer. As we inspect the new roads, I visit each town along the way to ensure our people are well and give them opportunity to voice any concerns they have. I discover a unified Malesiir where there had been rebellion. The trade officials Lorennt and I appointed have made improvements, and it shows in the production reports Erianna requested. I know what each township is capable of producing and can vouch for this year being more productive than the last.

The elders of the towns are pleased with the changes and extend their hospitality to us. They are grateful that they were not incriminated for the crimes they abetted last winter. In another year or two, when the plans for the Northern Province come to fruition, the people will be downright giddy that their plan for secession was quelled.

Our next stop in the weeks long journey is the new city that will become the center of trade in the north. Grandileer's vision for it was grand. A city as large as Malsihra along the coast to take advantage of a deep harbor. With its completion, our merchant ships will have a shorter route to both the Commonwealth, and the burden of Port Veritae, our only seaport of consequence, will be eased. While cleaning her office the day before the funeral, Erianna discovered the intended name for the new city along with its dedication written in the margin of the city plans.

Halden—For my dearest wife who saved our kingdom.

Halden is old Malesiirian for *Blessed*. The love note stretching across time brought a smile to my widowed queen's face even as she lowered her weeping veil for the remainder of the day.

In addition to Halden, Grandileer planned for two additional cities to be constructed once Halden and the expansion of Chishelm are complete. One shall lie along the river between the Northern and Central Provinces and be the last chink in the wall linking the North with the rest of the kingdom. The second will be a mill town constructed in the Southern Province to decrease the distance of our people's journey to process their grain. Erianna and Lorennt are determined to see Grandileer's dreams for Malesiir realized. I wholeheartedly support their plans for our magnificent kingdom.

This day, I lead a half company of fifty soldiers and craftsmen toward Halden to aid in platting the city and ensure the safety of the early inhabitants. We have not heard from them in several weeks. Their progress report is overdue. By my estimation, we should reach the location of Halden shortly after noon.

The forest quiets around us. Granite tosses his head. Prickles crawl up my spine. We are not alone in the woods. I raise my hand to alert the company but too late. Through the falling snow, a solitary rider clad in black materializes in the road. The man sits erect in the saddle, a dense compact horse beneath him. "Greetings, Commander Ironforge. I bid you carry a message for me."

My archers draw back their bows, training eyes on the man, at the ready for my word. "Identify yourself!" I tense anticipating the answer, certain I already know, but unwilling to kill someone without surety.

A white smile divides the shadows beneath his hood. "Tell Erianna Zavaan I shall see her soon. I am coming for my wife."

Ice plummets into my stomach while blood roars in my ears. I drop my arm for my archers as Granite surges beneath me. Reuel Zavaan wheels his mount and aims for the bleak forest. Arrows hiss through the air, but they are not solely from my men, rather they are launched from the forest on our flanks. A man screams as an arrow finds flesh. Most fall harmlessly into our formation. The archers are shooting blindly, too far back to be accurate, only intending to distract.

I rein Granite long enough to give orders. "Half of you pursue Zavaan! The rest protect the craftsmen!"

The captain in the company enacts my order while I cut through the forest. Zavaan is not far ahead. The fool. Risking exposure for what? A taunt? Rage sets a course from my heart to my head, muddling my thoughts. I will learn what Zavaan planned when he is beneath my boot, my sword sliding between his ribs. He ascends a steep mountain slope, finding paths in the forest I cannot discern. He must have plotted his escape in advance. Around us, I descry his Ruphiri charging up the mountain, each forging their own way, gaining ground and passing me. That slays my assumption.

Granite slips in the snow covered detritus. I balance my weight, guiding his head straight as he regains his footing. At this angle, a fall would mean rolling down the mountain, cracking bones against trees.

Granite's hindquarters dig in deep. He jumps forward, springing like a rabbit. His fore hooves find solid ground, and we are climbing again. I cannot risk unbalancing him by glancing back at my soldiers, but I hear their curses. Only an industrious few will be capable of making this climb.

Zavaan pulls away from me, gaining the ridge and faster ground. I push on, determined he will not slip through my fingers. I can catch him at the ridge. The day is not yet decided.

The ground levels. Tracks in the snow point us toward our quarry. Parallel paths through the snow converge into the one I follow. I allow Granite a dangerous amount of speed on terrain that is unfamiliar and could be hiding pitfalls. As long as we stay in the Ruphiri's tracks, there cannot be overmuch risk. The ridge opens, revealing another steep ascending slope, steeper descents on both sides, and a dozen horse tracks going in all directions.

I stop Granite. He is winded from the climb. All the tracks are identical. I scan far ahead, but discern no movement. Not that it would help. The Ruphiri all wear identical black.

Where would Zavaan have gone? Up? Less likely that I could pursue him on that slope. Good chance of his escape. Down? Another good chance for escape. I might be able to follow, but more likely Granite would go tail over ears if I try that. He has no practice sliding down mountainsides. Far too risky a gambit, for both he and I. The more level trails are possible, but they divide in five directions.

I never truly believed how fast Erianna claimed the Ruphiri bisected Malesiir from the coast where Zavaan captured her to the Ascent where she escaped. I blamed trauma for her unreasonable timetable. But Erianna did not exaggerate. If anything, she downplayed the truth. The Ruphiri move like wraiths in the forest.

They have escaped.
Again.
I bellow my anger. Guttural and wordless.
Zavaan is gone.

※ ※ ※

November 23th

The Ruphiri were harrying the construction of Halden. That is why we had no word from them for weeks. With our arrival, the Ruphiri abandoned their ankle biting that kept our people kicking at the Ruphiri rather than progressing on the city's construction. Only a few lives were lost because of them. I helped restore order and left the bulk of the company in Halden to protect the fledgling city. The craftsmen are scurrying to accomplish something between heavy snowfalls. If the only thing they are able to do is survey and observe the landscape, noting the way storms move into the harbor and selecting the best places to establish the docks, it will be worth it come spring when construction can begin in earnest.

Though I should have spent time in Halden, I could only think what would happen if Zavaan ambushed Erianna while I was away. He would disappear with her, and there would be little I could do to stop him. I rushed the conclusion of my assignment and pushed hard for home.

Not Parse Kítaran, where I once considered home. I rode for Erianna. She is home.

As I enter Malsihra, the captain stationed at the city gate reports that all has been quiet where the Ruphiri are concerned since I departed. It is a tremendous relief. Thus, I go the roundabout way to the castle to settle my ongoing bill with Mari the baker and buy a sack of cookies for the queen. Mari has been experimenting with new recipes for her most enthusiastic royal patron. She assures me these will be appreciated, so much so that they are now called *queen's cookies* for the crown shaped stamp in the center of each cookie. Granite approves of the recipe by tossing his head when I share one of the treats with him as a reward for tolerating my demanding pace. The queen is not the only member of my herd that I shamelessly bribe. Leelah accepts bribes too, but more often she takes the bribe then does whatever she pleases. Her children are more reliably behaved than she.

Lorennt summons me to his office when I arrive at the castle. He is more pleased to see me than I would have believed possible. Looking closer on him, I decide *pleased* might not be the right word. *Relieved* seems more accurate. The prince is weary, but there is an overwhelming contentment about him. "Married life seems to agree with you," I say while clasping his offered arm in greeting.

He smiles to himself. "It does. I should have taken Nev to wife a year ago."

Since Erianna is at the barracks training with Kragorn, Lorennt pours modest glasses of brandy for each of us. We settle in armchairs near the hearth and raise our glasses in silent toast.

"How is your wife these days, Highness?"

"She is fatigued and very near bringing our child into the world. Mother looks after her much of the time."

"Celiea has taken to her?" I drag in a slow sip of the golden liquid that bites and warms as it goes down. I rarely indulge in it these days.

"She has. It was bound to happen eventually. I think it is impossible to spend time with Nev and not be taken in by her guileless nature and inherent sweetness. Mother even thought to give all those infant gowns she and Erianna made to Nev. I had a room full of weeping women on my hands for the better part of that day, but they sorted out themselves."

"I am glad. I have never met a more likable person on the Continent than your Nev."

"Quite true." He eyes me over the rim of his glass. "But you prefer an imp in human flesh, do you not?"

I grin unrepentantly and take another sip.

He shifts his attention to the fire for a time, lost in thought. "Valor, I need your help looking after her. I thought I could do it all—look after Nev and Erianna and my parents and Malesiir—but I cannot." He swirls the liquid in his glass. "My brother had it all wrong. He entrusted his wife to me and Nev, though he would not have given Nev the credit she was due, and he looked after the kingdom. I do not want to relegate my wife in my heart. I saw what it did to Erianna, and I will not do that to Nev."

I nod but remain silent. He ought to prioritize his wife before the kingdom, though many would disagree.

"With the arrival of our babe, I know that even more of my time will be claimed. My sister is doing an excellent job being the high queen of our kingdom for the time being, but that in itself means she needs looking after."

For the time being… There is a very large fight looming between Erianna and Lorennt. If he thinks she shall willingly become the subordinate ruler, he does not know her as well as thought.

Unaware of my silent caution, Lorennt continues. "You were here to protect her when she rode into the city, but since then, she has set off on her own."

"Is she keeping secrets from you?"

"No." Lorennt winces and takes another swig. "But when I am not available, she does not curb her plans until a more convenient time arrises." He is generalizing, but this feels very specific.

"Stop talking circles, Lorennt," I demand as worry winds in my gut.

He sighs. "She woke me early a few weeks past with a scheme. I told her to tell me over breakfast and sent her on her way. But you know Erianna. Instead of waiting to discuss it with me, she went to the prison and met with the brigands."

I lean forward, staring down the prince.

"She sentenced most of them to manual labor rebuilding the west side and gave Anders charge over them. The others were tried and convicted of murder last week and hanged the next day. Since then, she has adjusted the imprisonment sentences of anyone convicted of a nonviolent crime to swell her labor force."

"You disapprove of her decision?"

"I disapprove of her going to the prison and making the decision without my approval."

"You told her that?"

"Oh, I told her." He winces again.

I glower.

"My point is this—I cannot keep pace with her anymore. A reasonable person would have known not to wake a bone tired man before dawn unless it was an emergency, but Erianna does not think to the conclusion of her impulsiveness until she is up to her ears in trouble."

How well I know it. She is logical and cool-headed in most things, but there is a thread of recklessness that runs through her too. It nearly always presents in regards to her own safety, which she neglects to factor into her plans. "Much of it is her personality, however, I think we often forget she is young and has only been under the yoke of responsibility since she came to Malesiir."

"I recognize that, and I do not want to embitter her or make her feel insignificant. Never that. But neither can I be the compatriot in her adventures anymore. I need to hand off that responsibility so I can give my wife and child the attention they are due." Lorennt's love for his family is obvious in his earnest expression. He never envisioned being the bearer of all this responsibility, but he is doing his best.

"What can I do to help?"

Lorennt leans forward, bracing his arms on his thighs, to make his request. "I need you to look after Erianna. I need you to prevent her from endangering herself and supervise her adventures."

I sit back in my chair, struck with the memory of Lorennt at one time ordering me not to even think on his sister. Now, he means to entrust her to my care.

"I know it is a great deal to ask of you," Lorennt says, thinking I need persuasion, "but I know, eventually, you will court Erianna. If you take care of her in the meantime and prove you are the sort of man I believe you to be, it will ease my mind significantly where she is concerned."

"I am honored," I reply around the lump in my throat. "Of course I will look after her."

CHAPTER THREE

VALOR

I enter dinner decidedly hopeful. Lorennt loves his sister so well that he is not willing to entrust her to just anyone. He means to keep an eye on how well I care for Erianna.

The great hall is full of nobility and royalty. I catch Nev's eye across the room and decide to greet her before finding my once-again charge. Unlike last time, the promise of more hovers on the horizon where my charge is concerned. My mouth twitches toward a smile at the thought. Being charged with her care by her brother is a huge step forward. It pleases me to no end.

Nev greets me with a fond hug. I cast my eyes to Lorennt to assure him I did not initiate this liberty with his wife and cautiously pat Nev on the back.

She laughs. "Oh, Valor, do not be ridiculous."

"Were you not the one who explained to me the jealous nature of your husband?" I remind her.

She laughs again. "I suppose, but I am glad to see you, and more glad that your meeting with Lorennt went well."

I hold the young woman at arms length, realizing what I did not before. "How much of my present good humor is owed to you?"

"I might have made Lorennt acknowledge what he already knew and suggested a solution that did not involve putting a leash on his sister."

"Lady Nev Rodiharian, you are a marvel," I declare. "You have my endless gratitude."

"You may retract that when you come to see how headstrong the woman you love is and how much mischief she can find."

"I cannot wait," I grin.

Nev smooths her hands over her Melon that now looks much more like a watermelon than a sweet melon.

I ask, "So, when are you going to share Melon with the rest of us?"

"Soon, I hope. I would rather have the babe outside than in, to be sure." Nev rests a hand on her belly. "The physician said it is nonsense to try to predict such things, but when Lorennt pressed him, he hazarded a guess that I would deliver before the solstice."

"Is there anything I can do to help you prepare? Would you like any of your friends from Parse to be here for the birth?" It should not be difficult to arrange if it is something she wants. The friends she made in Parse are more her family than the ones she cut ties from years ago.

Shortly after arriving in Parse this summer, I asked if Nev was an abbreviation for a longer given name. With shame she said, "Never. My full name is Never. I was a sickly babe so Mother named me Never because she so often said, 'That babe's Never gonna make it.' When I grew into a small child, she said, 'That girl will Never be worth nothing.' When I left home at fourteen, it was because I heard her say one too many times, 'That chit will Never leave if I don't marry her off.' I decided to go before she tossed me to the first willing man she found."

Nev fled to Malsihra and found a position in the castle as a chamber maid then worked her way up to lady's maid before Lorennt returned from his years of military service. They happened upon each other when he was hiding from his adoring throng of noblewomen. Lorennt was taken with her sweet, guileless nature and pursued her doggedly until she was convinced he was sincere in his suit. He set her up as Erianna's lady's maid for the benefits of the position and to give her an excuse to be in the royal wing.

Thus, Never of nowhere became Lady Nev Rodiharian, landed noblewoman of Limba, Prince's Consort, and mother of the Rodiharian heir. The Almighty certainly likes to take rejected, weak things and make them into something wondrous as only He can.

Nev mulls over my offer. "I would like Salome to be here, but I doubt she would be comfortable leaving Parse, and I do not want to offend Queen Celiea by displacing her with my mentor. But, If Leelah were willing to come before the solstice, I would very much like to have her here."

I take Nev's hand and bow. "That, I should be able to arrange."

She colors slightly at my formal deference to her and directs my attention across the room to my charge who is engaged with a young lord that seems familiar to me. "You ought to do something about that lordling. He is hounding Erianna. She has not been able to shake him like her usual admirers."

"Who is he?" I ask while my eyes feast on the woman I have longed for every day.

"That is Lord Jakab Sigure. He is Queen Celiea's nephew," Nev says, intending for me to find significance in his close ties to the Rodiharian family, "and a captain in the cavalry. He is visiting from Port Veritae."

"Is that so? I think it is time I greet my queen and the hound." My expression that promises trouble makes Nev laugh, but Lorennt excuses himself from his conversation to interrupt ours.

"Do not look at my wife like that," the prince orders.

"It is owing to your cousin that Valor is plotting his battle strategy." Nev slips her arms around Lorennt's waist.

Lorennt searches for the pair under discussion and huffs. "I told him to leave her be. She is in mourning for woe's sakes."

"Worry not, Lorennt. I will look after her." My long stride carries me across the room to my queen.

Erianna greets me with the warmest smile and takes my arm to keep me at her side without interrupting Lord Sigure's monologue. Sigure does his best to hold her attention but must concede defeat when Erianna makes the introduction between us.

Much the same as I did to her, her beautiful wintry eyes reacquaint themselves with my features. Hers have continued to improve from the sumptuous meals provided by the castle's kitchen staff. Were we alone, I might let my fingers trace the softened bones in her cheeks that blush becomingly under my perusal.

Instead, I touch the gold filigreed hilt at her hip. "Your weapons belt has a new addition."

Sigure frowns at the familiarity between us which makes me wonder what he wants from her? The prestige of her title? The thrill of a flirtation with a beautiful woman? Or is Celiea setting him up as Erianna next husband? I mean to find out.

"This is the sword you bought me for everyday use," Erianna explains. "I named her Daisy."

"Of course you did," I snicker. "And the glaive behind your chair on the dais?"

"Another of your gifts to me." Erianna's grateful smile tells that my money was well spent. "Violet is for special occasions. Battles, beheadings, and the like. I am quite fond of her."

"Both named for flowers?"

"Think how wonderful it will be when I say 'Fetch Violet' and then I am given my glaive to behead someone." Her bloodthirsty grin is displaced by a dramatic sigh. "Kragorn finds their names disrespectful since they are magnificent pieces of weaponry. He has no appreciation for irony."

I commiserate with her. "Appreciation of humor is not Kragorn's strongest point."

"My cousin's skill is quite impressive, though she has not taken me to ground yet," Sigure interjects.

"Because you cheat," Erianna deplores. "And if you continue doing so, you will have the distinct honor of being the first miscreant I behead with Violet."

She is not joking, though Sigure laughs indulgently as if she is. That rankles her. I pat her hand on my arm, acknowledging her present restraint. I bend my head to whisper in her ear, "I can hide his body where it will never be found."

That startles a giggle out of her and simultaneously curtails Sigure's chortling.

When it is time to commence dinner, I ascend the dais alongside my queen and help her gain her seat. Sigure, it seems, has been the one occupying the seat of honor next to the queen in my absence. He hesitates for a moment, then takes the vacant seat next to me.

Perfect.

The queen asks after the health of her kingdom once the viands have been laid out and the wine goblets filled. Out of deference to Erianna, who has just cause to dislike wine, I allow the maid to pass over my goblet and instead fill it and Erianna's with water from the pitcher on the table. It is no hardship to me, but it means a great deal to her. While we dine, I report on the progress in the North and the security of her towns.

When she turns to speak with Lorennt, I slip one of the cookies I bought on the edge of her plate then engage Sigure. "You are a relation of the Queen Abdicàt?"

"The second son of her younger sister," he states.

"Do you have many years left in your career?" This close, I determine he is at most three years older than Erianna. More of a pup than a true hound.

Sigure shrugs. "As many as I wish. The cavalry suits me. What of you?"

"What of me?" I reply with an arched brow, as if I find him impertinent.

His eyes narrow at the unfairness. "How long will my cousin allow you to serve as her Hand?"

"Assuming she does not decide to behead me with Violet? Interminably."

I hear Erianna snicker and glance across my shoulder. "Eavesdropping, Majesty?"

She licks the cookie crumbs off her fingers, drawing my eyes to her mouth. She ought not do that. "It is not eavesdropping in such a setting. If you do not wish to be overheard, then best not speak here."

"Unless one could speak without words. Then there would be no need to wait to say anything."

"Rubbish," Sigure mutters.

So he thinks, I wordlessly say to Erianna.

She presses her lips together to stifle her amusement.

We continue our individual conversations, and I surreptitiously set another cookie on the edge of my plate. Erianna makes a pleased noise a moment later.

I feign annoyance. "Are you stealing my dessert?"

"Is it stealing when they are named 'queen's cookies'?" She points to the crown stamped into the dough that mirrors the one atop her head.

"So they are. Mari says hello, by the way."

"Who is Mari?" Sigure asks.

"My favorite baker," Erianna replies. "I am afraid I have neglected the acquaintance of late."

"That is a shame," I say and take the half eaten cutlet of venison from her plate. "It sounds like you are in need of an outing."

"Only if you agree to reduce the number of guards underfoot," she complains. "I can barely move with the escort you assigned to me."

The threat Zavaan bid me deliver strikes a blow to my good humor. I try again to shake off the memory of the gaunt, abused version of this lively woman. The memory has tormented me these weeks we have been apart. "Let's discuss that later."

She frowns and sets her hand on my arm, hearing the undercurrent of my words.

"Later," I squeeze her fingers.

Sigure notes the exchange. "Something is amiss, Cousin?"

"Naught." She hides her concern behind her queenly mask and

returns her hand to her lap.

"Will you be staying much longer?" I ask Sigure, not bothering to conceal my annoyance.

"I have decided to accept my aunt's invitation to stay through the coronation. Court holds more appeal than it used to." He raises his wine glass in toast to Erianna then drinks deeply.

She rolls her eyes and not in the playful way she does at me. I smirk to myself. If *cousin* does not take care, he will find himself at one of the low tables regardless of his relations.

I slip another cookie onto the edge of my plate. Erianna snatches it with a grin and nibbles it while I swap our plates to eat what she left.

"Have military rations left empty places in your stomach?" She teases.

"Aye. It is good to be home."

"I thought you considered the valley your home?" She obscurely references Parse Kítaran where my cozy cabin is nestled between the arms of the mountains.

I set the spoon down and turn toward her, making my back a wall against Sigure's eavesdropping. My words are meant for her alone. "It feels like that sometimes. But other times the castle feels like my home. Other times home feels like a cave in the woods. Or the great hall in Grevnhold. Or a tidy little room at the Blue Heron."

Erianna blushes and looks up at me through her lashes.

"I am home," I murmur.

She catches her lower lip in her teeth. I pick up my spoon and set my sights on my plate. The high table is no place to chase Erianna's teeth from her lips with mine, though she tempts me mightily.

The tables are cleared of their burdens in preparation of the night's card games while we mingle. Lorennt and Nev bid all goodnight, leaving Erianna to oversee the evening. Her wistful gaze lingers on the stairs after they ascend out of sight.

I search for the telltale shadows under her eyes that are so commonplace I forget to consider her sleepless nights. "You want to go to bed?"

Her face instantly flames. "No."

I chuckle. "Forgive me. That sounded like an offer. It was not. I meant, do you want to sleep?" Seeing her embarrassment, I intuit her thoughts were more relational in nature. "I think I should have asked, do you miss being a wife?"

She nearly brushes me off, but then admits, "I miss certain aspects of it."

Before I can ask what aspects she does not miss, Erianna groans quietly and lifts imploring eyes to me. "Tell me your monicker becomes easier to bear."

Vestal. The term Anders assigned to me owing to my abstinence.

I raise my brows and slowly shake my head. "No. But you become accustomed to it."

She whimpers and steps closer to me. "I feel like I am slowly starving. I had no idea how much I would miss my husband's affection until it was taken from me."

I am surprised by her blunt yet accurate description. Being inherently modest, it is rare for Erianna to mention things of an intimate nature. Before advancing the topic, I search her eyes for permission which she gives. "Do you miss *affection* or your *husband*?"

Her brow furrows over the question before guilt seeps in. She fidgets with her grey mourning gown.

"You are allowed to be honest with yourself, Erianna. Nor will I judge you for your answer."

She laces her hands at her waist. There is more certainty in her expression than I thought to find. "I do miss him. And I miss the intimacy we shared. But I have let him go."

I attempt to check my overeager heart, but it is not listening. She will likely continue her mourning until the anniversary of his death, even if she does not feel it.

But if she does not feel it…

She curtails my musings better than I managed when she quietly says, "Even so, I am not sure I want to be a wife again."

"What do you mean?"

My confusion causes her to step back abruptly, closing the discussion as if she revealed something she had not intended. "Not here." The queen's mask is quickly and firmly in place with feigned good humor that few could replicate. "I think I shall have to remind you, Commander, why I am regarded as one of the best card players in Malsihra."

I resolve to pick up this conversation when she cannot divert it for legitimate or convenient reasons. In the meantime, I match her tone and lead her toward a table where Trent and Silla are seated, doling out cards. "I will remind you, Majesty, who it was that taught you to play."

"It was Trent, was it not?" She smirks over her shoulder as she settles on the bench. I give her a half smile and sit next to her.

Sigure, the fly that will not be shooed, joins us. "I think I would like to call in that doubles game you promised to me, Cousin."

It is funny that he believes continuously reminding Erianna of their distant marital kinship will allow him to sidle up to her.

It is even funnier when Trent puts the pup in his place by deliberately misunderstanding him. "We are *not* playing doubles. Commander and Majesty are an unbeatable pair. Your second would not thank you for instigating a match against them." Trent shuffles the deck. "My Lady, would you decide the game for us?"

Silla obliges, talking over Sigure's floundering. "Majesty, when are you going to cease procrastinating and collect your greaves from the saddler? It would be a shame if your 'fine legs' were injured while sparring." We four laugh while Sigure tries to catch the joke.

"I hear it is high time for a meaningless venture into the city." I invoke Silla's help. "Perhaps you can convince my queen."

She sets her fingers beneath her chin. "If the queen needs convincing, you are the one to do it. My pleadings have been fruitless."

"Is that so?" I turn to scold Erianna. "You have been ignoring the requests of your friend?"

Silla and Erianna both object to the the term *friend* being applied to them.

Trent folds his cards. "I am certain I have heard both of you name each other *friend* at one time or another. You simply have not acknowledged it to each other. I think you better admit right now how you feel and have done with it."

Silla and Erianna face off.

"I prefer the term *accomplice*." Erianna cants her head high.

"As do I." Silla throws Trent a challenging look that he devours, followed by their own unspoken exchange.

Have they…? I ask Erianna.

Not that I have heard, she replies.

"What will it take to convince you to set aside your responsibilities for an afternoon?"

"Bribery of the most compelling sort," Erianna says.

When she looks down at her cards, I produce another cookie and hold it loosely.

Erianna is astonished. "Are you hiding a bakery in your pocket?"

You are welcome to search me, I dare her.

She purses her lips, not rising to my bait. "A stop at Mari's is essential, but it will take more." She snatches the cookie.

"A dress for solstice?" I suggest, tossing my lousy pair of cards on the table.

"Yes!" Silla pounces upon the idea. "I am afraid we will not have our orders completed at the rate she is procrastinating placing them."

"Then we must see to it," I agree. "I also need a new shirt. Most of mine have roses embroidered in the strangest places."

Erianna's mouth twitches in a restrained smile, and she holds her palm up.

I drop another cookie into it. Her coy laughter brings another suggestion to mind.

"Maybe a *generous* dinner?" I tease, reminding her of our private jest when she generously warmed me after Kragorn insisted we bathe in the rain. I would gladly endure the cold if she would warm me in her arms.

She looks sidelong at me, reminding me of a more intimate memory. "Only if there is *dancing* to follow."

"You may count on it, my Queen." I wink.

Trent snorts. "Valor cannot dance."

Erianna's gaze flits to my mouth. "He dances very well."

"Only very well?" I ask.

"Satisfactorily?" She taunts, angling her head to the side.

My heart leaps. "You might as well say 'deplorably.'"

"Exceptionally?" she amends, her rose lips parting on a smile.

I lean closer to her. "I like 'exceptionally' but not stated as a question."

"Exceptionally," she drawls. Diamonds sparkle in the winter sky, framed by long dark lashes.

"Better," I breathe, watching a flush steal up her cheeks. Vivid memories of an earth moving kiss on a starry night steal over me. Her name is a plea on my lips as I lower my mouth to claim what she offers.

A kick to my shin jerks me around just as Silla sharply hisses, "Erianna!"

With a hard jolt, we return to the chatter in the great hall, leaving the solitude of our shared memory behind. Embarrassment overcomes us both that we were so carried away. Erianna takes her turn drawing two more cards while trying to pretend nothing happened. But our witnesses will not let it be so simple.

Trent is doing little to hide his mirth. Sigure looks murderous. But

Erianna is watching Silla who is scanning the great hall. A pointed glance is exchanged between them. Surreptitiously, Erianna follows the direction Silla indicates as do I.

Queen Celiea eyes her daughter in law with a mixture of disapproval and accusation. Erianna's expression falls even as she throws her shoulders back, holding herself higher. Silla leads a conversation on some inane subject to which I cannot attend. Erianna engages her with the utmost propriety then departs our table to spend the remainder of the evening making her way about the hall, speaking with influential nobles and giving her attention to her court.

When she finally calls the evening to an end, bidding the nobles to retire, she merely nods in my direction, dismissing me as well. Trent leads Silla from the great hall while I linger, waiting for the nobles disperse, hoping to apologize to Erianna. But her eyes skip over me when she glances around the room. Queen Celiea falls into step with her as she makes her way up the private stairs to the royal residences. I run my hands through my hair, lamenting what feels very much like taking advantage of Erianna's emotions when it was not what she wanted.

Though my body is weary from weeks of travel and nights interrupted with watch duty, I toss upon my bed, worrying over the apology as of yet unspoken and my obligation to allow Erianna to set the tone for our relationship.

Whatever that may be.

CHAPTER FOUR

ERIANNA

November 24th

With Mother's Celiea's scathing reproof burning in my ears, I consider the events that led to my "reprehensible display that disgraced our family and the memory of Leer whom I claimed to love." When she ranted that Leer was not even cold in his grave, it was every drop of self-possession in my being not to scream at Leer's grieved mother that he *is* cold, so very cold. I would know. I feel as if I have never warmed from the chill that pervaded my bones while holding his lifeless body in my arms.

But I bit my tongue. I hung my head. And I vowed not to shame our family or Leer's memory again.

Shaming my family may never have happened if Lorennt or Nev had the presence of mind to inform me that Valor had returned two weeks early. The surprise and joy I felt at his arrival was overwhelming. And then Valor had to behave like Valor with his teasing, his thoughtfulness, and his affectionate glances making me completely forget myself.

What is worse is that I am not certain who I am more embarrassed to see this morning—Valor, who I clearly remember telling I am starved for affection and then shamelessly flirted with and nearly kissed in the middle of the great hall, or Mother Celiea and the court that bore witness to our interlude.

I weigh the humiliation I will face in going down to the great hall for breakfast against the gossip I will initiate by *not* going. The perk of avoiding Valor tips the scales. I jot a missive to Lorennt that I have gone into the city to inspect progress on the west side and slip it under his door before escaping.

Thankfully, I am the first person to rise as has become my custom. Not even Valor is in the great hall. I also strike upon the luck of avoiding Lord Sigure who has been a bur on my side for two weeks.

My only difficulty comes when I mount Sacha. She is unaccustomed to the odd sensation of my glaive and sword rubbing her hindquarters. I left them at the castle yesterday when she balked at the feeling, but since I mean to ride to the west side today, I must have them. She jigs laterally as we ride under the portcullis testing my skills to bring her under control. I speak soothing words to her and grip the saddle with my thighs, freeing my hands to stroke her neck and rein her around. It does not help much.

My guard turns a critical eye to her antics. "Majesty, while you have a fine riding mare in that horse, I think she needs a heap more training before she should be treated like a destrier. You have not fought with sword or glaive from the saddle, yet she is already skittish."

"You might be right." As loath as I am to admit it, I should probably speak with the horse master about a well-mannered destrier for my personal use. I could ask Valor, but I have a suspicion that he would oppose the idea of me on the back of a war horse and thwart my efforts to obtain one. Leer certainly would have. He did not even allow me near Reaper, his destrier.

Hmm…

That bears considering.

I give Sacha's reins to a guard and stroll along the west side. With the labor I conscripted from the jail, progress has been rapid in clearing the remains of the old buildings. The foundations have been laid for the new construction under the supervision of the masons. If the weather holds and no unforeseen challenges arise, the optimistic reports say the structures could be completed by the new year. That gives me over a month to formulate a plan for furnishing and filling the interiors of the buildings, which is a problem for another day. I lavish praise on all those involved in the project and decide to reward the prisoners with dessert.

I return to the saddle and set my course for the barracks. In addition to a rigorous training session, I am hopeful that Kragorn has something to report about the investigation of our generals.

That is when my luck disappears.

Lord Sigure, who is also headed for the barracks, crosses my path. I growl to myself but proceed as if he was not a primary witness to my idiocy last night. He falls in with me, bidding me a perfectly normal, "Good morning, Cousin."

"Lord Sigure." I incline my head, shunning the familial claim. It is one of many things that he has employed to shift our acquaintance from the formal to the intimate. Unlike Valor's attention to me last night, Mother Celiea turns a blind eye on her nephew's advances toward me.

"You were missed at breakfast," Sigure says with an air of nonchalance.

"How nice."

"The obligations of a queen…" He makes the excuse for me.

"Precisely."

"Had nothing at all to do with avoiding your lover."

"My what?" I snarl, rounding on him. The movement smacks the end of my glaive against Sacha's hindquarter. She bucks, lurching into the horse ahead of us. I grab for the reins that I nearly lost as she tosses her head, rolling her eyes until only the whites are visible. At the first opportunity, I leap to the ground and rush to her head, calming the frightened mare. All is chaos as my guards clamor to rescue me from the wild horse, pushing past Sigure who is trying to grab Sacha's bridle.

Ninnies, one and all.

I bring Sacha's head down, cooing to her until her skin stops twitching and her ears come forward listening to the tone of my voice. "Let's walk the rest of the way, *hmm*? No more rotten weapons bothering you. That was not nice of me at all to spring them on you."

No one is quite sure what to make of the deference I show my horse, but I decline all the offers to ride their mounts with a wave of my hand.

Kragorn takes one look at me walking Sacha into the turnout pen and states, "You need a destrier."

"If only your succinct assessment was available this morning," I remark, then ask, "How long do you think it would take to transform Sacha into a destrier?"

"That is a question for your Hand." Kragorn glances around then his brows knit together. My very large shadow is nowhere in sight.

"I was feeling independent today," I explain.

Kragorn's mouth twitches, revealing his amusement. "What did he say to cross you?"

Since he will hear about it eventually, I head off the gossip by saying, "It is more of what we both said and did in the middle of a card game in the middle of the great hall. Nothing that you have not scolded us for before, but it was Mother Celiea who dealt my deserved reproach this time."

I expect Kragorn to add his own censure to Celiea's, but he turns contemplative. "I see."

"What do you see?"

He nods to the center training ring. "You and Sigure are in there today. Get your—"

I catch hold of his sleeve, tugging him to a stop. "Kragorn. Speak." Of all the abounding opinions I could hear, it is his I want. That he is reluctant to give it is unusual.

He crosses his arms over his chest, appraising me with a hard stare. "I think you ought to cast off mourning grey."

My brows reach for the sky. "It has only been four months."

He frowns, but does not say anything.

"It is customary to wait at least a year."

His stare does not waver.

"But..." I prompt.

He voices his opinion quietly. "But you had an arranged marriage. Aye, it grew to love despite extreme differences, but that does not mean it would be frowned upon for you to truncate your mourning. Better that than you and Valor walk a line you are not adept at walking to the scorn of your family for presenting a mourning that you no longer feel."

Well. I did ask.

My smile feels tight. "Thank you for your input." I turn toward the training ring he indicated.

"Is it your intention to remain unmarried?" He queries, bringing me to a stop.

It is a question I have barely asked myself. There is so much weight bound to the decision that I have avoided considering it, choosing instead to postpone the decision while I have the legitimate preoccupation of mourning. The thought of marrying again is fraught with unknowns, past hurts, and tender memories. I cannot fathom binding my life to another man. Unless, perhaps, that man is Valor.

"Have you sought the Creator's will?" Kragorn challenges me, not waiting for my answer, "Pray. Ask the Spirit of Truth to bring clarity and reveal His will. Then you will have peace one way or the other."

My spine slackens, knowing I have forgotten this essential thing. "I shall."

"Center ring," he directs. "And this time cut Sigure's legs out from under him. I am past tired of seeing him take you to ground." Which usually involves Sigure straddling me while pressing a weapon to my throat. Yet another thing he does that irritates me to no end.

I grin at Kragorn, pushing thoughts of Valor from my mind and imagine dropping Sigure face-first into the muddy ground. "I shall do my best."

※※※

Before dinner, I seek Valor like I should have done straight away this morning. My apology is not off my tongue before he says, "I am sorry for embarrassing you and imposing on your mourning. I should have used restraint. I know where we stand, but…" He huffs. "I am sorry. I am without excuse. Please forgive me."

I nearly allow him to own my mistakes, but the unsettled feeling in my heart will not be ignored. "I think you are taking all the blame when it could be split fairly evenly. I spoke on things I ought not have and wanted you to be what you are not."

My hearts churns all the worse at the half truth. I am embarrassed, but leading him to believe it occurred because of physical longing only is preposterous. I flirted with Valor and nearly kissed him because I want *him*. Not just anyone's affection. Not even Leer's. I want Valor. I want to be with him. I want more than his friendship. I want a life with him. Those feelings terrify me.

Maybe Valor hears the lie amid the truth. Maybe worse, he believes it. Either way, he takes a step back. "I understand." He seems to search for something to fill the silence that has never been awkward before but now is. "Were you training with Kragorn?"

I nod, grateful for the change of subject. "Aye. It went better today. I fought well until Sigure behaved like the miscreant he is. Anders was not amused and beat manners into 'cousin.'" I roll my eyes then grin. "Anders also told Sigure that if he addresses me as anything other than 'Majesty,' it will be a while before he can speak again."

The story meant to make Valor laugh and remove the awkward feeling between us does anything but that. Valor grinds his teeth, adding another layer of tension to his restrained demeanor. He looses a slow breath through his nose. "Good. How goes rebuilding on the west side?"

We speak inanely for several more minutes then walk to dinner in silence. I cannot remember a time when there was such strain between us. In an effort to redeem the court's opinion, Valor and I play through several rounds of cards while they scrutinize us for untoward behavior that cannot be found. Mother Celiea nods her approval, and the gossips are disappointed. Claiming fatigue, Valor excuses himself to retire early for the evening. I cannot help feeling he meant to avoid me as I avoided him. It stabs my heart.

Late into the night, I toss in my bed, unable to fall asleep. My conversation with Valor repeats in an endless loop while I pick it apart for hidden meaning. It was all so forced and unnatural. I hate it, yet I know it is my fault. If I could pinpoint exactly what I did wrong, I could fix it.

I imagine the conversation playing out a hundred different ways to try to produce a different outcome. When my sluggish mind renders the conversation entirely nonverbal, beginning and ending in a passionate kiss, I hastily turn aside from thoughts of Valor and set my mind to the difficulty of furnishing the west side.

My venture into the city to view the construction was heartening, but my people lack so much that it is unreasonable to believe we can build and furnish an entire block of buildings under our current strains. However, I promised our people they would not be destitute. They should not bear the consequences of my enemy's retribution.

Almighty, not for my benefit but for theirs. Show me how to provide for them. Please tell me what to do.

Kragorn's investigation into the possible collusion of one or more generals with Zavaan has proved as challenging as anticipated. Simply learning how the Ruphiri stole into this heavily guarded city that is surrounded by a curtain wall has proved impossible.

I groan and throw a pillow across the room.

Benighted crown! Accursed royal blood! I am abdicating come morning. Then I am going to leave Malsihra and gallop Sacha all the way to Leelah's house. I am going to soak in her newly completed bath tub until I am covered in wrinkles then I am going to fill it again. After that, I am going to drink tea and laugh with my friend and snuggle her sweet babes until my problems do not matter.

Aye. That is the best plan I have concocted in months. Tomorrow. *Things will look better tomorrow,* I promise myself and shut my eyes.

An idea niggles at me, just outside my mind's grasp. It keeps me hovering this side of sleep past the middle of night. Furnishings…

Where can I find furnishings…

I jolt upright, scattering my nest of pillows. I spring out of bed, pushing my feet into slippers while dragging on my robe. This will work! This is going to work!

My gleeful squeal echoes on the stairs as my feet carry me downward then across the great hall. I spin the plan through my head until I can bear the anticipation no longer and break into a run to sooner deliver me across the castle.

I rap my knuckles on Valor's door, bouncing on my toes. This solves so many problems! He is going to be thrilled. Well, maybe not thrilled. Lorennt was not pleased when I proposed a similar idea last winter, but Valor is not the indolent…

The door flies open and every blessed thought leaves my head. Valor fills the door frame with sleep tousled hair, a sword gripped in his hand, and missing his shirt.

"What is wrong?"

"Nothing," I say, suddenly breathless. From the run across the castle, of course. It has nothing to do with the powerful beauty of the man before me.

"Erianna, why are you here? Do you know what time it is?"

"I needed to speak with you." I catch my lower lip between my teeth, forcing my eyes to find his. "May I come in?"

Why in heavens did I add that? I shouldn't go in his room. But I want to.

Valor looks past me down the hall then ushers me into the dark chamber, leaving the door wide. In the flickering torchlight from the corridor I see him replace his sword in its scabbard. "What is so important that you had to wake me from the first full night's sleep I have had in days?" Valor crosses his arms over his chest, causing muscle to ripple beneath skin.

"Umm…" I moisten my lips. "I had an idea."

He raises an impatient eyebrow. "Do you plan on sharing it, or should I go back to bed?"

My eyes drift to the rumpled bed then back to him, brazenly gawking.

His other eyebrow rises too, and a half smile curves his lips.

Oh, I am in such trouble.

Slowly, he closes the distance between us. "Maybe you should go back to bed too."

The air crackles. I force my fingers into the folds of my robe to keep them from tracing the grooves defining the muscles from his chest to his waist. My eyes, however, do not obey. They linger, causing my body to grow warm.

Valor chuckles. "For shame, Erianna."

My face burns so badly I am sure he can feel the heat radiating off my cheeks. To hide my humiliation, my sassy tongue flings words at him before my mind approves them. "Perhaps I should take off my shirt and see if you are capable of coherent thought."

Valor's silver eyes reflect my idiocy back at me. "I am certain I could think of a few things to say."

I smirk. "I could say something myself," but my negligent mind returns and shuts my mouth on the rest of the thought that ended in *I want to kiss you.*

Valor leans closer to me. My chin tilts up, offering my mouth as if he is guiding me with his hands not only his presence. But he merely reaches past me to retrieve a shirt from atop his trunk then puts space between us and dons it.

Humiliation floods me for offering what he did not ask for and did not take, twice in as many days. Add to that my bald admission that I am more than attracted to him. Mercy, I have made a fool of myself! But I certainly leant credibility to the lie I told earlier, not that I am pleased about it one bit.

A spark bursts into life and catches upon the wick of the lantern. Valor stands across the room with his back to me, his palms pressed to the surface of his desk. "You have to the count of ten, Majesty, then I am throwing you out."

Think! I require of myself, pressing my hands to my cheeks. *What am I doing here?*

It returns to me in a flash. "I know how to furnish all of the buildings on the west side without spending a single copper."

Valor looks around in astonishment. "How?"

On an impulse I say, "It is something better shown than explained." Another half truth. I came down here with the intention of explaining my plan, but then I would be on my way back to my side of the castle in less than a minute. Alone. And I am desperate for another few minutes to restore the normalcy between us.

He leans against the desk, keeping as much distance between us as possible. "Now?"

His forbidding expression makes me reconsider, but I nod, holding my breath. He eyes me for a long moment then gathers up his weapons belt. I grin and collect the lantern, leading the way down the hall.

My guard, who I forgot followed me, feigns disinterest at what surely looked like a lovers' midnight tryst. I hold my head high as I stride past him. My guards can think what they want. They follow my every step and know that Valor and I do not have that sort of relationship.

When I hear Valor's door close, I pause and wait for him to gain my side.

"Where to, Majesty?" His tone is stiff. I will tolerate it no more. Valor is my safe place. The one person I can be honest with. Not that I am being honest with him, nevertheless, I am done with this awkwardness.

I walk backward, holding the lantern aloft. "It is a harrowing journey to a place few venture without a dearth of courage and an equal measure of recklessness."

He throws an eyebrow high. "Keep walking backward and you are going to fall."

"Then you must walk closer so you can catch me." My heart offers up the words my head seeks to deny. But it is true. That is what I want. Not that he understands what I really asked.

Valor is not amused. "Where are we going?"

"It is a surprise," I taunt and whirl around, skipping ahead.

"Imp," he grumbles.

Eventually, we reach the dusty stairs leading to the lowest level. I extend the lantern over the descent and persist with my foolishness, hoping he will play along soon. It is unlike him to be terse with me. "There our path leads, Valiant Warrior. Does your courage hold?"

"What is down there?" Valor asks, finally moved to genuine curiosity.

"You do not know? Is it possible I know more about this castle than you do?"

He dismisses my taunt. "I have lived in Malesiir for the better part of a decade, but the castle has only ever been a stopping point for me."

"Until now?" I ask, hoping he will assure me that what he said yesterday was true. My heart leapt when he told me that I was his home.

I feel the veneer of his reserve crack before I see it. Valor pushes fingers through his hair and turns desperate eyes on me. "What do you want from me, Erianna? Can't you understand how difficult it is for me to interpret your inconstancy? I need you to tell me plainly what you want, and I will be that to you."

My humor falls away as I comprehend what I have done. Valor has told me repeatedly how he feels about me. I am the one holding back. Except when I don't. Like last night. Like now.

Valor closes the distance between us, catches my chin in his hand. I lean my face into his palm, craving his affectionate touch. I want to be held so badly, to feel safe and warm. A sigh escapes me when Valor slowly strokes his thumb down my cheek.

"Is it desire you feel for me?"

I nod.

"Is it *only* desire?"

"No," I admit.

"Then what?"

A lump of fear rises in my throat to block the truth from being exposed. If I tell Valor what I want, he will give it to me. As much as I long to be caressed and loved by Valor, I am not ready to be his wife, and I cannot have one without the other.

Marriage is so much more than physical intimacy and friendship. It requires honesty, trust, and, for my part, submission. I cannot be honest with Valor about everything that happened between Leer and I, nor do I want him to learn from personal experience my deficiencies as a wife, of which there are many.

Valor and I are friends, confidants. But as friends, I am still in a position to do exactly as I please with the added authority my royal blood affords me. When we rode into the city to battle the Ruphiri, Valor told me not to go. As queen, I went whether he liked it or not. Had he been my husband, I would not have had that same privilege. Leer curtailed my plans far too frequently. For the first time in my life, I am free to make my own decisions, though I am a servant to my throne. The prospect of remarrying terrifies me.

A thought strikes me that is so horrendous all the rest of my objections nearly seem inconsequential. *What if I lose Valor?* By my own actions, in the course of our courtship, he could determine that he does not want me after all, and he could abandon me. Or even worse, he could die. Valor is *the* Commander. He is nearly guaranteed to be at the front of any and every battle. Memories of the outrageous stunt he and Anders executed in storming the brigands nest is exactly the sort of thing that could leave me widowed a second time. I could not bear it. I would not survive having my other half torn away from me again.

Valor's hand moves to cup the nape of my neck, pulling me closer. "What do you want from me?"

The scuff of boots on stone interrupts our intensely private conversation. I scramble to gather my royal demeanor and place the proper distance between Valor and I.

Valor's frustration is felt in a sigh that ends on a growl. I cannot avoid giving him an answer indefinitely. It is unfair to him.

My guard stations himself beneath the glow of a torch in the dimly lit corridor. "You would have me wait here, Majesty?"

"I would. We shall return shortly." I set my feet on the stairs, descending into the gloom. My heart pounds so loudly in my ears that I imagine the stairwell is amplifying it.

Valor sets his hand beneath my elbow as we descend which does not help the frantic rhythm of my heart. "You will think on it won't you?"

"I promise to." Kragorn's words about doing more than thinking on it resonate. I ought to ask the Almighty to cast light on the path He would have me walk. Truthfully, I am scared where that might lead me.

"I can be satisfied with that for the time being." Valor's allowance is beyond gracious.

"Thank you." The relief in my words makes him wince as though his reasonable questions were anything but.

He finds a lighter tone, putting us back on footing that I am familiar with. "If your guard has abandoned you, either he is confident of your safety wherever we are going, or you were not exaggerating about needing fortitude."

"It is both." I smirk, shifting my thoughts to the adventure before us. "Tell me, how do you feel about spiders?"

"Only slightly better than you feel about them."

"Best steel your nerves, Commander."

The stairs leading to this lower level are wide as if it originally had a use beyond storage. I wonder if it could be repurposed in some way. Dungeon is the only use that comes to mind, but maybe once it is emptied, we will have another idea. Valor halts on the landing before the ancient doors. They are nearly as large as the ones leading into the castle. He lifts the bar and pushes the groaning door open. We enter the pitch black cavern at the top of a second short flight of stairs.

I raise the wick of the lantern, causing light to spill across the first of three chambers the size of the great hall. "Behold! The furnishings of the west side."

Heaps of furniture of all kinds fill the expanse while diamonds and amethyst sparkle throughout. It might be pretty if I did not know that the fast moving amethysts are rats' eyes shining in the light, and the diamonds are from rodent hunting spiders.

Valor gapes at me.

"The Rodiharians have a tendency to hoard their belongings. For generations they have piled up things that fell out of use. I threatened to make Lorennt help me clear out this space last summer, but that did not happen. Do you think we could adequately furnish the west side with all this?"

"I think you could furnish half the city." He releases me and starts down the steps.

I huff and extend my hand for his assistance.

He is incredulous. "You are coming?"

"Of course," I lift the hem of my nightclothes and follow him downward.

He takes hold of the back of my arm. "You hate places like this."

"I am not agreeing to make my bed down here, but I will explore with you."

Admiration swells his words. "You are the bravest person I have ever known. I am so proud of you."

My full smile does not adequately express they way his praise bolsters my confidence. Only Valor knows how much fear I have overcome to be able to walk here.

He selects our path through the castoffs. "Other than the obvious vermin and foreboding of this place, why are your guards scared to come down here?"

"Are you sure you want to know?" I tease. "Maybe that story ought to wait until you are safely tucked beneath your covers."

"I do not like scary bedtime stories," he wheedles.

I roll my eyes. "A tale is told that on stormy nights the ghosts of the deposed Brannock kings visit these chambers and bang at the doors seeking revenge on the Rodiharian line and all those that serve them."

"And you brought us down here anyway?" He feigns terror.

"Lorennt told me the story after we spent several hours down here on a scavenger hunt. I decided that the only thing living down here is that sort of unpleasantness." I point to a large rat darting across our path.

"Very sensible of you," he commends.

Even so, I have not been down here since Lorennt told me the story.

We wander through the first chamber and into the second. About halfway through, I stop. Here is where we found the beautiful glass lanterns that will hang in the great hall for winter solstice.

Valor turns in place, surveying the relics. "How do you intend to clean and restore all of this? It would take copious amounts of time and labor…" He chortles. "Your conscripted army of brigands and prisoners?"

I shrug. "They stole from their people. The least they can do is restore something. Besides, I am still paying for their room and board."

"There is that. Does our adventure end here?"

"Not necessarily," I hedge. "I am curious about what is in the last chamber, but we broke some glass the last time we were down here and…" I point to the mess we made then lift my hem to reveal purple slippers with silver embroidery. The thin suede soles are flimsy protection against glass.

"A bit formal for the rest of your attire," he drolly notes before confusion rumples his features. "If you were planning on an adventure, why did you not wear boots? And better clothes for that matter?"

I avoid his gaze, looking down at the multicolored glass shards littering the floor. I hear them crunch before the toes of Valor's boots cross into my vision.

He knows. My scheme to be with him is frightfully obvious, and he will make me own to it. Then he will know what I feel for him. I shut my eyes to guard myself from revealing my heart in them. How will I explain my conflicted feelings without destroying what we already have?

But my present fears prove to be unfounded, because Valor is not Leer.

Without a word, Valor lifts me into his arms and carries me over the glass. He does not make me admit to what I did or chastise me for interrupting his sleep to drag him into the filthiest place in the castle for less than honest reasons. He bears with me, granting me the time I requested.

I lock one arm around his neck and hold out the lantern for us. When we are well past the debris, he sets me on my feet then places his hand beneath my arm, gently guiding me forward.

We make our way from the second chamber into the third in silence. The third room proves to be just as cavernous as the others, but it seems to have fallen out of use generations ago.

"Somewhere in this room is a hidden passage out of the castle," I say to fill the silence.

"Truly?" Valor halts, setting a hand on his sword.

"Lorennt said that it is well hidden and bricked over," I hasten to add, "but, aye. It leads to a tunnel that goes beneath the castle wall and opens somewhere on the mountain. I imagine after all this time it is impassable."

He relaxes his grip on the sword.

We weave through stacks of crumbling furnishings. There seems to be very little of value in this chamber. It is all too old and decimated by rodents. A thick layer of dust and droppings covers everything.

An ancient wardrobe protests when Valor brushes against it, causing a monstrous spider to scurry from between the doors to defend its home. We both startle then laugh nervously, giving the leggy predator a wide berth.

"What do those things eat?" Valor exclaims in a whisper.

"Rodents," I inform him, shuddering. He shudders too, but the act looks ridiculous on his large frame. My giggle is out of place in the ominous chamber. I have the impression that the vermin inhabitants lean toward the foreign sound. Lorennt's ghost story does not seem absurd anymore.

We edge around a barricade of spiderweb covered chairs. The lantern light bounces off something in a distant corner. I hold it aloft, focusing on the shape I thought I saw. For a second, I thought I saw a man.

"Did you see that?" My words are little more than breath.

"What?" He follows my line of sight, scanning the darkness. I shake my head and continue on.

The back wall of the chamber comes into view, revealing the roots of the castle. Rough hewn bricks taller than me form the cornerstones of the immense structure above.

Valor whistles long and low. "This place is older than I thought."

"It has been added to over the years, but no one knows who originally built it or when," I concur. The Rodiharians seized power from the Brannocks two centuries ago in a nasty bit of sibling rivalry that involved a treacherous Brannock princess murdering her older brother and establishing the Rodiharian line in her husband's name. It was not the Rodiharians' proudest moment, though some history books pretend that the princess had noble motives. Either way, she successfully ended the three hundred and fifty year rule of the

Brannock kings.

Prior to the Brannocks, power was won and lost in a bloody game of "king of the mountain" for about a century. No single family managed to hold power long enough for their children to take the throne. Little is known about the first monarchy that ruled in the centuries prior or what happened to them. They are thought to be the same ones who built the fortress in Grevnhold, but their name was lost to history. Staring at the megalithic foundation of my castle, it is not difficult to conclude that the same masons who built Grevnhold built this place. I wonder if this was the subterranean keep of the castle? Or has the landscape of Malsihra changed so drastically with the advance of time that what was once the ground level has become the lowest?

Valor leads the way around the exterior wall of the room. Another glimmer pulls my attention to the same corner as before. His hand tenses around my arm.

"You saw it too?" Anxiety pitches my voice higher.

"Something reflective. Maybe it is a chest of treasure," he muses but grips his sword as we edge around the room.

I quip, "We are not so fortunate as that." Though I wish we were.

The dank air grows colder the farther we go, raising the hair on the back of my neck. Debris of a different sort clutters the floor beneath our feet. Chunks of stone are piled against the wall. We follow the rubble until a gaping hole in the foundation of the castle comes into view. Beyond it is a black tunnel.

I grab a fistful of Valor's shirt to call his attention to what I am seeing, but he sees it too. The grim set of his mouth confirms my worst fears.

"You think Zavaan opened it," I whisper, my enemy's name sending a chill through me. He certainly had plenty of time to learn the secrets of this place.

Valor's hand finds mine, lacing our fingers together.

"Tell me what you are thinking," I murmur as he leads me toward the maw.

He stares down the dark length of the tunnel. "You do not want to know."

I step closer to his side. "This is how he did it. How he got the poison to her. How he knew so many intimate details though he had supposedly left the kingdom."

Valor's guides me away from the tunnel. "I think we have seen all there is to see tonight."

What he means is that he alone is no match for a score of Ruphiri lurking in the shadows. It is not safe for us to be down here.

We follow a new path back to the stairs. The door is so distant it appears as a small window of light across the expanse of the three chambers.

The cobwebs are thicker here. I shiver, thinking how easily the spiders could run up my slippered feet onto my bare legs. "Let's hurry. I think my courage and recklessness are spent."

Valor agrees, navigating us around a heap of furnishings so deteriorated it is impossible to know what they once were. Around the other side, flickering light glints off plate armor. My stomach drops to my toes while my eyes travel up the bulk of an immense soldier, waiting in silence to ambush us.

CHAPTER FIVE

ERIANNA

I reach for daggers that are not on my person while Valor pushes me behind him and frees his sword. With a single felling stroke, Valor cuts the fully plate armored man in two. The armor crashes to the ground, setting the chamber ringing with the sounds of metal. We gape in open mouthed horror, realizing our mistake too late as the rusty suit of armor springs apart on the floor, scattering thousands of spiders in every direction.

Shrieking, I stumble backward against the dross heap that begins to teeter. Valor grabs my hand, sprinting back the way we came while another crash sounds behind us throwing thick dust in the air. The light in the lantern wavers as we reach the foundation. Valor turns us opposite of the way we ought to go, but I see why when I glance back. Our blunder has unsettled the rotting piles and created a ripple effect through the room, toppling one heap into the next into the next. The spiders and rodents moving every direction are horrible, but more dangerous is the dust cloud filled with mold and a hundred years worth of vermin refuse.

Valor keeps us moving ahead of the dust by running along the perimeter, and I realize what he plans seconds before he stoops through the opening, propelling us deep into the stone tunnel too low for him to stand upright. He drags me down the tunnel until we round a bend.

The echoes from the chamber are deafening in the ancient passage. Valor pushes me against the wall and wraps his mantle around us both, excluding the choking dust. I squeeze my eyes shut, burying my face against his chest as holds me tight to him.

The cacophony quiets, but we wait for several more minutes while the dust settles. Distant shouts sound across the chamber, likely my guard wondering what has become of us.

I peel my eyes open only to realize the lantern I still grip has gone out. I try not to panic. "Where is your flint?"

Valor reaches a hand to the pouch on his weapons belt. I hear him fumble for a moment then swear. His palm slaps the wall behind me.

"Where is it?"

"I left it in my room."

"What!" Fear cracks my voice. "Why did you do that?"

"You did not tell me I would need it," he retorts.

"I brought the lantern, didn't I? Why would you not think to bring the flint!"

His apology lacks sincerity. "Forgive me, I was a bit distracted."

"By what, finding a shirt?" I mock.

"By you standing in my room begging me to kiss you!"

"I did not." I shove him.

"Lies do not become you, Erianna," he snaps.

The shouting in the chamber intensifies. Valor growls and grips my wrist, pulling me along after him. We cough the closer we near the tunnel entrance and cover our mouths with our garments.

"Majesty! Majesty!" My guard shouts.

"I have her! She is safe." Valor shouts back. "Our light has gone out. Bring a torch."

"Aye!"

I feel unpleasant things brush past my skirt then sharp little claws run across the top of my feet. I shriek, stomping in place to ward them off.

Valor pulls me directly behind him. "Stand in the middle. They will run along the walls."

I set my trembling hands on his back, waiting an interminable time for the guard to return.

"I have it, Commander!" Swearing punctuates his words, no doubt at the vermin rushing every way. "Where are you?"

"We are at the back left corner of the third chamber. There is a tunnel here that supposedly leads out of the castle proper."

"I am coming to you," the guard says.

"Do not bump anything!" Valor barks urgently. "We created a rubbish avalanche that way."

I close my eyes, preferring their natural dark to the unsettling feeling of being blind. I lay my forehead on Valor's back.

"He is nearly across," Valor reassures me.

More swearing explodes from the guard. "Commander, I see the tunnel, but I cannot reach you. I have to move some of this—"

"Do not!" Valor shouts. "You must not stir up more dust! It will poison the air," which Valor further fouls with curses. "Do you have flint?"

"Aye."

"Pitch it over."

The flint lands with a spark just inside the tunnel. Valor scoops it up and lights our lantern then dims the wick to a glow to preserve the oil. "There is fresh air in this tunnel. We are going to follow it out. It seems to run northwest. Tell Lorennt what happened and send a patrol onto the mountain to fetch us."

"Aye, Commander."

I raise my voice to be heard, willing it not to shake. "I forbid anyone else to attempt to come through the chambers after us. It is not safe. Tell Lorennt I am sorry for my misadventure. Now, get out of here."

"Aye, Majesty."

Valor turns to me, hunched over in the low passage. "Shall we?"

※ ※ ※

We wind through the tunnel, walking for what feels like hours. Sometimes the tunnel narrows such that I have to stoop in the constricted passage. At those times, Valor must fold in half to make it through.

Always, there are the rats. They scurry past us on the edges of the stone tunnel, pausing to look back at us, sniffing the air. They look hungry.

I keep my hand on Valor's back as we make our way forward in a roughly straight direction. The connection to him helps me not panic at the dank smell of stone.

"Erianna, close your eyes," Valor gruffly orders.

"Why?"

"Do it!" He barks.

I obey, gripping his mantle, and let him pull me forward. After a long minute he says, "You can open them."

I decide to ask him what he did not want me to see once we are out of this infernal tunnel and do not dwell on what it might have been.

Why in the three realms did I think finding this hidden passage would be a fine adventure! Erianna Rodiharian, ever the fool.

Valor stumbles as the ceiling lowers again. He swears, and I feel his muscles jumping beneath my hand.

"Are you well?" The awkward position must be terrible for him.

He grunts in reply, leading on.

The tunnel opens into a sort of antechamber. The height nearly permits Valor to stand upright and the width would allow three people to stand abreast. I wonder if it is a halfway point. If we have only gone halfway…

I moan at the thought. "May we rest a moment?"

Rather than answer, Valor kneels, stretching his back with his arms above his head. At his continued silence, I come around to face him. In spite of the chill air, beads of sweat have gathered on his brow. His face and shoulders are taught with more than just the exertion.

"Valor, what is wrong?"

He shakes his head, closing his eyes that are full of storm clouds.

"Tell me."

He drags in one ragged breath after another. His pulse hammers in his throat. "I do not like confined spaces."

The tunnel bothers him? "You never told me that."

"It never came up," he gripes.

My foolishness led him here. "I am so sorry, Valor. This is all my fault."

A tight smile spreads his mouth. "Still apologizing for things outside of your control."

"I *am* sorry. Will you please forgive me?"

His eyes pull open to meet mine. "There is nothing to forgive. I started this by hacking down a suit of armor."

My eyes must reveal more than my words because he admits, "I am not angry with you, Erianna. I am afraid. That uncontrollable, gut-deep fear… Trapped… Beneath an accursed mountain." Muscles twitch in his jaw as he wars against panic. "It is hard to breathe."

I understand now. Valor's deepest fears almost always present as anger. I touch his face, wiping away the perspiration with my fingertips.

Spirit of Truth, show me how to help him. Show me what to do.

I remember the times I was afraid of the oppressive stone rooms that reminded me of dungeons. The Almighty freed me of so much of my fear that I have not succumb to panic even in this place. But before that, when Valor held me, his touch and the scent of his skin overpowered the things that provoked my fear.

Hold him, the Spirit of Truth whispers to my heart.

I push my fingers through his sweat soaked hair and stand between his knees. Valor settles over his heels submitting to my touch. I wrap my arms around his head, gently holding him to me. I feel each breath shudder through him as he lays his head against my middle. I emulate what he does for me and hide him from this place as best I can. I ease his hair from his brow with soothing strokes. The mighty warrior quakes.

Valor's arms wrap around the backs of my legs. "You smell like summer. Like lavender."

"Do I?"

He nods. "But you look like winter. You are a beautiful contradiction."

Contrary I have been called by many, but never as a compliment. Valor sinks deeper into my heart with each passing day, no matter how much I fight it.

He holds me tighter. "My Winter Eyes. I have searched for you for so long."

Valor calms beneath my hands, thus I do not disturb him by asking for an explanation. By degrees, the tension ebbs out of him. I lose my fingers in his hair, wending the locks between them. He allows me to minister to him. His vulnerability does something to my heart that I cannot undo.

A song stirs my soul. The words long forgotten come to me like the turning of a page in my memory. My mother sang it often that last year of her life. Knowing what misery her life must have been, I understand it was the groaning of her burdened soul. The words spill from my mouth now in a fervent melody

"Hear my cry, Saving King; attend to my prayer. From the end of the earth will I cry to Thee. When my heart is overwhelmed, lead me to the rock that is higher than I. For You have been a shelter for me, a strong tower from the enemy. I will abide in Your house forever and take refuge in the shelter of Your wings."

Peace invades this miserable place. In spite of the rats, in spite of the oppressive dark, in spite of the stone tunnel that constricts ahead of us, in spite of all his fears, Valor looks up at me and smiles.

He breathes freely, rising on his knees to take my hands in his. "Father, lead us out of this mire. Thank you for Your peace. Please give us Your strength. Light our path."

"Amen," I whisper.

"Thank you, Erianna." Valor kisses my hands then frowns. With the backs of his fingers he strokes my cheek. "You should have told me you were cold." His mantle lands around my shoulders like a breath of fresh air. His warmth clings to the dense wool. He fastens it around me and forges ahead into the tight passage.

※※※

VALOR

The tunnel from the castle is miles long. I knew it would be. That knowledge did not prepare me for the trek. The gentle incline turns into a steep climb after another mile, and dripping water sounds just ahead. I grind my teeth against a wave of panic roiling my gut. Fear of being trapped in a flooded underground passage threatens to unman me and reduce me to a blubbering poltroon.

Small hands move over my back like a soothing balm. "Give us peace, Heavenly Father."

Erianna's beautiful song unlocked the fetters on my spirit. It echoes in my mind bringing to memory more of the precious hymns and prayers in the Holy Text. I add them to her plea, hoping that, somehow, we will come out of this.

"Where can I go from your Spirit? Where can I flee from your presence? If I go up to the heavens, You are there. If I make my bed in the depths, You are there."

If this is not the depths, I do not know what is. Yet even here, the Almighty sees us, and His Spirit is with us. The tunnel narrows again, I hunch low to the ground, ache shooting through my back and legs. This passage was not constructed with someone of my stature in mind.

Erianna grunts behind me. I hear her mutter to herself, but I cannot turn fully around to see why. "Are you alright?"

"Fine."

She is in pain too. It riles me that my ability to help her along is limited to verbal support. "Do you need to rest?"

"Once we are out of here. Keep going."

The water I feared is ahead. It puddles in what I presume is a shallow dip in the floor. The rats swim across it and continue unperturbed. "The tunnel likely passes under a stream." That would explain the lower roof here. I groan, folding in half and step into the frigid water. It is shallow, not even reaching above my boots. Water sloshes up the walls.

Erianna gasps when she steps into the water without the benefit of boots.

"Not far," I encourage.

The tunnel opens a bit while the incline becomes quite steep. If I judge rightly, we are climbing up through the mountain. I glance back at Erianna. She puffs her way along with her skirts pulled high over her knees, half crawling on hands and bare feet.

"Where are your slippers!"

"They gave up a while back. I think I shall burn all my slippers when I return. Every time I don slippers I regret it. They are useless."

"If you cut your feet, this filth will cause infection. Sit down immediately."

"We must get topside," she argues.

I sit, blocking her path. "What happened to the delightful princess that did what I asked because my instructions were reasonable?"

"That princess was naive. I do as I please nowadays." Bitterness underlies her jest.

"Do you not trust me?" I ask bluntly.

"I do. More than anyone else." She stops at my feet. "What do you want me to do?"

I reach out to her. "Come ahead of me. I will wrap your feet."

She scrabbles past and sits with a weary sigh. I take up the hem of my shirt with dagger in hand.

"Do not. Use my hem. Tis in my way anyhow."

"It is not as clean though." Before deciding, I move the light closer and take her feet in my hand searching for cuts or abrasions. Thankfully, though quite dirty, they are unharmed. I cut away two hands of fabric from her chemise and bind each foot in the fine linen. "Can you move freely?"

She nods, shivering over crossed arms.

"We must be close now. A warm bath and fresh clothes are not far off."

She forces a smile. "And sweet rolls. There will be sweet rolls for breakfast."

"I will hold you to that." I crawl around her and set a quick pace that will keep her warm until I can lend her my heat.

During the endless march, I weigh Erianna's words. Could it really be so simple? Does she not want to be a wife again, even mine, because she no longer trusts? She called herself naive, as if it was a flaw. It was not. It was endearing. Nor did her naivety extend to blind trust. She did not give her trust away easily even then. I fought each day to earn her trust. But we were separated. Then Grandileer betrayed her in the worst of ways.

Surely she does not believe she was naive for trusting her husband, for loving him? He deceived all of us. Could his betrayal have cut her so deeply that she is afraid to let someone near her again?

Smite me for a fool! I should have realized this sooner. Erianna is reticent because she is frightened.

I have taken for granted that she trusts me. I should not have. But now the real worry is this: When her mourning comes to an end, will she give me a chance or is she wholly determined not to remarry?

It will be an invalid worry if we do not make it out of here. My shoulders brush against the sides of the passage that shrinks miserably, limiting my mobility. Bands tighten my chest at the perception of being trapped. I cannot draw a full breath.

The passage levels out. I push on faster only to draw up suddenly at a wall of rock blocking my way. Light shimmers on quartz veins in the stone. It is not bricked. It is natural, solid rock. I close my eyes, breathing around the panic.

The passage was not fully excavated.

We have been headed for a dead end all along.

"This is it!" Erianna exclaims.

To put it succinctly.

The exit is blocked. We will have to turn back, descend miles into the earth with the filth of the chambers and vermin blocking our escape on the other end. We might not even make it that far without water to drink.

It was all for naught.

We are in an endless stone coffin.

I fall to my hands and knees. The dim lantern light cannot break through the darkness edging out my sight.

"Valor, what are you waiting for?" Erianna sidles around me. "You made it. We can leave now."

I shake my head. I led her to her death.

"Oh, Valor." She wraps her arms around me. "Everything is alright. Let me show you."

If I keep my eyes shut, I can imagine I stand with my woman in a summer meadow. Far better that than where we are.

"Valor. Find my eyes."

I might as well. I want her winter eyes to be the last thing I see in this life.

Clear, ice blue ringed by sapphire.

Incredible.

I never told her. Maybe I should have.

"I love your eyes."

"Winter eyes?" She questions why I said that earlier.

I did not mean to, though it was bound to happen eventually. I think it often enough. Those dreams are only ever a thought away from my mind. "It is what I called you before I knew your name."

"I do not understand. You knew my name before we met."

"I knew of Princess Erianna. I had no idea that she was the wintry-eyed woman for whom I was searching."

"Valor, you are not making sense."

She should know. She ought to know that she has been loved, that I loved her, even before I knew her name.

"Five years past, I wearied of seeking a wife. Courting women had lost its appeal. I wanted a companion, but I was dangerously close to casting off the moniker of vestal for Anders's sort of life." I search Erianna's face to see if I have offended her with my admission. She mostly looks confused. "I was lonely. I prayed that if the Creator had a wife for me, He would show me who she was. I wanted to know for whom I was looking. That night, I dreamed of your eyes."

I hear Erianna's strident inhale, but I have waded too deep to turn back.

"I woke knowing with absolute certainty the beauty of my wife's eyes. And I began searching for her. For you."

Those same eyes are full of confusion, fear, distrust. "That is impossible."

She knows I do not lie. If she knows nothing else about me, she knows that. "I scoured Malesiir, certain I would find my Winter Eyes on one of my assignments. When I was called back to Malsihra, I spent time at court and in the city. Searching. Endlessly searching. I enjoyed the hunt at first, wondering each morning if that would be the day I found you.

"Four long years your eyes haunted me. I prayed for you. I was faithful to you. And I loved you. Then I was sent to retrieve the Limban princess. And curse it all if Grandileer's bride didn't have the eyes of my wife."

Erianna's strangled acknowledgement lances my heart. "When I woke in the apothecary… You knew."

I hang my head, ashamed that I have to admit to her how great a coward I am. "I knew what you could be to me, though I denied it. I told myself it was coincidence. You were promised to someone else. It was impossible. Not that it mattered. I was falling in love with you before we even left Grass Lake. I have loved you for so long, Erianna."

She pulls away from me and the walls of the tunnel collapse on my shoulders. I try not to gasp. I do not want her to see me fall apart. I should be her strength.

"You lied to me."

"Never," I choke out.

"A lie of omission! How many times did I ask what you thought of me?"

I fall on my hands, shaking my head. If I had breath I would curse Grandileer for tainting her view. Not everyone lies.

"This feels an awful lot like a confession," she accuses. "Tell me I am wrong!"

"Wrong!" *Almighty give me air!* This cannot be how it ends between us.

"You have been keeping things from me! And now you tell me I am without choice about where our relationship will go?"

"You misunderstand—"

"I was forced to suffer one lying husband. I will not suffer another!"

Erianna flees from me, shuffling to the end of the passage. She stands upright next to the wall, jumps, and hauls herself out of sight.

CHAPTER SIX

VALOR

November 25th

Unable to call Erianna back to me, I crawl after her. Alongside the wall is a narrow gap in the ceiling. Without the benefit of a full breath, I struggle through it into a shallow cave. Muscles protest their straightening after hours hunched over. I stumble from the cave into the darkest hour before dawn. My lungs scream for fresh air. I gulp it down, but it is of secondary concern.

Where is she?

I scan the black forest for Erianna. This panic is worse, so much worse than the other. The mountain is steep. Depending on where we are, she could wander over the edge of a cliff if she is not cautious. It is too dark for her to go alone.

I croak her name, gulp another breath of air to break the bands of fear gripping my chest and bellow, "Erianna!"

A figure peels away from the shadows, heading downhill. "You left the lantern behind."

"Curse the lantern!" I stretch my legs, pushing them toward her.

Erianna jerks away when I reach for her arm. I move faster this time, catching hold of her. "Be angry with me if you must, but I will not let you fall off a mountain!"

She glares daggers. "Unhand me."

"Stay close."

Her reply is not an assent but a coarse suggestion.

"So be it. But make no mistake, if you wander off, I will bind you to me."

She yanks her arm free and walks away in silence, but she does remain near me.

Erianna's anger rolls off her in cold waves. There will be no reasoning with her in this mood. She will come to understand later. I hope.

I call myself six different kinds of an idiot. I should have known better than to tell her. After realizing that she is frightened of being a wife again, I told her that she was promised to me and would someday be mine. Was there a worse thing I could have said in that moment?

Probably not.

As a diversion, I try to think of a faster way to have sent her running. Nothing comes to mind. I blame my lapse in judgment on a lack of air and certainty we were going to die.

I just wanted her to know she was loved for who she is. She twisted that revelation into a pair of shackles it was never meant to be.

I snort. Erianna scowls across her shoulder at me. I mockingly return the expression.

If she does not realize by now that I love her, I am truly at a loss for other ways to communicate it.

Well, not completely at a loss. There is one path I have not gone down for both our sakes. Considering how we spent the last awful hours and the fractured ground we now stand upon, maybe it would have been better to take the kiss she offered in my room. And whatever came after.

My conscience pricks me for entertaining such thoughts. While I do desire her, so much that I must sometimes repent of where I allow my thoughts to go, I will not take her to my bed. Not even if she offers.

I have a strong suspicion that her views on intimacy's role in marriage are flawed. How could they not be after what Grandileer put her through? I want her to have absolute confidence in my love before she gives her body to me, and I will provide her with the safety of vows to do so.

Darkness gives way to gloaming, turning the forest blue. Erianna's cloth wrapped feet crunch through the snow. She must be unbearably cold. I certainly am. The burbling of a creek heralds its appearance. I veer in that direction. Erianna stiffly follows. We kneel at its edge, washing the grime from our hands, arms, and faces. The water is as ice, but we sip it, grateful to ease the thirst born of tromping through the musty tunnel.

"Not too much. You will—"

"Chill myself." Erianna tartly interjects. "I know."

It is a particular talent women possess to be able to flay a man with a mere glance. I am too exhausted to protest the injustice of my flogging.

"May I see your feet?" I phrase it as a request to win her capitulation. It does not.

"No."

I have half a mind do it without her consent, but she has been bullied too much for one lifetime. Nor does my greater strength excuse highhandedness. I prop my forearms across my thighs. "What will it take?"

"Pardon?"

"I am tired and want to rest, but you need to be looked after. Tell me what you require to gain your cooperation so that I can give it to you and tend your feet."

She stares blankly at me until her chin quivers. Without a word, she comes closer, sitting in easy reach. I unwrap the dingy cloths and toss them well away from the creek. Her feet are red and painfully cold and will be colder still. She huddles beneath my mantle as I briskly wash her feet in the stream. If I do not warm them, I fear she will loose some of her toes to winter's bite. With the night losing to the day, I recognize our location on the mountain and form a plan.

I cut more strips of fabric from her chemise, raising the length of it to her knees. She blushes until I cover her bare skin with the robe then rewrap her feet. She does not resist my help climbing the frozen bank of the stream and walks compliantly at my side until we find the place I seek. I guide her over an outcropping that juts from the mountain to reveal Malsihra nestled in the valley below. The walk down to the city and back around to the gates would take a couple of hours, but we are both exhausted, and she is dangerously cold.

"What are we doing?" She asks.

"Waiting for Lorennt to come pluck us off the mountain. We will see him easily from here."

She nods and lowers next to me which will not do.

"Sorry, Majesty. It is too cold for that."

Erianna mutters under her breath but sits on my lap, facing me, and drapes my mantle around us. I unwind the fabric from her feet and tuck them against my legs to protect them from freezing. The cold morning air drifts between our bodies, preventing heat from accumulating. I untie her robe and slip my arms inside around her waist, pulling her closer. Obstinate as ever, she resists.

"Woman, either cozy up to me or I will think of another way to put the rose back in your lips."

She narrows her eyes and brings her body against mine, burying her face in my neck and, going a step further, tucks her icy hands under my shirt to rest against my stomach. I stifle a yelp at the chill of her fingers against my skin. She is far too cold. Fearing for her toes, I wrap a hand around her feet.

"Oh, you are bonfire," Erianna murmurs, drawing closer to me. Her warm breaths float across my neck then fall down over my chest where her soft body is pressed against mine.

I loose a string of creative curses in my head to turn my thoughts aside from where they were headed. Lorennt had better hurry. I am but a man. I can endure sweet torture for a finite time.

Erianna grows heavy in my arms, drifting toward sleep. From the very beginning, that first time we shared the rented room in Grass Lake, she has slept easier with me near. In turn, her ease drives out my restlessness. Maybe that is what we have both needed for months. A deep, full night's sleep. Fatigue weighs down my eyelids. The next time she wakes me in the middle of the night, I shall take her back to my bed to use as a pillow.

But I cannot sleep now. I must keep watch.

I rub the sleep from my eyes against the wool hood covering her head. She responds with a contented sigh while her fingers find the grooves in my abdomen and begin tracing them. I relish her touch for a moment, but she has no idea what she idly does to me. Or maybe I am remembering the naive princess. The careful space she has mostly maintained between us attests to her loss of naivety. So does that look she gave me last night.

With a divine amount of self control, I swallow a plea for her to keep going and instead embarrass her into stopping. "So, you got what you wanted after all."

"*Hmm*?" She asks, pressing her hands flat against me and sliding them languorously up my body.

"Erianna!" I growl.

She comes awake and withdraws her warmed hands and arms from beneath my shirt. She raises her red stained face to glare at me as if her wantonness is somehow my fault. "If you say even one word about this *ever*, I swear I will unman you."

That is better.

I keep my lips sealed and offer a patronizing smile that toes the line on what she would consider "one word." She raises a scarred brow, daring me to add another "word" to the conversation. I do not. Satisfied, she lowers her head to my shoulder and folds her arms between us.

My thoughts roll back to that miserable tunnel and the humiliating weakness I revealed to her. That is what led me into our current state of hostility.

"Your elbow is unnecessary. I think I did the job quite thoroughly myself."

"You are injured?" Concern is apparent in her tone.

"My pride," I clarify, "and your opinion of me suffers. I am sorry I was undone."

"Because you were afraid?"

Distaste curls my lip where she cannot see it. I dip my chin against her head in acknowledgment. Over and again I have told the men I command that there is no shame in fear. It is a healthy response to danger and necessary for survival. However, it should never take control of ones actions. Men do not surrender to fear. Yet that is exactly what I did.

Though Erianna is furious with me, she cannot help herself from consoling when it is in her power. She lays her palm over my heart. It is her own endearing gesture of receiving or bestowing truth. "I do not think your fear unmanned you in the least. Nor do I think of you as weak for showing weakness. My opinion of you was not harmed by that."

"But it was harmed." I lay my hand overtop of hers when she would have pulled away. "I did not lie to you. I vow I have never lied to you. Not even by omission."

"Stop," she tugs against my hand.

"If you think back, you will realize that I told you as much as I could at the time. The only accusation you can brand me with is *coward*. If I had not been so frightened by the truth, I could have fought to free you from the beginning. You must know—"

"Please! I am not ready to discuss this!"

I let her pull away. The depth of my regretful sigh makes her body rise and fall against my chest. "I am sorry I upset you."

She folds her arms again.

I intended to tell her one day. I truly did. Someday, when she is my wife, I would have told her. She has had so little power to decide her own future, I did not want her to feel like I was forcing her to marry me. But I bungled it. All because I wanted her to know how fully she is loved.

I am an idiot.

"Leer never told me of what he was afraid," Erianna says. "He saw me fall apart so many times because of my fears, and he helped me through them. But I never got to do the same for him. He never even told me."

I let the silence stretch out but am incapable of letting her feel sadness when I have the power to move it away from her. "Falcons. He was afraid of falcons."

She lifts her quizzical gaze. "The hunting birds?"

I grin and nod. "I learned of it when he, Lorennt and I went hawking. He made excuses about the gloves not fitting properly and avoided all contact with the birds until Lorennt teased him for still being afraid of them, which was Lorennt's fault. The story goes that in their youthful rivalries, Grandileer, being seven years older than Lorennt, always came out the victor. Through a series of underhanded schemes, Lorennt lured Grandileer to the falcon mews after tucking scraps of meat into his pockets, unbeknownst to him, of course."

"Of course." I feel her smile against my neck.

"Lorennt locked him in there and fled, leaving his brother to be attacked by falcons intent on retrieving the scraps of meat at any cost. Grandileer was relieved to learn that was why the birds were clawing at his pants."

Erianna exclaims, "That was what those scars were from! He had a few strange scars that did not look like they came from weapons. He said he earned them when Lorennt and he were scrapping." Her amusement fades. "Why did he not tell me?"

"I would guess in that instance he did not want you to know he was afraid of birds. He would have hated to appear weak in your eyes."

She hides her face against me. "But I hate lies."

I hesitate, then kiss her head. "I know."

Spirit of Truth, please show her that I did not lie to her. Reveal to her that I will not disregard her, or place her wellbeing second, or ever be unfaithful to her. Please let her see that I will always endeavor to love her as Your Son loves His bride. Give me the chance to prove myself to her.

I hold Erianna as the sun chases away the night in a beautiful show of golden color. "I sometimes come up here to watch the sun rise. Can you see it?"

She curls into me, turning to watch the sun crest the distant mountains. The rays illuminate Malsihra in a wave of light.

The rest of the verse I recited warms my soul, so I share it with her. *"If I rise on the wings of the dawn, if I settle on the far side of the sea, even there Your hand will guide me, Your right hand will hold me fast."*

Her breaths stutter through her. I did not mean to make her cry.

I rest my chin on her head. "He holds you safe, Beloved. He has never lost sight of you, not for a single moment. He will never let you go."

Her words are muffled with tears. "The far side of the sea was so awful. I am scared to go back there." So awful that she was willing to escape by any means necessary, even her own death.

I set my hand beneath her jaw, lifting her face toward mine. "You are not alone this time. He preserved you through those trials, and He will sustain you through your future trials. It is in some of my darkest nights that I have known Him more purely than in the brightest dawn."

There is much uncertainty in her eyes. I want to erase it with a word or a touch, but that is outside the realm of my power. I stroke her tear streaked cheek with my thumb and draw her back to my chest so she can know my heart that echoes the Almighty's love for her.

On the distant low path ascending the mountain, riders in Malesiirian colors fan out, searching for their queen. I cover Erianna's ear and bring my fingers to my mouth whistling shrilly until the riders halt, scanning the mountainside. I wave to them and someone whistles back.

"Your bath and sweet rolls are minutes away, Brave One."

"Lorennt, will chew my ear off first."

"No, it will be me who takes the reprimand, and I am well with that."

Erianna did not do anything that deserves reprimanding—her poor choice in adventuring clothes aside. As the riders draw near, I call her attention to the silver haired Rodiharian riding hard at the fore. "That looks like Boldizar to me, not Lorennt."

Cold air rushes to fill the space between us as she sits upright, training her eyes on him. She gasps. "It is!"

I wrap her tightly in my mantle and ignore her token protest made through chattering teeth while I carry her through the brush. Before I can reach the narrow path, Boldizar leaps to the ground, running toward his daughter. He takes her from me with a look that demands explanation.

"She is well, merely cold and in need of shoes."

Relief washes over his lined face and tears touch the corners of his eyes. He kisses his daughter's brow, holding her secure in his arms.

Erianna's eyes do not stray from his face. "You came for me," she says in amazement, trying to make sense of why he would. She still does not understand how completely she is loved.

Boldizar imbues the fullness of love only a father knows into two words. "My daughter." He kisses her brow again, striding toward his horse and scanning the surrounding woods for any danger to his precious child. He settles her upon the saddle and waves to one of the soldiers who hurries forward with blankets. Boldizar wraps Erianna snuggly and offers her a water skin. Once he is sure she lacks nothing, he swings to the saddle, holding his heart-daughter close.

I endured one of my worst nightmares without tears, but the sight of my beloved held safe in her father's arms moves me to them now. I turn my back, gazing at the dawn through the skeletal branches.

Thank you, Heavenly Father. Thank you so much for giving her a father to love her as the man she sprung from never did. Thank you for restoring tenfold the love of the family she lacked.

※※※

Boldizar relinquishes Erianna to the tearful welcome of Nev and Celiea. Riders were sent out to recall Lorennt and the other search parties with the message that Erianna was found. Seeing how much agitation her misadventure caused her family, Erianna is chagrinned. She assumed all that awaited her upon her return was a scolding from Lorennt for being foolhardy. I am not surprised in the least. If I had not been with her, I would be beside myself with worry for her safe return.

What does surprise is the baleful look Boldizar levels at me after his daughter is taken above stairs. His hand grips his sword in bald threat. "Meet me in my study in a quarter hour."

"Yes, Your Majesty." I bow to him.

I do not have the benefit of more than a wash basin to remove the filth of the underground while I mull over what earned me Boldizar's wrath. Lorennt knows firsthand that going with Erianna on her adventures is wiser than sending her back to bed. She might have gone without escort and landed herself in even more trouble.

Boldizar does not leave me in suspense once I attend him in his study. "What are your intentions toward my daughter, Valor

Ironforge?"

The dropping of my title and his glare a shade away from violence throws me back in time to the sins of my youth. Boldizar glares at me like the angered father of a maiden daughter whose honor I have ruined. The guilt of the youth I was finds me in my lack-witted state. Did I ruin this man's daughter?

The man I am knocks the youth aside and laughs at the absurdity of the situation. Unfortunately, I do not contain my humor. "I think we are a bit old to be having this discussion, Your Majesty. Especially since it is in regards to Her Majesty, my blood sworn sovereign."

Boldizar does not share my humor. "I fail to see how my daughter's honor is laughable *especially since* you have besmirched it in the past."

That quells my amusement.

I harden my expression. "My queen's honor concerns me greatly. Knowing the rumors in circulation about the nature of our relationship, we have been above reproach in our conduct."

Boldizar does not invite me to sit with him but keeps me standing for my reproof. "I am not speaking of rumors. You err in believing I am uninformed about the sordid actions of you and Leer. I know full well the tug of war you fought over my daughter and why he summoned you to the seaside castle. Now I say again, and for the last time, what are your intentions toward her?"

It takes more energy than I currently poses to remain impassive. "With respect, Majesty, my queen knows how I feel and that is all I will say."

The king springs to his feet advancing on me. "Then you have sullied my daughter?"

"No," I growl. "I shall never disrespect her."

"Yet she sought you in the middle of night for noble reasons? In her bed clothes, no less!"

Somewhere on the other side of the castle, Erianna is blushing furiously with no idea why.

"My queen is an honorable woman," I retort. "She came to discuss provisions for her displaced people and wished to show me how she intends to furnish all the buildings on the west side."

"In the middle of night?"

I shrug. "She is enthusiastic."

Boldizar returns to his chair by the fireplace. "Lorennt and I have been inundated with men, young and old, seeking permission to court Erianna."

The shift in conversation unbalances me. "She never said—"

"She does not know."

My mind reels. Already the old vultures are circling, trying to take hold of the title of *queen's consort*. And the pups like Sigure want to take hold of her.

"You seem agitated, Commander."

"She is in mourning! How dare they impose on her!" My volume rises with my temper.

Boldizar placidly steeples his fingers. "Join me."

I begin to pace. "Who has asked for her hand?"

He names half a dozen young lords whose requests are easily written off as infatuation or power grabbing—Lord Sigure among them—a few despicable ancient men, a general...

"Wait," I interrupt the King Abdicàt, "Did you say General Kannik?"

He affirms it with a nod.

"General Kannik wanted to serve her to the Ruphiri as a means to get rid of them! Now he wants to marry her?"

Boldizar taps his fingertips together. "He reasons that Erianna needs a strong counterbalance to her 'sentimental feminine nature.'"

My blood boils. "He means to subdue her! He would make my queen a puppet to his will!" Boldizar is far too calm for my liking. Where is the concerned father from five minutes past? Lorennt would gladly help me string Kannik from the tallest tree before entrusting Erianna to him. I might do just that for his even asking to court her with such insults.

"You may be right." Boldizar's brow furrows in thought. "But what role should the husband of a queen have?"

"Her husband should protect her and free her to make the decisions she must. She needs someone to listen to her and respect her thoughts. He should bolster her, not superimpose his will on her."

"You mean let her be the leader in the marriage?"

"No, she must have a husband confident in his leadership. But she needs to be led with love, not might. He should be willing to serve the kingdom alongside her, lighten her burdens."

"Anything else?"

"She should be cherished and loved as the Saving Son loves his people."

"*Hmm*... That is a long list." With a satisfied smile, Boldizar tightens his snare around my feet. "You seem to have given the subject a goodly amount of thought. Do you have any suggestions on who might fit that description?"

I stare at Erianna's father who looks thoroughly amused. I should have known better. He riled me, baited me, then let me reveal what I had not meant to out of respect for her wishes.

This time, when Boldizar points at the chair opposite him, I sit.

With a groan, I dig the heels of my hands into my eyes. I need sleep. This would not have happened if I had a full night's sleep at my disposal. The cause of my sleeplessness is probably already sighing into her pillow, bathed and with a full stomach, no less. It is a good thing there are no hidden passages to the royal wing of the castle. I might sneak into her room and curl up at the foot of her bed like an overlarge dog.

"During your years serving Malesiir, you have proved your character. You are a man of honor and integrity, Commander Ironforge. Thus, I ask again. What do you feel for my daughter?" Boldizar's steady gaze requires a direct answer with no more evasions.

If he knows in full what transpired between Erianna and I, as told by Leer, I presume, then my simple answer will not surprise him. "I love her. I want to marry her."

Not only does the King Abdicàt expect my answer, he knows where the difficulty truly lies. "What if she will not have you?"

Something I do not want to consider, but knowing her misgivings, I ought to. The promise I made to her when she considered fleeing from Malsihra returns to me. Though she has taken up the mantle of queen, my promise still stands. "I shall be her constant companion and serve as her Hand. Wherever she goes, I go."

Boldizar is pleased. "It is a wonder that you did not seek my permission to court her, though I am aware you have an understanding of sorts with Lorennt."

"With respect, Majesty, Erianna has had everything in her life decided for her. I do not think anyone has the right to tell her who she is allowed to marry this time."

"I happen to agree with you," Boldizar says. "I want my daughter to be happily married and cared for. I see where her life is headed, and she will need a partner for what the Almighty has planned. That is why I charge you with courting my daughter and taking her to wife."

I stare slack-jawed. I am in need of sleep worse than I thought. Did Grandileer's father charge me with wedding Erianna? I sputter, "You want me to… But I don't… She is in mourning for *your son*!"

He sighs. "Erianna has been mourning the death of her short-lived, tempestuous marriage alongside her daughter for over six months. I would not fault her for moving on with her life. She is too young to be widowed. It grieves my heart endlessly to see her in the clothes of an old woman, her vibrancy shadowed by a weeping veil."

Verily, he does appear equally grieved for his daughter still among the living as he is for his son lost behind the veil of eternity. Boldizar, however, is not the only person for whom Erianna feels concern. "I do not think Queen Celiea would agree."

Boldizar's attention centers on me. "Why do you say that?"

I am surprised he has not heard of it yet. I recount what happened in the great hall and what I infer transpired between Celiea and Erianna thereafter. The king hangs his head in his hand, aged by time and sorrow. It is several minutes before he collects himself and regains his words. His struggle is a visceral reminder of Erianna's stilted sentences. I will never allow her to be broken and abused again. Staying at her side as either husband or companion is the only way I know to prevent her from being harmed.

Boldizar returns to our conversation. "My poor Celiea. Grief has done cruel things to her. She has lost more children than a mother can rightly bear. But I shall speak with her. And Erianna." He rises from the chair with far more joints popping than those of his knees and shakes my hand. "Thank you for looking after my daughter last eve, Valor. Though I would prefer it if you would curb her nighttime wanderings rather than encourage them. My children have a predilection for carnal sin. It would be best to avoid such temptation."

"Aye, Your Majesty." I cannot refute his claim with the phantom of Erianna's touch occupying my mind.

I walk by rote to my room and collapse into bed, my thoughts caught in a whirlwind.

Boldizar charged me with wedding Erianna. How shall I convince her?

CHAPTER SEVEN

ERIANNA

November 27th

I mull over father's words from this morning. After breakfast we went for a walk and spent time together in conversation that was both honest and encouraging. One thing in particular stood out among the rest. Gazing upon the frozen forest gilded with fresh snow, Father took my hands and kissed the top of my head. "Erianna, do not let Celiea's grief prevent you from moving forward with your own life. Her grief is not yours. Nor are the burdens you bear the ones she must carry. Be brave, Dear One. Walk the path the Creator has laid out for you with whomever He has given you to make the journey. You ought not be alone."

I shuffle the papers on my desk and stack them again. The weight behind father's words was not lost on me, but chewing on them has only resulted in a lip bloodied by my bad habit. I am no closer to having peace about my next step, though I am relieved I have his support.

My breath huffs as I dab at my lip. I wish I could skip ahead to a tidy resolution of the numerous problems facing me so that I know what I must do to reach a favorable outcome. But not all outcomes are favorable to my way of thinking, even if they are the ones the Creator has planned. Somehow, our brokenness and desperate situations are places where He shows up so mightily that His light is seen all the better through our cracked and shattered places, like a candle beneath a broken clay vessel. I could not see the fullness of His wondrous perfection until I was broken beyond my or anyone else's ability to repair. Then His love poured out and remade me.

I bask in the remembrance of that marvelous day and decide to trust that He will be just as present this day and in the ones to come.

Valor and Lorennt enter with tight expressions portending trouble. I loose a silent prayer heavenward as Lorennt motions me to join them by the fire. Valor prepares me for the vein of trouble with a few words. "You never asked why I told you to close your eyes in the tunnel."

Zavaan is to be the topic of discussion. It occurred to me when I recalled those measureless hours that Valor was protecting me from something, and that something probably had to do with the last man in the tunnel. I wave my hand, giving him leave to tell me what I know I do not want to hear.

Valor continues, "We stumbled upon the remains of a woman. I sent a pair of guards back through the tunnel yesterday to retrieve what was left of her. After a considerable amount of work for which you owe Silla three more favors, she discovered that the remains belonged to a serving woman who worked in the kitchens for the past several years. She resigned her position in May after telling her husband that she was leaving him to be with her lover."

"Let me guess," Lorennt mutters.

Valor inclines his head. "He managed to keep it hushed, but Zavaan had an affair with the woman."

"And then murdered her," I conclude.

"Or had one of his henchmen tie off his loose end," Lorennt suggests.

I shake my head. "No. If he was involved with the woman, he did it himself." *The cold steel of a bloodied dagger kisses my cheek... Lust blends with death in the umber of Zavaan's eyes.* Bile rises in my throat. "He enjoys killing. Especially if it is personal. I am not sure why."

"I hope you never know why," Valor rumbles with a depthless fury toward this man who set himself up as my enemy—*our* enemy. "Beyond that, I am inclined to agree with Erianna. Bronis might have been capable of such violence, but he, like myself, was a bit large to fit through those tunnels."

I do not want to know, but I ask anyway. "It was a gruesome thing?"

Valor softly pleads, "Do not ask anything more."

I don't.

Lorennt summarizes, "This woman was Zavaan's informant within the castle until he no longer needed her, then he disposed of her."

"And," Valor holds my gaze, "the woman was close friends with Jaleh."

My fingers grip the arms of the chair. "This serving woman was the missing connection, the one we could not find."

"Aye," Valor confirms.

We did not know how Jaleh obtained the poisons or why Zavaan would claim to have planted the idea in her mind. According to Silla, Zavaan never had any direct contact with Jaleh. If this serving woman confided in Zavaan, he could have easily used her to pass the poison to Jaleh. But Zavaan underestimated Jaleh's hatred for me. He took quite a risk giving her such a strong tincture. Killing me would have foiled his plans.

Silla and Trent have searched tirelessly for any connections Zavaan made to my court or to my army that would continue to give him access to sensitive information. Unfortunately, he concealed his tracks very well. Posing as Gavin Chase, Trade Ambassador of the Commonwealth, he circulated through my court making the acquaintance of everyone but befriending no one. The whole of my court claim passing knowledge of him, but no one *knew* him. It would be simpler if he had been reclusive. He even trained in the barracks with the soldiers, absorbing what, at the time, seemed like innocuous information about the workings of the Malesiirian military while also learning their fighting styles.

I cringe each time I ponder how much he learned of us last winter.

"Do you think he has used the tunnel recently?" I ask.

Valor watches me in that deep way of his, sensitive to the current of my feelings. "It is difficult to say, but I do not believe so. The dust was thick through the center of the tunnel. I could not discern any evidence of its recent use."

"But he could use it again," Lorennt voices the troubling thought, then orders, "I want the tunnel sealed. It holds no strategic value to us. It is only a weakness."

"I agree," I murmur.

Valor accepts the order with a bow of his head. "I will see it done."

"Is there anything else?" I hate discussions of Zavaan. I want him to be erased from my life and expunged from my memory.

Valor eases back in his chair. "Nothing of importance. If you have no objections, I plan on going with Kragorn to retrieve his family after this business is concluded. And Tirzah. She wrote to ensure I do not forget to collect her."

Something uncoils in my belly that I do not care to name. After mere days of being returned from his assignment that lasted long weeks,

Valor is ready to leave again. At Tirzah's behest, no less! It does not sit well with me. Is he anxious to see her?

A more logical voice attempts to uproot the seeds of betrayal in my heart. Maybe Valor's leaving has nothing to do with Tirzah. Maybe she is an afterthought as he makes it sound, and his real motive is to help the Tareths.

Or maybe I am an idiot.

The air in the room becomes uncomfortably taught. Lorennt shifts his gaze between us with growing bemusement while Valor awaits my permission with keen interest at my prolonged silence.

If I ask him not to go, would he? Probably, but that does not matter because he wants to go. Leelah and Kragorn will need all the help they can get. It would be selfish of me to deny them his assistance, whatever his motive is for leaving. Nor will I be a petulant woman who whines to keep a man at her side. If he wants to go, let him.

I force myself to incline my head giving my assent. Before Valor can pursue the source of my obvious unease, I rise. "I am most anxious to see them. If you will excuse me, I must draft a letter for Leelah."

CHAPTER EIGHT

ERIANNA

December 2nd

"You ought to take another lady's maid," Silla says as she enters my chambers without the preamble of knocking.

"A good morning to you too," I counter, eyeing her perfectly groomed appearance in direct contrast to my half dressed state. "You are early. I intended for you to join me after breakfast. There was no cause to rush up here at daybreak."

"Be at ease. It was no inconvenience for me," she waves a dismissive hand.

"Perhaps *I* am inconvenienced," I counter tartly, striding into my dressing room.

She ignores the barb and follows, sorting through my mourning dresses. "You do intend to grace the court with your presence, do you not?"

The timbre of her voice conveys more than the casual question. "I do. Why do you ask?"

She spreads the fabric of a gown I frequently wear between her hands then pushes it away in disgust. "You should obtain better dresses. These are beyond drab."

"They are mourning dresses, Silla. They are supposed to be drab." I reach for my training clothes. Since they are hues of grey, I consider them appropriate mourning attire. Thick wool hose hug my skin before I layer on pants, tunic, overdress, and cuirass. I plan on training or riding at some point today. Donning my light armor simply saves time.

Silla lets fall the solemn skirt of another mourning gown. "You hate them."

"I do not 'hate them.'"

Her expression is all skepticism. "You wear that threadbare garb more often than garments befitting a queen."

I strap my smallest dagger to my thigh then retrieve my weapons belt bearing Daisy and the twin daggers. "This is hardly 'threadbare.' Besides, I always dress in gowns for dinner."

My vambraces sit at the ready next to my beautiful glaive, Violet. They seem a bit much for breakfast so I leave them be. But on days that I hold court in the great hall, Violet resides in a stand on the dais. Whether or not my glaive's presence has any bearing on the court's opinion, I cannot know, but I feel better knowing she is at hand.

"You advance the gossip with your..." she searches for the word, "*unconventional* mourning attire."

"I see. May I assume you are referring to the gossip regarding the unfortunate display with Valor?"

"Which display?" She challenges. "When you nearly kissed? Perhaps the day after when you pretended to be polite strangers after avoiding him?" She taps her chin. "No, you must mean the following day when you arrived barefoot in your bedclothes after spending the evening in his company." She chuckles. "You looked like the spoils of war being carried into the keep."

I round on her. "I take your meaning."

"If you did, you would not need to ask me what the gossip is. You would apprehend it without being told."

A flush born of ire and embarrassment overtakes my complexion. "I know there is conjecture that Valor and I have met beneath the sheets. I am asking you specifically how this affects the court's opinion, which is our arrangement if you will recall."

"Very well, Majesty." Silla calmly informs me, "Owning to the combination thereof, the court has determined that you deign to wear mourning clothes to appease the Rodiharians while, in truth, you are eager to entertain male attention."

She continues speaking over my aghast exclamation. "Since you have not rebuffed the commander's advances in a meaningful way, the noblemen are intent upon making their own gambits to claim your hand—or at least gain your bed. Lord Sigure is leading the charge to obtain permission from Boldizar to court you."

"The audacity!" Hot indignation burns through me. "I am the High Queen of Malesiir, quite possibly the woman with the most power on the Continent, yet it is still the male members of my family who hold the power to give consent or denial to my suitors!"

Silla commiserates. "You may be High Queen, but you are still a woman."

I scoff, "And Valor wonders why I am not rushing into marriage."

"A woman would be foolish to rebuff his suit." She says it drolly, but I believe she might be earnest. It is always a mix of truth and nonsense with her.

I pace the length of my dressing room, considering my options. Since Father encouraged me to move on, I have a strong suspicion that he will give Sigure permission to court me, possibly others. Lorennt might be persuaded to intercede on my behalf, but that smacks of weakness. I will not be weak again.

If I plead my case to Mother Celiea, she may be able to sway Father. I doubt she is overeager to see me remarried. Although, wasn't it she who invited her nephew to extend his stay? In hopes that a fondness would grow between us? A pounding ache begins behind my eyes. Leer warned me that she was crafty.

"For a society that upholds propriety as the pinnacle of civilized culture, there is nothing proper about making overtures toward a mourning widow," I grumble.

"Then why did you allow Valor to do so?" Silla queries, perhaps more to point out my own instigation of these events than a curiosity to define what goes between Valor and I. As such, I do not reply.

I am in a position to be maneuvered like some doe-eyed ingenue because of societal flaws. It offends mightily. I am the Warrior Queen, capable of deciding for myself when and whom I will court. If ever I wish it.

My pacing brings me around the room to my mourning gowns hanging in a neat row. I huff, trailing a hand over the somber fabric. Poor shields these when the one wearing them possesses notoriety. To me, they are a symbol of respect for Leer. Even if my heart pulls me toward another man, it was one with Leer first.

How can I honor him while making a mockery of mourning by fending off the advances of other men? Grudgingly, I acknowledge the truth that my behavior has been the foundation of my current predicament. As Kragorn recommended, it would be better to abandon my state of mourning than further shame the Rodiharian name.

Spirit of Truth, lead me forward, I quickly pray. *You know my heart in this.*

I unbuckle my belt and shuck off my training clothes. "This is my decision. I will not be forced into a courtship. Not with anyone."

Silla's vulpine smile curls the corners of her lips. She crosses to the opposite side of the dressing room where a collection of my favorite dresses gather dust.

"The rose gown, if it is not too wrinkled," I direct her search.

She withdraws the richly dyed gown to examine it. "It is passable, but you ought to have them all pressed straightaway."

I exchange my wool stockings for the proper undergarments while Silla tugs on the gown to remove a few creases. Without prompting, she aids me in my preparations. The fellowship provides me with much needed assurance in the face of the daunting horde below stairs.

In turn, I attempt to support Silla. "How have relations with your father been of late?"

Her nimble fingers falter on the buttons though her answer is bland. "Unpleasant. As I expect them to be."

My sympathy is genuine. Lord Hugler is a harsh man given to spewing his vitriol on Silla and her mother. It is my belief that Mother Celiea extended sanctuary and permanent residence to Silla after her second failed betrothal to protect her from the physical pain of Lord Hugler's disapproval. It is there in the things not spoken by Silla, and the protective glances of Mother Celiea when she observes Silla and Lord Hugler conversing. Mother Celiea and Lady Hugler gained Lord Hugler's cooperation when it was intimated that a match between Silla and Lorennt was likely, though Silla took up residence in the castle some years before Lorennt returned from serving in the military. The details are somewhat murky. Not even Leer would explain much on the arrangement beyond what I gathered on my own.

"How is your mother?" I inquire. "I hope her presence has been a comfort to your aunt and that she is recovering from her illness." A sudden illness caused Lady Hugler to leave for Port Veritae shortly after Lorennt's wedding. It was a great disappointment to Silla.

Concern pinches Silla's eyes. "Mother has recovered to a degree, though there is still a lingering cough. She will be staying in Port Veritae through the winter."

"That is good news, but I am sorry your mother will be away." Lady Hugler's company has never been odious like that of some of the other noblewomen. Her quiet, gentle manner is pleasing. Mother Celiea favors Lady Hugler in particular when she is in attendance during the winter season.

"It is a shame." Silla circles me to view the front of the gown. With a sharp nod she steps back. "What will you do with your hair?"

I sigh through my nose. Silla habitually shuns my efforts to build a friendship with her. That does not mean I am willing to abandon my attempts. "What does Trent make of your father?"

A twinge of regret crosses her expression. "Trent loathes him."

With good reason. It is doubtful that Lord Hugler would give his permission for a match between the two. Trent is from a respectable but lowborn family. Arguing that he could more than adequately provide for Silla would not change Lord Hugler's mind. Hugler is set on an advantageous match for his only child. That Trent would make Silla a loving, honorable husband is inconsequential.

"If there is anything I can do..."

Silla's smile is wry. "Focus your efforts on your own troubles, Majesty. I will attend to mine."

I tease, "What sort of accomplice would I be if I left you to flounder?"

She ignores my offer, instead making one of her own. "Shall I warn Celiea of your colorful apparel?"

I scrutinize my appearance in the mirror. "And undermine my reputation for the unpredictable? I think not."

She chuckles and passes me my weapons belt.

"Just the accoutrement I needed." The weight of steel on my hips sets me at ease. "Lest the noblemen forget who they are dealing with."

Silla nods her approval. "Woe to them."

CHAPTER NINE

VALOR

December 4th

Traveling with Leelah and Tirzah is nothing like traveling with Erianna. Erianna prefers to throw her favorite soap and a few belongings in a pack then figure the rest out later. Leelah and Tirzah's belongings alone weigh down one pack horse. The children's weigh down another. In spite of that, Leelah panics as we are nearing the pass out of the valley, demanding that she has forgotten something of vital importance and sends Kragorn back to retrieve it. When the trip that can take as few as two days stretches into four, Kragorn reminds me that I volunteered to come along and I am obliged to help my family besides.

Tirzah teases me while I restlessly sharpen my daggers, "Can you not be parted from Erianna for a few days without going to pieces?"

"No," Kragorn interjects. "He cannot."

"It has been over a week," I reply. "Maintaining my weapons is not 'going to pieces.'"

"You will see her tomorrow," Tirzah twiddles her fingers in the air as if it is of no consequence then settles into her bed roll.

Tirzah's company has become barely tolerable these past few days. Erianna has less than nothing to worry about where that woman is concerned. She will realize that when we return, and I can lay another of her fears to rest. I am certain that is what placed me on uneven footing with her before I left.

"Kragorn," Leelah whines, tossing back her blankets.

"Yes, honey-sop?" The past few days of travel have proved Kragorn's patience with his pregnant wife is truly boundless. Leelah wore my nerves thin after the first day.

"The ground is too hard." Leelah moans. "I cannot sleep like this."

"I am going to check on the horses," I inform anyone listening.

"Oh no!" Micah shouts. "I forgot Majie's seeds!"

Karris reminds him yet again, "No, you didn't! They are in your pack, in the leather pouch."

"Are you sure?" The boy whines.

"Yes!" Ivy and Lois shout.

Almighty, preserve me.

※※※

December 5th

The castle grounds are decked in fresh swags of bright colors to welcome the queen's friends and noble guests. Trumpeters herald our welcome onto the castle grounds. The children exclaimed the entire ride through the capital city and now bounce in their seats at the grandeur of the castle ahead. The upper bailey teems with nobility waiting to greet the newest arrivals. This time of year is a reunion for friends who have little opportunity to see each other the rest of the year. I help Kragorn and Leelah heard their brood up the steps into the great hall beneath an arch of pine boughs. The lady of the castle has been busy.

Lorennt and Nev are seated at the high table across the hall. When the children see her, they break into a run, squealing their glee. All is a flurry as Leelah and Tirzah barely restrain themselves from doing the same. Nev descends the dais to catch them in hugs.

Lorennt, however, is engrossed in a conversation with Sigure whose frustration carries his words to me.

"...will not be reasoned with! I tried! You must do something before she breaks her neck!"

Lorennt glances across the room then fixates on me, his apprehension lessening. "Oh, good. Commander, your timing is fortuitous."

Sigure slaps a palm to the table. "You think he can manage her when I have failed?"

"We shall soon see," Lorennt challenges me.

But Sigure insists, "No. You must go, Lorennt!"

"Where is she?" I ask the prince.

"Training ring nearest the stable."

I turn on my heel and head back the way I came.

Sigure storms down the dais, matching my stride. "This woman might be more trouble than she is worth," he grumbles to himself.

"Keep thinking that," I encourage him. If he has already run to Lorennt to manage Erianna, then he certainly is not cut of the right cloth to court her. Besides, how much trouble could Erianna possibly have found in broad daylight on the castle grounds?

The mixed gathering of soldiers, servants and nobles observing the scene in the training ring forewarns I might not like what I find. Nobles complain as I weave between the crowd to gain a place at the fence then stifle their objections when they recognize who is blocking their view. My heart stops in my chest at what I behold.

Erianna is riding Reaper.

No, that is inaccurate. Erianna is barely staying seated on the warhorse who is making a game of un-seating her. The mean-tempered bay destrier bucks beneath the petite woman struggling—and failing—to bring him under her control. It is moments like this that I am vividly reminded what drove me to tie her up.

Sigure demands, "You had better do something about this, or I will kill that horse before it kills her!"

I happen to agree with his assessment. Reaper is onerous under the best of circumstances in the hands of an experienced rider. In this situation, he is deadly.

I hop the fence and approach the horse with measured, confident strides. He sees me before Erianna does and lurches to the side, shooting across the training ring. Erianna's knuckles are white on the pommel of the saddle as she tries to hang on. I curse Grandileer. He wanted a destrier only he could control, and he created it.

"Reaper is coming along," Erianna spares a moment to look at me with a determined smile. I could shake her senseless.

Reaper lays his ears flat, contesting her statement, and charges me. I stand my ground then jump to the side at the last moment, grabbing for his reins but missing. He runs on his toes, jigging from side to side in a maneuver used to dodge arrows. Erianna's strength is dwindling, and the horse perceives it. He comes to a sudden stop, dropping his nose to the ground. I watch in horror as Erianna flies through the air over the destrier's neck. She lands in a roll and springs to her feet, sprinting toward the fence as Reaper charges her. I dash across the ring to intercept him, but Reaper is faster. A breath before she is crushed beneath his shod hooves, Erianna springs between the rails of the fence then drops to her knees. The foul beast bares his teeth at her and paws the ground in challenge.

Sigure pulls a shaking but foolishly optimistic Erianna upright as I climb out of the ring, ignoring Reaper's clarion whistled challenge. I will deal with that brute later. There is an addle-brained queen I must see to first.

"Maybe if we put him back on the lead rope, he will be manageable," She suggests to Sigure but casts an anxious glance at me.

"Maybe as stew he would be manageable!" Sigure retorts.

"You are overreacting again," she argues. "He simply needs more time to adjust to me."

"Clear the training yard!" I bark at the onlookers. They scurry like so many rats as I stalk around the ring. Erianna catches the scent of my anger and stiffens her spine, preparing to fight. The cool water of her presence turns to raging rapids as she squares off against me. We glare at each other until only one member of the audience remains.

"Leave," I order Sigure.

He crosses his arms over his chest like a stubborn child. I do not have the patience for him at the moment, nor the wherewithal to discern his role in this, though I could guess. "We will have words later, Sigure, but first I will speak with my queen."

He glowers at me for another moment then relents, washing his hands of Erianna's trouble.

I grind my jaw, trying to release my anger before it explodes on Erianna. She does not aid my efforts.

"Shall I fetch the lead rope so you can tie me up?" She taunts, drawing her two handed sword. "I promise I will not be easily subdued this time."

"I thought you forgave me for that," I snap.

"I did, but that does not mean I will forget what you are capable of!"

"What *I* am capable of? *You* are behaving recklessly! You broke our pact!"

Erianna does not deny it, nor does she show any remorse. Her betrayal slaps me in the face. She made a calculated decision.

My voice drops to a lethal whisper. "Did you intentionally wait to train Reaper until I was away?" I already know the answer, but I want her to admit it.

"I do not need your *permission* to ride my horse!" She spits the word like it tastes vile on her tongue.

Erianna's fears, my fears, both our anger will torch every bridge between us in this moment if I do not do act wisely. Desperate, I plead, *Almighty, guide me. Turn aside the destruction.*

The ever-faithful Spirit of Truth whispers to my heart, *Fools give full vent to their anger…*

But a wise man quietly holds it back, I remind myself of that hardest lesson for me to learn. If there is one thing that I have wrestled with longer and harder than anything else, it is my temper, especially when fueled by fear.

Perfect Love drives out fear, He counsels.

That perfect Love is alive in me. It is greater than my fear and my anger. I focus my gaze on Erianna, balanced over her feet with the brandished steel gleaming in the sun. This is not what I will allow our arguments to disintegrate into. Never again will they take this form.

I draw a deep breath to subdue the rage in me. On the exhale, my inward battle for control is won.

But now I must combat Erianna's fears.

"Put it away," I calmly instruct.

Her face is harsh with defiance as she holds her position.

"Are you hurt?"

Not yet, her eyes voice her blatant fear though her words are little more than a string of curses.

I cover the distance between us faster than she can back away. With my bare hand, I grasp the blade of her sword, ignoring its bite, and pull her against me. She struggles to free herself, but I hug her tight. "You frightened me, Erianna."

"I can manage my own horse!"

I release her slowly so that her struggle does not land her in the mucky ground. "That is not your horse."

"He is now," she glances at my hand restraining her sword and startles. Rivulets of blood drip into the mud. "You imbecile! What have you done!"

I remove my hand from the blade. "I needed to be closer to you."

She looks at me like I am mad.

"Why are you riding Reaper?"

Some of the color drains from Erianna's face as she stares at my blood on her sword. "I need a destrier. Sacha spooks at my weapons."

"That is understandable, but why did you choose that horse? Because it was Leer's?"

Her head snaps up. "He is a fine destrier and has been confined to a sedentary life far too long. I will not stand by while he rots in a box because he is difficult."

She felt empathy for him. Reaper is every bit as trapped as Erianna is, both without Grandileer who brought them here and trained them to their roles. I shift my gaze to the destrier who defends the training ring as his territory. I remember well when Grandileer and I trained our destriers together. Even then, I argued that Reaper did not understand his relationship to man. Grandileer was not bothered that Reaper thought himself dominant over man so long as he submitted to his master. Reaper's incomplete training paired with his temperamental nature has now become a serious problem. Other than being used as an occasional stud, the horse is fulfilling no purpose locked in the stable. Erianna has a point. He is too fine to let waste away.

I push my fingers through my hair with a growl and go for the lead rope.

"What are you doing?"

"Your horse is tired. He will not learn anything else today. It would be better to start fresh with him tomorrow. We can discuss the best ways to gentle him after dinner."

"We?"

"Of course 'we.' Did you think I would let you do this alone?" I work the horse into a corner, using the lead rope to herd him. Merely that is difficult, but I persist until I catch him.

Erianna watches mutely. Her expression clouds with conflicted emotions as she falls in step with me toward the stable. "I do not understand."

"What do you not understand?"

"You. I do not understand *you*," she states.

"Because you are comparing me to Grandileer." I place Reaper in the care of the horse master with several instructions for his care then usher Erianna ahead of me. "This will not be easy. It might be another week or more before we attempt to ride him. If you want a destrier to use in the meantime—"

"I want Reaper."

"Then we will do our best. All I ask is that you do not train him if I am not present." I catch her eye, emphasizing what she must hear. "Please note that I said 'ask' not 'demand.'"

Erianna's pride does not want to yield, but her good sense wins out in the end. "You will help me train him?"

"I give you my word."

Erianna consents to the bargain. "Then I give you mine."

I bind a cloth around my hand and fumble to tuck in the ends single-handedly. After watching me struggle, Erianna impatiently tugs my hand to her and knots the cloth.

To lighten the mood between us, I say, "The next time I volunteer to travel with the Tareth brood, knock some sense into me."

She raises the eyebrow bisected with a scar. "You are not one to complain. Was it so terrible?"

I trace the line of the scar with a fingertip. It decidedly adds to her warrior repute without detracting from her beauty. "You recall the chaos of being confined to their house? Well, imagine all of that while stuck in the saddle traveling at a snail's pace for four days with two women who hate riding and sleeping on the ground. I have endured worse but not willingly."

She bats my hand away from her face. "I had the misfortune of being called upon to resolve not two, not three, but *four* crises involving decorations. There were also a myriad of spats between the nobles that needed resolution, and, once, Nev kept us up all night long with labor pains that went away come morning."

"Thus—comparatively speaking—riding an ornery destrier was a pleasant change?"

"Decidedly pleasant," she concurs.

We barely make it from the vestibule into the great hall when Erianna is assaulted.

I wave a staying hand at the queen's guard who moves to intercept the red-headed terror dodging nobles as she hurtles across the room. Leelah is talking at a gallop before she even gains Erianna's side and throws her arms about her. "I cannot believe the first thing I hear of you is that you are causing a ruckus by riding a wild destrier and everyone is placing bets on which bone you will break first but I could only laugh because that is exactly something I would expect of you and I am so happy you have not become a complete bore with all these rules and responsibilities and I am so happy to see you!" Leelah finally takes a breath which Erianna fills with laughter.

Of course Leelah would approve of Erianna's recklessness. I grumble, "You are not a good influence on my queen, Leelah Tareth."

"Oh, who asked you!" Leelah retorts.

"Who indeed?" Erianna seconds her friend's opinion, quickly regaining her self-possession under Leelah's influence.

I wag a finger at Leelah, emboldened by the many witnesses that will prevent her retaliation. "You behave or I will have no qualms about trussing you up and returning you to the high valley."

Leelah's eyes glitter. "Oh ho, we are in the castle now instead of my kitchen so you mistakenly believe you have the authority to speak thusly? But remind me, whose domain is this?"

"It is mine," Erianna grins fiendishly. "Leelah, you have my blessing to beat my Hand with whatever bludgeons you can lay hold of if he offends you."

I glance between the two of them and cast my eyes about, hoping to rally support from Kragorn, but, as usual, he makes himself scarce when his wife needs to be scolded. Rather than locating support for me, reinforcements for the women heads this way in the form of Tirzah.

She saunters forward, linking her arm with Erianna's. "Why Valor, you look no better for having seen Erianna. Was your reunion lacking?"

The change that comes over my queen in that moment is marked. Erianna stiffens, her mischievous smile becoming one of false curves.

I reply to Tirzah, hoping to gloss over Erianna's strain. "Our reunions always seem to involve weapons in one of our hands, usually hers," I tease my queen.

Her response attains to joviality but misses the target. "Then perhaps you ought to make more of an effort to arrive on my good side."

I cannot help but notice that she pulls away from Tirzah as she speaks. Subtle as it may be, her feet even find balance beneath her hips as if, on some level, she anticipates a fight. I glance at Leelah, who also notices the change in her friend. Behind her back, Leelah shoos me away.

I bow to the women. "I can see I should have stopped at Mari's on the way here."

Leelah closes the circle between Erianna and Tirzah while I hasten toward Lorennt, certain he is expecting a report on Erianna's latest pastime. Hopefully, between Leelah and I, we can convince Erianna that she has nothing to fear from Tirzah, only the opportunity to gain a friend if she can set aside her prior hurts that have everything to do with her first husband and naught to do with Tirzah or myself.

CHAPTER TEN

ERIANNA

"Will this suit you?" I nervously ask Leelah after showing her into Leer and my redesigned suite. I removed the table and some of the shelves from the dressing room to accommodate small beds for Lois, Ivy, and Micah. I had a babe's bed placed in the large bedroom for Fialla with additional trunks for their belongings and a breakfast table. "Karris may stay in my room if she likes. I know how much she wishes to be older and thought she may enjoy being my companion while she is here."

"She will love that, thank you," Leelah hugs my shoulders again. "This is all wonderful! I cannot believe how large the rooms are!" Leelah exclaims, walking through each space. She notes the steam rising from the surface of the full tub in the bathing room. "Did you have a bath sent up for me?"

"I thought you would enjoy it after days on the road. Dinner is a formal affair—"

"But—"

I hold up a hand to allay her concern. "Before dinner, we may go to the storeroom of gowns to select anything you like for your and the children's use."

"You have thought of everything!" Leelah gushes, displacing my nervousness until she adds, "but Tirzah must come too. She has less than I."

My notable pause before replying causes Leelah's eyes to sharpen. I smile to mask my agitation. "She may come as well, if Lady Silla has not already seen to her needs. Silla promised to look after Tirzah while she is here, thus I placed Tirzah in the room adjacent hers." And I did not have to bribe Silla to do so. She was intrigued by a new player in the castle.

"You will help Tirzah, will you not?" Leelah gauges my reaction. "She is not pursuing Valor, so you needn't let the past where that is concerned bother you."

I rearrange the pillows on the couch. "As I have already said, I will help her and make a few introductions. Silla knows absolutely everyone in the castle, and Trent knows all the soldiers. Tirzah could not hope for a better informed pair to ease her entry into court. She will be well looked after." So well, in fact, that I will know what she is about at every hour of the day. I have not deluded myself into thinking my caution specifically with Tirzah is justified. I know it is leftover from what Leer did. Nevertheless, I do not see how my caution will harm anyone as long as Silla and I are discreet.

Leelah seems satisfied with my answer and enters the bathing room. "Valor said you are still in mourning."

I plop onto the couch in the parlor. "I was when he left, but no longer."

"What changed?" She asks, easing into her bath.

I play with the tassel on a pillow I dragged into my lap while I explain what transpired these past few weeks.

"I am happy for you. It is good that you are moving forward. And," she drawls, "now you are free to accept Valor's suit, which will make both of you very happy."

"I do not think I am ready to do that."

"Why in heavens not?" Leelah exclaims. "You nearly kissed him!"

I included an accounting of that night and my tales from the tunnel in the letter couriered by Valor. I needed to tell someone who would not hesitate to give me her opinion on the matter. Yet I find myself reluctant to expound on it. "There are lots of reasons," I hedge.

"I have time. Let's here these *excuses*."

I chuckle, set at ease by Leelah's no-nonsense nature. "Well, in that case…"

※※※

Leelah pleaded that I not put the table manners of her children on display for the entire court by seating them on the dais. I laughed and gave her a choice of the low tables. Nev kindly brought Tirzah to sit with her and Karris walked at Valor's side as his guest. I am nearly bursting to have them all with me.

Karris and I took care with our appearance before dinner, styling our hair into a loose braid woven through with ribbons to match our gowns. Taking the Tareth girls through the room full of gowns was such fun. Having grown up accustomed to the best clothing, I did not realize how delighted they would be by the experience of choosing whatever they wished.

Karris repeatedly runs her hands down the folds of the deep green satin gown that Kragorn is cross with me for allowing her to wear. He scowls every time he looks at his daughter growing into a young woman. She does look quite lovely. I do not doubt she will have her choice of young lords to dance with through the upcoming festivities. Of course, once they realize who Karris's male relatives are, they will be too intimidated to behave other than perfect gentlemen.

I chose a lavender gown fashioned by the late Mistress Getty for the evening. It was one of her earliest creations and reminds me of her in all the best ways. I smile to myself while looking around the great hall overflowing with my people, friends, and family. The air is scented with pine from the evergreen boughs draped over the mantles of the fireplaces. I scoop a bite of stew from my bowl, anticipating the winter season this year. Even the flocking nobility do not dampen my mood. It is pleasant for the room to be filled with cheerful voices instead of the gloom of mourning.

"You are shining this evening," Valor murmurs in my ear. "Any reason in particular that you are so lighthearted?"

"Beyond the obvious," I nod to the low table where my friends are seated, "I am learning to see joy."

"I saw the verse framed in your office."

See I am doing a new thing! Now it springs up; do you not perceive it? I am making a way in the wilderness and streams in the wasteland.

I set it on my desk the day I put away my mourning clothes. After numerous exchanges with my family and the nobility, I locked myself in my office with the Holy Texts until I found my footing. The days that followed have driven me to my knees again and again. "I am trying to perceive the new thing He is making of our lives and our kingdom. There is a way forward and streams to preserve us, but I cannot see it with my eyes. I must see with my spirit what the Almighty is doing."

"What have you seen?" Valor asks.

I smile wryly. "That I cannot perceive what He wants me to do if I am staunchly telling Him what I *will not* do."

His voice drops to a rumble. "What does He want you to do?"

I glance sidelong at him. "Eat your stew."

Valor grins and bends to his bowl.

Since we are seated on the dais before everyone, I decide to inform him of the latest bit of nonsense plaguing me. The audience should prevent him from committing a hasty murder. "In the interest of fair play, I ought to tell you that Lord Sigure has declared himself and was given permission to court me."

Valor chokes on his stew. "You are entertaining the suit of that pup?" He exclaims, causing several people to look up, including Sigure.

"Hush!" I hiss trying to maintain an even demeanor which is difficult to do with Valor's eyes boring into me and Sigure grinning from down the table. When the attention shifts away from us, I quietly continue. "I did not say that. He is *attempting* to court me. I have told him quite plainly that I have no interest in his suit. The pompous fool has ignored my wishes and follows me around exactly like an irritating pup."

Valor is mollified. "You have no interest in him."

"None."

I try to return to my meal, but I cannot shake the challenge Leelah laid on me. After listening to all my "excuses," she called me to task for believing the lies planted by the enemy that I am not enough for Valor. In her blunt, honest way, she told me that if I would let go of my past hurts and trust Valor with my heart, he would give me the love that I long for and help me heal. Valor himself promised me that months back at Lorennt's wedding.

"You are trembling." Valor discreetly takes my hand beneath the table. "Has anyone else pressed you with an unwelcome suit?"

My heart thuds as his fingers stroke my palm, lingering over the scar from the promise that he made to me when I was at my lowest. *I will jealously fight for you… I will esteem you…* His love and friendship have remained steadfast though I have been inconstant.

My fears snake out like chains to shackle me. *You are going to disappoint him! How could you ever be enough for one such as he? Marriage will change everything. He will not allow his wife the same liberties he allows his friend.*

Leelah was right. These fears reek of the lies of the enemy. How have I allowed fear to once more become part of my existence? Deep inside, I begin to fight as Leelah challenged me to do. Over the clinking chains, I proclaim truth and feel them loosen. *I am a child of the Everlasting King. He has redeemed me through His own death and resurrection. I trust in Him, not in man, certainly not in myself. If He leads me toward Valor, there I will follow.*

"Erianna?" Valor insists. I feel a storm building beneath his skin from thinking other men have discomfited me. If Leer was my shield, then Valor is my sword.

I squeeze his hand and offer him a smile. "No one has pushed a suit on me. Some are testing the waters, but they have found them... wintery." I wink setting my hand atop the table.

He probes my gaze for additional meaning that he will not find. Not yet. I am merely testing the waters myself, unprepared to dive into what he wants to give me.

"Perhaps we should return to less evocative topics for the time being," I suggest. "Such as how to gentle an ill-tempered destrier."

Resigned to the fact that he cannot sway me from claiming Reaper, Valor explains the finer points of gentling a horse during the remainder of dinner. My heart brims to hear him speak passionately on the subject, knowing that we will be tackling this adventure together. It has been so long since we have done anything like this.

After dinner, our usual card game is exchanged for spirited rounds of dice with the children. Micah demonstrates the best way to toss dice that looks a bit like cheating to me, but no one has the stamina to argue Micah around to being reasonable at this hour, so we let him be. Ivy is shy in the new setting with strangers and retreats to the safety of Valor's lap while we play. Long before the children are ready, Leelah and Kragorn take them up to bed—excepting Karris who remains with me.

To Karris's way of thinking, being on first name standing with the queen softens the blow her young heart sustains at seeing Trent's open admiration for Silla. She dismisses him with a narrow stare and a toss of her head. It is such a Leelah-like mannerism that I chortle. Most of the families with children of Karris's age, which she proudly tells me is thirteen after her birthday several weeks past, have not yet arrived, but I introduce her to those in attendance.

Valor grants Karris her freedom by not intimidating her new acquaintances with his formidable presence. He engages in his own conversations, but I feel his eyes often upon me, undoubtedly watching to see who would dare "test the waters" with his queen in his presence. No one dares.

CHAPTER ELEVEN

ERIANNA

December 7th

Kragorn takes one look at Tirzah, Leelah, Silla and myself assembled in the great hall then flees up the stairs. spouting some nonsense about strong personalities and helping Karris watch the children while we shop for gowns. Leelah smirks. Trent looks worried. Valor is amused.

"I, for one, have never been to such a grand city before." Tirzah hooks her arm with mine. "I hope you plan on giving me a thorough tour while we have the opportunity."

The impertinent woman is living in *my* court in *my* castle, yet she still refuses to use my title when addressing me. Even my closest friends understand the necessity of such before the soldiers and nobility, but Tirzah is intent on shunning court manners.

I return her smile. "How could I do anything less?"

Silla's vulpine grin makes an appearance as she pokes at my irritation. "How, indeed, *Majesty*?" After attaching herself to Tirzah, Silla's appraisal of the woman has been most informative. Tirzah, it seems, has two goals in mind for this visit and does not attempt to conceal them. Firstly, she intends to fully avail herself of my hospitality, and, secondly, she desires to find a husband. With the myriad options available to her, from studying in the trove of the royal library to visiting the apothecary shops in the city, her goals are as trivial as the rest of the unwed noblewomen who all come to court for husband hunting.

In my opinion, Tirzah is a bit of a flirt. Leelah says it is simply her manner, but I want to do something decidedly *unqueenly* whenever she turns her playful smile on Valor—or Trent, for that matter. Tirzah seems to be perpetually amused by all of us.

"Cuyler," Silla latches herself to his arm. "Have you found a docile mount for me yet?"

"I am afraid not, my Lady." Trent pulls her hand tighter around his arm. "Would you be put out by riding with me today?"

"Not entirely."

Valor catches my eye. *Their merry chase is coming to a close.*

One would think, I shrug. *They like the banter too much to declare themselves.*

He chuckles.

"How do you do that?" Tirzah drawls in her annoying way. "You two conversed without saying a word."

How dare she call attention to it! This is something special between Valor and me! I disengage myself from her. "Commander, are we ready?"

He swallows a broad smile, adopting something more subdued. "Aye, my Queen."

"You always title her 'my Queen.' Why? Why not *Majesty*?" Tirzah wonders.

"Full of questions this morning, aren't you?" Valor offers us each an arm. He is Tirzah's official guardian while she is in Malsihra. Even so, if he wishes to escort me, then he escorts me alone. I will not share. Nor do I require help descending a few measly steps.

I grip the hilt of my dagger, striding past Tirzah and the churl. Sacha nickers a greeting. I kiss her nose and give her an apple I saved from breakfast.

Tirzah stops to pet her neck. "I still think she would look nice hitched to a little cart. Such a shame she cannot drive."

"I suppose." Is there nothing of mine on which this impertinent woman will not voice her opinion? I swing into the saddle and lead the way out of the upper bailey without a backward glance. My guards form the line around me in the lower bailey.

Silla and I preemptively laid out a strategy for this venture. We begin with the shops she and I need to visit while Leelah and Tirzah search for ready-made gowns that can be altered to their measurements. Leelah is quite tall, so it is several tries before she finds the right gown. Tirzah has even less luck. Silla and I bicker over what shops would be best while Valor asks Tirzah what the trouble is.

I could not see straight when I learned that Valor would be purchasing Tirzah's solstice gown. The gossip such a move will instigate is almost unfathomable. Silla and I made a wager that someone will ask me how long they have been betrothed. Her jests about the situation distracted me from my injured pride.

My memories of Valor and I shopping in Grass Lake are among some of my most treasured. It is the main reason I cannot bear to part with the training clothes he bought me. They mean so much more to me.

Since he is accompanying Tirzah and doing the same for her, I question if it meant as much to him. Perhaps it did not. Perhaps he is simply generous. Not a bad quality, but why must it be in this way?

Tirzah arches an eyebrow at Valor. "You think buying a gown is a simple task?"

"Why should it not be?" He wonders.

"Well… How shall I explain?" She cocks a hand on her hip. "I am too 'lovely,' as you put it, for a regular gown to be altered for me."

Valor's brows pull together, then he blushes as comprehension settles. The churl actually blushes! And at some point he called her figure "lovely."

Tirzah huffs. "If only I were formed like your queen. She has the choicest of picks." *Because her figure is unremarkable,* she does not say aloud, but the look she gives me says plenty.

I hate her.

"Perhaps we should break for the noon meal?" Leelah suggests, pulling me away from Silla before we can devise retribution for Tirzah's statement. Leelah murmurs, "Tirzah did not mean that how it sounded. She envies the admiration you receive from the men at court."

What nonsense! She meant it exactly as it sounded. "I know a number of excellent taverns. What would you all like to eat?" I ask the group, ignoring Leelah's defense of her friend.

Leelah pierces me with her cat eyes. "You promised to help her."

"No," I hiss, riled into a response I did not intend to give. "You and Valor spoke on my behalf. I promised nothing of the sort. I am obligated because of you two."

"I expected better of you," Leelah scolds. "You are being petty."

Not yet, but I am going to be.

"Somewhere with a decent soup," Valor requests, ignorant of our aside. The others agree. Silla and I lead the way.

After the meal, I casually ask Silla, "Do you not think Mistress Weirford is the best option for Tirzah?"

Silla fairly cackles, perceiving my scheme. "To be sure. She never disappoints." The dressmaker's talents are as legendary among my court as are the rates she charges for her services. Valor, however, does not know that.

Leelah believes I took her reprimand to heart and is pleased when I personally assist Tirzah at the seamstress's shop. I impress upon Mistress Weirford that Tirzah's gown be the height of fashion. The seamstress obliges me and assures me she can have the gown completed in time for the solstice—for an additional fee, of course. Despite Tirzah being the recipient of this gown, I enjoy the experience. Her violet eyes and rich brown hair make an excellent palette. Designing gowns is diverting.

Once all the arrangements have been made, there is only one thing left to do. Mistress Weirford's assistant is writing out the bill to send to castle when I halt her and summon Valor from the receiving area at the front of the shop. "Please send the bill to Commander Ironforge. This is his gift to the lady."

"Indeed?" Mistress Weirford is all surprise. "The gossip was that he favored you. Someone in particular told me that he keeps an open bill for you in her shop."

"The Commander is a generous man," I say noncommittally as he gains my side.

"All settled?" Valor asks.

"Pending your approval." I wave him forward and step aside with Mistress Weirford.

Tirzah glides toward us with a genuine smile. "Valor, I cannot thank you enough."

"Did you get what you want?"

"I will now," she implies.

He checks her enthusiasm. "You are putting too much stock in a gown."

I interject, "It is quite a gown."

The assistant slides the bill to Valor while going over the details. Mistress Weirford leans close to me. "Put a bird in my ear, Majesty. Is it true you are being courted by the queen's nephew, Lord Sigure?"

"So he tells me," I reply archly.

We share a laugh as Valor takes up a pen to sign the bill. The pen hovers midair. Valor glances at me. I smile like an adder.

Tirzah reads the sum and gasps. "Valor, no! That is too much. I could not—"

He puts his name on the paper. "I am a man of my word, Tirzah."

She hugs his waist with excessive gratitude that turns my stomach. Trapped by my own mischief, I cannot look away without the dressmaker taking notice when Valor wraps his arm around her shoulders and bends his head to her, speaking too softly to overhear. Tirzah nods fervently then seeks out Leelah to share her joy.

Mistress Weirford *tut tuts* watching the exchange. "Ah, well. I shall have to set the tale aright after this. He clearly favors another. Are they formally betrothed, or is he still making his overtures?"

Whatever satisfaction I meant to find by gouging Valor's accounts disappears with that statement. I knew Valor would not be able to purchase a gown for Tirzah—a lovely eligible woman—without the city buzzing with mixed reports of whom he favors, particularly because my mourning has ended.

I hold my head high as I walk out of the shop. Leelah lavishes praise on me for what she thinks was an honorable thing I did. Tirzah is also pleased with me for assisting in the design, claiming my expertise was invaluable.

"How stands our wager?" Silla murmurs.

"I won." Though it is a poor comfort to my heart.

"As expected," she replies. "Your Commander is a fool."

I might be a bigger one.

Valor tugs me aside while Trent helps the women into their saddles. "You could have simply told me you were upset."

"I am not upset."

"You are lying through your teeth," he growls. "If you would be honest with me, I could have—"

"What?" I snap.

He draws out his patience like a knife on a whetstone. "I would have adjusted any of these plans until you were comfortable. You have no cause to be jealous."

That makes me sound pathetic. "Thank you, Commander Ironforge. Your reassurances have done my pride immeasurable good." My tone drips sarcasm as I step around him with a haughty tilt of my head.

He stops me with his mouth against my ear. "There is no mask you can hide behind to prevent me from finding you. Not the warrior, not the queen, not the jealous lover." His harsh challenge rattles me.

"*Lover*?" I disparage the claim. "Is that what you imagine we are?"

Valor's temper slips free. He cannot abide when I feign ignorance of obvious truth. His hand encircles my upper arm, and he marches me toward Sacha. "We will discuss this later without an audience."

My menacing glare warns his assistance with mounting is unwelcome. "There is nothing to discuss." I climb into my saddle and adjust the length of my dress, paying no heed to the inquiring glances of my friends.

When Valor corners me after dinner, I flatly inform him that I will not speak further about Tirzah and consider the matter closed. He allows it and does not apologize for pushing me to befriend the woman. I do not apologize for costing him two month's salary.

CHAPTER TWELVE

ERIANNA

December 12th

These early mornings paired with late nights might be the end of me. I leave Karris slumbering in our cozy room and don my training clothes and fur lined cloak. The training yard is bitingly cold at this heathen hour. Once I work Reaper and the sun rises, I will feel a bit warmer, but Malesiirian winters make me long for a sweltering day in the Commonwealth.

My guard follows me as I trudge to the stables. Valor has been kind enough to let me grab a few more minutes sleep by preparing Reaper. This morning is to be special though. Valor wants to see how Reaper behaves out of the training yard. To test this, I will be riding Reaper on the castle's forest trails while Valor accompanies me riding a borrowed gelding from the stables. He believes it is much too soon to add the distraction of another stallion to the training lessons. Granite and Reaper clashed particularly badly when Valor and Leer were breaking them years ago. I am not surprised. Granite has a habit of becoming the dominant stallion in any herd. Reaper does not take orders from anyone.

Valor has the two horses tacked and waiting in the cross ties when I find him in the stables. "Took you long enough, *Majesty*." He means *layabout*. "Thought I might need to drag you out of bed." Valor's ability to wake up at any hour of the day or night and come fully awake within minutes is a talent I both envy for myself and despise in him. Rather than think up a witty rejoinder, I throw him a rude gesture.

"You better rub the sleep from your eyes or Reaper will toss you around the castle grounds like one of Lois's dolls."

"Sure, sure." My jaw cracks on a yawn.

Valor smacks my head then lands a fist into my cuirass-clad stomach.

I block his next blow as irritation drives the grogginess far from me. "Woe's sakes, Churl! Do you want to be beaten before dawn?"

He grins unrepentantly. "Good morning, *Majesty*. Nice to see you awake."

I mutter curses at him as I lead Reaper from the stable. The frighteningly intelligent animal seems to know something different is in the cards for him this day. I can tell because he is compliant. He never is.

Valor explains the plans to my personal guard and the paths we will take then orders him to remain behind. That alone puts a smile on my face as I check Reaper's tack. I rarely have a moment to myself these days. Valor's presence is so soothing that I do not count him as another person.

Valor leads the way on the sorrel gelding, setting the pace. Reaper does not like it and makes his complaints known by pushing through the bit to bump into the gelding. I bring him to an immediate stop and command him to back up three steps to show him my displeasure. He tosses his head in defiance, but I do not relent. He obeys then we continue. These stops and starts are becoming less frequent. Reaper is learning to follow my leadership which has been the largest obstacle. Every time he tests my dominance, I must enforce my standing as his herd leader. This often means sending him to his corner of the training ring for a time out until he is ready to heed or making him back up several steps thereby yielding to my authority. He has not appreciated being deposed from his lofty position, but I hope, one day, he will accept me and I can trust him as Valor trusts Granite.

The other thing that has been of great benefit is using verbal cues while training Reaper. Leer trained him to respond to commands in the old Malesiirian language—something Sigure and I did not know. Almost no one speaks it, thus I need not fear another giving commands to my horse.

After a time, Valor instructs me to take the lead. Reaper surges for the gap in the path, forcing me to check him yet again. I have grown used to his antics.

Each training session has been a productive, positive experience under Valor's guidance. Sigure was nearly incompetent, though he insisted he had experience training destriers.

I am not certain what transpired between Valor and Sigure, neither will own to anything, but Sigure has kept his distance and nearly abandoned his dogged pursuit of me. Valor seems a tad smug about the situation, leaving few doubts that he is the welcome wedge between Sigure and I. Not that he has used his advantageous position to press his own suit on me. He seems to be waiting for something. Leelah says it is receptiveness on my part.

My self-proclaimed best friend has much to say on the subject which surprises me. Nev and I speak honestly, but she does not pry. Leelah does not seem to think there should be any secrets between us. It is strange having a bosom friend again after losing Liddy what seems like two lifetimes ago. It is also wonderful. Leelah and I have sat up late into the nights since she arrived laughing and talking. Sometimes Valor and Kragorn join us in the Tareth's parlor. It is during these hours in the company of our friends that some of the barriers between Valor and I fall away, and our old way of interacting as more than friends emerges. But come morning, we return to what we are now. Whatever that is. My head aches when I spend too long trying to wrap tidy little bows of definition around Valor and I. Later. I will sort us out later.

"I have something amusing to show you. Think of it as an alternative to your plan of escaping to Parse Kítaran." Valor points me down a game path in the woods.

Starlight has given way to the gloaming of dawn, revealing snow shrouded evergreens. I have been all over these woods, but I do not recognize this particular path. It leads to a tributary of the stream that cuts through the castle grounds. We dismount and tie off the horses after watering them.

With his trouble-filled half smile, Valor hauls himself into the branches of a massive spruce growing alongside the stream. Curious, I follow him upward. High in the canopy, I discover a wooden platform. Valor guides me around the tree and helps me through an opening in the floor into a little wooden room with glass windows. In the east, the horizon is beginning to glow behind the mountains. I skirt the tree in the middle of the room, looking out over the forest.

Valor taps the glass windows and shakes the walls to test the integrity of the building. "Lorennt was not jesting when he said princes make better forts than urchins. That is five silvers I will never see again."

"Do you mind!" I exclaim, grabbing hold of the trunk when I hear the wood creak.

"Do not worry. It will not come down that easily. Lorennt put it to the test last winter."

"Oh, did he?" I drolly mock.

Valor grins. "Go ahead. Ask me how."

"How?" I humor him.

"I shall give you a hint—Nev helped." He wags his eyebrows.

"You are a rogue of the first order," I retort, seeing where this is headed.

His laugh floods the air around me. I suddenly long to feel his laugh roll through me as it used to when we lay side by side at night, talking softly after nightmares woke me. Valor did not let me go back to sleep until I laughed. But more than my own laughter, it was his laugh rumbling through his chest that set me at ease, warming me on those chill nights. I lower my eyes to the floor, blushing at the memory. Mercy, I was naive! I used to sleep curled into his side without my thoughts straying. Now he cannot laugh without my thoughts cartwheeling toward sleeping in his arms again and skipping gaily from there down paths we have never journeyed together.

"What are you thinking about?" Valor asks, sitting at my feet and leaning back against the tree trunk.

I shrug and join him. "The past."

Valor's reply is a bland, "Ah."

It is not until several minutes of silence pass that I realize he must believe I was thinking of Leer. I do not correct him. It is easier that way. It does not require me to be brave.

We watch the sun illuminate the sky above and the forest floor below. We are at the very edge of the castle grounds, so near that I can discern the curtain wall encircling the castle and city. It is precisely like Lorennt to build his treehouse as far from the castle as possible. He likes his peace and quiet too.

Speaking of, I smirk up at the warrior dozing with his head lolled to the side. Bless him, he is worn through. He must have been up earlier than usual today to tack both horses. I return my gaze to the forest, enjoying the tranquility of the moment.

Movement near the wall draws my notice. I stare at the spot, assuming it to be rabbits or some such, but I discern the shape to be too large to be any sort of small game. Crouched low to the ground and hidden in shadow, it could be a mountain lion. They are unusual on the grounds, but not unheard of. Fear trips my pulse. The horses!

"Valor," I whisper, rousing him.

"*Hmm*," he grunts. "Sorry, I—"

"Look at the wall, just there." I direct his attention.

He comes alert, shaking the sleep from his head. Soundlessly, he adjusts his position to view it from a better angle. As we watch, the sun disperses the shadows, revealing two cloaked men. Realizing their hiding place is exposed, the men rise and stalk to a place further along the base of the wall in the shadow of one of its buttresses.

The bottom falls out of my stomach and roaring fills my ears. I shake violently and draw my knees to my chest, never taking my eyes from my enemy. A cry escapes my mouth. I muffle it with my knees. Valor's head whips around to me.

"He found me," I utter. "He said… said…" I whine, curling in on myself as undiluted terror rushes through my veins.

Valor's hands grip my arms, dragging me forward. I am reminded of my vow. I swore I would kill him. I have to go down there and face him, but I am not ready. He is not supposed to be here! I am not prepared! I am not ready! He will kill me. Worse. He will keep me.

You are mine, Little Queen.

I dig my nails into the old timbers, burying splinters in my fingertips as Valor drags me forward. I cannot go!

Valor jostles me, urgently whispering my name.

I shake my head. I cannot. "I am sorry!"

"Is that him, Erianna?"

I nod.

"That is Zavaan?"

"*Shhh*!" I hiss, panic stricken. "He will hear you!"

I cannot take my gaze from the *Vragh*. If he sees me, my life is over.

Valor interrupts my line of sight. "You are safe. I will not let him near you. You are not alone this time."

I stare mutely at him.

"Do you recognize the other man?"

I shake my head once.

"This is important, Erianna. Try."

I shake my head again. The only reason I recognize Zavaan is because I know how he moves. His build. Height. The feel of his hands on my skin…

I shudder. I am far too intimately knowledgable of that man.

"Alright. We need know how he got in, and who he is talking to. Besides that, if there is even a chance that I can take him by surprise, I must do it. I cannot let this opportunity escape. Do you understand?"

"*Vreh Král Vragh.*" I ordered him to do it. We were supposed to face Zavaan together.

"That's right. You will stay here. They do not know you are here. You are safe. I am going after him. I need you to keep your eyes on them. Pay attention to where they go on the chance they slip past me. You must do this." Valor's hands attempt to uncurl mine from the painfully tight grip I have unconsciously taken on his shirt.

"Do not!" I plead, going back on what I just agreed to. "Do not leave me!"

He glances back at the hidden figures, warring with himself. Resolve steels his hands around mine. "I must do this. And you must let me." His fingers slip inside mine and pry them loose.

Valor disappears through the floor of the treehouse, deaf to my pleas, giving me no false assurances of his safe return. He cannot give them to me.

He does not lie.

I am going to lose him.

※ ※ ※

VALOR

It breaks my heart to leave her, but this must be done. She would order me to do this if she could. I climb down the tree without rustling the branches or loosing the white powder clinging to the tips of the limbs. It is unbelievable that Zavaan is here! I would not believe it except for Erianna's visceral response to seeing the men. She looked like she did when…

No. I cannot think there now, not with the enemy so near. The horses stand on alert by the stream, flicking their ears back and forth. I edge around the path, cutting across the forest floor, glimpsing the wall between the bare trees. I keep to areas of sufficient cover that will allow me to close in on the men. Wholly focused on the task, I home in on the buttress, searching for the figures hidden in shadow. They are nowhere to be found.

I glance down the length of wall, considering the possibility that I miscalculated their position. More likely, they moved while I was approaching. I skirt along the forest, reasoning where they would have gone next. Further back. They would have gone deeper into cover if their business was not concluded. But if it was…

How in the blazing depths did Zavaan get onto the castle grounds! I have become fanatical about the security of the castle proper since the attack on the west side.

I creep back into the forest, hurrying to the next buttress. The snow is iced over, crunching underfoot. If they hear me, there is a solid chance that Zavaan will vanish before I close in on him. But the other man? If he is an informant, which is the only reasonable assumption under these circumstances, he will flee to the castle, hiding under our noses. I press deeper into the forest, minding my steps. We need them both. Whoever has been aiding Zavaan will be held accountable for the crimes he abetted. Unless Zavaan kills him first.

That scene in the tunnel pushes to the fore of my mind. *Was it a gruesome thing?* Erianna asked, knowing that suffering would be a trademark of Zavaan's kill. It was beyond gruesome. It turned my stomach months after the murder even though vermin had reduced the woman's body to bones shrouded with the tatters of a dress. Blood stains coated both walls. The woman's skull was shattered, her bones jutting out at wrong angles. Zavaan took his time breaking the woman that he had been bedding for months. And he was the last man to lay hands on my Erianna. The mere distant sight of him caused her to panic.

My feet stall on the cold ground. My eyes seek her in the treetops. I feel torn in two. She needs me to hold her together right now, to make her feel safe. But if I do not bring down Zavaan, her safety is illusory. Each day that he lives, the danger to Erianna grows along with the number of his victims.

Before I reach the next buttress, the crunch of snow jerks my head around. One of the cloaked men is sprinting into the forest. Instinct tells me it is the accomplice. Zavaan would never allow himself to be seen. I scan the wall and the forest one last time, but Zavaan is nowhere in sight. My curses steam in the air as I break into a run. From her vantage, Erianna will have seen where Zavaan went, at least the general direction of his escape. If I waste time searching for him, this traitor will escape. His lead is already huge. I cannot allow it to grow. I pound through the forest, gaining bit by bit. If only his hood would fall back to afford me some idea of who he is. But it does not. Nor does he glance back at me to gauge his lead. He knows his neck is going to be stretched when I discover his identity. He attempts to lose me in the forest, but I know these woods like—

"Stop!" Erianna's commanding shout cracks across the quiet morning, bringing me to an immediate halt.

But she was not speaking to me.

"If you surrender your death will be merciful, *Vragh*!"

I spin around, looking back to the wall, but cannot pick her out this deep in the forest.

Then I hear his voice plainly on the still morning air. "Hello, Wife."

I thought I knew fear.

I was wrong.

My feet carry me back over the ground I covered while my eyes jump between breaks in the trees until I catch a glimpse of them. Erianna stands ready to fight with daggers drawn, snarling upward. Midway up the thirty foot curtain wall, Zavaan clings with nothing but his fingers and booted toes to the hewn stones. My mind argues with my eyes that such a thing is impossible.

I call on every ounce of strength in my body to propel me over the frozen ground.

"Come down here," Erianna demands.

No! Run, Erianna! I silently scream as I creep through the trees as quickly and quietly as I can. At the risk of spooking him into harming her, I remain out of sight, dodging between trees, praying heaven down on her.

In one lithe movement, Zavaan leaps to the ground, landing in a crouch. Erianna startles back, maintaining the distance between them, but she does not flee. The brave beautiful idiot.

"No embrace for your husband? I confess, I am disappointed. Aren't you the least bit pleased to see me?" He opens his arms, moving toward her.

Erianna angles her daggers, holding her ground. "On your knees!"

"You first," he drawls.

Erianna hurls her dagger so quickly, I do not anticipate the movement, but Zavaan does. The dagger glances off his vambrace.

He laughs with sick delight, then draws his own dagger with exaggerated slowness. "Erianna Zavaan. It has been too long since I have had the pleasure of your company. Of course, there are a few matters we must attend to first." He traces a finger from the tip of the dagger down to the cross guard. Erianna stares, momentarily frozen until Zavaan replaces the dagger in its scabbard.

Erianna shakes herself and frees the dagger strapped to her thigh. "On your knees."

"Not today, Little Queen." He takes a step toward her then pauses. "You are supposed to be training the dead king's destrier. What has brought you all the way out here? And where is that paragon of self-righteousness you have tricked into serving you? Did he abandon you already? Learn how filthy you really are?"

"Be silent!" Erianna's voice quavers in the middle.

If the Deceiver has a mouthpiece, it is unquestionably Reuel Zavaan. He preys on her every fear, accusing her of every sin.

"Oh, my foolish Little Queen. I have heard how close you two have become, that you abandoned your mourning too soon. Was it for Ironforge? Did he tell you he loves you? Lie to you like Leer did? He does not want you. How could he? He does not know what you have done."

"He does," Erianna says soberly.

"He will change his mind. You are not who he wants either. He will cast you aside every morning just as Leer did. How did that make you feel, knowing that you could not satisfy him?" Zavaan chuckles. "Maybe he will also bed his lover on the day you wed him."

"You know nothing!" Erianna's anguished scream splits my heart wide open. The one truth amid all the lies.

She never told me. But Zavaan knew. He made it his objective to know how to slay Erianna in the most effective ways.

Zavaan's predatory smile is wickedness itself as he advances on her.

I am still too far! *Almighty, stop him! Stop him before he destroys her!*

"You were not enough for Leer. You will never be enough for Valor." Zavaan reaches for Erianna as he stalks toward her, poison dripping from his tongue. "But have I not been considerate of you? Have I not been gracious? You had best come with me. I will look after you. And you must stop neglecting your Limban people. They are in a bad way."

Erianna stumbles in her backward retreat from Zavaan. *So close!* I am nearly in range. If I could get close enough to hurl a dagger into his evil excuse for a heart… But I must time it correctly.

"Come here, Erianna."

She shakes her head, staggering faster and shouts across the frosty air. "*Utok*!"

"Enough foolishness! Come here!" Zavaan lunges for Erianna as Reaper breaks through the trees, issuing his clarion battle cry and charging Zavaan.

Zavaan is so surprised that he misses his chance to snare Erianna. She clears out of the destrier's path while hurling daggers backward to hold Zavaan at bay as he pursues her. He must slow to deflect them. I bellow, breaking free of the trees that concealed my advance. My dagger hurtles forward, flashing the light of the dawn on steel. It falls short as expected, but it shifts Zavaan's attention to me. He bares his teeth in a fit of rage as his prey escapes while he stands to be crushed between the onslaught of warrior and warhorse. Zavaan weighs his odds while setting a hand on his sword. Reaper lays his ears flat against his head, baring his own teeth at the enemy. He may not like Erianna or I much at all, but he instinctively hates Zavaan and will trample the murderer given the chance.

"Who goes there!" A guard making his rounds shouts from the top of the wall.

The decision made for him, Zavaan does not waste breath on words but launches himself at the stone wall. With frightening dexterity, he ascends the thirty foot wall like a spider, gripping the grooves between the blocks. I hurl another dagger at the knave. Hindered by his armor, it finds a shallow home in his shoulder.

"Stop him!" I command the guard running on the wall-walk. My third dagger narrowly misses Zavaan's leg as he swings atop the wall.

"Your life is forfeit, Coward!" I roar.

Zavaan pulls my dagger from his shoulder and flings it down at me. I sidestep, drawing two more.

His sadistic smile spreads wide. "Say your goodbyes to my wife while you can, Ironforge. Soon enough she will blame you as the cause of her pain."

I rear back to sink the daggers into his eyes, but he disappears. The guard atop the wall slides to a stop and hurls his spear into the forest on the other side of the wall. No shriek of pain follows, only the dull sound of metal kissing earth.

"Rally a patrol immediately!" I order. "Tear apart the mountain! Track him down! That is the leader of the Ruphiri."

"Aye, Commander!" The guard rushes on without a backward glance.

Zavaan's parting words have the dual effect of riling me and stoking Erianna's fear. His wife. *His wife.* That will be true when the seas boil and the mountains melt. I bend over my knees, chest heaving, heart thumping painfully.

Reaper paws the ground, turning his head to the side to eye the wall. He brings his forefeet off the ground as if estimating the jump needed to carry him over it to continue his deadly charge. His determined spirit reminds me of his new owner. Maybe they are well suited after all. I pat a hand on his neck in thanks. His timely entry saved our queen. I am surprised she thought to bring him as surety against Zavaan. It was a wise decision amid the recklessness of facing the demon alone.

I gather our daggers littering the ground while attempting to cage my anger at Zavaan and fresh anger at the faithless Grandileer—even a bit of anger at Erianna for not staying in the cursed treehouse like I ordered. My anger is the last thing she needs to face in this moment.

Tracks in the snow lead beneath the boughs of a drooping evergreen. I crawl beneath the tree on all fours to find Erianna knotted at its base, staring vacantly. She flinches when I reach for her. I drop my hand.

"He was here." The words shake past her chattering teeth. "We sealed the tunnel, and he was here."

I would ask if she is alright, but the words would be foolish when she is obviously not. She squirms, rubs her hands over her arms, wipes her face on her bent knees.

"Would you like me to hold you?" I offer without moving.

Erianna's eyes reflect pain before she closes them, hiding her constricted expression. "Please do not touch me."

Her refusal brings me to the realization that I was asking as much for myself as I was for her. I want to hold her. I want to make her feel safe. She wanted that before I left her.

It had to be done. I tell myself. *I had to try.*

But Erianna's pleas that I not leave her echo in my mind with all the desperation of one who knows what it is to be alone.

"He was lying, Erianna. I did not leave you. I was fighting *for* you. I am here."

She holds herself tighter.

I unclasp my mantle and carefully settle it around her shoulders without touching her.

"Take it back."

I frown, certain I misunderstood. "What?"

"I do not want your mantle. Take it back."

I am stunned. She cannot mean that. The gesture seems insignificant, but it means much between us. It always has. It is everything that I have unconditionally given to her. My protection. My support. My friendship. The assurance that I will care for her. Erianna knows that.

She is not rejecting the warmth of my mantle.

She is rejecting *me*.

I watch her crawl stiffly from under the tree. When she rises, she pushes my mantle from her shoulders dropping it to the ground like an offensive rag.

"*Nakt*!" Erianna calls for Reaper.

I pick up the discarded offering and am on my feet chasing after her, desperate to mend the breach between us that I do not understand. "Talk to me, my Friend."

She ignores me, stalking up the path, calling for Reaper again.

Why is she doing this? I circle back to the venomous bite of Zavaan's words. "You know he told you lies. I did not abandon you. I will never abandon you. I love you. No one else."

Winter has never felt so cold as the look she levels at me. "Retrieve your horse, Commander. I am ready to return to the castle. Lorennt must be told what transpired."

I fist my mantle. Resentment rises up to twist the knife she plunged into my heart. Stupidly, I reach for her again.

"Do not touch me!" She grips the hilt of her dagger.

I am going to lose her again. I do not even know why. Fear and anger bleed together then seize my tongue. "Why did you not stay in the treehouse like I told you? If you had listened to me, we could have avoided all of this!" And she would not be looking at me like I am the one who betrayed her.

Erianna turns her back on me.

I watch her walk away from me again, the loss made all the worse for what I have so intentionally cultivated with her this last week. I thought we were in agreement, that we were moving forward together. But I was deluding myself.

My strength is sapped from the battle. There are too many obstacles between us. It is too long, too arduous. Defeat seems imminent.

I do not know what else to do.

CHAPTER THIRTEEN

VALOR

Breakfast is underway in the great hall when we enter. The queen's severe bearing stifles the conversations humming in the room. Erianna does not break stride as she crosses to the dais. Her hushed words bring Lorennt to his feet. She signals for Kragorn, Trent, and Boldizar to accompany us to the war room. The doors close, sealing us in with the dread emanating from the men.

Erianna clenches her hands at her sides. "Zavaan was on the castle grounds less than an hour ago."

Shock hobbles the exclamations of the others. Frankly, we have all become so accustomed to bad news becoming worse news that true disbelief is beyond us.

"We spied Zavaan meeting with someone from the castle near the corner of the north and west walls. Valor attempted to take the men by surprise, but they shifted positions before he could close in on them. The man from the castle went one way, Zavaan went the other. From my vantage, I knew Valor would not know which way Zavaan went, thus I pursued Zavaan while Valor ran down the other man." Erianna pauses, blinking several times, and soberly reports, "I am sorry to say they both escaped."

"Were you harmed?" Boldizar asks, perceptive as ever and placing priority where it ought to be.

"No." Erianna does not meet her father's eyes. "But we do know Zavaan entered the grounds by scaling the curtain wall without ropes or aid of any kind."

"That is impossible," Lorennt says, rattled by this unwelcome talent of our enemy.

I confirm Erianna's outlandish assertion. "I saw him do it. Even a dagger stuck in his shoulder did not shake his grip on the wall."

"Thus it stands to reason," Erianna proceeds, "that the rest of the Ruphiri could have entered the city months past in a similar fashion. And we now have confirmation that a Malesiirian aided Zavaan."

"But if our walls are not a barricade against them…" Trent lets the thought hang unpleasantly in the air.

My hand closes around my sword hilt, not that it provides much reassurance. My weapons were useless this morning. "I ordered a patrol to pursue Zavaan, but the amount of guards on the walls needs to be doubled. Possibly tripled."

Kragorn nods, undertaking the responsibility of shoring up our defenses against this unsettling skill of our enemy.

"Did you identify the man with Zavaan?" Lorennt asks me.

"I did not."

"Erianna?" He asks.

She is a frozen pillar. Somber. Unmoving.

I extend my hand to brush her arm, hoping to gently bring her back from whatever nightmare she is reliving. Inches from contact, Erianna clasps her hands at her waist, increasing the distance between us. I close my eyes, gnashing my teeth, and withdraw my hand. It does not go unnoticed. The men look between the two of us, prying into the sudden estrangement. I am not a man who admits defeat. I fight with all my strength until my last breath. But in this moment, I want to surrender.

Erianna rejoins the conversation. "I do not know with whom Zavaan met, but I am certain he was brown haired and of a similar height to Zavaan."

Lorennt disparages her information. "That description could fit a hundred people on the castle grounds alone. How are we to hone that?"

"Begin with the generals," Erianna instructs Kragorn. "If none of the generals fit the description, move to the captains. It is unlikely Zavaan would be working with a servant this time. He needs more detailed tactical information."

Kragorn grunts his agreement.

Lorennt resumes his questioning. "What else happened? Did Zavaan see you? Speak to you?"

"I failed to bring him down." The slightest catch is notable in Erianna's words.

"What else?" Lorennt presses.

I subtly shake my head to turn him aside.

He sees the gesture and demands, "Erianna what happened?"

Without inflection she states, "I spoke with Zavaan. He attempted to convince me to leave with him. He fled when Valor and the guard cornered him."

"What did he say?" Lorennt persists.

Erianna turns to Boldizar. "Can you think of any generals who have reason to be discontent? Anything we are not seeing that you do?"

Boldizar shakes his head then taps his finger to his temple.

"He will think on it," Erianna translates. She looks around the room, avoiding my gaze. "If there is nothing else," she says in dismissal and slips from the room, ignoring Lorennt.

He is on the verge of running her down, so I motion him to my side and wait for the others to depart. Summarily, I reiterate Zavaan's condemnation of Erianna and the stake he drove into her heart. Lorennt's explicit death threats and curses against Zavaan are no worse than my own.

Since she will not tell me, I ask Lorennt how deep the wounds in Erianna go. "Did Zavaan speak true? Did Grandileer bed Jaleh on their wedding day?"

Lorennt's jaw flexes. "That morning. I know because Nev was called upon to attend Erianna whenever Jaleh was..." He shakes his head in disgust.

My words are little more than a rumble. "Then he consummated their marriage that night?"

Lorennt's protracted silence is all the answer I need.

I storm toward the door.

The acidic lies of the Deceiver slip through my vulnerability. *Grandileer and Zavaan ruined her. Your girl is gone. Give up. She is too broken. You should not continue suffering for her sake when there is no hope.*

※※※

Not a pel is left standing in the training yard by the time I return to the castle. The guards keep a healthy distance from me, fearful that I might satiate my bloodlust with those of flesh rather than inanimate wooden posts. The patrols' hunt for Zavaan was unsuccessful despite Trent's assistance with tracking. I am sorely tempted to hunt for him on my own for as long as it takes to find him, but fealty, loyalty, or perhaps stupidity, drags my miserable bones back to the castle to brood in the Tareth's parlor.

As the children ready for dinner, I let the sounds of their scampering drown out my thoughts. Leelah sits on the opposite side of the room, fussing over Lois's hair, while Ivy waits impatiently for her turn. Kragorn apprised his wife of the situation this morning, and I, thereby, avoided questions from Leelah I would rather not answer.

Karris bursting onto the scene does not raise an eyebrow in any of us. The Tareth children have a habit of coming and going like miniature whirlwinds.

Leelah tasks her within seconds of her appearance. "Karris, help me find the ribbons that match the girls' dresses. I have misplaced them and—"

"Mother."

"I am certain I left them in this drawer, but I cannot—"

"Mother."

"They are my ropes to tie up the brigands!" Micah exults, brandishing a mass of ribbons knotted around small carved soldiers. "I bound up the lot of them just like Father and Uncle did!"

Leelah groans. "Micah, you must not take—"

"Mother!" Karris raises her voice above the noise.

Leelah snaps, "What is it, Karris?"

"I think..." She glances at me, then back at her mother. "I think something is wrong with Erianna."

Karris has our full attention.

"Why do you say that?" Leelah asks.

"She... Can you come speak with her please?" Karris fidgets nervously.

Leelah sets aside the brush. "Of course, Darling. Wait here with the children."

I watch Leelah leave, wanting to go with her but knowing Erianna would not welcome my help.

"Did something happen to her this morning?"

I lift my gaze to Karris's. "There was an intruder on the castle grounds."

"Who?"

Karris is aware in a general sense what happened to Erianna over the last few years. Thus, when I tell her it was Zavaan, compassion moves her features. "Poor Erianna. That must have been so frightening for her. At least you were with her."

For all the good it did.

"She has been fretful today."

"Is that why you asked your mother to speak with her?"

Karris shakes her head, blushing.

"Then why?"

Embarrassed, she shifts on her feet then whispers, "She will not get out of the bath to dress for dinner. She keeps saying she is not finished bathing yet, but she has scrubbed her skin raw. I heard her crying."

Pain gouges my heart. I hang my head in my hands, maintaining composure while inwardly I am wrecked.

Karris pats my shoulder. "She is going to be alright, Uncle. Mother will help her."

"I am sure she will try," I somewhat agree to settle Karris. But the word resounding through my head will not be squelched.

Ruined.

For the first time, I find validity in what Erianna has been telling me for months. Her scars may be too deep. Maybe her trust in people was so fundamentally shattered that she will never recover enough of it to have a relationship. Maybe we can never be what we should have been. Maybe that burden is on me for not protecting her from Grandileer and Zavaan.

I should have never let her go. I lost my girl, my fairytale princess. That sweet, innocent woman was irreparably broken. Ruined.

All the proof of that is in her absolute rejection of me. In less than one minute, Zavaan destroyed five months of healing. How can I combat that sort of power? Even if we manage to route the Ruphiri and hang the villain, will Erianna ever again have peace or be free of what he did to her? Or is she ruined?

※※※

ERIANNA

The cold knife drags across my face. Curves down my jaw trailing blood... Zavaan's hands move over my body, knowing me in ways only my husband should... My hands are on him, too, knowing him...

I swallow convulsively, and attack my skin with renewed vigor, but the soap isn't helping.

Valor's eyes, full of affection that I cannot accept—not like this... His arms open to me, offering safety. Love. Protection... Giving me the shelter of his friendship even though I cannot give him what he wants…

I cry, scrubbing at my palms.

The rag is snatched from me.

Instinctively, I shield my face with my arms. When no blow lands, I glance between them. Leelah stands alongside the tub with crossed arms. Water drips from the rag to the floor.

"Give that back. I am not finished."

She huffs. "It won't work. You cannot wash away that feeling. Believe me. I have tried."

That is not what I want to hear. Frantically, I reach for it. "Please, give it back! I am not clean yet!"

A solid reprimand leaps from her amber eyes. "My mistake. I thought you were clean. Have you been lying to us all?"

I sink lower in the opaque water. "I do not understand."

"The Savior lifted every sin from your soul and body the very moment He redeemed you. It is not yours to bear anymore. You have been made clean. You know this," Leelah challenges me to remember. "Furthermore, Zavaan's sin against you does not make you unclean."

Shame burns along my skin. "Then why do I feel this way?"

"Because what was done to you was vile. Because the Accuser wants you to question the love of the Creator and His redemptive power. If he can keep you bound with shame then you will never walk freely in the life the Creator has planned for you. Shame is even more crippling than fear.

"You must reject his lies. You know the truth. Keep telling yourself the truth and calling on the Creator. He is with you. He is near to the broken-hearted. He will lift you out of this pit once again."

The image of Zavaan's cruel smile in the dark of the cave snares my mind. He was not even lustful in the normal sense. His lust was for the ruining of me. His pleasure was in dethroning Leer and stealing me from my husband. He lusted for power, for control. My shriek of misery echoes in the bathing room. "I cannot forget the feel of his hands on me! I hate it!"

Sympathy fills Leelah's voice. "I understand. That will pass. Especially once Valor's hands dull that memory."

"No," I snap. "Valor cannot touch me."

"Why not? Do you not want him?"

"Of course I do," I brokenly admit. "But he must not."

"Why?"

"I will sully him. I am so used. I have nothing left to give him."

Leelah is not surprised by my wretched confession. "I know what you are feeling, Erianna, but it is a lie. You have been made clean of your sins. And the ravishing actions of those men did not make you dirty. Valor knows that."

I watch my tears drip into my bathwater, rippling the surface. "How could he want me after what I have done? What they did to me? He deserves better. I cannot believe that the Almighty would shackle him with me."

The bench next to the tub creaks as Leelah sits down, settling into her words. They are imbued with deep conviction. "I shall tell you what Kragorn told me. I felt sorry for him, too, told him that he must be cursed for being bound to me. What he told me I never forgot, and it drastically changed my way of thinking. He said, 'Leelah, if the Creator has seen fit to entrust me with you, His beloved daughter, then I must have proven myself incredibly worthy to be given such an honor. Because He knows your beautiful heart and your fragile places. He would not trust just any man to care for you in your sojourn on this earth. I consider myself to have found the highest favor in His eyes by being gifted with you.'"

Kragorn's view of the wife the Creator gave him is so beautiful. He acknowledged all of who she is, the good and the broken. "He considered himself blessed with you, not cursed."

Leelah smiles. "He did. He still does. And each time the Creator brings us another daughter with a dark past and a broken heart, Kragorn rages at the evil done them but still sees each daughter as a gift. Then he devotes himself to healing their hearts with the pure, unconditional love of a good father. He also vows that he will be incredibly choosy about what men he allows to marry his girls when they are grown."

I return her smile and sniffle my way through my words as I wipe my face clean of tears. "I think that is happening faster than he is prepared to admit where Karris is concerned."

Leelah laughs brightly. "Oh, he was ready to wallop you when Karris came downstairs looking like a young woman. He will not be handing off his little girl anytime soon."

I exhale, leaning my head back against the rim of the tub.

She holds up the rag. "Do you still need this?"

I shake my head, sloshing water. "No. But I do not feel like I can fully embrace what you have said yet. I do not know if it is because my heart is so raw, or my faith is too weak."

Leelah takes my hand in hers. "If it is a matter of growing your faith, then you can share mine until yours is stronger. Like me, you are a fighter. But this enemy is within your own mind. You cannot fight it with steel. Only faith, truth, and prayer will vanquish it. Those are the weapons that will allow you to take captive the thoughts plaguing you and bring them into submission to the Almighty."

A flower blooms in the desolation of my heart, promising spring will come eventually. "Thank you. I am so glad you are my best friend."

Leelah's smile is tender. "I am glad, too." She reaches for a towel while I rinse the suds from my hair. "Have you spoken honestly with Valor about any of this?"

The question alone makes me want to hide. "No. He knows what happened," especially since Zavaan so explicitly spoke of my shame in being the second woman my husband bedded on my wedding day, and most days thereafter, "but I truly hate talking about any of this. What would I tell him?"

"That is for you to decide," she says, moving into the dressing room as I withdraw from the tepid water. "But I think you ought to tell him something. He has been positively morose this afternoon—moping in my sitting room the last hour. Pathetic. What did you say to him?"

Guilt stabs my conscience. "I pushed him away."

"Hmm," Leelah stares me down as I enter the dressing room. "You must have been forceful about it. I have not seen him like this since he came home this past spring certain you were permanently out of his reach."

"He was that hurt?" I ask softly.

She confirms it. "You need to make amends. Soon. And that is going to require a large dose of truth on your part. By the way, why did you not stay in the treehouse? Weren't you frightened of facing Zavaan?"

"I was terrified," I murmur, feeling a shadow of that fear even now. "But I could not let Valor face him alone. I was so, so frightened that he had seen Valor and was plotting to take him unawares. I had to protect Valor."

"That is what I thought," Leelah says with a satisfied nod as she walks across the dressing room.

Dread uncurls from my belly, wrapping tendrils around my lungs. This feeling drove me from the treehouse. "Leelah, what if I lose him? I cannot—" Tears plummet down my cheeks. "What if—" I struggle to make the words leave my mouth. They are crushing to think, let alone speak. "What if Valor dies?"

"Someday, he will. You both will." Tears gather on her lashes, mirroring my own. "We love warriors, Erianna. They are called to defend others with their lives. We might lose them tomorrow, or in a week, or in fifty years. Only the Creator knows. But, if you try to protect your heart by keeping Valor at a distance, then you are depriving yourself of the joy and love the Creator has gifted you today." Before leaving, she turns back in the threshold, daring me to be brave. "Take hold of it. Take hold of it with both hands, and live."

I dress as quickly as possible, resolved to speak with Valor before dinner. I do not want him to be miserable. If explaining myself can alleviate any of what he feels, I must try. Unfortunately, the opportunity is taken from me. Karris informs us he left for the city to inspect the defenses and did not anticipate returning until very late. Leelah's pointed look leaves no room to doubt the reason he is absent. He wishes to avoid me.

CHAPTER FOURTEEN

VALOR

December 13th

"A weeks's worth of meals for a full night's sleep!" I grumble, rising from my bed to answer the pounding on my door, having only slept one measly hour after hiding at the barracks with Anders. Not that he was a great lot of help for my wounded heart. He dragged me into the city after assuring me that the proper measures had been taken to guard the walls. A meal in a seedy tavern and losing a large sum to a talented card player did nothing to assuage my black mood, though it was preferable to sitting through an unbearable meal on the dais.

I open my door to find one of Erianna's guards. "Commander," he salutes, "Her Majesty apologizes for interrupting your sleep. She says that Lady Nev is laboring, and if you would like to wait with the family in the Tareth's room you are welcome."

I thank the guard for delivering the message then stand behind the closed door, wavering. I asked Erianna to tell me this news so I could wait with the family, knowing both Lorennt and Erianna could use support on the occasion. Not that I imagine she will accept such from me now. But she did send for me…

I groan and pull on clothes, wondering if I am the glutton for misery that Anders jests I am. I enter the Tareth's parlor where Boldizar and Kragorn wait while Lorennt paces a circle in the carpet. He turns anxiously at my entrance. "Have you heard anything?"

"Aye. Your wife is laboring. Did you know?" I ask.

Irritation flashes across his face. "You are delightful. Sense of humor like Erianna. Churlish lout."

"'Churlish oaf' if you want to quote your sister properly," I correct, presenting an outlet for his tension.

"I am certain I could fill a book with things to call you. Two books if I include the profane," he retorts.

"Only two? That is disappointing. Anders has three."

"But his descriptors are solely profane," Kragorn remarks, taking first pick of the three volumes that I brought to pass the time.

I sit on the couch and cross one foot over the other, flipping through the pages of a book to find a chapter I would not mind rereading.

"What do you have there?" Boldizar asks.

I hold up the book I selected, *A History of the Commonwealth*, and the other book, *Famous Battles in Malesiirian History.*

He points to the first. "Do you mind?"

"Not at all," I pass it to him and search for a battle about which I remember the least.

"How can you read at a time like this," Lorennt complains. The poor man looks near pulling out his own hair.

"It is difficult at first," I allow. "But if you practice slowly sounding out the words, then try reading them aloud—sometimes that helps—eventually, you will become proficient."

He glares daggers at me. "I know what you are trying to do, but I am plagued with memories of Erianna bleeding out and praying that does not become Nev. So leave me be."

That seals my lips.

We pass an hour in tense silence until Karris enters.

"Well?" Lorennt cuts her off before she can get out a word.

Karris tries again. "She is doing well. The physician says the labor is progressing apace."

"Apace! What in—"

Kragorn clears his throat.

Lorennt corrects himself. "Her pains began at dinner. How much longer will it be?"

"Presently," Karris grins, spinning on her heel to return to Lorennt's room with the women.

Lorennt swears once she cannot hear it.

"These things take time, Son," Boldizar calms him. "If the babe comes ere dawn, that will be quite a feat."

Lorennt drops into an arm chair, pinching the bridge of his nose. "Valor, have you any news from the city?"

"After the guard was increased on the walls, Anders sent a patrol to attempt to sneak in from without. Even knowing the weak spots in the defense, the patrol was spotted without fail. Anders says a mouse could not climb the curtain wall without being spotted."

"Good." He sighs, glancing about the room. "The situation with the generals?"

Kragorn puts a thumb between the pages of his book, marking his place. "That is going to be more difficult than Erianna believes. I have interviewed all the generals in the city. Most have proof of being elsewhere at that time. None fit the description perfectly nor do they have motive."

"Not even Kannik?" Boldizar asks.

"No. I will be interviewing all the captains tomorrow. Valor will be speaking with the castle guard."

Lorennt nods, pondering the information for a moment. "What if the clue was less obvious. Have we considered past generals? They would still have connections to information and could move about freely. Not all of the older generation love our Warrior Queen. Put together a list of those as well."

"I could do that, if you do not object," Boldizar offers, looking to Kragorn and I for approval. It has always surprised me how willingly Boldizar handed over the reins to Grandileer, aiding where he could without imposing on his son's reign. It was a commendably graceful transition in leadership.

"That would be helpful," Kragorn says, never too proud to accept help. It was a lesson he instilled in me long ago.

Boldizar inquires, "How has Erianna fared after encountering Zavaan?"

All the eyes settle on me, assuming I will know the answer. Resignedly, I admit, "I have not spoken with her since our meeting this morning."

Their stares intensify. I close the book cradled in my hand and engage Lorennt, expecting my reproof to come from him.

He does not disappoint. "Why not?"

"She made it clear that she wanted to be left alone."

He looks at me like I spoke in Limban. "That does not sound like her."

"I was surprised myself," I state, attempting to end the discussion.

"She was looking for you before dinner. And after," Kragorn says. "Something about an apology."

I lock eyes with him. The scold he levels at me for hiding is unmistakable. I incline my head in acknowledgment. Kragorn is not appeased. If anything, his silent rebuke compounds.

Another interminable hour passes in silence.

"Did you hear something?" Lorennt perks up. With the door to the hall open, faint sounds echo down the corridor. Lorennt goes to his feet when the muffled sounds of a woman in pain grow louder, then quiet with the closing of a door.

Karris appears long enough to say, "The babe is coming! Hopefully not much longer."

Lorennt's face is ashen as Nev's pain is heard then muffled by the closed door. "I have never heard Nev scream before. Not once. She rarely raises her voice."

"That is the way of having babes. It is natural." Boldizar squeezes his son's shoulder. "Not long. They are in good hands."

Lorennt looks worse as a good half hour ticks past. He sits on the edge of the table and wipes sweating palms on his pants. The door opens down the hall again.

Erianna storms into the room, billowing winter fury. "If you make your wife endure this alone, I will beat you senseless! You get in there and stop acting like a coward! If she can do what she is doing then you can at least have the decency to hold her hand through it!"

She is gone without a glance spared for the rest of us, leaving Lorennt shaking.

"Am… am… I allowed to do that?"

"I was with my wife when she delivered Micah," Kragorn says. "I plan on being with her for this babe, too."

Lorennt is frozen. "I do not know anything about… What would I do?"

"You do not need to know anything," Kragorn advises. "Be present for her. Lend her your strength and encourage her. She only needs your support."

Lorennt nods.

"Go to her, Lorennt," I prompt. "Hold her. Be with her to greet your child."

He nods again, finds his feet, fixes his courage, and strides from the room. We hear the door open and close.

Boldizar chortles. "Celiea's sense of propriety will not like a man in the birthing room."

"Leelah and Erianna have never put much stock in propriety," Kragorn declares, sinking into the cushions of his chair, perhaps considering how he will be in Lorennt's place come summer.

"She was scared," I say, staring at the open door. "That was pure bravado. Erianna is terrified for Nev."

Kragorn glares at me overtop his book. "A shame you are hiding from her. She probably could have used some support of her own."

"I am here now," I retort.

Boldizar glances between us then makes his way from the room. "I could do with a bite. Erianna always hides cookies or some such in her parlor."

Kragorn leans forward, hardly waiting for Boldizar to leave. "Is this to be the end? You have surrendered? I know a Valor from a year ago who would have cut off his own arm to be in your position."

I match his stance. "It is more complicated than that. She rejected my help and my friendship, never mind I told her I love her. She is not the same woman with whom I fell in love. My girl would never have behaved how she did this morning."

"You knew that she was changed from the moment you found her. You knew things would be different. What sent you running? Is it your pride? She bruised it and now—"

"You know me better than that!" I rage to my feet. "I do not know what to do! I lost her this morning! She saw Zavaan and fell apart. She swallowed his lies and would not let me near her! How can I overcome that? I do not know what else to do."

Kragorn lowers his voice. "Is she broken?"

My shoulders slump.

"Well? You think, even after the undeniable redemption you saw transform her, that this is insurmountable?"

"They ruined her," my voice cracks. "I do not know that I can help her heal."

"So you ran away. Instead of letting her pain hurt you, you ran."

"I needed time." I lower to the couch.

"Let me be perfectly clear," the intensity of Kragorn's voice snares my attention. "When you marry, you take on every single one of your wife's burdens, including her past. You cannot erase it. You bear it with her and remove as many of her burdens as you can. You lay down your life for her each and every day. You do not get to run when her words cut you. And you do not get to take away your support if she becomes cold.

"I know you are capable of demonstrating the love and consideration you ought to show. But now is when reflecting the character of the Saving Son becomes truly hard. It means sacrificing yourself for her. And you are right. There may be certain places in Erianna that take a lifetime to heal. There may even be some things from which she can never fully recover. But if you love her, if she is the wife the Creator has given you, then you will marry her knowing full well who she is and what it means to be her husband. And you will *never* allow her to feel less-than because of her fragile places."

Conviction lashes my back. I told Erianna I would not leave her, but today I hid from her. I should have been steadfast. She did not get to escape the pain afflicting her. If she were my wife, flesh of my flesh, bone of my bone, I would have to face that with her. It *should* pain me because it pains her. *Almighty, forgive me. Make me strong for the fight.*

"Now that is done," Kragorn characteristically follows up his chastisement with encouragement, "you need to speak with her. She feels badly about this morning. You will, too, once you know why she behaved as she did."

My head snaps up. "You know?"

"Leelah told me. Which is why I know you need to be ready to fight for her as soon as she tells you." Kragorn's scowl softens to almost a smile. "You can win this fight. It will not be too difficult once you understand."

"That is a relief," I dryly mock. "With next to no sleep for two days, I have to fight for my woman."

He chuckles. "If I can offer you one piece of advice, it is this: Do not get carried away."

"Thank you. That is so informative. I think I will ask Leelah for her advice next time."

"Leelah would say, 'Prove it.'" He grins, knowing that is equally obtuse.

Annoyed, I prop a pillow behind my head and cross my arms. "Wake me when the babe arrives."

※ ※ ※

ERIANNA

I cool Nev's sweat soaked brow with a wet rag. "You did so well Nev."

"Aye, she did," Lorennt kisses his wife then tucks her head under his chin. "A son Nev. You gave me a son."

The precious babe sleeps against his mother's breast, safe and whole. I touch his tiny fists, marveling over my nephew. "He is perfect."

"We want you to name him," Lorennt requests. "You have done so much for us, Erianna. It would make us happy if you would."

Tears pool in my eyes. I always knew he would be the one to take the throne. In a way, Leer and I were both right. "Laszlo Rodiharian, for his great-grandfather. The name Leer and I would have given if we had a son." I kiss his downy hair. "You are the fulfillment of my hopes, Laszlo."

"It is fitting," Lorennt agrees.

"Not 'Melon?'" Nev teases. "I suppose that would not suit a prince." As she says the words, the shock of what she said overcomes her. Nev-of-no-surname who was Never to have survived is the mother of the prince of Malesiir, heir to the kingdom. She begins to cry, completely overwhelmed.

Lorennt passes the babe to me. With a meaningful glance at Nev, he suggests, "Why don't you do the honors of introducing Laszlo."

"It would be my pleasure." I exit quietly while Lorennt comforts his wife. My relief that he came to attend the birth was second only to Nev's. I felt inadequate to the task of supporting Nev through the arduous birth with my own fears raging, and Mother Celiea was in much the same state as I. Physician Cervil's stoic demeanor was decidedly unhelpful to Nev or myself, and Leelah was busy directing Nev through the delivery. But when Lorennt calmly entered and confidently took up a place at his wife's side, whispering encouragement to her, Nev had the support she needed, and I was permitted to inwardly fall apart.

I meander down the corridor, snuggling Laszlo. He smells soft and new. Mother Celiea bathed and swaddled her grandson while we tended Nev following the delivery. Cervil and Leelah assured us Nev would fully recover and there was no cause for concern.

There is quite a party going on in the Tareth's parlor when I enter with the guest of honor. Someone apparently raided my hoarded queen's cookies and brought tea up from the kitchen. I proudly display our sleepy little prince to his grandparents and the Tareths. He is, of course, declared perfect. Father is especially pleased with Laszlo's name, the name of his own father.

Valor admires him from a distance then takes a seat on the couch. After what I said this morning, I can hardly fault his reticence.

Until now, I have possessively held Laszlo, but I want Valor to share this with me. "Would you like to hold him?" I ask, joining Valor on the couch.

His gaze on me is uncertain, attempting to make sense of my thoughts as he nods. I place Laszlo in his large, calloused hands, treasuring the way they cradle the babe so tenderly. A smile overtakes him as he admires my nephew. "Lorennt did himself proud. This is a good lad."

The babe's breaths puff out of him, quivering his lower lip. I tap the dimple in his chin. He chases my finger, mewling, then sucks contentedly on my knuckle, fisting his little hands to his chest.

I scoot closer to Valor, resting my arm on his to comfortably reach the babe. "Do you mind?"

"Do you?" He counters, bewildered by me.

To answer, I lean my shoulder against him. "I owe you an explanation. Could you make time to speak with me later?"

"Of course. I am sorry I was not here for dinner. Kragorn said you looked for me then."

"Thank you for being here now."

We sit together peaceably, watching Laszlo sleep. He is a perfect babe. I am so pleased to share him with Valor.

When Lorennt enters a short while later, after all the congratulations have been given, Mother Celiea asks, "How is Nev?"

"Sound asleep." He chuckles. "You would think she just did something exhausting. Fell asleep in the middle of a sentence." He crosses to where we snuggle the babe and lifts him from Valor's hands, beaming at his son. "This boy is mine, Valor. You shall have to have your own."

I dry my knuckle on my dress, biting down hard on my lip. Valor wraps his arm around my shoulders, holding me tightly against the thoughtless words. "You have a fine son, Lorennt. There is no denying that."

My eyes do not leave Laszlo as his father carries him proudly about the room. Too soon, he leaves and takes the babe with him. I think I manage to smile at Lorennt and say something about visiting later. I look down at my empty arms. I wrap them around my flat stomach, but can only think of when Illyanna fit there.

I make my mouth smile. Get my feet beneath me. Say as normally as possible, "There are a couple hours left before I must be at breakfast. I mean to use them sleeping." Then I flee.

This day has been altogether too much.

I reach the safety of my parlor and lock myself in before curling up on my couch to weep into a pillow. I am happy for Lorennt and Nev. I am so pleased with Laszlo, that he is here, safe, and whole. Truly I am. But I feel bereft all the same.

The lock clicks open. "It is because of you I learned to pick locks. How appropriate that you give me a reason to use the skill." Valor sits on the low table opposite me, lacing his hands together between his knees.

"I am sorry," the words gush out. "I am so sorry. I cannot do that for you. I cannot place your child in your arms."

Valor's heart was set on being a father ten years ago when he got his lover with child. She stole that from him. The way he looked at Laszlo made me keenly aware of what Valor will give up by choosing me—yet one more thing I cannot give him.

Valor's words are decided and even. "Then I shall put a babe in your arms, as Kragorn has done for Leelah."

"Does that not bother you?" How could it not? Every man wants a son to bear his name.

"Not for me. But for you, yes. I know it cuts you deeply." He weighs his words before expounding. "Is Karris any less Kragorn's daughter than Fialla? Does he love her any less?"

"No, but—"

"Being an orphan myself, I know how desperately they need loving homes. It has always been my hope to take in a child, as Hellah did for me, whether or not my wife bears my children." The affectionate pride in Valor's words soothes some of the ache in me. "Unless I do not know you at all, I think you would love a child wholeheartedly no matter how he came to be yours. The consideration you have lavished on Jace and the orphans of this city is proof aplenty. But may we come back to this topic later?"

At my nod, he initiates the conversation I meant to have with him. "What bothers me is your rejection. After everything we have been through, one minute with Zavaan sent you running from me, as if I had betrayed you." My face crumbles hearing that is what he thought. "It breaks my heart that you are still suffering so badly from his violation. I did not know. I wish you had told me."

Honesty, I demand of myself. *Be honest.* "I have not felt like that for some time. Mostly because I try not to think about it. I could wallow in the past if I let myself. But I do not want to. I want to forget all of that and move forward. And we were. That made it hurt all the worse. This morning, I was not prepared to face him. I was safe with you. We were in my home, doing something we enjoy." I shudder. "Then he was there. Suddenly, I was back in that cave… I felt defiled again. And guilty." Shame flays me. "I could not let you dirty yourself by touching me."

My words hang in the air, so ugly that I instantly want to take them back. But Valor does not recoil.

"Let me be perfectly clear before anything else is said." Valor takes my hands in his, pulling me upright. "You are clean. Zavaan's lies are from the deepest pit of hell. Cast them from your mind."

I stare at our entwined hands, fearful to search his eyes. What if he is only speaking what he knows to be true? Is he disappointed with me nonetheless?

Valor brings my hand up, pressing it to his heart. "Find my eyes, Erianna."

Reluctantly, I obey. They are beautiful and so familiar. I know every nuance of them. How they change color and honestly reflect his feelings.

"When I see you, what do I feel?" His right hand moves slowly up my arm and catches an escaped lock of hair, trailing it through his fingers.

"Admiration," I decide, noting how he lingers over the single lock of my hair.

"Not just for your beauty, which makes me stupid at times, but for your character. Your mettle. Your quick wit."

The backs of his fingers feather over my brow, my temple, down to my cheek. "What do I feel?" He caresses my face while his eyes memorize my features. He feels something undeniably soft and warm while looking at me. I know what I would name it, but I do not want to put the word in his mouth.

"Love," he speaks from his heart. "I love you. Can you not see that?"

"I see it."

Valor then traces the line of my jaw with his fingertips, outlines the bow of my lips. His touch flows down my neck to the hollow of my throat, leaving tingling trails of heat. Hovering over my skin he follows my collarbone. His fingers stop, but his eyes move lower, drinking in my figure, then raise to mine. "What do I feel?" His words are only breath.

I blush at the molten silver. "Desire."

"That word is inadequate to express what I feel for you. But it will do for now."

My blush deepens, and I drop my eyes. His finger beneath my chin lifts my eyes again to his. "We are not done." His hand grips my waist, the other sprawls open on my back. He pulls me across the distance between us, seating me on his leg. He bends his brow to mine, sharing breath with me. Something fierce moves in his gaze, filling the silver with iron. "What do I feel?"

I linger over this feeling of his, discerning its name. "Possessiveness?"

Valor nods, touching his mouth to my brow. Into the crown of my hair, he murmurs, "I want your heart, Erianna. I want the privilege of calling you mine. I want all of your days. I want to wake smelling lavender and for every barrier between us to be gone."

I feel the intensity of his claim move through me. It fills my heart and gently speaks to my brokenness, too, asking me to let him in. I twine my arms around his neck. "You are the only one to whom I want to belong."

Valor's exhale fans the little hairs framing my face. "Good."

I lay my head on his shoulder, setting my nose against his throat. I breathe him in and sigh with pleasure. I long to put the past behind me, thus I speak the first thought that occurs to me, something I hope will let him glimpse my heart. "I like how you smell, too."

"Oh?" The word rumbles in his throat.

"You smell of salt."

"That would be from sweat," he remarks snidely.

I shake my head, feeling the rasp of stubble on my skin. "Even freshly washed, you smell salty."

"Then I must need better soap," he jests.

Or help washing. I smile, but I keep that thought to myself. "You also smell of fresh air, like the breeze over the Hillcountry."

"Truly?" He is surprised.

"*Mhmm.* And you smell like sunshine."

"*Sunshine*?" He barks. "You cannot tell a warrior he smells like sunshine! It is insulting."

I giggle at his reaction. "Do not take offense. I like sunshine. You have always smelled thusly to me. It has pulled me out of more than one nightmare. You are steadying." With a bit more boldness, I admit, "When I am in your arms, everything else becomes insignificant. The world shrinks to only you and I."

Valor rubs a slow circle over my back. I sigh into him, content to stay like this as long as he allows it. "I want to court you, Erianna. Please give me the chance to lay claim to your heart."

Be brave. Trust, the Spirit of Truth whispers to my soul.

I loose my arms from Valor's neck, but he pulls me closer, pleading, "A chance, Erianna."

"There is still too much between us. You must understand what you are asking." I kiss his cheek. "I am not saying no, but you must do something for me first." I pull his arms from around me and lead him to the trunk in the corner. I dig to the bottom and withdraw the stack of papers bundled with twine. "Here."

Valor takes the stack and looks up in wonder. "Your journal."

"I want you to understand. I want you to know, to be sure about me. There are things I have not told you. They are in there."

My soul laid bare. That is what I am offering him. And one last chance for him to turn back from me before I cannot let him go.

"No more barriers." He soberly acknowledges what this means.

"No more."

VALOR

December 12th

Long after the castle has gone to sleep, I set aside Erianna's journal smoothing the pages filled with her beautiful script that illustrate the most poignant moments of her life. I asked for no barriers between us. She honored that request. And I am overwhelmed.

This is not the dispassionate accounting of events she related to me months back. This is what she lived, how she felt, her emotions then and now. She reveals everything to me, her whole life right up to the moment Zavaan takes her captive. It is so much to grasp.

My inaccurate belief that I do not hold her heart is demolished. Erianna never ceased loving me. As it should, her love for me changed during her marriage, but never disappeared. That was one reason she did not allow me to read this sooner. She was not ready for me to know.

I asked her to see herself through my eyes. Having the ability to see myself through her eyes is incredible. She rarely speaks of how she admires me, but it is here in unabashed honesty. She is profuse in her praise of me. I sit taller in my chair reading it, fairly crowing with the favor I have found in her sight. Her oft spoken declaration that I am her favorite person is the absolute truth yet insufficiently encompasses what she feels for me, how much she respects me. It is a heady thing to know the woman I love loves me too.

Moreover, I now understand of what she is terrified. It physically pains me to read how she was carved up, body and soul. Her wounds go so deep, down to her very identity. Praise be to the Almighty for redeeming her and giving her true identity in Him. She would not be among the living if He had not.

The worthless princess.

The mother who could not save her daughter.

The wife who questioned if her husband preferred the other woman in his bed.

For all her spirit and audacity, Erianna is achingly insecure.

She thought she knew the man she married, who they were together, and what she meant to him. It shredded her to learn what he did. All the confidence that she gained in his love and in her positions as wife and queen gave way on a foundation of sand. Then Zavaan worked his evil on her in that most broken place.

Erianna understands who she is to me in our friendship. Those boundaries feel safe to her. Familiar. She is frightened that if we remove those lines, blurry as they are, I will find her wanting. By exposing her life and her thoughts to me, she is giving me a chance to decide if I am sure I want her.

Erianna is not ruined. She is defensive. She has been protecting her heart from allowing me the opportunity to break it and from losing me again, something she is certain is inevitable. Sadly, I cannot promise she will not lose me. She might. I might lose her. The Almighty calls us all home eventually. I hope it is after a long life filled with joy, but there are no guarantees. However, I can promise that I will never sunder her heart.

Part Two

All Things New

CHAPTER FIFTEEN

ERIANNA

December 13th

Papers litter my desk. I sort them into piles of priority. "If there is one thing I could eliminate from my duties, it would be the need for paperwork."

Valor catches the point of the dagger he tossed into the air. "I would have gambled on you eliminating the nobility. Is your decision based on what is irritating you at the moment?"

"Obviously," I reply. The weight of the unspoken is tormenting me. Since giving Valor my journal early yesterday morning, we have not discussed it. I should be patient, but I expected he would have said something about it. A sympathetic or disdainful look. Or, at the least, mentioned that he had begun reading it. He has said nothing.

"We have roughly an hour before chapel begins," he notes, rocking back in his chair while playing catch. He has been fidgety this morning —more than usual. Perhaps that is an indicator. Maybe I have caused him to be uncomfortable with me. If so, why be here? Of his own accord, he joined me, uninvited, to an early breakfast in the kitchen then followed me to my office. I have become convinced my personal guard reports my movements to him. It would annoy me to no end except I like his company, and I know his intention is to keep me safe. Zavaan's arrival unnerved him, too, not that he would admit it.

"In that case, put yourself to some use instead of daring chance. After all, I wanted to go for a walk. You thought I ought to be productive with my morning." I push a pile toward him.

"I am honing my coordination, not daring chance," he counters.

"I am not of a mood to suture you when you miss."

"Then I will not miss."

I roll my eyes. His confidence can be irksome at times.

A stack of letters awaits my perusal. I have half a mind to throw the ones from the lesser nobility in the fire unopened. "I delegate to you the task of responding to these."

"More requests for an audience?" He tosses the dagger in his right hand and catches it with his left.

"Everyone wants to come to court. Everyone wants an audience with me. Everyone thinks they can gain land allotments and favors from me that Leer never gave them."

"So do what he did. Allow them to come to court on certain days in alphabetical order. You do not have to meet them all, but you can allow them to come in groups so you are not overwhelmed. Stride around in full armor with Daisy at your side then use Violet for a beheading their first day at court. That will set an excellent tone for their visit."

"*Hmm…*" I tap the stack of letters. "The idea has merit. But where would I find that many people to behead?"

"Start with the pup." Valor does not hesitate to put Sigure's head on the chopping block.

"Lord Sigure has been remarkably well behaved of late, something you well know since you arranged it."

Valor grins, not taking his eyes from the dagger flying through the air. "Are you insinuating I would threaten the Queen Abdicàt's nephew?"

I quirk a brow. "You said 'threaten,' not I."

"Finish your work so we may go to chapel." He fixes his laughing gaze on me, letting the dagger fall toward his chest. I gasp and lunge forward, snatching it out of the air. He chuckles.

"That was not funny," I scold, tucking his dagger into my weapons belt. "Now it is in time-out until you can behave."

The front legs of his chair thump to the floor. "Aye, my Queen."

He sets to work opposite me while I ensure none of the letters require my immediate attention. My name written in an uneven scrawl marches across a page. I flip the letter over and break Valor's seal. Could it be a delayed correspondence from his last assignment? No. It is dated from yesterday. My heart stammers.

Erianna,

Thank you for letting me see your heart and removing the barriers between us. I will not betray your trust.

"Love is as strong as death, its jealousy unyielding as the grave. It burns like blazing fire, like a mighty flame. Many waters cannot quench love; rivers cannot wash it away. If one were to give all the wealth of his house for love, it would be utterly scorned."

That is the love I have for you, Erianna. Scars and all. I will not yield. I will not leave you or let you leave me. My love for you is unquenchable. You are beautiful to me. Perfect in my eyes. Chaste and virtuous until I take you as my wife, no matter what happened in the past. You were given new life. All things have been made new.

I vow to protect your heart as fiercely as I protect your life. My love will be a fortress around you and I will be the garrison to defend you on all sides. You are precious to me. You have stolen my heart. Seal it with your love.

You are mine, Beloved. I am yours. Bone of my bone. Flesh of my flesh. With every day of my life, I will love you.

Valor

His gaze waits for mine when I look up through my tears. He does not waver as he rises and extends his left hand to me. *Bone of my bone. Flesh of my flesh.* The words the first man spoke to his wife when the Creator entrusted him with her. When they still lived in paradise. When everything was new.

Valor is giving me a new beginning, echoing the Creator's love for me.

"All things are new?" I ask tremulously.

"All things are new." He promises.

"Blood of my blood," I place my scarred hand in his, remembering his commitment to me. "Heart of my heart." My promise to him.

"Evermore, Beloved," Valor pulls me into his embrace, enfolding me with his love.

I set my hand on his cheek, letting go of my heart, giving it fully to him. "You will not let me fall."

"Fall?" Valor kisses my eyes, banishing my tears. "No, Erianna. I am going to help you fly."

His lips brush over mine, binding my future to his with a kiss.

※※※

VALOR

"She appears settled," Kragorn decides as we walk through the manicured castle grounds hidden beneath a fresh blanket of snow. Erianna does indeed move like a weight has been lifted from her shoulders. Only now, glancing back at me with a smile, open and sweet, can I see how guarded she has been toward me.

"Do you plan on informing the court today?" He asks, molding a snowball between his hands.

"We spoke with her family after breakfast. Celiea was the only one displeased with the news. She favored her nephew for Erianna."

"Understandable."

"Indeed." Nor was I offended. "As for the court, Erianna wishes to wait before being subjected to the deluge of gossip. As she put it, 'Can we not just be happy for a few days?'"

Kragorn grunts.

"You disapprove?"

He tosses the snowball in the air. "Do not give them fodder for speculation. That would be worse than facing it head on." He lobs it at his son. Micah spins about, his own snowball in hand, blaming his sisters. Kragorn pitches another his direction. Micah bellows, charging his father. Kragorn lets himself be taken to ground by the boy eager to test his strength. The skirmish ends with Micah riding on top of his father's shoulders, proclaiming how big he is.

"Micah," Erianna calls out. "Do you think this spot will be suitable for our orchard?"

"So long as nothin' bothers the little trees. They are breakable." Micah slides down Kragorn's back.

"I will give an order that none are to touch them," Erianna assures him.

Micah cocks his head to the side, doubting Erianna's ability to give such an order. He cannot reconcile Majie being High Queen of Malesiir.

"Valor, go fetch us a stick so that we can mark where the seeds were planted," Leelah instructs.

I obey as Erianna and Micah climb over the hedge that marks the boundaries of the garden bed and plant the apple seeds. I drive the stick into the frozen ground where Micah points.

"Now you will not forget where they are planted," Leelah says, unconsciously settling a hand on her belly that does not yet reveal her condition. It seems to be the habit of women with child, always reminding themselves of what they hold close. Erianna notices Leelah's hand and smiles.

The way she held her nephew this morn while we visited with

Lorennt and Nev, the longing she could not conceal, put it firmly in my mind that I must give her a babe of her own soon. Even in Malesiir, too many people cast off their unwanted children or leave newly borns in the forest to die. As much as I traverse the kingdom, it should not be too challenging to find a babe in need of a home. Still I cannot put it entirely from my mind that, perhaps, after Erianna has been allowed to heal, in a few years I may be able to give her a child born of her own body. But I will not suggest such a thing to her. That is distant in our future, and I know her heart cannot bear any more broken dreams where children are concerned. Until then, I will tend the seed of hope for her.

"You know, Majie," Leelah sets her hands on her hips, looking about the grounds, "I think this space is underutilized."

Erianna follows Leelah's gaze. "How so?"

"The orchard is a start, it could be tastefully incorporated amongst the formal garden without detracting from it. You could also better utilize the horse paddocks, setting aside some for pasture with careful planning. Do you have many nut trees in the forest?"

"No, it is primarily evergreens."

Leelah tuts. "That is a waste. Nut trees would be much more useful. You could allow turkeys and hogs to fatten on the mast in autumn."

"And…" Kragorn nudges my side, knowing what will be suggested next.

"Beyond that," Leelah warms to the topic, "you absolutely must have goats for meat and milk. You could substitute so much of the purchased staples with things produced on the castle grounds."

"You believe so?" Erianna is intrigued.

"Without a doubt!" Leelah assures her. "But you must have a place for your goats. Perhaps convert a block of the stables. Or build them a shelter in the forest."

Kragorn snorts. Then he chuckles. I stare at him. He bursts into a full, resounding laugh and claps my shoulder. "I have spent the better part of a decade keeping Leelah out of the castle. Then you go and make her best friends with the queen!" He guffaws. "There are going to be goat kids in the great hall! Chickens nesting in the formal gardens!" He throws his arms wide. "Fruit trees *everywhere*!" Kragorn folds in half, sighing nasally between bouts of laughter. "You did it, Valor! This one is all your fault!"

Leelah glares at her husband's dramatics then waves dismissively. "Never mind him."

Erianna looks between them and sides with Leelah. No surprise there. "I have been meaning to ask you about our management of goods in the kitchen. Your pottage was lauded, and I would like your opinion on what else could be improved."

Kragorn falls down laughing. The children seize the opportunity and pile atop their father with battle cries. Leelah and Erianna discuss the finer points of kitchen management while I rally to my brother's aid, tossing his children into snowdrifts.

CHAPTER SIXTEEN

ERIANNA

December 17th

I bound from my bed with the verve of a woman soon to greet her love. Mornings are not so terrible with the promise of Valor's embrace awaiting me in the stable. My winter layers go on quickly, my hair I plait while crossing the great hall.

"Wait for me in the training yard," I instruct my guard.

A knowing look flickers about his face before he salutes.

"Something on your mind?" I challenge.

"Naught that I would repeat, Majesty," he strides toward the training yard, repressing a smile.

The stablehands are already at work, cleaning stalls and feeding horses. I make my way toward the block where Reaper's stall is, but a low whistle turns me aside to an aisle already cleaned. I nod in greeting to the lads I pass, peaking into the empty stalls. A little further down, I spy a bit of blue wrapped around one of the stall doors.

I tug the loops of my scarf free from the door with a grin. It is more worn than I remembered. I play with the tassels on the short edges and trace the lighter threads woven into the dark sapphire cloth. There was a time I thought I would never see it again.

"I thought you might want it back," my favorite voice rumbles behind me.

"I do. However," I toss my braid over my shoulder, not letting him see my smile. "You whistled for me like a horse. That does not inspire warm feelings in me."

Fresh straw wafts on the air as he draws near. "A shame. Then you will not like this at all." He takes the scarf, stretching it between his hands, and tugs me toward him with the length of it spanning my waist. I spin around, huffing my indignation at being led like a horse. Valor's teasing eyes crinkle at the corners. I stubbornly drag my heels, pretending I do not have any intention of throwing myself into his arms momentarily. He laughs and pulls me into the vacant stall across the aisle.

"So you have me." I cross my arms, affecting annoyance. "Now what?"

Valor kisses my cheek. "I have missed teasing you."

"You mean pestering?" I scold him with an arched brow.

He kisses it. "And flirting with you."

My mouth twitches, containing a smile.

"And holding you." He folds me in his arms, bringing me closer still. "And most of all…" He kisses the corner of my mouth stealing my breath.

Will he kiss my lips next? He has not since that singular promising kiss days ago, chaste as it was.

"Most of all?" I prompt, locking my arms around his neck.

He lowers his mouth to my ear as if to impart a secret, but the action chases every thought save him from my mind. How does he render me simple with his touch? I have been kissed before. Hundreds of times. But I can barely string a handful of words together with Valor so near, his breath warming my neck, his body heating mine. Heavens, he is like holding a live coal!

"Are you paying attention?" He teases, not the least bit ignorant of the effect he has upon me. He rather enjoys stealing my words. "I am attempting to have a conversation with you."

"You have my undivided attention," I vow, tilting my head so his rough jaw rasps against my cheek.

Valor presses a kiss to the tender place beneath my ear. The piteous whimper that parts my lips may as well be a full conversation in which I beg for more such affection. I must get a hold of myself before Valor decides I am absolutely pathetic. He told me that he did not mean to rush the kisses and caresses between us, wanting instead to savor our courtship. I thought it sweet at the time, but oh, I want to be kissed! Not that I have not treasured the tenderness of his lips against my cheek and hand, the kisses he drops on top of my head. But I want more.

A deep breath of air pulled in through my mouth, not my nose—that would be disastrous with him so near—helps clear my head the littlest bit. Space. I need space. Immediately.

I loose my arms from his neck, opting instead to rest my hands on his broad shoulders and pick up the thread of conversation. "What you missed most?"

Valor sets me back, his grin full of trouble. "What I missed most of all was your laugh."

The wry turn of my mouth conveys my disbelief. "You have heard me laugh. Sakes, *you* make me laugh all the time."

He shakes his head slowly. "Not this laugh."

"I have more than one laugh?" Now he is being ridiculous.

He nods, shifting his stance ever so slightly to corner me in the stall.

I prop my hands on my hips, staring him down. "You would not dare."

He crouches and shakes out his hands.

I dismiss his nonsense with a wave, edging around him toward the door. Before I take one more step, Valor's fingers are flying over my sides, tickling peals of laughter free. His arm hooks around my waist when I would have dropped to the ground giggling.

"Mercy!" I cry off. "I… cannot… breathe!"

He grants it, burying his face in my neck, a smile in his voice. "That laugh. I have wanted to make you laugh like that."

I feel I might burst from the wave of happiness swelling in me. Valor finds joy in my company.

I giggle again. "I am your favorite, too."

"Just figured that out, did you?" He smirks.

I nod, giggling.

"My beautiful idiot," he hugs me tightly.

I lean into his heat at my back, wrapping my arms over his. "There is something else you missed."

"Quite a few things, but what do you have in mind?" Valor sets his chin on my shoulder.

I look at him from the corner of my eye. "You once made a game of causing me to blush."

Valor's eyes light up as if I just gave him a present. "I did at that." He straightens and turns me to face him. "But what would it take to make you blush nowadays? Certainly more than a passing comment about intimacy or how beautiful I find you."

I step free of his embrace with a playful taunt. "I leave it to you to figure out." I sidle into the aisle. "Are the horses ready or have you been remiss?"

"Oh no, my Queen. You do not get to escape after dropping that gauntlet." He tugs me back into the stall, eyeing me over crossed arms. I hold my head high, determined to maintain my composure no matter what he concocts.

He looks me up and down, grinning that trouble filled half smile. "What happened to your plan of buying new training clothes?"

I cannot see where he is possibly headed, but I play along. "I meant to, but these have history. Besides, Nev helped me darn the little holes. They have plenty of life left in them."

"What a relief," his smile stretches wider. "I thoroughly enjoy the way they hug your shapely legs. Heats my blood on these chilly mornings."

I roll my eyes, no where near blushing. "That is contrived."

Valor's brows rise. "You think so?" He sets my palm over his heart to prove his point. How it pounds! His fingers trace my jaw, lifting my chin. His lips touch my brow then part as he sighs into my hair. "Ah, I surrender."

"Surrender?" My heart seeks to beat in time with his beneath the fingers he lowers to my throat.

"You have distracted me from our game, so I surrender."

I smile into his palm. "I think you distracted yourself."

His thumb brushes over my lips. "You tempt me from my purpose with your sweetness."

I kiss the pad of his thumb. "What if…" The thought does not move further. I do not want to risk his rejection. He already told me how he feels. And in the last several months, I have invited half a dozen kisses that he has honorably deferred.

"If…?"

I turn pleading eyes on him, hoping he will intuit the rest.

"Oh, do not look at me like that, Beloved. I vow I will not disregard your feelings." The tender regard written on his face gives me the needed dose of boldness to make my request.

I draw a breath filled with the salt and sun of Valor. "What if we savor our courtship with…" I swallow, feeling a blush burn my cheeks. "*Dancing*."

Several heartbeats pass. "Is that what you want?"

I nod, unwinding like a dropped spool while I await his answer.

"You must know how I long to kiss you," he fervently whispers. "But as I warned you months back, I do not want to lead either of us into too much temptation. I do not trust myself, yet the responsibility for setting boundaries falls entirely on me."

I frown. "Nev trusted me to hold her accountable. You think I do not know what we ought not do?"

"That is not what I meant at all, though it easier to advise than to do, or *not do,* in this case." Valor gently explains, "You have never needed to concern yourself with boundaries. Because of your betrothal, the moment you met your husband nothing was forbidden to you."

"That is true, I suppose, but I know that a kiss *is* the boundary." Even as I say the words, I ask myself, *But how* much *of a kiss?*

Valor nods his agreement, but his eyes are on my lips. With a flush of chagrin, I amend, "A controlled kiss."

His silver eyes meet mine. "I love you too much to be the source of any more of your regrets where physical intimacy is concerned. The privilege of calling you my beloved is enough."

A sense of contentment and joy warms me from inside. My palm settles over his heart. "Valor. I love you."

A deep rumble moves through his chest. "Those words on your lips are sweeter than a kiss."

I offer him my mouth, smiling. "Judge for yourself."

"Only a kiss," Valor murmurs more to himself than me. He takes his time, setting his lips slowly to mine. My heart beats as erratic as a butterflies wings. Each brush lingers, so warm and gentle. The sun soaked scent of his skin sinks into me, warming me like a summer's day. I let go of myself in his arms, knowing only him. He lifts me off my feet, tilting my face, bringing me closer, and—

"Commander!"

Valor pauses, breathing hard against my mouth.

"Valor," I whisper his name, a quiet plea to ignore the world a bit longer.

He barely sets his lips to mine when Trent again calls out, "Commander!" This time closer than before.

"I will dismember him for this," Valor growls, returning me to my feet. I hold to him, giggling at his ire that far outpaces my irritation with Trent.

Valor drops his hand to my back and guides me into the aisle. Trent is only a few stalls down when we emerge.

"Ah, there you are." Wisely, Trent does not immediately close the distance between himself and the thunderstorm at my side. "The stablehands said the queen came this way—good morning, Erianna," he grins at my flushed complexion, "so I figured you would be here also."

"What could possibly be so important that you could not await me in the training yard where I will soon be," Valor asks in his lethally soft voice.

"A matter of urgency," Trent replies. "Or else I would not have interrupted."

Valor glares as Trent brandishes a missive like a peace offering. Valor receives it, scans it, and looks up in astonishment. "This is from a reliable source?"

"No. It was delivered anonymously, thus I came to find you. He leaves today on a patrol. Would you have me delay him? Send him to meet with you?"

"Aye. In the royal office after breakfast," Valor orders, passing the paper to me.

I quickly digest the missive then declare, "I also have a few questions for the general."

※※※

VALOR

General Kannik sits opposite Erianna at her desk. I stand behind her, leaning against the wall to observe the proceedings. Thanks to the first hand account Trent delivered this morning, anonymous though it was, evidence exists potentially linking Kannik to the attack on the west side and thereby Zavaan.

Kannik crosses his ankle over his knee, gazing about the office in a proprietary way, then returns his eyes to Erianna. We decided he might respond better to her, so she leads the questioning.

"General Kannik, I dislike mincing words, so I will be blunt. As you know, an investigation has been in progress to determine how the Ruphiri breached our walls in October, thus far without results. However," she enunciates the word for effect, "new witnesses have stepped forward placing you on the west side just before the attack."

Kannik does not flinch at the revelation.

Erianna waits for him to give some sort of acknowledgement before prompting him to it. "Were you there?"

"Aye," he states.

A minute stretches out, neither of them breaking eye contact.

"Had you a reason for being there?" She asks.

"Aye."

"Would you care to share it?"

"No."

Erianna's conversational tone holds. "You do understand you are casting yourself in a derogatory light?"

His mouth curves into a smile. "Aye."

"Is this a game to you, General?" Her voice is chilling.

"Not yet." General Kannik settles back in the chair, bouncing his foot.

"Why were you on the west side that eve?"

"Because I obliged myself to be." His eyes slide down as much of Erianna as is revealed above the desk. "I must say, Majesty, I expected this meeting to be regarding something else entirely."

"I have not changed my mind about turning myself over to the Ruphiri. Tell, why were you on the west side?"

"You do not know what I mean?" Kannik tilts his head to the side, considering the queen. "Ah, I see. He never told you."

Not willing to allow the man to taunt Erianna with secrets, I interject in a bored tone, "My Queen, General Kannik was among the men who sought King Boldizar's permission to court you. It was not given."

"I see." Erianna drums her fingers on the desk.

"Her Majesty asked you a question. Answer it," I demand.

"It was a matter of personal business," Kannik addresses me, then her, "that has nothing to do with the Ruphiri or an alliance between us."

"While I dislike prying into the personal affairs of my people, I am afraid I must insist you reveal your purpose on the west side," Erianna requires.

"Very well." Kannik's expression is nothing less than placatory, as if he is doing the queen a favor by cooperating. "Though unnecessary, I have made myself responsible for a whelp I sowed on a trull. I went that eve to ensure they had sufficient money for the month. They live on the west side."

"Were they harmed in the attack?" Erianna's apprehension is plain, though he seems to not care in the least.

"They survived."

Erianna manages to contain her repulsion at his callousness, but her fingers drum faster. "You have nothing to say regarding the Ruphiri?"

"I serve Malesiir. I would never have permitted the Ruphiri to ravage our city," Kannik declares. "Nor will I apologize for considering the plan of trading you for Malesiir's protection. However, their attacks here and on our ships proved they want to destroy Malesiir, not merely capture you."

"How good of you to realize that," she derides.

Kannik braces his forearms on the desk, narrowing the space between them while increasing the familiarity. "You need me, Erianna. You need my experience and dedication to this kingdom. With my help, your rule would be strengthened. I could balance your emotional nature and free you to return to your primary responsibilities as lady of the castle."

My temper flexes at his impudence. "That, my Queen, is why your father did not offend you with Kannik's request to court you."

"Wise of him," she utters, then looks back at me. "I wonder, have you seen Violet about? I have need of her."

I grin. "Say the word, my Queen. There is nothing I would like more than to make the arrangements."

She matches my malevolent smile, turns back to Kannik, and demands, "I wish to know the name of the woman so that your story may be confirmed."

He is affronted. "My word is not enough?"

"Not in situations of this magnitude. No one is above investigation."

"You would make an enemy of me so readily?" He threatens.

Erianna does not retreat. "I would protect the kingdom you claim to serve."

"Claim?" Kannik balls his fists and slowly comes to his feet. "After revealing the honorable thing I do and offering you the benefit of my marriage even though you are less than—"

I plant my hands on either side of Erianna, surrounding her, putting my face inches from Kannik's. "You forget to whom you speak, General. You are dismissed. I expect the name of the woman delivered to Her Majesty within the hour, or I shall come for it."

Erianna's fingers cease drumming the desk with the feel of me guarding her.

Kannik looks between us. Ire twists his mouth. "Oh, I see the way of it. You spiteful woman! You take your revenge on Grandileer by laying down for this baseborn—"

My first punch breaks his nose. The second takes him off his feet. I stalk around the desk and seize Kannik by the throat. His eyes bulge like a fish on land while I drag him into the corridor. Erianna's guard comes to attention, drawing his sword. I drop Kannik at his feet.

"Escort this putrid excuse of a man off the castle grounds. He is not to be allowed near the queen again. If he seeks an audience with her, I am to be notified immediately."

"Aye, Commander."

Hate burns in Kannik's eyes as the guard none too gently hauls him to his feet and marches him out of sight. I slam the door to the office.

Erianna leans against the desk, looking slightly amused. "You know, I can break noses, too. A friend taught me how."

"Then you will have to be quicker to swing than I!" I bite out while pacing the length of the office, fuming. "And I still expect you to if I am not present."

"He was telling the truth, wasn't he?"

I snap my gaze to hers.

"About the attack," she clarifies. "He did not help the Ruphiri."

I clench my fists and continue pacing. "Maybe."

"Valor," she chides, extending her hand to me.

I go to her, taking her hand and bringing her against my chest. She is unruffled by his accusation. I inhale the scent of a summer's day and exhale half of my anger. "He was telling the truth about that."

"The other was complete rot."

"That goes without saying," I wind my fingers into her hair, loosening the crossings of her braid.

She huffs with annoyance. "Everyday I must fix my plait because of you."

"Then leave your hair down so I can admire it." I kiss the top of her head and hear her contented sigh in answer. My thoughts return to our interrupted kiss this morning. Almighty, she is sweet.

"But then my hair would get in my way," she complains. "For all those important tasks I must attend to. Like decorating. And menu planning. And beheading." She counts them off on her fingers, tapping each against my chest.

I chuckle, feeling my tension melt. "You are good for me."

"Our one trail has led nowhere," she worries. "I truly hoped Kannik was the culprit."

"Me too."

"Ah, well. No beheadings today. What is next to do?"

My hand kneads the back of her neck, easing the tension she is about to feel. "It is time we make our courtship known."

As expected, Erianna's muscles go taut beneath my hand. "Today?"

"Today." I press my thumb into the knot forming at the base of her neck and loosen it. "Kannik knows. Your guards know. And plenty of others undoubtedly suspect. I will not allow anyone to question your integrity. We tell them today."

She sighs deeply and rests her forehead on my chest, trusting me with this decision. "All right."

※ ※ ※

ERIANNA

I don my brocade armor for dinner. I tug every fold of weighty satin into perfect placement then spend an inordinate amount of time arranging my hair until I am satisfied that the woman reflected in my mirror is the High Queen of Malesiir. The black and gold of my gown is austere, far more staid than the vibrant colors I have indulged in of late. But I cannot allow even a hint of playfulness in my appearance tonight. The court must take me seriously.

From the crowns displayed in neat rows, I lift a diadem and settle it behind the braid circling my head so that the gold peaks rise proudly and organically upward. *A blooded queen,* the ornamentation declares. *A powerful queen,* the weapons hanging from my hips emphasize.

The door opens into the foyer, admitting Leelah. "Karris, are you ready?"

The girl ruefully sets aside the novel I lent her. "Must we go now? I am nearly to the end of the chapter. Rupert and Jenelise are finally going to be reconciled!"

From the dressing room I call out, "What chapter are you on, Karris?"

"Fifteen."

I smile. "Best go to dinner. You are only getting into the thick of it."

She groans.

Leelah pokes her head through the open doorway. "What romantic nonsense have you given my daughter to read?"

My hands smooth the fall of fabric from the fitted waist. "I resent you calling my beloved characters 'nonsense.' They are a delightful pair who overcome much in the pursuit of love." I turn round, asking for her opinion on my appearance with raised brows.

She eyes me curiously. "Why don't you look… Regal. The coronation isn't tonight, is it?"

I welcome the descriptor. "Regal is good. And no. My coronation gown is ten times as impressive as this."

"Then what is the occasion?"

Karris squeezes into the doorway next to her mother. "She is telling the court about her and uncle. And she is nervous."

"About time," Leelah approves. "But I do not understand why you are nervous?"

"Because I am willfully making a target of myself."

"You are sure that is it? You are not having doubts about Valor?"

"Of course not. It is only the court that makes me nervous."

"*Hmm.*" She sharpens those eerily perceptive amber eyes on me. "Karris—"

"*Ugh!*" Karris's outburst is instantaneous. "What could you possibly have to scold Erianna for that I cannot hear?"

Leelah stares down at her eldest until the girl relents with a huff. "Fine. I shall go help Father with the children. Micah is probably throwing things out the window again."

"Doing what?" I exclaim. Even a pillow thrown down on a person from that great height would be quite painful.

"Never mind." Leelah wags her finger at me to distract me from the antics of her children. "What truly has you so anxious?"

She does not understand the court games or the venom of their gossip. If she did, she would not be ignorant of the mischief Tirzah has caused me. "Truly, it is the court. I wish to waylay any gossip by reminding them exactly whom they are speculating about." I pat Daisy's hilt for emphasis.

"You are making too much of the opinion of the court. I agree they have a narrow view of the world, but I have not found them to be as backbiting as you made them out to be."

Nor would she. I have not repeated the things Silla told me they say about her. I want Leelah to enjoy her time in my castle and to protect her from the dark side of the glamour. "Perhaps you are right." I give her a genuine smile. "I am glad you are here, Leelah."

She returns my smile. "As am I."

My smile slides away when Leelah rushes toward the commotion of her children in the corridor.

Am I making too much of the court's opinion? I chew on my lower lip and decide to seek out the opinion of one who will understand.

My knuckles tap on Lorennt's door, but the sound goes unheard beneath the wailing of the infant inside. Though tempted to knock louder, the muffled sounds of the new parents trying to soothe their babe make my hand lower to my side. Lorennt has his own concerns demanding his attention. Compared to that, my worries are petty. I fix my courage and determine to proceed with my original plan.

Halfway down the corridor, Lorennt steps out. "Erianna! I am glad I caught you."

Completely missing my own relieved expression, he says, "Laszlo is out of sorts. Nev and I will not be at dinner tonight. Could you have trays sent up for us? Thank you." He pats my shoulder and is in motion before I can get a word in.

To his back I ask, "Is Laszlo ill?"

"Merely colic," he replies before disappearing.

I massage my temples and head for the stairs, needing Valor's steady presence to settle my nerves.

But it is not his reassurance that greets me as I alight in the great hall.

"Erianna. I must speak with you at once."

Mother Celiea's forbidding expression makes me inwardly groan. "Of course, Mother."

She leads me into an alcove with regal composure that falls away as soon as none but I can see her. "Boldizar told me what you mean to announce tonight. I demand that you reconsider. There is no reason to make a hasty decision based on infatuation."

I knew she was not pleased, but I am taken aback by the level of her disapproval. "I am not 'infatuated' with Valor. I am in love with him. Nor have I made this decision in haste."

She continues as though I had not spoken. "When you inevitably come to your senses, you will regret what you are about to do. Surely you realize the rumors this will incite! It will be all the worse when you accept the suit of a legitimate prospect."

My words pass my teeth like a dagger drawn from a scabbard. "Valor is both legitimate by birth and respected among the highest circles within our kingdom. Just because he is not your choice for me does not preclude him from being mine."

Mother Celiea bristles with indignation. "What does Lorennt have to say about this?"

"He was the first to approve of Valor."

"Then where is he?"

"Helping Nev with Laszlo."

"It will not look proper if he is absent should you decide to do this. At lest wait until he is crowned king. If you do not reconsider by then, it will go better for you if your king announces a courtship between you and Leer's Hand. Doing it now appears as if you mean to legitimize an illicit relationship before your king can refuse it."

Her words ignite my temper, causing me to ignore the sensible counsel she offered sprinkled among the rubbish. "Valor is *my* Hand, not Leer's. And I do not need to hide behind Lorennt's crown. I have one of my own."

Before I can utter something hurtful to one I dearly love, I walk away.

Mother Celiea's reproach is only the beginning. If she makes her displeasure of our courtship known to all, they will feel no restraint in adding their own censure. She knows how that would undermine me. I hope that she would not do such a thing. Surely her love for me outweighs her disapproval of Valor? I discreetly look back to see her already in conversation with Lord Sigure, her emotions plainly stamped across her face. I walk faster.

Valor's gentle clasp of my arm arrests my retreat to the dais. His hand slides down to mine in a chaste caress that calms some of my inner turmoil. "My Queen." The words are spoken as an endearment.

His eyes rove my face then skim my choice of attire. "In fighting form, are you?"

I lace my fingers with his. "It seems appropriate. I have been in the hall less than three minutes and already traded barbs with someone."

He searches overtop my head for the offender. Mother Celiea's disapproving look must give her away, for Valor inclines his head respectfully, but then, very intentionally raises my hand to his mouth and brushes a kiss across my knuckles, all without breaking eye contact with the Queen Abdicàt across the room. "She will come around eventually."

I smirk. "Ironic. She said the same thing about me."

"Even so, I am sure you and I can out stubborn a single monarch."

My reply is quiet. "We have failed in that before."

Valor's eyes are quick to find mine. "This time is different for a variety of reasons, foremost among them being I refuse to surrender you ever again."

The confidence in his eyes is rich soil for the tender shoots of my own. "All right."

"All right." He kisses my hand again, just for me. "Together, Beloved."

I smile for his sake. "Together."

Valor's grip on me does not slacken as we ascend the dais. Even that small intimacy does not go unnoticed.

Valor seats me at the center of the high table, causing the rest of the great hall's occupants to find their own seats. Once all have settled, I raise my voice to be clearly heard. "Before I commence this night's meal, I wish to make an announcement." The few sentences I rehearsed feel awkward in my mouth. Perhaps I should have swallowed my pride and entrusted this to Lorennt or Father. Regrettably, it is too late to bow out now.

"It pleases me to announce that I have accepted the suit extended to me by Commander Ironforge. He has distinguished himself in my estimation, and I have every confidence that he will continue to serve Malesiir with the same dedication he has displayed heretofore should he become my consort." I extend my hand toward the kitchen doors. They are opened for servants who file into the great hall, their arms laden with food. "Good eve."

"Good eve" is chanted back to me as Valor reclaims my hand.

"Well done," he murmurs in my ear.

"I am no good at speeches. Leer was much better at them." At all of this, really.

"His had more formal pomp," Valor agrees, "but I like your directness. You do not mince words."

I nod my head in thanks. And sink my teeth into my lower lip.

"You are overthinking," Valor chides. "We are heading off trouble this way, and if some should arise, I will face it with you."

"I know." But I do not know. Not with Mother Celiea's disappointment weighing so heavily. Nor with the court gossips so plainly looking between me and the low table where Tirzah is seated. "I trust you," I reaffirm, then pull my hand from Valor's so that I may take up my water goblet.

CHAPTER SEVENTEEN

ERIANNA

December 19th

"She just tromped in, begging for mashed fruits for her babe, then afore I know, she is doling out orders and rearranging the workings of my kitchen!" The woman's ample proportions strain the seams of her frock as she puffs her way through her tale. "And then! When I ask on whose authority she comes down to *my* kitchen giving *me* orders, she says, 'I am the General. Take your complaints to Queen Erianna, if you have any.'" Cook fans her face. "What did you do it for, Majesty? For what did you send that harpy to my domain? Have I offended you? Proved myself unworthy of my position?"

I massage my temple. Perhaps asking Leelah for help was not such a well-laid plan. Kragorn's uproarious laughter comes to mind. *Kept his wife from the castle, indeed.* "Cook, Mistress Tareth is my friend. She is general of her own domain and is accustomed to doling out orders. She did not mean to offend, and I certainly did not. I mentioned to her that perhaps her experience with frugality and some of her original recipes would be of use to you. Her potage was well received, was it not?"

Grudgingly, Cook gives a noncommittal assent.

"Were all of her suggestions amiss?"

"Not all," she huffs indignantly.

"Then you have my leave to keep the good and dismiss the bad." I smile, hoping that settles it.

It does not.

Cook heaves a great breath, drawing up to her full height that is half a hand shorter than mine. "I simply cannot abide such undermining in my kitchen. If she persists, or if any others come down to give me orders and throw about chaos, then I shall seek employment elsewhere."

"Cook, please understand," I soothe, "I do not want to lose you. Had I known you would be offended, I would not have made the suggestion to Mistress Tareth. I did not see the harm in it. As you know, I have Prince Lorennt and Commander Ironforge and a bevy of others to advise me in running this kingdom. They are essential to me. So you see, there is no shame in considering the suggestions of others."

She purses her lips, nodding to herself in an internal debate. "I hear what you say, Majesty, but it seems we are at odds. I shall tender my resignation immediately."

"Are you trying to make your queen cry?" I change tactics abruptly. "Or do you wish me to beg?"

Cook is taken aback. "Majesty?"

I implore with my hands, imbuing my words with not entirely feigned distress. "We are in the midst of preparing for a winter storm. Solstice is in two days, New Year's and Lorennt's coronation eleven days past that. My cook abandoning me in my time of greatest need will absolutely bring me to tears."

"Oh, Majesty, no!" Cook rushes to take my hands. "I didn't mean it, I would never leave you in such straights."

I inhale a shaky breath. "Thank you, Cook. Without you, our people would roast me on a spit in the great hall." That prediction might have been too much sauce on my dramatics, so I quickly press on. "I will clear up the miscommunication with Mistress Tareth immediately. Should she ever give you trouble again, send word to my Hand. Commander Ironforge will bodily remove her from the kitchen if it becomes necessary. You have my word." And it will serve him right for not properly warning me about Leelah's sort of help.

"Thank you, Majesty. And don't you fret. All the preparations for the winter season are coming along just fine. Just fine." Cook pats my hands reassuringly and bows her way out of the office.

That disaster narrowly averted, I flop into my chair.

My steward, who remained silent throughout the exchange, nearly smiles. "Do you think the grounds keeper and the poultry master will also be easily settled?"

"She has been to all of them?" I exclaim. "Is Commander Ironforge still about the grounds?"

The steward nods.

"Then you send him in Mistress Tareth's wake and tell him to make amends with the staff. Be sure to give him my regards."

"Aye, Majesty. And what of *my* affront?"

I gape. "Did Leelah come to you as well?"

"She made a few suggestions about the use of space within the castle."

"You have my condolences," I grumble.

"If I may, was it not Mistress Tareth with whom you resided this summer?"

"It was, and as I say, my most *empathetic* condolences."

He chortles, then catches himself. The sober man never reverts to such human displays.

I roll my eyes. "Almighty, bless the woman. There is no one like her."

"Would you like to hear Commander Ironforge's report on the proceedings?"

"Please," I wave my steward to be seated. As he prefers, he remains standing. I have barely seen Valor for the past two days. The beast of winter festivities has taken over our lives along with a steadily falling snow that has complicated everything.

"The commander reports that he has encountered no suspicious persons seeking access to the castle. The nobility continue to arrive and many that live within the city have sought permission to take rooms in the castle in the event that the falling snow makes roads impassable or should a blizzard arrise."

"A reasonable concern. I trust that the commander gave them permission?"

"He did." The steward links his hands behind his back, the only shift in his position since he arrived.

I fidget with the blue scarf woven into my braided hair. "Have we reached capacity for the castle?"

"No, Majesty. There are still thirty or so vacant rooms. I cannot recall the last time the castle hosted so many guests. Not even the year past were there so many in attendance."

"Delightful. Does the commander think it likely we will be snowbound by solstice?"

"He is concerned and has assigned soldiers to suspend their training at arms to aid the grounds keeper in shoveling snow from the pathways. He also advises you to 'pack extra blankets for the treehouse.' I assume that means something to you?"

My head drops into my hand. "It means that we are going to be snowbound with the castle filled to the rafters. Please warn Cook of this and order the master of the pantry to increase our reserves. I would rather not resort to eating the horses."

"Aye, Your Majesty."

"Is there anything else? Good news, preferably?"

He bows. "Tirzah of the High Valley requests an audience with you."

"Truly?" I have spoken precious little with her since her arrival. Only over cards or when she in company with someone I *do* want to see, like Leelah. Yet somehow, in all of those instances, she managed a snide insult or two, veiled of course. As much as I dislike her presence, she seems to have taken every effort to make herself odious to me. Not that Valor or Leelah notice. Nor do they notice the way she persists in smiling at Valor like he is some delightfully amusing morsel. He is, of course, but he is *my* morsel. The one time I deigned to call Leelah's attention to it, she did not see anything suspicious about how Tirzah looked at Valor. I was reprimanded for my preconceived and defensive notions. Nev might have been called upon as an unbiased voice, after all, she knows the full of it and would have honestly told if the fault was mine or Tirzah's. Unfortunately, Laszlo occupies a great deal of her day, and she never seems to be present when I have need of her wisdom. It seems wrong to burden her with my qualms during our short visits. Thus, I have determined to watch and wait.

"Aye, Majesty. She awaits you in the corridor."

"And you are just informing me?" I come to my feet.

"I advised her to wait in the great hall until your business was complete, but she said what she needed to discuss with you was important and preferred to wait."

"Send her in immediately, after which you are dismissed." What could she possibly wish to discuss?

I hold my head high as Tirzah enters. The probing look she gives me is undoubtedly to determine if I intentionally caused her to wait in the chill corridor. Whether she believes me or not, I face the accusation head on. "My steward only just informed me that you wished to speak with me. Please come to the fire." I motion her to an armchair to warm herself.

She does not press her suspicion. "A queen is quite busy."

"Indeed." I think of Valor and the scant moments we have seen each other. The kiss left unfinished. "What can I do for you, Tirzah?"

"How well do you know Silla?" She prefaces.

"Quite well. Why do you ask?" Has Tirzah realized Silla is watching her?

Tirzah eyes me. "Do you trust her?"

"Why do you ask?" I slowly repeat myself.

With her typical candor Tirzah explains herself. "She has been behaving strangely and has been secretive. She leaves her room at the oddest hours. And—"

I raise my hand. This is regarding Silla's spying. I should have known Tirzah would notice such things by being next door to her. "Thank you for your concerns, but I trust Silla."

"I do not think you should," Tirzah insists.

"I know what Silla is about, and I ask that you not interfere."

She snorts derisively. "You do? Even her secretive meetings with a man of average height, lean build, and greying brown hair? They spoke forcefully. In her room. At night."

"Haughty expression? Perpetual frown?" I inquire. She nods. "That is Lord Hugler. Her father."

"Oh." She did not know that.

"As you probably noticed, their relationship is strained. Hence, she lives at court with me year round."

"I see," Tirzah drawls. "She is your friend. Still, I believe you need to know what I overheard."

Though I am curious, especially since Silla has rebuffed all conversations I initiate about her father, I do not feel right about hearing secondhand from a contemptible witness what was spoken. "If Silla wishes me to know, she will tell me directly. You do not need to tattle." My patience dwindles. "Was there something of real importance you wished to discuss?"

Tirzah glares at me. "You will not hear what I have to say?"

"If it has anything to do with Silla, no, I will not."

"You are making a mistake, Erianna."

"Thank you for your concerns, but I believe there is nothing of consequence you have to say. If you will excuse me…" I rise, lacing my hands before me. It is as pointed a dismissal as I can give without blatantly telling her to leave.

Tirzah rises, holding her head high. "So be it. Your trouble is on your own head." She glides toward the door then turns back. "It is quite obvious that you have no desire to be my friend, and I am done trying to be yours. I have tried to make amends with you, though I have never wronged you. I wash my hands of you, *Your Majesty*." The door closes firmly behind her.

The arrogance! What could she mean by saying she has tried to be my friend? She has been impertinent since she arrived. She cannot return to Parse Kítaran soon enough.

I pull my cloak tighter around me. Even the roaring fire cannot chase all the chill from the air. I lean into the window embrasure and blow my breath on the frosty glass pane. I wipe the moisture away with my sleeve and gaze on the stark landscape. Dark grey storm clouds roll over the mountain range, bringing the dreaded snowstorm Valor forewarned. I hope it holds off long enough to complete the preparations.

CHAPTER EIGHTEEN

ERIANNA

December 20th

The storm broke over Malsihra in a blinding white fury during the night and still rages.

Anders lays a conciliatory hand on my shoulder. "Sorry, Majie. There's nothing for it now."

Wind howls, whipping snow across the bailey in a ferocious white haze. Anders closes the iron clad door in the vestibule and takes my arm, escorting me to a fireplace.

"How long has Valor been out in that?" I pluck at the coarse fabric of Anders's sleeve.

"Not long enough for you to worry," he assures me. "He's crossed the kingdom in conditions like this."

That does not ease my anxiety. While we wait for Valor, the great hall fills with those early risers who attend Gathering in the chapel. Even within this stronghold, the moan of the wind can be heard. I abandon my post by the hearth after ordering a maid to bring mulled ciders to warm us. I return to the vestibule and brace myself as I step into the swirling white to await Valor under the arbor of pine boughs. My eyes ache from searching the storm for him. But finally, my worries slide away as Valor's hunched shape ascends the iced steps.

His hand around my arm propels me back inside. "You beautiful idiot. What are you doing standing outside in a blizzard?"

I brush snow from his cloak as he unwraps a wool scarf from his face. "Waiting for you, of course." Frost clings to his eyelashes and wind chapped skin.

Valor pulls me into his side and kisses the top of my head. "For being so reckless with yourself, you certainly worry overmuch for others."

Anders tromps into the vestibule. "Well?"

"The gears to the portcullis are frozen shut. We are locked in until they can be thawed," Valor reports. "Meeting in the chapel would be unwise. No one should leave the castle without necessity."

"You did," I chide, pinching his side.

"With *necessity*," he asserts. "Stop fretting, Beloved."

"Could we hold the Gathering in the great hall? Like we did at the Tareth's home?" I suggest.

"Aye. Kragorn will lead if you like. The teaching elder was at the barracks praying with an ailing soldier when the storm hit. I advised him to stay put."

"Wise," I agree. "But now we are locked in the castle for who knows how long. I must speak with the steward to ensure everything was taken care of before the storm."

"I already have," Valor says. "The only thing left for you to do is dust off your deck of cards."

If only. "This is not like the Tareth home during the autumn rains, you know. There is no respite from the work. I must preside over all these people and give consequence to their complaints and wade through the conversations they will spring on me about land allotments, tax breaks due to losses, fortifications of cities, and on, and on."

After my explanation, the weight of Valor's gaze becomes heavier than usual. The storms in his eyes seem to swirl as he stares at me, taking my measure. There is a question behind it all that he has not asked, does not even hint at. I have no idea what it is.

"Before you go getting all glum," Anders interrupts the full silence, "why don't you just turn today's amusement over to me, so you don't have to worry none about it."

Anders looks far too devious for my liking. "Under no circumstances may you turn my castle into a… a…"

"Den of iniquity?" Valor helpfully suggests.

"Aye, that. I absolutely forbid it."

Anders does not possess the moral scruples to be insulted by our assumption. Rather, he is mildly disappointed. "Ah, well. Just a polite tourney of games then. And after noon, we'll hold a soldiers melee to give 'em all a show."

"We are holding the sword tournament the day after solstice," I remind him.

"I recall but I might be busy that day," Anders argues. "So I must give these propriety constricted noblewomen a display of my swordsmanship *today* to secure my dance partners for solstice. Overwhelm them with my warrior prowess and all that."

I glance at Valor, mildly disconcerted that Anders may not be speaking entirely literally.

Valor smirks. "The only thing you are likely to overwhelm them with is your odor. When was the last time you bathed?"

Anders scrunches up his face in concentration.

I roll my eyes. "If you have to think on it, it has been too long."

"I take your meaning. But may I arrange the melee?"

"Only if I get to participate with Violet," I stipulate.

"A paired melee," Valor counters. "And Erianna is with me. Someone has to watch her back." He punctuates his declaration with a kiss to the top of my head.

My heart flutters. The onerous task of contending with the gossip of the court is offset by the affection Valor lavishes upon me. "Agreed."

"Maybe we can even get the princeling to join." Anders waggles his brows.

"We must do that," I heartily second. "It has been far too long since I walloped Lorennt."

※※※

Anders descends on the great hall late in the afternoon, reorganizing the room to create a tournament ring. The long tables outline the boundaries of the ring, and the benches are set in rows for the onlookers. The air thrums with excitement that I feel in my limbs. I bounce on the balls of my feet in full armor, waiting for the rest of our contestants. Ironically, I was outfitted in my gear faster than Lorennt or any of my soldiers—for which I will be sure to tease them.

While I wait, I check the fit of the leather guard over the curved steel of Violet's blade. I do not want to accidentally impale any of my friends.

Mother Celiea clucks her disapproval. "You ought not be exhibiting yourself in such a manner. It is unbecoming behavior for a queen."

"But not for a prince?" I ask as Lorennt appears at the foot of the stairs in his light armor.

"Do not be obtuse, Erianna. You know why it is wrong for you. Why do you persist in this manner?"

"Because I like hitting things," I tease.

"You could be seriously injured."

"Do not fret, Aunt," Lord Sigure interrupts my clever rejoinder. "I will look after Erianna." He sets his hands on my shoulders in a gesture meant to sway Celiea. "Besides, we always hold back when we spar with her. No one wants to see her harmed, me least of all."

I glare at him over my shoulder and jerk out of his grasp. "Preemptively laying out your excuses for when I fell you? Tell me, Sigure. Where do you hide your skirt?" I examine his legs.

"Erianna!" Mother Celiea gasps.

Sigure chuckles, but I see the vindictive gleam in his eyes. "Not to worry, Aunt. I enjoy her jests. Like the ongoing one where she pretends to court a commoner. Do you not also find it amusing?"

"I cannot say that I do," Mother Celiea sides with her nephew in belittling my relationship with Valor.

It stings. Deeply.

"Did you fit the sheath well?" Sigure seizes Violet to examine the bladed end.

"Touch my glaive again and I will shame you before the match has even begun!"

"Do not rile her, Jakab." Lorennt steps between us. "Unlike most people, she fights better when she is angry."

I spin on my heel, stalking across the great hall before Sigure provokes me into making a spectacle with him. My patience with his pointless attempt at courting me has dried up. I am done playing at civility.

Leelah and Kragorn have found excellent seats for the melee at the side of the makeshift tourney ring. Tirzah, who sits alongside Leelah, acts as though she does not notice me despite the exuberant cries of the children.

"Are you gonna fight, Majie?" Micah asks, jumping to his feet on top of the bench. "Is that your glaive? Can I see it?"

Naturally, the weapons master's son would know the specific name for the polearm, unlike me when he placed one in my hands the first time. I pass it to Micah, keeping a hand on the top when it teeters ominously toward other bystanders. "I *am* going to fight. Your Uncle and I are on a team."

"It is called a *double's match,* Majie," he condescends to inform me. "He is your *partner*."

I grin. "Thank you for telling me."

"Father's not fighting 'cause Mother can't," Lois inserts herself between Micah and I, tugging on my arm. "She said it was only right that he stay with her out of 'solitarity.'"

"*Solidarity,* Love," Leelah corrects, patting her husband's leg. "It is a needless risk for me to take with the babe. But next year, Majie and I will be in the tourney together. Show them just how dangerous women can be."

Kragorn frowns. "If you mean to take Majie as your partner next year, then why am I sitting out this year?"

"*Solitarity,*" Lois informs her father.

We all laugh.

"What she said," Leelah chuckles and drops a kiss on his cheek.

"You ready?" I feel Valor's hand settle on my waist. Even through my hardened cuirass, his touch seems to burn through to my skin.

The look I give him brings out his trouble filled half smile.

Tirzah is suddenly interested in the conversation now that Valor has joined it. "Who is participating?"

I arch my brow at her. She ignores me, attending solely to Valor's response.

"Trent and Anders, Prince Lorennt and Lord Sigure, my queen and myself."

Because I am in the melee, Valor did not want any men participating that he did not explicitly trust sparring against me. Furthermore, none of the men involved will be embarrassed if I bring them to ground. Excepting Sigure, perhaps. Honestly, I hope I can put a notch in his pride. He has certainly nettled mine. The last time we sparred, he knocked my feet from beneath me, straddled me, and pressed Violet against my throat, trying to force me to yield. Needless to say, I struggled beneath him in the mud and adamantly refused. Kragorn was forced to intervene when neither Sigure nor I would relent. That shameful event was the turning point in my patience with Sigure. But I did not relate it to Valor. I do not need him to intervene between my "cousin" and me. I am perfectly capable of handling the pup.

"Quite a lineup," Tirzah drawls. "Who is favored to win?"

"It will come down to Valor and Anders," Kragorn states.

I glare at him. He shrugs.

"I think you are underestimating just how bloodthirsty Violet is," Valor contests. I love him a bit more for it.

"Violet?" Tirzah queries.

"Majie's glaive," Kragorn disparages, still sore that I named such a fine weapon after a diminutive flower.

Tirzah's smile is derisive. "How… Whimsical."

I look to see if Valor noticed, but he is occupied with Micah's pleading to enter the tourney as his second. Leelah, likewise, is occupied with her son. I huff my annoyance at Tirzah. She chuckles.

Large hands land on my and Valor's shoulders. "You done preening? I want to cross swords." Anders shakes us and says in what he probably thinks is a whisper, "I have some noble skirts to set aflutter."

"Don't you mean noble *hearts*?" I ask.

He grins at me. "Sure. Hearts."

I throw my elbow into his side.

"That's cheating!" He shouts. "Maiming a contestant before the tourney. You are gonna get yourself disqualified, Majie."

"The High Queen cannot be disqualified," I regally declare. "I am allowed to maim anyone at anytime I deem appropriate."

Tirzah's laugh stands out among the rest. "Sounds like cheating to me."

Valor does not miss the look I give her this time. Nor the fact that I am excessively armed. He takes hold of my itching sword hand. "Lead the way, Captain Anders."

Anders stalks toward the dais, nodding deferentially at a few noblewomen, plotting his conquests, undoubtedly. My eyes attempt to follow his, but are snared by Valor's scolding gaze. "Tirzah was only teasing like the rest of us. Why are you so determined to take offense at everything she says? You wrong her by doing so."

I know it is childish, but I pull my hand from his grasp and take a two handed grip on Violet and let that stand in for my response. Better that than the retort on the tip of my tongue.

Valor seeks my gaze that I withhold from him. Finally, he shakes his head. "I think you need this melee even more than the rest of us."

Before I can ask him what *that* means, Father claps his hands, calling for attention. He looks simply delighted to be overseeing the match. Nev and Mother Celiea sit to either side of him, one looking as pleased as Father, the other casting her disapproving gaze my way. I return my attention to Father.

"Welcome to our first indoor melee match. Captain Rhain Anders had the excellent idea to provide us with some entertainment on this inclement day. Though it storms outside, we can be thankful for roaring hearths and bottomless mulled cider to keep us warm indoors."

A cheer runs through the crowd, though his assertion is not quite true. Our supplies of mulled cider definitely have a limit with which I am particularly acquainted. Cook has orders to dilute it with water if our supplies run low, which they well may. Better that then switching to mulled wine.

"For those unfamiliar with a melee, the rules are quite simple. Our paired contestants shall face each other simultaneously in the tourney ring until there is only one team, or representative of a team, left standing."

Father seems to have missed his duties as king, for he launches into the introductions of our teams with flair. Valor notices too.

"How badly do you think Celiea would react if we invite Boldizar to join the melee?"

I whisper back, "As a contestant? Boldizar would never."

"Why not? He is more than competent. Likely could take down Sigure. Maybe Trent."

"You jest!"

Valor spares me a sidelong grin. "Boldizar and I met over swords the day after we told them of our courtship. He insisted upon learning firsthand whether or not I would be able to keep his eldest daughter safe."

My mouth falls open. Valor chuckles.

Boldizar spreads his arms wide. "I wish all of our contestants luck!"

We salute the King Abdicàt with our hands fisted over our hearts.

"I presume you want the pup and the princeling?" Valor asks as we stride to our side of the tourney ring.

"In that order," I affirm.

"Position Anders between us and it will go easier. Trent is wily. Keep him in your line of sight at all times. Do not let anyone separate us."

"Aye, Commander."

Though it is only a tourney match, the men entering the ring take it every bit as seriously as a battle to the death. Valor begins taking deep, rapid breaths. I hone my vision down to the four men opposing us. Years past, I would have run from the ferocious warriors before me. Now, I number among them. A menacing grin tugs at my mouth. My boots grind into the flagstones. My fingers flex on my glaive. Across the ring, Sigure eyes me. Slowly. Then he dismisses me with a smirk. I bare my teeth at him.

"Attend!" Valor snaps.

I shift my focus back to the warrior at my side, prepared to follow him into the melee.

"At the ready!" King Boldizar's voice shouts our benediction. "For Honor! For Victory! For Malesiir!"

Valor's war cry echoes through me, wakening my battle fever, though I rush into the fray two steps behind him with nothing but a blood thirsty grin. He positions us at the edge of the fighting where I can make the best use of Violet, prodding and poking the others into the path of Valor's blade. Lorennt, however, goes wide of our tactics and decides to take me out of the fray early, circumventing the battle and leaving Sigure to tangle with Trent.

I catch the arc of Lorennt's blade and do not stop moving as I push his blade up and away. He takes the momentum I gave him to swing his sword around and up, cutting in too close to my body. Thankfully, my reflexes are faster than his. I increase the distance between us to make the most of the leverage of my glaive which is the true strength of my weapon. My glaive connects again with his sword followed by a thrust that nearly ends the contest. His eyes widen at my skills that have grown by leaps and bounds under Kragorn's steadfast tutelage.

Rather than taking offense at my smug smile, Lorennt teases, "Fie on you, Warrior Queen!"

I cackle through the blows I exchange with my brother.

Until the hair on the back of my neck prickles.

On nothing more than intuition, I swing Violet behind my back and evade the perceived threat. A blade glances off the glaive, scouring a line across my beautiful cuirass, marring the leather. When I come round, Jakab Sigure's gloating face waits me. "Go don your skirt, Lady. The tourney ring is no place for you," he mocks.

I hiss while presenting him with the mace end of Violet that I hope cracks the bones in his legs. He leaps over her, setting the crowd to cheering at his theatrics.

"Oy, Prince," Trent shouts. "You are mine!"

Which saves me from facing the two simultaneously. I shoot a look of thanks toward Trent. His stalwart nod goes beyond the bounds of the melee. He wants me to have a chance to fell Sigure.

Past Trent and Lorennt, Valor and Anders trade furious blows. Anders wards off a swing from Valor, whose quick footwork positions Lorennt between the two of them.

The skill of the swordsmen is so impressive that I long to be a bystander to their match, but I feel that they are all working in concert to give me this chance to win my dignity back from Sigure.

It is an opportunity I will not waste.

"Come close, Erianna," Sigure taunts. "You know this match will end with you beneath me as did our last."

Though I am certain he intends to propel me into recklessness, he does not know the true form my battle fever takes.

He does not know that deep inside, I have frozen steel.

The roar of the crowd fades into the background as I plot this step and the next and the one after that. As anticipated, Sigure initiates the same hewing strokes that have brought me down in the past. I do not let my defense falter as he makes me parry with large, tiring movements. The placement of each step is critical for what I have planned.

His vindictive look comes to the forefront once more. "When you cease dallying with the commoner, I will bring you to heel."

I laugh derisively though my blood froths. "My rejection must be eating at you terribly. Or is it that Valor has bested you and claimed my heart purely on his own merit while all your noble superiority and kinship could not sway me to even consider you?"

His lip curls as he delivers the downward cut I expect. I maneuver him like a pawn, ensuring the way behind him is clear. Then his sword angles upward, catching the pole of my glaive where it is grasped between my hands. He yanks it backward, dragging me against his body so that he may press his physical advantage.

This is where I have lost many of our previous matches. I refused to surrender Violet, my greatest advantage over him. In the ensuing struggle, he used his advantageous strength to off-balance me. In the last match, he dropped me to the ground, pressing my own weapon against my neck while straddling me, cutting off my air so that I could not throw him.

But this time, I meet his victorious grin with one of my own.

And I let go of Violet.

She sails through the air behind Sigure, my greatest advantage over him wrenched from my grasp, clattering across the tourney ring. Dismayed gasps sound from many. But I am far from done.

My skill as a warrior extends far beyond my proficiency with a glaive. Sigure, however, fails to acknowledge the threat I am. While he is busy congratulating himself, I draw the twin daggers from my hips.

The crowd roars, knowing what Sigure does not.

I plant my feet beneath me and attack. My fists fly with daggers angled downward. Every exposed bit of his flesh is vulnerable with me beneath his guard. He cannot bring his sword to bear against me in such close quarters. The blades of my daggers turn red with Sigure's blood that I let from his vulnerable upper arms and legs.

He does not dishonor himself by turning squeamish at the sight of his blood dripping to the floor. But he does dishonor himself by the vicious slur at my womanhood and the attempt to backhand my face. I catch his blow on my vambraces and throw all my weight into him, deciding to defame his pride as he has previously done mine.

Sigure is thrown off balance. With a yelp he stumbles backward, grabbing at me in a failed gamble to right himself. I follow him to ground sitting on his chest, pinning his arms beneath my knees.

"Remember this," I snarl then strike his temple with the pommel of my dagger that bears the honored title Malesiir bestowed upon me, affirmed this day a year later.

Warrior Queen.

Sigure's head slumps to the side. Rendering him senseless is an excessive use of force by the rules of the tournament, but I dare anyone who witnessed him try to backhand me to fault me for it.

Though a resounding chant of *Warrior Queen* shakes the walls, the battle is not won.

Valor is caught between Trent and Anders, fending them off with a sword in one hand and a dagger in the other. One of them must have taken Lorennt out of the match.

I surge off the ground, sprinting toward Violet so quickly that I slide, overshooting my weapon. My fingertips touch flagstones as I drop into a crouch to redirect myself. Scooping Violet off the ground, I witness Trent doing exactly as Valor warned he would, circling my warrior's back to gain an advantage over him.

A battlecry tears out of my throat. My warrior will not go down with a sword in his back!

I charge Trent. Violet sings through the air with deadly speed. Trent ducks the blow that would have taken him off his feet. I spin with the momentum, dipping the mace end down defensively. My arms rattle with the force of Trent's hewing cut. What he lacks in bulk, he makes up for with precision. He meters his offense, seeking an advantage over me.

I retreat, bringing Violet's sheathed blade between us, holding him at bay so that I may ease my winded lungs while seeking an opening.

Though I dare not let my attention stray for long, I see swords flashing with awe inspiring skill between Valor and Anders who are both flecked with blood.

In the spare second I shifted my focus, Trent has snuck beneath my guard. Red flows from my my unprotected upper arm. The pain waits for the battle fever to leave my body before it will make itself known. But gasps from the crowd bring Valor's demanding gaze to mine. I flee to his side, setting him at my back while he defends against the onslaught from Anders.

My mind scrambles for a tactic to play. Trent is lightning fast and lethally accurate. Though not the strongest of the three men, he is certainly stronger than me. Placing myself against Anders is laughable with him in such a frenzy.

I am a liability to Valor.

Without Trent and I in the fray, Valor would be able to focus solely on Anders. I adjust my stance for my final attack that will hopefully be enough to take Trent down with me.

"No!" Valor shouts, noting the subtle shifts in me. "Together or not at all!"

"Then make a play, or it will be not at all!" I contest my commander's order.

"Trust me," he demands, setting his back to mine. I feel the change in his stance and, though I cannot see him, I know how he moves so well that I can tell his intention. I ready myself.

Valor pushes hard on his off-foot at the same time as I do, trusting him to be the counterbalance to the maneuver he is asking of me. I let the glaive slip outward taking a grip near the mace end as Valor spins us around, switching opponents. Anders's surprised face registers a sliver of a second before the sheathed blade of Violet is sweeping his feet from beneath him. The seasoned warrior maintains the grasp of his sword, though he drops to one knee with a painful thud. I follow Violet's momentum around for another quarter turn before Valor arrests it with a hand at the center of the pole, guiding it into place at Trent's throat. A glance across my shoulder assures me Valor's sword tip rests at Anders's throat.

Anders's white toothed grin contrasts his dark, shaggy beard. With unblemished honor, he lowers his sword. "I yield!"

Trent likewise bows his head with a broad grin. "I yield!"

We won.

Valor and I won.

My arms shake the second I relax my grip on the battle song thrumming in my veins. Valor turns me about to face him, moving concerned eyes over my bloodied arm and trembling body.

Then he smiles.

The great hall is a riot of noise and color as ladies throw their kerchiefs into the ring and men cheer. Above the chaos, Father pronounces Valor and I the winners of the melee.

But it all fades into the background. My world distills down to the man before me.

Valor catches me up as I throw myself into his arms. He holds me so tight that I believe no one shall ever take me away from him. With a room full of witnesses, he lays claim to the kiss I have offered so many times.

I bask in the heat and love he pours into this kiss, into me. I return it in full measure until he sets me on my feet, laughing against my mouth when I do not release him. He moves my arms from his neck to his waist, which is wise because he has left my senses in such glowing disarray that I am dizzy. Valor folds me in his arms, muting the world around me that is raucous with cheers and whistling.

All that I hear is his heart.

It is all I want to hear.

CHAPTER NINETEEN

VALOR

December 21st

I wait with nervous anticipation at the bottom of the stairs beneath a ceiling of rainbows. Erianna's touch is evident across the castle. From the beauty of the room to the relaxed boundaries between social classes, Erianna's advent into Malesiir has been a blessing. I have enjoyed watching her gracefully maneuver the court, love on her people, and leave a mark on this kingdom. I knew she was capable. Erianna has become every inch the queen I knew she could be.

But I cannot help wondering if this is where she is meant to stay. I saw the stress fractures form in the Warrior Queen when she was told her world would shrink to the span of her immense castle for the duration of the storm. *Caged*. The word jumped from her eyes while she fastidiously maintained her composure throughout preparations for the storm then again yesterday as she spoke of her responsibilities.

Not a day passes that she does not rove the grounds. There is a wildness to her that she contains in Malsihra. I had the privilege of seeing her race headlong over hilltops and sleep under open sky. I watched her ride nimbly between the monolithic trees in the Pinewoods. I want to release her to do that again. But first, I must kill the Wolves baying for her blood.

Boldizar and Celiea are announced from the opposite side of the great hall. Not long now. Boldizar nods to me as they ascend the dais, an amused smile on his face. What future does he see for Erianna? He said she would need me, I assumed as the queen consort and her Hand. Could it be something else?

A trumpet brings the great hall to attention. Prince Lorennt, Lady

Nev, and Prince Laszlo, tied to his mother in a scarf from Grass Lake, descend the stairs. The Malesiirian royal family. This is undoubtedly where they belong. Even Nev is a perfect fit among the Rodiharians. She tightens the bonds between the common class and noble class while Lorennt is thoroughly noble and has the heart of a soldier. Little Laszlo is the embodiment of all that our kingdom is becoming.

The trumpet sounds again, announcing the High Queen of Malesiir. I hold my breath until the toes of her boots come into view. Then I chuckle.

The other day, I caught Erianna toting a crate which looked to contain every pair of slippers she owns. She raised her scarred brow, daring me to comment. She used to raise her right brow to issue a challenge, but she has switched to the left now that a scar cuts through it—I knew she would like that stigma. I could not resist the overpowering urge to tease her for making good on her threat to dispose of all her slippers. So I stopped her, peered into the box, and selected a pair.

"What do you need those for?" She challenged.

Soberly, I explained, "The floorboards in my house are rough. I might want to rub my woman's feet sometime. I cannot do that through boots."

Erianna pursued her lips crossly, but a blush stole up her cheeks. She took the slippers from me, slapped a different pair in my hands, then continued on her way. But I saw the grin she tried to hide.

Lorennt and Nev pass me, but my eyes do not stray from the skirt of flowing, sapphire satin grasped in small hands. Long tresses the color of a raven's wing fall to her slender waist. My heart pounds in my throat. I swallow it back down, but it will not stay put. The perfectly tailored gown clasps her arms and silhouettes the soft curves of her figure. My mouth goes dry. A smile plays on rose lips set in porcelain skin that seems luminous this evening. Her eyes find mine and do not let me go as she descends another step.

It was not a burden those precious two times she asked me to hold her and not let go. It is simply the physical extension of what she has done to me since I began dreaming of her. Even in the Limban court when I judged her harshly, she captured my attention. Even when she was not mine to adore. She has held me all these years and not let me go.

I take Erianna's hand for the final stairs. She stands between my boots, elegant and perfect. All I can do is stare.

"Have I left you speechless?" She jests, not believing it. One day I will convince her of what she does to me.

I nod as I raise her hand, placing a single kiss on her fingers.

Her cheeks flush. "Truly?"

"I… You…" I take a breath. "Beautiful."

Her smile contains a hint of hesitancy. "You are pleased? The gown is plain by court standards, but I thought you would prefer the simplicity of it to something more extravagant."

The room is full of ostentatiously dressed women, glittering with their attempts to outdo each other. Erianna is set apart from them by her uncommon beauty, the gown an accent to what she already possesses. "You are radiant, Beloved."

She smiles, gripping my arms for balance as she stands on tip-toe to kiss my cheek. I lower my head to her, amazed that I have this woman's love.

I guide Erianna to the dais where she performs her duty of welcoming the guests to the solstice celebration and commences the feast. I notice the lack of weapons on her hips as she fluidly gains her chair.

"Daisy was not invited to the celebration?"

"I find a weapons belt to be a cumbersome dance partner. Besides, you are my sword. For what do I need Daisy?"

Her sword. I like that descriptor. "I find it difficult to believe the Warrior Queen abandoned all her weapons." I reach across her lap and brush her thigh, feeling the dagger hidden there for assurances. I dislike the idea of her being unarmed.

"Smart woman," I commend her.

Erianna returns the touch beneath the table by tapping her toe against the leg of my boot where a dagger is concealed. "You are a walking arsenal. As long as you share, I can have additional blades without worry."

There is something intimate about her knowing where all my weapons are hidden.

"Then I am to have the pleasure of you at my side all evening?" I take her hand in mine while plates are set before us.

Her anticipation at the thought lights her eyes. "I cannot think of anywhere I would rather be. However, I probably ought to socialize with the court and my generals. Would you keep me company?"

"It is adorable that you still think I will not choose to be with you every moment I am allowed."

The evening waxes full with expectations when I lead Erianna to the dance floor after Lorennt and Nev conclude the opening dance. To think that Trent ever teased Erianna for being graceless is laughable. She moves like water to the music swelling through the room. I ask her to expound upon the basic steps I know. With subtle instructions, she teaches me, making me look more competent than I am. Leading Erianna feels natural. I lose count of the number of dances we pass in each others arms. She is tireless. I am mesmerized by her grace. Enthralled by her vivacity.

I pull her to her toes at the conclusion of a song, savoring the way she fits my arms. She sways, leaning into me, then giggles like a child. "I am dizzy. And winded." Her chest rises and falls rapidly against mine, pulling the blue satin taught. Not for the first time, I wonder how long I must court Erianna before making her my wife. Is two weeks sufficient?

Notes spiral down, summoning couples to the floor as the next set begins. I tuck her hand around my arm and guide her to the edge of the room. We have barely reached the sidelines when Anders appears bearing a water goblet for Erianna. "Commander, do you plan on hoardin' the best dance partner for the whole evenin'? Hardly seems fair." He winks at Erianna.

She grins. "It is I who have apprehended Valor. I fear if I turn him loose the ladies of my court will be upon him and refuse to return him to me. I saw them fighting over you for the last set. The warriors of the melee are in high demand."

"They were?" I ask in surprise.

Erianna cocks her head to the side. "How could you not see it? We passed right by them. I feared I would have to relieve you of a dagger to bring an end to the women squabbling over Anders before their claws came out."

In utter disbelief, I regard my friend whom at the best of times could be described as unkempt. "*You* incited a riot among noblewomen? And not because they were disputing who would be the first to slap you?"

Anders smooths his beard that was combed for the evening. I think he even bathed. "They were quite impressed with my swordplay. Seems I earned some admirers. They prefer a man to these refined coxcombs."

His plan actually worked. Perhaps Anders knows more about women than I have given him credit for.

Erianna begins to say something then snaps her mouth shut, glaring past our little circle. I follow her line of sight to an encroaching group of women. Several hesitate at the ominous expression of their queen, but a few pluck up their courage and lead the pack. They huddle around Anders, vying for the honor of being his next partner. He gives consequence to each of them in turn, creating something of a frenzy.

As the women round on each other, Anders snares Erianna by the arm, pulling her toward the twirling mass of capes and skirts. "I am sorry to disappoint you, Ladies, but I cannot deny the queen a dance." He leans in to whisper to none of them in particular, "Though for you I wish I could." They all puff up like peahens then glare at one another, arguing over to whom the compliment was paid. The roguish grin Anders throws them puts mine to shame. The ladies sigh gustily, accrediting him with chivalrous qualities I know for a fact he does not possess.

Because Anders's ultimate goal is to see how many skirts he can lift before the end of winter, I warn them, "He is a rake."

"What could you possibly mean?" One of the glittering peahens inquires.

"I have known Captain Anders for a long while, and I think you ought to know he is an accomplished lecher."

They gasp with offended sensibilities at my pointed explanation. Denials are voiced, and they leave me alone to hold Erianna's water goblet. Well, I tried. Their foolishness be on their own heads.

I assure myself Erianna is still with Anders before draining her water goblet and moving to refill it. The flirtatious glances of a dozen women find me, but each time another lady whispers in the flirt's ear presumably deterring her friend when she would have approached me. Repeatedly the women's eyes seek the queen at the center of the room where Anders teaches her the steps to a commoner's dance. I can pick out her laugh amid the sea of voices when he lifts her high off her feet at the crescendo of the piece.

"I do not think you will find another partner now that the queen has claimed you."

I follow that voice around over my shoulder. Tirzah is resplendent in the gown Erianna designed for her. It is as lavish as the other noblewomen's but far more tasteful. The color shifts indecisively in the flickering light from black to purple, inviting the eye to linger and in so doing, calling attention to the woman. It is comforting to know Erianna's ire at me did not strike Tirzah.

"That suits me," I reply. "Have you enjoyed the evening? I doubt you have been wanting for partners. You look lovely."

"Thank you. I have had more offers than I could possibly accept." She nods her head back to the last trio of women that made to approach me. "Do you know what they told me when it was known I meant to speak with you?"

"That I am the queen's suitor and ill-tempered besides?" I guess with a smirk.

She replies with a sharp smile of her own. "Naught of your character. Only that it is unwise to cross the queen where her lover is concerned unless one wishes to find oneself dead."

I glower at Tirzah. So that is what they whisper about. I have never heard it spoken of openly but by Kannik. Nor should it be. "That is ridiculous."

"But rooted in truth, *hmm*?" She pries.

"Leave it be," I gruffly command. "You do not know where you tread."

"Maybe," she admits. "But I know your queen threw me out of her office two days past. There was no mistaking that."

"What—" I begin, but heads pique toward our conversation, sniffing out choice gossip like dogs picking up scraps. I lead Tirzah to a remote corner of the room, distant from those who besmirch my queen. Conscious of my volume, I continue. "Why did she throw you out?"

"Because she is jealous, petty, and arrogant?" Tirzah posits to my growing displeasure. "But you know her better than I, so perhaps you should judge her motives."

"Why did you seek her?"

Tirzah takes exception to my tone and responds drolly, "Because, wretch that I am, I feared for her life."

Apprehension brings my head up, seeking Erianna again. Her petite stature hides her from my view, but I discern Anders still in the middle of the dance. The royal guards remain at the doors along with a score of other guards posted about the hall. Then there are the soldiers in attendance as guests that make up a quarter of the room's occupants. She is safe.

Tirzah sees me take stock of the room and awaits the question I press to her. "Tell me everything."

She shakes her head derisively, and I think she means to deny me. "I should not. After all, I attempted to voice my concerns to *Her Majesty*," she mocks, crossing her arms, "and she would hear none of it." Tirzah looks toward the dais. "However. I have a care for Leelah, Nev, and even you. Thus, I sought you out."

I want to shake the explanation loose to speed it from her lips, but I preach patience to myself.

"The week past I overheard a conversation not meant for me between Lady Silla and her father, Lord Hugler. As I passed by her door, I heard raised voices and thought it odd a man would be in Silla's room that was not Cuyler. But as I listened, I realized it was no friendly meeting. She was attempting to deter him from something dangerous. She asked if he wanted the kingdom to burn. He cited what he did was for the greater good. They both abhor the thought of a peasant on the throne and do not like the Limban woman there either. He said it should have been Silla on the throne, but she let two princes slip through her fingers. He told her to honor her blood and do what she must. She said she had cast suspicions elsewhere and that he could not ask her to do more than that. He said she must then left."

I feel struck. It was not by chance our investigations bore no fruit. They were poisoned from the start by one we depended upon for information. What of Trent? He is pursuing this woman, and she has been receptive to him, returned his affection.

No. I scrub a hand down my face, reeling with the depth of Silla's treachery. Trent was deceived. She played him, too. The anonymous tip about Kannik? That had to be from her. But what is Lord Hugler's place in this?

I grip Tirzah's shoulder, bending closer to her. "You are certain it was Lord Hugler? Beyond a doubt?"

She nods. "I waited in my room for him to pass by. I watched through a crack in the door. When I described him to Erianna, she said it was Silla's father and would hear no more of what I had to say."

Why would Erianna blindly—

Not now. That is a question to put to her later. "What was it Silla asked him? Why was she angered with him? Recount it exactly."

Tirzah tries not to shrink from the intensity in my eyes. I cannot afford to waste time with her fear. Of me? Of the gravity of what she revealed? It does not matter. "Please, Tirzah. I believe you. Please."

She masters herself and quietly repeats, "She said, 'Do you want the kingdom to burn?'"

My blood runs cold. Lord Hugler had a hand in the attack on Malsihra. Somehow, he aided the Ruphiri. "By the depths!" I snarl. Tirzah tries to step away from me, but I pull her deeper into the shadows, stepping into an alcove. "Be still," I demand. "You have nothing to fear from me." Leelah was correct. My anger frightens women. Excepting Erianna. She is not afraid of my anger. Quite the opposite. She struggles not to fear my love.

I search her out on the dance floor, but again I cannot find her. I search instead for Anders, knowing he will not leave her side until she is returned to me. He stands near a refreshment table with Erianna. She holds to his arm, her queen's mask firmly in place looking this way. Trying to peel apart the shadows.

Because I have disappeared with Tirzah.

I say something so profane that the sting of Tirzah's hand lands hot across my cheek. "Do not spew such filth in my presence!"

I grit my teeth, beating back my anger instead of letting it escape in any form. If I do not appear shortly, Erianna will never give me the opportunity to explain this. "Is there any chance Silla knows you overheard?"

"None," she says.

"Have you noticed anything else, overheard anything else, insignificant as it may seem?"

Tirzah huffs. "As I told Erianna, Silla has been acting strangely. Coming and going at all hours, servants speaking to her as if they report to her. She is too keen. I do not trust her."

Acting strangely? That could simply be from fulfilling her duties as spy. The servants? Likely her informants. Coming and going? Probably the spying, but perhaps not.

"I told Erianna this and she dismissed it and would not let me repeat a word of the exchange I overheard."

"What reason did she give?" I ask, wondering how Erianna could simply dismiss this.

"Reason?" Tirzah scoffs. "None. She said she knew what Silla was about. I assumed they were friends, though I warned her not to trust Silla. She told me to leave her office. That I had nothing further to say. She was so haughty."

I growl under my breath. Erianna's misplaced trust in Silla could see her killed. But why would Silla betray her?

"Are we done?" Tirzah asks, tugging against the grip I still have on her arm.

"Nearly. There is one more thing I need you to do." I tug her after me so she cannot flee and step out of the shadows, walking the fringes of the room toward Erianna.

"What are you doing?" Tirzah hisses. "I have naught to say to her!"

I do not reply. She will understand momentarily.

Erianna steadfastly watches the dancers in the room, ignoring whatever words Anders speaks to her.

I drag Tirzah the last few steps until I gain Erianna's side. The women will not look at each other or at me. Anders does though. His hands are fisted at his sides, and his jaw is locked. The only thing restraining him from flaying me is the confusion setting furrows around his eyes. Accursed shadows! My exchange with Tirzah must have appeared horribly wayward.

"My Queen, I must speak with you immediately. In your office."

She does not move.

"It is vitally important. I heard from Tirzah what you would not."

Erianna winces almost imperceptibly at Tirzah's name from my lips. I want to take her in my arms, to remove her pain, but she is unpredictable. She would either weep or she would try to beat me senseless. Both would draw attention to us, making this worse from every angle.

"Erianna. Now," I demand, attempting to incite her to action.

So slowly, she looks up at me. Her eyes settle on my cheek. She opens her hand, hovering it over my skin, identifying the mark. "Of course it is about that. A logical explanation." But her eyes are riddled with doubt. *Have I lost you?*

Before I can formulate a response, unspoken or otherwise, she returns her hand to Anders's arm and leads the way toward her office.

CHAPTER TWENTY

VALOR

"Turn aside anyone who comes down this hallway," I instruct Erianna's guard. "We must not be overheard."

Anders stokes the fire to life in the hearth, chasing the chill from the air but not from my beloved. She is a pillar of ice.

"Why must I be here?" Tirzah stomps toward me. "Surely, you are capable of explaining this without me."

I take Tirzah's arm, though she objects, and place her before Erianna.

"Ask her." I tell Erianna who stares through us. "I need you with me for this, and I know I do not have you. Since you will not believe me, you must ask her."

"You told me you are mine." It sounds like an accusation, as if she has already determined I betrayed her. Her fears present more danger to our future than Zavaan ever could.

Before bitterness can make its way from my heart to my tongue, Erianna raises a shaking hand, staying my destructive words.

With a look of fierce determination, she closes her eyes to wage war against her fears and doubts. I give her the moments she needs until her eyes find mine, battle weary yet earnest. "Tell me the truth. Whatever it may be. I will choose to believe you."

"Tirzah overheard a conversation that points to the identity of Zavaan's informant. I pulled her aside so that none could eavesdrop on such sensitive information. She struck me for speaking profanely when it occurred to me what my taking her into the shadows must look like from your perspective."

"Wait," Tirzah interjects. "Did you think that I dallied with Valor?"

Erianna flinches at the blunt question, her confirmation causing Tirzah to lurch backward and fling more painful words. "Would you have killed me if I had?"

Erianna's brow puckers in confusion, then smooths as her sin once more strikes her. "So that is what the noblewomen are saying. Silla would not tell me."

I could strike Tirzah.

Anger fuels Tirzah's words, causing her to abandon the slow, drawling way she speaks. "What kind of woman do you think I am that I would take what is not mine? Furthermore, what sort of man do you believe Valor is to dally with me when he loves you? Why did you accept his suit if you think so poorly of him?"

If I am startled by Tirzah's defense of my character, I am stunned by Anders's incrimination. "She doesn't think poor of him, but it looked bad, you two being huddled in the dark together just as soon as Majie was not lookin'. Specially after Valor bought you that dress, and you bein' coy with him."

Tirzah shakes her head. "I did not—"

"Did not know what you did?" Erianna rallies her attack, crackling with temper. "Did not mean anything by your flirtatious overtures toward Valor? All the while snidely insulting me at every turn."

I do not understand. Tirzah has behaved no differently toward me recently than she has ever behaved. It is simply her way.

Tirzah glances toward the door then bristles, choosing to hold her ground. "I did not. You are making much of nothing."

Erianna sneers. "You claimed to wish for a friendship with me. Those are not the actions of a friend! So do not act surprised if I dismiss your assertions against Silla who *is* loyal to me and instead think the worst of you."

Tirzah opens her mouth to retort then snaps it closed. Erianna holds her head higher, victorious.

The truth slaps me in the face. Tirzah has been baiting her all this time where Leelah and I could not see it. Erianna tolerated it until the other day when she perceived Tirzah was attacking Silla. That is why she told Tirzah to leave her office. Erianna never defended herself, never explained her animosity toward Tirzah. She simply let Leelah and I scold her for not befriending Tirzah. The same as Grandileer pushed her to befriend Jaleh.

Benighted fool! I thought by asking her to aid Tirzah she would conclude there is nothing between Tirzah and I but well-wishes for each other. I intended to help Erianna overcome her fear. I had no idea I was watering the seeds of doubt.

"You have never liked me," Tirzah accuses Erianna. "And perhaps I *have* nettled you for not giving me a chance. It hardly seems fair, considering all you have been given simply because of your royal birth."

Erianna chuckles humorlessly beneath the weight of the golden crown crushing her head. She would trade places with Tirzah this very moment if she could.

"But that does not change what I heard." Tirzah implores me with her hands. "Please, tell her, Valor. I do not want her and Nev's deaths on my conscience."

Erianna looks at me. I wish she did not. Her eyes call me to account. *Can you not see what you have done? This is not only my fault.*

I fist my hands, restraining myself from touching her. It would be so simple to play on her emotions to earn her forgiveness, but I will not. "I have mishandled this. I am sorry, Erianna. I am more sorry that we cannot resolve this at the present moment. But if we do not act now on what Tirzah heard, more lives will be lost."

"So be it." Erianna turns inward, setting aside her pain and anger, relegating them however she manages for survival. "For the good of Malesiir," she whispers to herself. It cuts me to the marrow. It was Grandileer's mantra when he excused his behavior that placed his wife second to his kingdom. Erianna grips the hilt of her hidden dagger through the fabric of her gown, bunching the blue satin too thin for winter. The only way the gown could possibly be adequate is if the motion of dancing were warming her. Or if she were in my arms, letting me warm her. For a few blissful hours, that was what we enjoyed.

In the course of reading her journal, I learned that, until tonight, she has not worn sapphire blue since wedding Grandileer, because it was my favorite color on her. The loyalty of such an act touched me deeply. She must have decided to wear it again for me a month ago when she ordered the gown.

Erianna returns to us, unyielding as a winter storm. "Tirzah. What did you overhear?"

Tirzah repeats what she told me. Erianna analyzes the details as if we are not discussing her trusted friend. It is chilling. I know that I can become driven, harsh even, when I am acting as the commander and Hand, but I do not like to see my intuitive, soft hearted woman become unfeeling. Being the queen has hardened her. Being betrayed left her disillusioned with love. This life razed my innocent princess.

Erianna listens raptly then adds her thoughts to the details Tirzah provides. "Lord Hugler is a cruel man. That is why Lady Silla resides at court. There is a chance that he has manipulated Silla into helping him under threat of some form or other. It is difficult to resist coercion when one fears the man they are against, especially their father."

I did not know that about Silla. It is an unhappy commonality between she and Erianna.

"However, there could be more to it. Lord Hugler owns several properties in Malsihra." Erianna unlocks the massive cabinet she recently organized then takes a seat at her desk, looking through a box of land deeds until she finds those belonging to Lord Hugler. She hands them to me while scanning another stack of papers.

The properties were purchased by Hugler nearly thirty years ago. They are scattered about the city, but of note is one location on the west side. The deed indicates that it is close to the curtain wall and would have escaped the fires. It cannot be coincidence. I share the find with Anders. He swears causing Tirzah to cross her arms in annoyance.

"Look at this," Erianna calls me to her side. I brace my hand on the desk, leaning over her shoulder. Her finger taps a map of the family estate in the Central Province belonging to Lord Hugler. It lies near Port Veritae. Erianna flips the page, revealing another document. "Lord Hugler requested additional lands from Boldizar to increase his family holdings and was denied. Shortly after Leer took the throne, he made the request again and was likewise denied." Grandileer's seal marks the bottom of the page. "He also tried several times to make himself advantageous alliances by betrothing Lady Silla. When those fell apart, he allowed her to take residence at court with the aim of securing her a marriage to a prince." She scrutinizes the pages a second time and concludes, "Lord Hugler has been trying to increase his wealth and power for a long time. I do not doubt he is bitter toward the Rhodiharians for undermining those schemes."

"Wasn't Hugler a general under Boldizar?" Anders asks.

Our attention jolts to Anders.

"Was he?" I ask. "You have been enlisted twenty more years than I."

"And yet I had you on the ropes yesterday, Boy." Anders lands the jab with a grin. "Hugler served as the master of Old Fort. General Hugler..." He repeats the name to himself, then nods. "Aye. That sounds right."

"Curse that maggoty worthless cullion!" Erianna flings the vile words like daggers.

Tirzah sets her hands on her hips. "Must you all speak like knaves?"

Anders thumbs the Malesiirian crest on his formal military tunic. "We're soldiers, Darlin.'"

"Not her," Tirzah argues, pointing at Erianna.

"She's more a soldier for this kingdom than any of us," Anders soberly replies, championing our queen. "You've no idea what that woman has sacrificed for this kingdom."

Tirzah's arrogance is knocked askew.

"Could Lord Hugler have been the man Zavaan was meeting with?" I wonder.

Erianna chews on it. "Quite possibly."

"We need to search his property on the west side," I say to Anders.

"Mining?" He voices my theory. I concur, turning to the window. I dry the pane and stare into the moonlight. The snow falls steadily, but the blinding winds have subsided.

"We go there tonight. After the celebration," I decide, hoping the gears to the portcullis have been thawed.

"It will carry through till dawn," Erianna informs me. "The longest night of the year."

"We best have a look at the family estate too," Anders says. "Could be the Wolves have been waiting out the storm there. Caves only provide so much shelter. And they've still got to eat."

"What of Lady Hugler?" I ask, not recalling seeing her at court recently.

"Her sister became ill," Erianna supplies the answer. "She is spending the winter with her in Port Veritae."

"All right. We take the opportunity to go to the estate, too," I agree. "But we must not show our cards. We need to do this without arousing suspicion. Silla will not be easy to slip past. That also means we cannot alert Trent until we know for certain."

Anders rubs his hands together, anticipating the challenge. "How we going to sneak past our spymasters?"

"*Spymasters*?" Tirzah exclaims to Anders's chagrin.

I glare at him while Erianna states, "Trent is Valor's spymaster. Silla is mine."

"Then you have been thoroughly duped by her," Tirzah remarks.

Erianna does not let the barb find flesh, but I am riled on her behalf. "Keep such candor to yourself," I growl at Tirzah. Her fists return to her hips with a defiant smirk.

"We could say we are headed to the barracks for a few days," Anders suggests. "Or to see how the construction at Chishelm fared through the blizzard."

"Simple enough." I think through the plan. "But Trent will be suspicious. He knows we made arrangements to stay through the coronation."

Anders shrugs. "So we bring him. Or tell him it has to do with the Wolves. He would accept that."

"Then he would tell Silla we have a lead that we did not explain to him," I point out the flaw. "Nor do I want to leave Erianna without an ally at court. Especially if Silla is her enemy."

Anders grunts. We toss ideas around, but continually come back to Trent being a problem. Even if we were to take him along, Silla would demand a plausible explanation for his absence which we could not give. If we were to tell him what we suspect of Silla, he could not help but behave differently toward her. We must keep him in the dark, terrible as it is.

I rest my eyes on Erianna, seeking reprieve from our scheming. She is distant, lost in herself. I crouch beside her, drawing a finger over the back of her hand to bring her gently back from wherever she has gone. "Beloved."

The vague look dissipates from her expression, but it remains devoid of emotion. "We hide your absence with gossip," she murmurs, not as far afield as I thought.

"How so?" I match her soft tone.

"Like Anders said. It looks bad."

"What does?"

Her eyes settle on the woman warming herself at the hearth. "You and Tirzah."

I grit my teeth, scrabbling for the restraint to calmly, if tightly, say, "Erianna, you said you believe me."

"Have you not heard the gossip these past weeks?" She inquires dispassionately. "There are bets on how soon I will be scorned again. They think it a sure thing since the commander brought a beautiful woman to court under his protection. I heard Lady Gavlund say, 'The queen must be cold in bed or lacking sufficient wiles to hold a man's interest for long.'"

Fury like lightning destroys my restraint. "They said that to you! Why did you not tell me?"

She ignores my questions. "It will be a simple thing to convince them that their gossip is founded."

"Why would I want that? We are attempting to work around Trent and Silla, not maneuver the whole accursed court!"

Not moved in the least, she replies, "Because if you leave, I can tell Trent and Silla that we fought and I do not wish to discuss it. They will believe that, and it will not surprise Trent if Anders goes with you."

Tirzah stalks toward Erianna, rife with indignation. "Your plan is to let everyone believe that you took Valor to task for having a tryst with me so he has an excuse to run out of the castle with his tail between his legs? Are you daft? That would ruin all our reputations!"

"No." Erianna glowers at Tirzah. "I can protect your reputation *if* you swear to keep all of this a secret."

"How do you—"

"I was not finished," Erianna frigidly declares. "You will keep this a secret, play along in whatever capacity I require, *and* you will cease your coy behavior toward Valor."

Tirzah stares her down. "How do you propose to protect my reputation when you cannot even protect your own?"

With that question, I know Erianna's mind and realize how much more she will suffer for our kingdom to legitimize my disappearance. I rise to face Tirzah, gripping the back of Erianna's chair. "My queen will not protect her reputation. She will sacrifice her reputation and mine for the sake of yours and to protect Malesiir."

"What do you mean?"

"It is quite simple," Erianna laces her fingers atop the desk. "Valor made an unwelcome advance toward you this evening. You resisted and struck him. He attempted to conceal it by bringing you before me and laying the blame on you. Being the scorned, violent woman I am, I saw through his ploy. We fought, then I cast him out of the castle in a fit of jealous temper. But I will bring you to my side at meal tomorrow, showing the court I find no fault with you. You will be victimized but blameless. Valor will be held in contempt while I bear the brunt of the gossip and speculation."

Tirzah is taken aback. "You mean to announce this to the court?"

"No. This is what they will assume based on our behavior. Trent and Silla will hear that Valor and I fought, and I asked him to leave. That is a version of the truth. However, Lorennt must be told everything so he does not attempt to kill Valor."

"Leelah will require the truth, too," I add then tie up her loathsome, but effective plan. "When I return with evidence of Lord Hugler's treachery and hopefully the Ruphiri in custody, Erianna and I will explain the truth of things, or simply make amends with each other in a public way so that the court does not realize we have played them."

"The latter," Erianna decides.

But I stipulate, "That depends upon how vicious the gossips are to you, Beloved."

Erianna's eyes thaw as they search the depths of mine.

Anders claps his hands together in anticipation. The promise of a looming battle takes precedence over his second favorite activity—chasing women. "We can gather a contingent of soldiers on the way to the estate so Hugler does not catch wind of it. Let's hunt some Wolves!"

I do not break from Erianna's gaze as I direct the others. "Anders, go ready and meet me at my room. Tirzah, wait for Erianna in the corridor."

When the door clicks shut, I draw Erianna to her feet. "I think you ought to know I hate this plan. I hate that your name will be slandered across Malsihra until I return and set it right."

She tries to dispel my concern, but her voice is lifeless. "I will be fine. I have survived far worse."

I pull her into my arms. She comes to me but is as unyielding as steel and twice as sharp. "This is real, Beloved. No matter what they say, no matter what you fear, this is real."

"I know that," she says without inflection.

"Do you?" I chafe my hands on her arms that are prickled with cold beneath the thin satin. "I am sorry I am leaving tonight."

"I am too. But it would be foolish to waste this opportunity."

Erianna does not say there will be more solstices. She is personally acquainted with that folly. I thread my fingers in the thick locks she left unbound for me that are constrained only by the crown perched on her brow. There is so much to say, too much for these few minutes. "Will you forgive me for all that happened with Tirzah? I did not know the gossip I instigated or that she was being unkind to you. I am unaccustomed to considering how my actions will be perceived. I weigh my motives carefully before acting, but being in the eye of the court adds a level I have never needed to consider. I need your help to navigate this."

I feel her soften to me. "I forgive you. Will you forgive me for doubting you? I know you have never betrayed me and that I am faulting you for Leer's sins. It is wrong of me."

"It is true I am paying the penalty for his sins, but you are paying it too. You have lost faith in love. I think that you might have trusted me more before I began pursuing you. What makes matters worse is that you are so afraid of losing me, so certain that it will happen, that you are terrified of holding onto me."

Tears gather in the corners of her eyes as her walls crumble. "Each time I think I have conquered my fears, I find I have only maimed them, not destroyed them."

"I forgive you." I catch the tears that roll down her cheeks, numbering them. "It is difficult to destroy something when those around you constantly resurrect your doubts. And my misguided meddling did not help."

A ghost of a smile alights on her face.

"Now that I understand, I will be more sensitive, but I need you to be more honest. Your honesty points my sword in the direction of the enemy we face. When we battle together, we will triumph, just like yesterday." I hold her tightly, vowing to make certain her laughter outnumbers her tears.

"You will not return in time for Lorennt's coronation," Erianna notes.

"It is unlikely," I regretfully agree. "But I will do all I can to return with a present of trussed up Wolves."

"See that you do."

This is not how I planned on having this conversation, it is barely more than a conceived notion in my own mind, but if I do not return before the coronation, Erianna needs to settle this in her heart without me. "Beloved. I want you to weigh the merits of maintaining your position as High Queen. Lorennt believes he is going to assume the role as High King, and I know that you intend to fight him to hold onto it. But before you do, consider carefully if that is what you truly want. I will not tell you what to do, but I want you to be sure of your own mind before the coronation. Think toward the future and decide if this is what you desire." Her muddled expression meets mine, wondering why I have brought this up, now of all times, but she allows me to continue. "And if you feel that you need guidance in this, I want you to seek Boldizar. He is wiser than we are. Speak with him before you decide anything."

"I shall," Erianna agrees.

We have just one more moment. I intend to make it memorable, but her stiff posture compels me to ask, "May I kiss you?" I want to salvage what I can of this night before I am speeding across a frozen wilderness and she is thrust into the backbiting masses.

She grants my request with half a nod, though I saw conflict in her eyes.

I kiss her gently, assuring her between breaths that I love her. She leans into me, warming to my touch. But I want to do more. I want to show her how weak her doubts are against the strength of my heart.

"You are not cold," I assure her, touching my lips to the tender skin of her neck. Erianna grips my shoulders, turning her head to the side, exposing more soft skin to my kisses. I move my fingers through her hair, sliding them over the satin gown, following the contours of her back down to the flare of her hips. I pull her flush against me. "And you most certainly are woman enough to hold my interest for a lifetime."

This fear of Erianna's is dealt a fatal blow. Trusting myself only because of the constraints of time and obligation, I reacquaint myself with the honeyed taste of her, kissing her more deeply than I ever have before. She returns my kiss fervently, hinting at the passion of which she is capable as she melts against me, holding me as tightly as I hold her. One minute stretches into three as I defy the press of time with my woman in my arms. Becoming one with her will make the last decade of longing seem insignificant.

Although that day is in sight, it is not this day.

I pull back slowly, scattering kisses on her beautiful face that I will be denied sight of for too long. She lays her head on my chest gazing up at me with love in her eyes. I touch the bow of her lips, admiring her well-kissed mouth and the flush of her skin. "I hate that I am always saying goodbye to you."

Her eyes echo the sentiment as she kisses my finger against her lips. It takes all of my self-control not to lift her off her feet and steal away with her instead of seeing this miserable plan through.

"Are you ready to throw me out of your castle like the churlish oaf I am?" I make light of what is going to be a wretched evening for both of us.

"No," she smiles sadly. "But we best get on with it."

I lead her to the center of the room and relax my muscles. "Not my nose, please."

"Hush, Churl." Erianna forms a fist.

The Warrior Queen grits her teeth and punches her wayward lover in the face. My lip splits against her knuckles, pain superimposing a flash of light upon my vision. Blood drips into my mouth and down my chin.

"Your jaw is as hard as it looks," Erianna grumbles, rubbing her sore knuckles.

I examine them, then kiss the redness spreading outward, proud of her despite being the object of her exhibition of skill. "Nicely done, Beloved. Someone taught you to throw a perfect punch."

She grins. "Unfortunately for him."

"Come along you delightful imp." My hand links with hers for one last moment then I stoically release her into the cold embrace of her castle. I linger to speak with her guard, wanting to leave Erianna with some warmth before I go.

CHAPTER TWENTY-ONE

ERIANNA

I part from Valor without a backward glance, though I catch notes of his murmured conversation with my personal guard. Tirzah walks at my side in silence until the great hall looms ahead.

"Press your lips together," she advises. "They are too red. You do not look like you have been fighting."

I do as she recommends, hiding my heart behind the forbidding Warrior Queen before striding into the great hall.

This is not real, I counsel myself as the not-so-furtive whispers begin. *From this night until Valor returns, all is an act.*

Lorennt is easy to locate. He has been watching for my return with Nev. They hasten to me without appearing to do so.

"Erianna, what is going on?" Nev whispers, puzzling over Tirzah at my side and glancing back where Valor has not yet appeared.

I pitch my voice low. "I will explain all tomorrow, but, until then, know things are not as they seem."

Lorennt takes his cue from my sober demeanor. I force myself to converse with Tirzah until a murmur through the room alerts me to Anders and Valor's arrival, though I do not need the warning. Valor's gaze upon me is all the warning I require.

I glare at the one who calls me Beloved, standing so stiffly my spine aches. The room quiets to watch as Valor stares apologetically at me. The ravenous looks of the gossipmongers presume it is the look of one who is wayward. Only I know it is the look of one who feels he is leaving me alone to face the lesser of two enemies while he faces the greater. But it must be. He gives me what protection he can by lowering his head as if ashamed by his misdeeds then turns his back and steps into the snowy winter night.

The doors bang closed in the deafening silence. The echoing boom barely fades before the speculation begins in earnest. I harden my heart to the cruel words bouncing off the rafters. A necessary evil.

Silla and Trent make their way toward me. I demand of myself not to judge her yet. Nothing is certain. We do not have all the details. But the bitter, caustic taste of her betrayal is on my tongue. I wish I was not so familiar with that taste.

Leelah is fast on their heels, gaining my side when they do. "Where is Valor going?" She takes the hand unconsciously fisted at my side to look at my knuckles and gasps. "Did you do that to him?"

"I do not want to talk about it," I mutter. Leelah's interference could quickly turn this into more of a spectacle than it needs to be and raise suspicions that must not be brought to light.

As predicted, she presses. "Erianna—"

"Yes! I did that to him. I told him to leave the castle."

"Tirzah?" Leelah asks her friend.

"May we speak of this later?" Tirzah says, playing the part of a victim well. I wonder how she became such an accomplished performer.

"No, I think we need to discuss this now," Leelah demands.

Tirzah looks at me for permission. I grant it, and the women depart.

Trent lays a hand on my shoulder, proving how stalwart a friend he has become to me in these past few months. Silla gives him a worried look that seems genuine. It will be difficult not to openly question every word and expression of hers until Valor provides me with the truth of the matter.

My heart seizes with fear for him and longing to be by his side.

The rumors gain volume as I stare at the doors that bar my love into the freezing night. The chill in my limbs makes me long for a warmer gown and heavy mantle.

As if summoned by thought, one of my guards approaches bearing my fur lined cloak.

My blue scarf is folded inside.

Tender feelings that will fuel the gossips bring tears to my eyes. I conceal them with the action of donning this token of Valor's love to keep me warm until he returns.

※ ※ ※

* * *

VALOR

The city sleeps in juxtaposition to the clamor in the castle. The privilege of being noble means the ability to afford plenty of fuel to chase the winter night from a room. The poor do not have that luxury. Blankets and body heat are their best weapons against the cold.

We arrive at Lord Hugler's property on the west side within the hour despite the mountains of snow blocking the streets. The front door has a board sealing shut the crumbling tenement house. We skirt the building, peaking through broken windows as we go. The back door of the home is not boarded. I kneel before the lock and plunder it while Anders keeps watch. Only the moon witnesses our dealings. We ensure it by stepping into deep shadow when the guards pass by atop the curtain wall.

The lock clicks open. The interior is so dark it is difficult to discern shapes. We pause in the threshold, drawing swords. The scent of the air is more informative. Musty. Earthy. With the pungent odor of dog urine. Our eyes adjust. Reasoning puts names to the shadows.

A rotting staircase clings to the exterior wall of the building. Anders touches the lowest step with his boot. It creaks and groans, pleading that he not bring his considerable weight to bear on it. We leave it be.

I twist the sole of my boot on the floor. A thick layer of grit rasps beneath it. I advance through the lower room. Near center, a rug sags in the floor. Anders halts next to it while I continue to the back of the house. A door hangs half off its hinges. Some broken furnishings gathering dust is all the room holds. I back track to Anders.

I hold my sword at the ready as he bends to grasp a corner of the rug. With a jerk, he flings the rug aside revealing a gaping chasm in the earth. Jagged edges of floor boards outline the darkness, resembling the toothy mouth of a great fish I once saw. No sound echoes down the tunnel. Anders tears off a strip of the moldy rug and wraps it around a chunk of floor board that was cast away from the hole during excavation. The makeshift torch ignites after several attempts. While I stand guard, Anders drops into the shallow hole. He hunches over, exploring the length of it which must be a goodly distance judging by the amount of time he is gone.

Anders's shuffling steps signal his return. The tunnel glows golden until he stomps out the torch before clambering out. "Tunnel runs clear under the wall. Pops up about a half mile outside the city. Nothin' there now, but smells like dog. Tracks from wolves and men run the length of the tunnel."

This is how they did it. It was no hastily planned thing. They must have worked on this for months before breaching the walls the night of Lorennt's wedding. Possibly began digging before the king's murder when our patrols were not as aggressive in their watch.

The damage they could have done, beyond what they have already done, is staggering. Praise the Almighty they have not utilized this yet. Or perhaps they have. Perhaps Zavaan has been waiting for Erianna to ride into the city so he can scoop her up and disappear with her.

We depart the west side as quietly as we came, leaving the door unlocked for the guards that will address the breach come morning.

CHAPTER TWENTY-TWO

ERIANNA

December 22nd

"I do not believe that is the whole story," Karris argues while we dress the morning after the solstice. "Uncle loves you. You love him. You could not have tossed him out."

Karris's youthful dream that lovers would never be so cold toward one another is more difficult to contradict than the court's jaded opinions were to manipulate.

"Besides," Karris drags a brush to the ends of her hair while I plait mine and tuck the length under as if I prepare for battle, "Uncle and Tirzah barely tolerate each other. Whatever reason they had for talking in the dark, it certainly was nothing more than that. It is impossible that they kissed like everyone seems to think. Uncle would never kiss a woman that did not want to be kissed."

Her logic is more sound than mine was last night. Almighty bless Leelah and Kragorn for teaching sense to their children.

"So when are you going to tell me what truly happened?" Karris demands, mimicking her mother's look that persuades her children to confess their misdeeds.

A knock echoes in the foyer. I tug my skirt down, straightening the bodice of my dress. It is a black, stately thing Leer once described as imposing. I want to be imposing today. Maybe if I look it, I will feel it. "You are a smart girl, Karris. But I cannot answer your questions satisfactorily. And I must ask that you not poke holes in everyone's impression of what happened last night. It is vitally important that they be allowed to think the worst of Valor and I."

"You leave me no choice but to ask Nev what happened," Karris forewarns.

"Absolutely not! Karris, do not speak of this with anyone! Not Nev or your mother or Trent. No one!" I point my finger at her as I answer the door. My personal guard awaits with a note for me.

"Your Majesty, this just arrived from the porter at the city gate." He passes me a folded scrap of parchment inked with Valor's scrawl.

B,

W S suspicion confirmed. Address immediately. You stay. Distract H. Proceeding apace.

A M L,

C O

I smile over the closing. *All My Love, Churlish Oaf.* Only Valor would turn my insult into an endearment. "Karris, please fetch your father." I will send Kragorn to the barricade the tunnel. He may cover his departure by organizing the prisoners into labor groups to shovel snow from the main thoroughfares. I wish to go with him, but I will trust Valor's judgement. Perhaps Kragorn will be able to interpret why Valor insists I remain in the castle. For the time being, I have a coronation to prepare and a noble family to distract.

※ ※ ※

December 27th

I curl into the supple leather armchair in Father's library. Hiding in here affords the isolation I cannot find in the rest of the castle. The past six days have presented me with more musings on the state of my life and flaws therein than I have listened to the prior six months. Some of the court have been particularly nasty toward me. Lord Sigure glutted himself on my perceived misery before Tirzah interjected herself into the situation. Whatever were her personal reasons for disliking me, she has set them aside to become my advocate amongst the mockers of the court. It is a change that pleases Leelah, though she chastised Tirzah and I for waiting for a cataclysm to resolve our differences.

"Daughter," Boldizar greets me. "Everyone is wondering where you are. They expected you were in the stables. What are you doing here?"

My lips tilt into a sardonic smile as he settles opposite the lounge I claimed. "I *was* in the stables. I came up here to regrow the flesh they stripped from my bones when they found me."

He frowns. "You youths take such drastic action when a more moderate route could have been found. But it is always do or die with the young."

I wink. "Maybe the old see their folly in us and *that* is the greater part of the distate you feel."

He chuckles, making Leer's wise eyes twinkle in his aged face. *I miss talking with Leer.* The thought takes me by surprise, but I do not cast it aside. I wish I could sit across that chess board from Leer once more and discuss our lives and vision for the kingdom like we had a lifetime to see those dreams come to fruition. Did I savor those times to the fullest when I had them? Probably not. I was too busy looking forward to the future and complaining about the present to recognize what I had. Regrets solidify my purpose to not make such mistakes again.

"You are far away," Father comments.

"I was reminded of Leer. Of dreaming with him about our future."

"Happy memories then."

"Those are the ones I hold at the forefront. I want to remember him for what we were to each other. For the way he molded me into the queen I am. I am grateful for Leer having been in my life."

"He was grateful for you, too," Father reminds me. We sit companionably for a time, drifting in the currents of memory.

"What do you dream of with Valor?" Father asks.

The personal question does not offend because it comes from love. Moreover, I am pleased to have someone to talk to that has a longer view of life. Perspective. "Would you understand if I said I am reluctant to dream? After all the hollow hopes Leer and I shared, I am hesitant to look too far into the future with Valor."

"I do understand. But you cannot stop dreaming when life takes a different shape than what you dreamed. You need dreams to motivate you, to make you want to change the present and achieve the impossible. Your Valor knows that well. He dared to dream you would one day be his though you were embroiled in grief and it seemed impossible."

Valor's dreams of me go so much deeper than Father knows, something I still struggle to reconcile, thus I have not spoken of those dreams with him. How could he have known that I would one day be his wife? In what ways did that influence his actions? Would he have treated me differently had he not known? I doubt he could answer such questions. Perhaps I ought to simply accept that he did know, and however his knowing influenced our relationship was for the best.

Though I wish he had told me of it long ago, before I wed Leer.

I think back to my decision to honor my betrothal when Valor would have rather I agreed to let him steal me away. How did he manage to grant me the freedom of choosing my path while believing he risked his own predestined future? Had I known, would I have still chosen to marry Leer?

No. I would not have. It would have been the excuse I needed to break faith. I stare at the man sitting opposite me. If I had not wed Leer, I would not have gained the Rodiharian family. Or Nev. Perhaps Lorennt and Nev would not have married without my influence…

My head aches attempting to plot all the crossroads and course corrections from what might have been. Valor claims he nearly became a whoremonger years past, but knowing I awaited him in the future gave him the hope he needed to continue living a righteous life. When he thought he lost me to Leer, he dove into a bottle and refused to climb out for months. His torment believing that he had forever given up his wife crushed him.

Why then, did he let me go? He claimed it was because he was a coward, but I cannot believe that about him. He let me choose. He let me…

Tears prick my eyes when I arrive at the answer. Since Valor stormed into my life and lifted my broken spirit off a prison floor, he has fought for my freedom each and every day. Freedom from Limba. Freedom from the poisonous tincture. Freedom from fear. Freedom from my own sin.

When it came time for me to make the choice that would influence the rest of our lives, he could not bear to take away my freedom by telling me I was promised to him. He gambled his future so that I would be free.

An ache cascades through my heart depositing immutable gratitude in its wake. Have I ever realized how much Valor loves me?

I untie my blue scarf from my waist where I have worn it as a sash and wrap it around my shoulders. How can being bound by love be so freeing?

It is for freedom's sake that I have set you free, the Spirit of Truth whispers to my heart.

Of course. I dry my eyes with the edge of the scarf. Valor's love is an echo of the Saving Son's love for me, He who laid down His life to purchase my freedom from the eternal shackles of sin that bound me to the Deceiver.

Thank you, Almighty, for Your love. Thank you for sending Valor to live out such love in my life.

Father stirs the fire and places another log upon the grate. He settles back into his chair, watching it catch the blaze. "Of what does Valor dream now that you are his?"

I gnaw my lower lip, considering it. We have been so entrenched with the blasted Ruphiri and the work of being Queen and Hand that we have not slowed to speak of it, but I know Valor is dreaming. He sees the things that I want and plans to make them happen. With Valor, it seems less a matter of *if* we will do a thing than *when* we will. He is not content to let my dreams disintegrate.

"We dream of returning to the Commonwealth someday. I loved the Hillcountry and Pinewoods. There are more places he wants to take me." And there is another dream that Valor nourishes each time I must give Laszlo back to his parents. "Valor means to give me child of my heart."

Father is pleased. "You dream of being together. Of a family."

"Aye."

"Those are good dreams—things you ought to pursue wholeheartedly. How will being queen help you achieve those things? Will Valor continue being your Hand though that will require him to be absent from you much of the time?"

Valor's words as he departed return to me. *I hate that I am always saying goodbye to you.*

Once Valor and I marry, could I return to living like this? Being parted from him for long stretches of time? It would be much the same as Leelah lives. But I would be here, contending with the court and the affairs of the kingdom, unable to devote my days to my child as Leelah does. The thought is a stone in my belly. Perhaps Valor would content himself with living in Malsihra with me. The thought is no sooner formed than I think of all the reasons he enjoys being Hand. Even if he were to be only the commander, head of the military in Malsihra and overseer for the kingdom, he would be restless. I cannot blame him. The castle can be suffocating.

"Erianna, Daughter of my Heart." Father fills the space between us with loving kindness. "Ever you will be that to me. You will always have a place in this family. Nothing shall change that. Thus, I want you to answer me honestly. Do you want to be queen?"

He makes it sound as if it is a choice. It is not. "I *am* queen. It is the life I was born to and married into. It is my responsibility."

Father sighs deeply. "Sometimes I see you speak, but I hear my son. More than Lorennt ever did, you absorbed Grandileer's thoughts. His ideals. But I asked for yours. What do *you* want?"

Valor asked me that, too. First about our relationship, then about mine to my crown. Am I so indecisive that I do not know my own mind? Or have I too easily accepted what I am told I should feel and continued on the path my feet were on because I do not see a way to turn aside from the inevitable? Have I been reacting to the circumstances placed before me rather than acting to make my own way?

I know I have been reacting. My whole life has felt like a wide path going towards an end that I cannot see. I did not choose it. I cannot change it. I can only make minute decisions on where to place my feet. What obstacles to avoid. What hurdles to leap. Have I been plodding onward when all the while I have had the power to affect change?

Questions beget questions. Father does not press me. He allows me time to think then voice what I will. What I ask is a question that I did not believe necessitated answering. Suddenly, I feel that I missed something by not closer examining my crafty mother-in-law's motives.

"Why does Mother Celiea want me to marry Lord Sigure? Even though she knows my preference for Valor, though she knows Valor is good for me, I still have the feeling she would rather I choose Sigure though he has behaved less than chivalrous of late."

Father looks on me with a measure of pride, as if I have finally begun to think. "Why indeed, Erianna."

"Because he is her relation? If I marry Sigure my bonds to the Rodiharian family will be tightened? Or is it Valor to whom she is opposed because of prejudice?" Father does not answer. Rather, it is as if Leer sits across from me with a chess board between us, imparting some lesson of strategic value. *Ugh,* these Rodiharian men! Lorennt is the only one of the lot that is forthright.

"Because..." I line up the ebony pieces in my mind. I weigh each motive, then light upon one heavier than the rest. "All of those reasons are valid. But Sigure is something that neither Valor or I am—not truly. He is Malesiirian by blood."

Father smiles and inclines his head for me to continue.

I do not like the next thought that could topple my ivory queen. "Is that why Celiea presses a Malesiirian man toward me? Why you have asked if I want to be queen? Why Lorennt assumes I will yield the highest throne to him? Because you all want a blooded Malesiirian on the throne?" Without giving him a chance to respond, a colder thought seizes my tongue. "Does my family intend to force me to abdicate my throne?"

"We want what is best for Malesiir. That may be you. Nor can anyone force you from your throne without overwhelming cause. The unfortunate facts are that in the eyes of the court, you have made decisions that leave them unsettled with your rule. However, you have won the hearts of the commoners, and, for the most part, the military. If you wed Valor—which I hope you will—the bonds with the commoner, with the military, even the rest of the Continent, will be strengthened. But it will come at the cost of estranging the nobility. I know you believe they are less than essential, but your view of them is narrow. They provide a sizable portion of the taxes and their industry propels the kingdom."

"Through the work of the commoners," I argue.

"That is true, but it is also through their administration of inherited estates, the coin they spend, the servants they employ, and the ships they purchase to carry goods across the Continent. One day, they may be unnecessary. The shift of power Leer initiated for the betterment of Malesiir is the first step toward that end. But it will not be in your lifetime. Maybe not even your grandchildren's."

My heart squeezes as it ever does when the mention of my progeny comes about. That is another consideration. "My branch of the Rodiharian line will never bear fruit. That is something you, Celiea, and Lorennt know but no one else does. It is another reason you would have Lorennt become high king. He has already produced an heir. I cannot."

"It does not preclude you from being queen or high queen, for that matter," Father compassionately explains without protecting me from the harsh facts. "You could name Laszlo your successor without contest. However, it would be a better transition for Lorennt to hand his son the throne as I did."

I feel pressed on all sides. The court assumes I will yield the throne. My family thinks I should. Valor must think something similar or he would not have brought the issue to my attention. Reuel Zavaan is determined to rip me from Malesiir.

Father takes a knee before me, raising my downcast eyes. "We are not against you, Daughter. We are on the same side. If you can tell me that you dream of shepherding Malesiir until you have reached a ripe old age, that Valor will be your unwavering support in doing so, and that more than anything you want to be Queen of Malesiir, then we will give you our full support, regardless of the difficulties you face."

Can I say that? I challenge myself. *Can Lorennt, for that matter?* With Nev at his side, aye, he can. He loves Nev first, but together they love Malesiir and will dedicate their lives to this kingdom. Lorennt has always known he would rule. As a prince beneath Grandileer, true, but the moment Lorennt returned from his tenure in the military, he bore the full weight of his crown. He is loved by the military as one of them. The nobility respect him as a Rodiharian. And the commoners feel they matter to him because he wed Nev. Lorennt's branch unites the kingdom as Leer and I strove to do.

"I cannot say that," I admit quietly. "I believe Valor will be my steadfast support, as husband and Hand, but this has never been the life of my choosing. It is what I was born to. What Leer made me into. But I wanted to be something else." The lush valley of Parse Kítaran rises in my mind, cut through by a life giving river that leads to a log home nestled in the arms of the forest. I see Valor's incomplete blacksmith forge collecting dust in a stall. The barn larger than his home to begin a stud farm. The glowing promise of a babe of our own.

But a sizable portion of my heart is here. With my Rodiharian family. "Then what is left to me? Lady of the Castle? That ought to be Nev's place. She will not hold a crown, but Lady of the Castle is hers. If Lorennt takes a Hand of his own, then Valor and I are redundant." The remnants of the life I built with Leer are crumbling around me. It should feel freeing to know I can walk away. It does not.

Tears clog my throat and spill their heat from my eyes. "What was the point of all this? Why did the Creator bring me to Malesiir if not to be its queen?"

"Why? I cannot know all His reasons, but I will share what I have discerned." Father takes a seat on the edge of the hearth. "Beyond the redemption he brought to you and Leer through your marriage and the blessings of it that included Illyanna, He used you to bring Nev and Lorennt together. You needed a family that loves you, and we needed you too, Erianna. Outside of that, you began the process of uniting the kingdom in a way that it has not been before. All for the better. Do you not agree?"

I cannot deny it. Those are blessings in my life. I am whole in a way that I was not before Malesiir. Not even with Valor.

Father stares at his folded hands. His eyes shine bright as he blinks away moisture. "And…" He struggles to gather his words, emotion stealing them from him.

"Take your time," I say. "I am not going anywhere."

My reassurance has the opposite effect I intended. He drops his chin to his chest, age lines deepening with sorrow on his dear face. I slide down next to him on the hearth, remaining by his side as he finds what he meant to say. "You are Queen Erianna Rodiharian Vrock. The link between two powerful kingdoms. Leer helped you come into your own."

"You all did," I amend.

"Aye. You are more than you were when you came to us. You have grown. And now, you are prepared."

"For what?" I ask, utterly bemused.

"To return to Limba as its queen."

CHAPTER TWENTY-THREE

VALOR

December 28th

We have the advantage. That is a rare thing these days. I look once more upon the map of the Hugler's modest estate. The legal document mapping the boundaries of their lands does not provide a description of the interior of the buildings, however, from what I can see, it is mostly unchanged since the document was drafted fifty years ago. The defensive fortifications include a five walled palisade with bastions projecting from each corner. The gate is set beneath a gatehouse built in the center of the palisade's southern wall. The poorly disguised sally port faces west—an easy jaunt from the branches of the forest. It is there our force led by Anders will breach the estate. But first, we must determine if our quarry is within.

For that, we need bait.

At daybreak, I ride upon the manned gatehouse with a third of our considerable company. This contingent fifty strong is larger than the usual number of soldiers in a patrol. The showing of force will persuade the Ruphiri that I am cocksure for thinking I can subdue them with a number slightly double theirs. I am not. The other hundred soldiers hidden with Anders are my insurance. I have no intention of allowing a single Ruphiri to escape.

"Who goes there?" An armored guard calls from the gatehouse.

"Commander Ironforge, Hand of the Queen. I demand that you open to my patrol and make ready to be searched."

"A search?" He calls back while the second guard sidles away. "On what grounds do you demand entrance to a private estate?"

"I do so at the behest of Her Majesty the Queen. Now open or we will enter by force!"

"That will not be necessary," he says. "I only await orders from the keeper of the estate in Lord Hugler's absence."

I bet he does.

"My patience will not last long," I warn. At the count of one hundred, we will go through. The Ruphiri cannot be permitted time to ready for our incursion. When I reach the count of seventy three, the other guard returns.

"My master's steward bids you enter. We are instructing the villagers to stand aside."

"Villagers? For what are they present?" I ask.

"They sought shelter from the storm. Some of their dwellings did not withstand the load of snow upon their roofs."

Or they are disguised Ruphiri, like as not.

The gate is unbarred with the shifting of timbers. It creaks slowly outward.

"Advance!" I wave to the cavalry behind me. The pounding of fifty horses' hooves and ringing of chain mail masks the sounds of Anders forcing his way through the sally port.

We ride into the midst of the bailey and our luck fails. The walled estate is packed tight with wide-eyed villagers clutching children to their sides. Tents and belongings are piled everywhere while livestock mill about braying their concern.

Human shields.

If the Ruphiri are here, then we can be assured they will employ the same tactics they did on the west side. They know we care more about protecting our people than we do about capturing them. I scan the faces in the crowd, attempting to match any of the men to Erianna's descriptions of the Ruphiri. I cannot.

"Where is the steward? Bring him forward!" I demand.

A balding man exits the manor house that spreads congruent wings to either side of a keep. Smoke curls lazily from the many chimneys. "Commander Ironforge. Welcome. For what have you come to the Hugler Estate?"

"I search for a band of miscreants. They call themselves the Ruphiri, though others name them Wolves for the animals they tame. Have you seen any matching that description?" I direct my question to the steward, holding my eyes to him, but I unfocus my gaze so that I may catch movement from the villagers in my periphery. They do not disappoint. To my left a mother claps a hand over her child's mouth.

The steward's affected puzzlement is lacking. "Ruphiri? Wolves? I have not seen any matching that description. Why do you believe they are here?"

"My reasons are my own. But believe me," I grasp the hilt of my sword. "They are founded."

Perspiration beads the man's brow. "Would you care to search the estate for yourself? Lord Hugler has naught to hide."

He offers far too readily. I eye him sharply, calculating that Anders has had sufficient time to position the company. The longer I let this go on, the more likely the Ruphiri will find a way to escape or turn the situation to their advantage. Casting my furious gaze around the bailey, I bellow, "Reuel Zavaan! Show yourself, you craven milksop!"

The steward leaps a foot in the air and scurries into the crowd. My nearest soldier thwarts his escape.

"You make this worse for yourself if you do not show your face! You have no where to run! Face me as a man if you dare! Not the flaccid worm you are!"

From the stables, smithy, manor, and gardens, from beneath every rock, Ruphiri slither into the crowd with drawn swords that are quickly pressed to the necks of women and children. Archers hang nocked arrows out of the embrasures in the bastions, aimed not at us, but at the innocents. Judging by the number of blades glinting in the morning light, either Zavaan or Hugler has bloated the number of Ruphiri with mercenaries.

The doors to the keep of the manor are flung wide. With languid movements, Zavaan enters the bailey. "Valor! So good to see you again. We had little opportunity to speak when last we met. I anticipate a long conversation between us this day."

His black cape billows in the winter wind. Eyes like embers burn in his wicked face. His countenance bespeaks his genuine excitement that I have barged into his midst. "But first, how fares my wife? Still calling my name in the wee hours of the night as I do hers? I miss her dreadfully."

I let him see my fury. It is not feigned. Karris told me that since their recent encounter on the castle grounds, Erianna wakes most nights screaming *Král Vragh*. Come morning, Erianna does not speak to me about it. She applies cosmetics to the bruises beneath her eyes and pretends she is fine. I am not sure if she hopes to fool me or herself.

"Send the villagers from the bailey and let us see this to its conclusion," I growl.

"Why would I do that?" Zavaan muses, wandering toward the crowd. One of the Ruphiri shoves a woman forward. She stumbles into Zavaan's waiting paws. He brings her to stand alongside him with his arm wrapped around her waist that is round with child. She cries, frantically tugging away from Zavaan while a man in the crowd struggles against the kiss of a sword at his throat.

"*Shh, shh,*" Zavaan caresses her face. "Hush, my Dear. This will be over soon—one way or another."

Zavaan's taunt finds its mark, burrowing straight into my heart. Though we have the advantage of force, he does not hesitate to use threats against the villagers to return control of the situation to himself. This is how he controls people. Through cunning manipulation of our emotions. He knows we will not sacrifice the villagers. What is he unwilling to sacrifice? His men? No. He sent them into the capital to wreak havoc on our city knowing not all of them would escape. But he held back. When Erianna and I encountered him on the castle grounds, the moment his defeat was likely, he fled.

Zavaan will not sacrifice himself. All other things are expendable.

That means he thinks that he can escape capture this day, possibly along with some of his men. I need to prove that is not the case. The moment they begin killing, we begin killing, then Anders will enter the fray with Zavaan as our highest priority target. But the casualties will be unconscionable.

I ignore the woman in Zavaan's grasp, not allowing him to leverage her against me as he intends. My bearing displays confidence and power, the only language Zavaan understands. "I am prepared to accept your immediate surrender. Drop your weapons."

Zavaan chortles. "What is it you once told my wife?" He pulls the woman against his chest and fists her hair, wrenching her head to the side to cruelly whisper, "Make me."

Self loathing raises my gorge. Erianna was right again. Zavaan did watch us at the training arena in Grass Lake. He saw me use her fear to provoke her to action. Watching Zavaan attempt to provoke me through this frightened woman is despicable.

But I do not let him see that he has affected me. I shove it down, focus on the task. This is not about me. It is not even about Erianna right now. It is about freeing these people without bloodshed. My hope of capturing every single one of the Ruphiri is dust on the wind, but I shall not permit them all to escape this encounter.

"So be it." I bet on Zavaan not reacting rashly. All that I know of him speaks of a man so calculating that emotion has no place in his being. Terrifying as that fact is, it will play to my advantage if wielded properly. However, if my judgment is wrong, the innocents between us will be slaughtered.

My piercing whistle summons Anders and his company into the bailey. In moments fifty soldiers encircle the Ruphiri with drawn swords. No less then ten archers train arrows on Zavaan, the rest sight the Ruphiri archers in the bastions. My soldiers hold position, choosing enemy targets and planning their way through the villagers. The Ruphiri drag their hostages into the thick crowd of villagers who knock each other down while trying to put distance between themselves and the enemy. Within the stables, wolves begin to yip and howl throwing the livestock into a frenzy.

"Every one hold!" I bark at soldiers and villagers alike, grappling to maintain control. The slip of one blade is all the spark needed to ignite this conflagration.

Zavaan stands like a hawk in the midst of the chaos. His head swivels, formulating a new strategy to counteract mine as if watching the drama unfold from some remote vantage. Anders wears a menacing snarl behind Zavaan, sword poised, awaiting my order to disembowel the murderer.

Zavaan smiles at me. He knows my next play, why I have not filled his body with arrows. "You lack the ruthlessness of the dead king."

"Almighty be praised," I concur. "Take your men. The mercenaries and wolves stay."

"My wolves and horses come with me," Zavaan bargains as easily as if it is a card table between us, the stakes paltry, the outcome insignificant.

"Not the wolves. Dane, go release the horses," I instruct the soldier at my right.

For the time that it takes to accomplish the task, Zavaan toys with the woman in his arms. She cries and her husband roars. I watch coldly without averting my gaze. When Zavaan accepts that I will not be riled, he bores of the woman and ceases his perverse caresses, though his grip does not slacken. The silence stretches painfully until Dane opens the stable door and chases the horses into the bailey. Without benefit of tether or tack, they funnel toward the open gate, rushing for the forest.

"Mercenaries, drop your weapons," I demand, "and step back." At a nod from Zavaan, they comply. The number identifying themselves as mercenaries is far less than it ought to be. We have kept careful count of the Ruphiri trespassing in our kingdom. I cannot believe that we have so grossly miscounted. At least half of the men identifying themselves as Ruphiri must be mercenaries trying to escape the noose. It does not signify. It will be sorted out relatively soon.

With the mercenaries pressed against the palisade, I speak the bitter words that will free my enemy and, hopefully, protect the innocents. "You have your horses. Now go."

With their human shields clutched to their chests, the Ruphiri edge toward the gate. I turn Granite to follow their progress, preparing for duplicity. Before crossing beneath the gatehouse, the Ruphiri release their captives who sprint into the embrace of their families. When the husband of the woman Zavaan holds is released from the Ruphiri that held a sword to his throat, he charges Zavaan. I vault from the saddle, intercepting the enraged man. He tries to go through me to rescue his wife from Zavaan's hold. Little does he know that his actions are the ones that will ensure Zavaan snaps her neck. I plant my fist into the man's jaw, knocking him unconscious. Zavaan chuckles.

"Valor," he drawls. "Ironic. *Valiant* you are not."

I do not let him find flesh with his taunts. Zavaan backs toward the gate with the woman.

"That will do. Release her."

Zavaan sniffs the woman. His lip curls in distaste. "Squalor. Ash. So unlike my wife." Zavaan smiles at me, searching for the least reaction. I do not give him one. "My wife smells like a garden. Like lavender." His eyelids lower, reveling in the memory. "Lavender. And fear."

My fists clench of their own accord. Zavaan laughs, finally satisfied with our exchange, then shoves the woman toward me with all his might. I lunge forward to arrest her headlong flight before the hands she instinctively thrusts out to break her fall snap at her wrists. She trembles violently, shoving away from me. I set her aright, freeing her to rush to her husband as I pursue Zavaan.

Simultaneously, Anders gives the signal and our archers loose nocked arrows on the few remaining Ruphiri before they harm any villagers. I whistle three times. My other fifty soldiers hiding in the woods spring from behind snowbanks to engage the escaping villains. They were positioned to net any Ruphiri that managed to slip past us. Now they become the primary fighting force.

The clash of swords rings through the trees while chaos in the estate at my back creates a clamor of distracting noise and motion. But I am singleminded in purpose.

Zavaan.

Where is Zavaan? I scan the forest, but he is nowhere in sight. I drop my eyes to the ground, searching for his tracks, but they are obscured amid the myriad others.

No! I will not lose him again! Almighty, guide me! He must not escape!

I feel a *pull* to go left and obey, hurrying forward between dense briar patches that stretch out claws to snare my cloak. I stay to the middle of the path, following the pull that urges me on. The shifting light in the forest highlights tracks running away from the estate. I keep after them and find the length of the stride between impressions in the snow matches my own. It cannot be Zavaan. His stride should be less than mine, relative to his height. Nevertheless, the pull does not slacken, so I do not abandon my pursuit.

The tracks curve around to the south then stop abruptly. I do not have time to consider where the man has gone before I hear steel parting air. Instinctively, I drop and roll, but not before my off shoulder is slashed. My feet find level ground, propelling me back around to face my opponent.

I catch his attack on the cross guard of my sword, shoving him back. The lanky Ruphiri is not unbalanced in the least. His feet flow with the force of my shove to quickly ground him and receive the oncoming arc of my blade. My mind absorbs the details of his build and structure as he fights with his two handed longsword.

Though of comparable height to me, he is slighter of build. The structure of his attack is flawless, perfectly centered, optimally engaging the power of his cuts to deal the most damage. We cut, parry, thrust in a match that will not be easily decided. More details of the man fly at me, as I formulate my strategy. An antagonistic sneer is fixed on a face that does not change in preparation of his attacks. His feet follow the movement of his hips rather than leading his steps, making it nearly impossible to anticipate the timing of his attacks. Breathing deep, he times his breaths with his movements to engage each cut, but not in a rhythm overtly revealing of intention.

Shallow nicks in both of our upper bodies and extremities turn the honed edges of our blades scarlet. The tip of my blade scrapes his sword arm, my thrust that was intended to pierce his wicked heart diverted. The cutting edge of his sword scores my thigh where I impede it from severing my limb.

Frustration divides my focus. I ought to be hunting Zavaan not exchanging hews with this knave!

The glimmer of satisfaction in my opponent's eyes returns my focus to the present before he seizes the advantage my frustration affords. I tamp all emotion down into a tight knot, bound with a strength of will that does not betray me.

Our contest becomes one of stamina when our equally matched skills do not yield an easy victor. Judging by the amount of blood sliding down my upper arm and body, the cut in my shoulder—though not something that yet pains owing to battle fever—is something I must account for as it will inevitably hinder me in a lengthy contest. This weakness negates my superior strength that could be used advantageously to tire my opponent.

Drawing his own conclusions about the necessity of involving other factors to secure victory, the Ruphiri attempts to utilize our environment to gain the upper hand. He advances, pushing me back to my detriment. My heel encounters the unyielding obstacle of a tree at my back. I fend off one cut after another, meant to lock my blade against the trunk of the tree. Either I must move or use this position to my advantage. And an advantage I sorely need before fortune or outside factors provide the resolution, for good or ill, of this match. My position presents greater risk but also greater reward if I dare to claim it.

In preparation of exacting my scheme, I use several clashes of steel to allow myself to be pushed back against the trunk of the tree. The sneering Ruphiri delights in the fruition of his plan to trap me. But he does not feel what I feel.

The solid tree at my back feels like the small steady hands of my beloved, calming the uproar in me and reminding me I must return to her.

When my opponent brings his sword down to cleave my head from my neck, I use the extra grounding force of the tree at my back to stop the onslaught of death. Our swords bind between us. Now the tree becomes my advantage allowing me to leverage my superior strength in a meaningful way. He attempts to pull away as I press the bind of our swords, but before he can, I relinquish the two handed grip of my sword to my dominant hand. Surprise cannot find a home on his face before I draw the dagger from my vambrace and strike for his hands' grip on the hilt of his sword.

In a spray of blood and satisfying yowl of pain, one of his fingers is severed from his left hand.

I surge forward, knocking his sword out of his compromised grip and bringing mine to rest against his throat.

Our labored breaths billow in the cold air as we stare at each other for long moments. The Ruphiri clutches the stump of his finger to stem the flow of blood as he appraises me. A rapacious grin reveals teeth that are crooked yet white, if not all accounted for. His civilized words contrast with a barbarous tone. "Well met, Valor Ironforge, Hand of the Queen."

Who is this man? Not a hint of the Ruphiri accent lurks in his voice, but neither does he have the look of a Malesiirian. "And you are?"

His smile only settles into one of self-satisfaction though he remains utterly at my mercy.

Of what has he to be smug? I glance about, ensuring I have not neglected the presence of another enemy but only hear the pounding of my cavalry advancing into the forest.

When soldiers spring from their mounts to bind my prisoner, I lower my sword from his throat.

Gazing about the bloodied snow, my mind seizes upon the purpose that brought us into this contest.

Zavaan.

Orienting myself, I trace the path that led me here then expand my search laterally until I locate a second set of tracks sprinting parallel away from the estate.

"To me!" I command a pair of soldiers and set off at a run.

The tracks are readily visible for several miles as Zavaan's primary concern was distance not evasion. But with distance won, evasion was given priority. Late into the day, we scour the forest for traces of Zavaan. Eventually, the pursuit leads to a shallow stream. We follow its winding path east and west for miles, scanning the banks for signs that he exited. My search becomes frantic as day wanes into night with snowflakes descending like soft cold kisses that melt on heated skin but linger on frozen earth. The cloak of night brings my fruitless hunt to close. By morning, winter's kiss will have thoroughly hidden the trespasses of man.

Exhaustion and pain from wounds long ignored plague my return to the Hugler estate. Anders welcomes me at the palisade gate. My thunderous look forestalls questions regarding my search for the *Král Vragh*.

"As it happens," Anders reports while we cross the courtyard, "the Ruphiri rounded up the inhabitants of the nearest village on the chance that what happened today happened. We released them back to their homes. Some of the women are worse for their capture," he adds darkly.

The prisoners are bound in plain view with a fire to warm the huddled lot of them. My eyes land on the bound form of one man in particular who laughs at my empty handed return that he arranged. All the emotion knotted inside me comes loose. Stalking toward him, I bend and shove the end of my dagger into the fire. The flames lick the steel, tasting it greedily, endlessly hungering for food.

I step behind my bound opponent and yank the cloth away from where it is clotted to the stump of his finger. He shouts in pain. Swiftly, I press the fired flat of my dagger to the bleeding digit, feeling more satisfaction than I should at the scent of his burning flesh and agonized scream as I cauterize the wound.

Exerting control on my vengeance, I wipe my blade through the snow when the task is done instead of branding his skin with the instrument of my wrath.

"Many thanks," he pants, swaying in place.

"You will be drawn and quartered alongside your master. I do not wish you to expire from infection before then."

Anders looks on approvingly. "In my grandfather's day, they did far worse to them that forced themselves on a woman. It's a shame old King Laszlo abandoned that punishment as barbaric when he rewrote the punitive laws after finding religion."

The temptation to ignore justice is seductive. Resolutely, I turn away from it. That is not who I am.

"There's something you need to see," Anders says, leading the way into the keep of the manor house.

I follow him up the stairs and down a long hallway into the east wing of the house. Muffled sobbing filters through the timbered door.

Anders raps softly before pushing into the room. "My Lady, Commander Ironforge has returned."

A weeping mass of skirts rises from the bed at my entrance. The frail woman with ash blond hair is a slighter, aged version of her daughter.

"Commander! Thank the Creator!" She sighs in relief, manages a few wobbling steps, then collapses into a chair.

I kneel before her, thoroughly confused. No man in his right mind would allow his wife to be under the same roof as Reuel Zavaan. Were we wrong? Did Zavaan capture the estate or was he invited? "Lady Hugler. What on earth are you doing here?"

CHAPTER TWENTY-FOUR

ERIANNA

January 1st

Dawn breaks over my home on the first day of the new year. It is not the gilded morning of a year ago when my husband's arms enfolded me, and I put my trust in his certainty of what the future held for us. That morning I sang of the gifts the Creator had given me, the way He brought me out of Limba and spared me from my enemies while Leer's warmth surrounded me.

The only thing this morning and that have in common is the bitter cold.

My heart tests the bonds of its bone cage, stretching painfully as too much hope in the tangible floods my memories. I clench my hands to keep them from straying to my womb that once held life. My lungs fill with frosty air. Too much hope in the tangible. The exhale relieves me of those dreams, drawing upon the sharp pain of reality to deflate my heart. My eyes drift over the crenelations, falling down to the snow packed graveyard far below.

Long gone.

Perhaps not in the measurements of time, as my court likes to remind me when they run out of other ways to besmirch my character, but long gone in the distance my soul has traversed since I crawled across the stone floor and the world I knew gave way beneath me, hope bleeding out as quickly as my lifeblood.

My heart tries to swell again, prematurely. I do not let it. I need to feel this. Today is pivotal. I will give the past its due.

I cannot distinguish his words, but I remember his tone. The regret. The sorrow. Above all else, the love. My Leer. It was achingly short, our blessed marriage. But I would not wish it away. I view it for what it was without the haze of what might have been. Imperfect, but sweet. And I am grateful.

Here I let my memories increase their pace, not lingering on the darkness. There is no need to remember that in detail.

Then grey eyes, a storm within a storm, pierce the darkness taking my hand, refusing to let me live in the crushing depths at the bottom of the sea. My own instrument of grace.

A smile plays on my lips. My warrior. My friend. Now my love.

But not my hope. Never that. Because Valor introduced me to Living Hope. To Hope that exists outside of the tangible realm, though He regularly invades our lives in tangible ways.

My Salvation. My Redeemer.

It was hard. Being remade was no easy thing. My redemption was not without pain. But it cannot be taken from me. That makes what I must do bearable.

The wind blows colder, stirring snow flurries. *Turn back,* it warns. *Not too late. Stay where it is safe.*

But I cannot. My hope is not in the future or in the strength of the man at my side or in the love of my family. My hope comes from faith in the Almighty. He is my Hope. I will follow Him even if He leads me into the wilderness. Surely His gifts are good, generous beyond measure, but He is the greatest gift.

Peace, His Spirit whispers to my thrashing heart. *Peace,* He speaks to the turbulence of my soul. In the ensuing stillness, He extends a gentle invitation that warms me from the inside. *Follow Me. I will never leave you, nor forsake you.*

I close my eyes and take a step forward held securely in the arms of the Almighty.

※ ※ ※

The gown was altered, the long train done away with. Artisans spent tedious hours shortening the hemline and reworking all the embroidery at the bottom of the gown to blend with the new length. When I reach my arms into the sleeves and the heavy weight of my coronation gown settles on my shoulders, it feels right. I stare into the mirror, feeling like I belong beneath the queen's robes. A Malesiirian queen in full. It stole over me quietly, the accepting of this burden. Somewhere in the last year, I learned who I am and who I am not.

I ascend the dais ahead of my royal family. My place is at the center of this austere occasion. Nev mounts the steps with Laszlo, the crown prince cooing at his mother. Father and Mother Celiea are next, both praying this is the last coronation they will see in their lifetime. Though we rejoice with Lorennt, Leer's absence is keenly felt by all of us.

They are seated on thrones at my back while I remain standing to welcome Lorennt who awaits in the antechamber. The honor of crowning him falls on me.

An excited child's voice speaks in the hush of the great hall. "Look! There's Majie!" Micah waves at me from his bench where he stands peering over the heads in front of him. I let a smile slip through my royal demeanor and wink at Micah. He grins and winks back, blinking both eyes at once, and thumps into his seat. Leelah bends to his ear to remind him for the hundredth time today that he must be quiet through the ceremony. He pays her little heed, too excited by the novelty of it all.

"All rise," I call to our people.

The doors are opened before Prince Lorennt. He strides down the aisle, tall and proud. He is regal. Kingly. Not a drop of the indolent prince remains.

Lorennt pledges his troth to the kingdom, vows to uphold Malesiir, and lays claim to the throne by virtue of his royal blood. I recite the ancient words in the old Malesiirian tongue, charging Lorennt with the heavy burden he bears. He acknowledges it full well. I am struck with the similarity between this and a wedding. The groom vowing to serve and to protect his bride with his life and always act in her best interests, even though that involves personal sacrifice.

Lorennt ascends each step until his people receive his vows, voicing their acceptance of him as their king. When he kneels on the last step, I place my hand on his head and raise the invocation to the Creator, praying for His blessing upon Lorennt's reign, his lineage, and all of Malesiir.

I take a deep breath, touching the hilt of Leer's dagger in my scabbard. For a fleeting moment I can feel Leer's arms around me, holding my back to his chest, steadying me. It brings tears to my eyes. Our reign has delineated down to this one moment. All that came before is done. A new era begins.

Lorennt takes my hands after the blessing and kisses them.

"Leer would be so proud of you," I whisper as a single tear streaks down my cheek. "I shall forever be glad to call you my king."

"Thank you," he murmurs.

I step back toward my throne and take Leer's crown, the king's crown, from the white velvet seat. The ornate golden symbol of all that has transpired this day settles on Lorennt's brow. "It is my honor to present His Royal Majesty, King Lorennt Rodiharian. Long live the king!"

I go to my knees, bowing before the High King of Malesiir, letting go once and for all of the future that was laid out for me since I was ten years old.

CHAPTER TWENTY-FIVE

VALOR

January 5th

At noon I stalk into the great hall, every fiber of my being alert. Lord Hugler is in attendance seated at one of the low tables. That can only mean one of two things. Either Erianna successfully intercepted Zavaan's correspondance warning Lord Hugler that his collusion was known, or Zavaan determined that Hugler's usefulness was spent and never sent a warning.

I stop halfway across the hall amid the mutterings of the nobility. Lorennt is seated in the High King's chair and Erianna sits placidly at his right. An inward smile forms behind my foreboding expression. She relinquished control.

I fist my hand over my heart and bow deeply, waiting for royal acknowledgement.

"Commander Ironforge," Lorennt gives my welcome. "You have returned from your assignment. Come forward."

More murmurings. *Assignment?* The befuddled nobility echo the king.

I rise, giving Erianna my eyes. Hers are a jumble of emotions though her face betrays none of them. Relief at my safe return. Trepidation at what I have to tell. Anxious hope that my mission was successful. Dread at what inevitably happens next.

Surprisingly, Tirzah sits at Erianna's right in a place of honor—and not begrudgingly so. She whispers something to the queen and Erianna inclines her head to receive it. With a slight shake of her head, Erianna replies setting Tirzah's lips into a stern line. Tirzah implores me with her eyes, trying to communicate something vital, but I do not catch it. She casts her eyes around, looking for an aid. When I near the dais, I notice Tirzah staring pointedly down the high table. I follow her gaze to find Sigure smugly eyeing the queen. Tirzah picks up her fork and discretely smashes a roasted potato while glaring at Sigure. I begin to understand and nod my head at Tirzah. But she is not finished. She takes up her knife and dices her food into little pieces while glaring all around the great hall. Sigure was the worst, but the whole court has been brutal to my beloved, so much so that the women who were combatants have declared some sort of truce to weather the conflict. Erianna sets her hand on Tirzah's arm, stilling her movements, but not before I decide here and now to quell the gossip with finality for both their sakes.

The Huglers and the court can hang.

"Your Majesties," I bow again. "I hope you will forgive my absence from the coronation and for leaving the solstice in such a manner. It was a regrettable necessity to route the traitor from your court."

"You were missed, Commander," Nev inserts sweetly.

"Thank you, Milady. I hope I am permitted to be where my heart always is from now on." I shift my gaze back to Erianna, but the present task preoccupies her more than my affectionate words. I loathe always being the bearer of bad news to her.

"You found what we suspected?" Erianna asks.

"I did, my Queen."

"Then let us proceed." She rises from her seat. "Lord Hugler, Lady Silla. Come forward."

Silla pales as they walk toward the dais. Lord Hugler is all defiance.

"What is the meaning of this, Your Majesty?" He addresses Lorennt. Lorennt does not dignify his impertinence with an answer.

Erianna grips the hilt of her sword. "Commander Ironforge, please present the evidence you have uncovered."

My voice carries for all to hear. "On October the Eleventh, Malsihra was breached and attacked by the Ruphiri. We have long suspected that they were aided from within the city, though we could not find proof. Our investigations into the matter were assisted by Lady Silla who has served as an informant to you. A few weeks past, a witness overheard an incriminating conversation between Lady Silla and Lord Hugler then brought it to my attention."

A trembling Silla winces beneath the scorching gaze of Tirzah. Silla has never seemed less in control than in this moment as her mountain of lies is swept away.

"Not wishing to insult a respected member of the nobility, on my Queen's orders Captain Anders and I left to investigate the allegation that pointed to collusion between Lord Hugler, Lady Silla, and the Ruphiri."

Lord Hugler raves, "This defamation of my character will end immediately! I will not allow such—"

"Be silent!" Lorennt snaps. "We will hear all the evidence before coming to a decision."

At his nod, I continue. "We discovered a tunnel leading from the inside of one of Lord Hugler's derelict properties beneath the curtain wall with clear signs of the tunnel being used by wolves." The great hall gasps collectively and looses a wave of chatter. I raise my voice to be heard. "Not feeling this to be sufficient proof, I set out for the Hugler's family estate near Port Veritae."

Silla presses a hand to her mouth, her eyes wide in fright.

"We apprehended eleven Ruphiri men at the Hugler estate, ten mercenaries, and five members of the household who resisted our search of the property. They are being held in the castle's jail. In addition, we found Lady Hugler at the estate. She claims to have been kept against her will—"

"There!" Lord Hugler points at me. "My wife was a hostage! It is impossible—"

"*After* being sent there at Lord Hugler's order," I cut him off. "The rest of the evidence I uncovered is more conclusive. Here are letters found at the estate from Lord Hugler to Reuel Zavaan and his corresponding replies were found this morning at Lord Hugler's residence in the city. They detail what Lord Hugler receives in exchange for his collusion with the Ruphiri." I relinquish them to Erianna. It was a stroke of cunning on Zavaan's part to keep the correspondence. It makes it quite simple to convict Lord Hugler.

She opens the letters and gives the appearance of examining them, but her eyes do not move over the words. She passes them to Lorennt who does glance over them with mounting ire.

"Your Majesty," Silla humbly interjects, "if I may—"

"You may not," Erianna cleaves her plea in two. "I find this information most disturbing and sufficient to have you both incarcerated until a trial can be held. Do you agree, Your Majesty?"

Lorennt grits his jaw and only permits himself to nod when he would rather impale Lord Hugler on his sword. Part of Zavaan's bargain was to murder Nev thereby clearing the way for a new queen to take the throne as Lorennt's wife.

Erianna motions the guards forward. "I shall attend to this task personally," she informs Lorennt and descends the dais to take hold of my outstretched hand.

"Do remember," the king growls, "we do not afford noble lawbreakers privileged treatment. Treason is treason."

Silla sways at the mention of treason.

Lord Hugler fixes his disdain upon his daughter. "Cease your dramatics ere you make fools of us!"

But to my eye, there is nothing dramatic in Silla's bearing. She is coming apart. When her father looks more apt to strike her than aid her, a guard comes forward to support Silla.

Erianna clutches my hand like a rope in a flood while we march her friend toward the jail. I lace her fingers with mine, binding us more tightly, then touch my lips to her knuckles in silent greeting and solidarity. If the thick application of cosmetics to her haggard face is any indication, she needs every assurance I can give her.

Standing at attention outside the jail are Trent and Anders. We did not want our friend to learn of his lady's betrayal publicly, thus Anders summoned him from the great hall before I entered. My heart is heavy for him. I have never seen him give a woman the devotion he has shown to Silla. The typical badge of his relationships is brevity.

Silla turns her pleading to Trent, letting go of the guard to reach for him. Trent is a stone as the guard propels Silla through the fortified doors.

The jailer silently leads the way to a waiting cell for Lord Hugler and Silla opposite the one containing Lady Hugler. Silla's face is relieved at seeing her mother safe and unharmed. That is, until the guards deposit Silla into the cell with her father. Genuine panic brings Silla around. She grips the iron bars that clang shut. A key scrapes in the lock. "Erianna. Please. Not this too."

Something passes between the women, a bond capable of spanning the rift of betrayal.

From the mercy of one victim to another, Erianna orders the jailer, "Move Lady Silla to Lady Hugler's cell. Lord Hugler is not to be allowed in the same cell as the women."

A guard retrieves Silla and transfers her to the opposite one containing her mother. Silla's shoulders slump in relief as mother and daughter embrace. "Thank you, Your Majesty."

※※※

* * *

ERIANNA

With my guards in tow I listen silently as Valor recounts the details he omitted before the court. Valor's thumb runs the length of mine in slow reassuring strokes as the narrative becomes darker still. Human shields. An entire village at the mercy of the Ruphiri. Lord Hugler bargaining for Nev's murder. I shudder. Aiming my hatred at Zavaan and Lord Hugler leaves little room to feel the wound Silla dealt me. Poor Trent does not have that luxury.

The reek of unwashed bodies is worse in this block of the jail. Valor indicates the cell containing some of the worst villains to which this kingdom has been subjected. I retrieve a torch from the sconce on the wall and push it between the rusted bars. The glow illuminates the hardened eyes of each man like so many animals in the dark.

Seven of the men I recognize from my time with Zavaan. In spite of the haze that came before and the torrent of emotions that came after, I recall in stark clarity each moment with Zavaan. Unfortunately. Likewise, I remember the faces of each of the twenty nine Ruphiri men in his vile pack. Thus, I can say with certainty that four of these men garbed as the rest are new recruits—mercenaries, Valor suspects. They have not spoken a word since being captured, not even to each other. That bodes ill for our interrogations.

"Do you know who I am?" I ask the newcomers in Limban. The men I recognize eye me balefully. A man situated in the far corner smirks. I repeat myself, demanding an answer.

The man asks the known Ruphiri in the common tongue, "What does she want? Does she expect us to bow?" A few chuckle in response, but not all of them speak the common tongue.

I ask a question I know he will not refuse to answer if he does, in fact, understand me. "What is my name?"

His eyes drift downward over my body, lingering long enough that I hear Valor's teeth grind. His eyes return to my face, taking his time there too. Despite his lascivious perusal, I sigh in relief. Given the opportunity to pair my name with his master's, he remains silent.

He is a Malesiirian recruit to the Ruphiri ranks, not an unknown Ruphiri. These men are likely some of the many brigands that Zavaan utilized over the past year. Malesiir has its own malefactors the same as any other kingdom. Their appearance is nothing to be concerned about.

"We will speak at length after a few days of thirst lighten your tongues," I say to the rest. "Until then enjoy the complimentary vermin as a demonstration of my welcome."

Hatred wafts from the cell. Given the slimmest chance any of the Ruphiri would snap my royal neck. I find that satisfying in a way that should make me question my sanity.

I reunite the torch with its scone and move toward the mercenaries' cell to address them. "If any of you wish to make a statement at the trial for Lord Hugler detailing your involvement then I will consider —"

"*Královna,*" a voice croons from the Ruphiri's cell. My blood runs cold as the newcomer rises from his corner, stalking forward on silent feet. Not even the dry chicken bone he treads upon makes a sound. He speaks in the Ruphiri's guttural dialect of Limban. "What if I wish to speak with you now, Erianna Zavaan?" The others do not stop him. They simply watch.

I feel each doomed footfall as I return to stand before him. Valor's stiffened arm does not allow me within lunging distance of the cage. We learned that lesson already.

"If you have something to say to me, I will hear it," I reply in Limban.

"So haughty for one so young," he smiles, revealing a mouth full of crooked teeth. "Is that what has Reuel salivating for you? Power ripe for the picking?"

"Who are you? Where did you come from?"

He spreads his hands palms up to show they are empty, then settles each finger one at a time around the bars of the door. The middle finger on his left hand is missing. Only a bandaged stump remains. "Have none of your advisors warned you about asking more than one question at a time? It makes you appear weak. Desperate for information."

Leer warned me of that. But I *am* afraid. And desperate. "You wished to speak with me. Speak." The demand is delivered with the lethal softness Valor uses to intimidate others. I hope I mimicked it correctly.

He chuckles again. "So that is it. All that willfulness wrapped up in an alluring little package. You would make an excellent third wife for me if you manage to slip free of the *Král Vragh.*"

"You have lost two wives already?" I do not particularly care, but such knowledge can be useful in a negotiation.

"Lost," he rolls the word in his mouth, cocking his head to the side.

A chill runs down my spine. "You murdered them. Like Zavaan murders women."

He shakes his head with a snort. "No. That bit of wickedness is Zavaan's alone. His thirst for blood is unmatched. Yet he seems to believe it will be a long time before he kills you. Could you tame him, do you think? I wonder…" The way he looks at me is despicable. Like a broodmare in her prime. "No, I have not *lost* my wives. They are safe at home in the Spires. Along with my *hetaeraz*."

My skin crawls. "*Hetaeraz*?"

"Similar to a concubine, but with more privileges. Women of lesser parentage can only attain that rank in a warlord's house. They are all most fortunate to belong to me."

"I know what the word means." How much have the Ruphiri changed since they moved into the Spires? Have they so thoroughly abandoned tradition that they have descended into barbarism? Warlords and harems and pillaging. "Does Zavaan have multiple wives?" I want to know how much this man will speak about his *kyzar*.

He chortles but hate burns in his eyes. "As you already noted, Zavaan's previous marriages were *short lived*."

Bile churns the food in my stomach. "I see. But your wives fare better?" I challenge.

The warlord takes another step toward the bars. "I like women, *Královna*. I would not waste their beauty or revel in their misery."

I sneer. "Yet you keep a harem? Is that not 'reveling in their misery'?"

He draws himself to his full, considerable height and drops his hands from the bars. "I am a warlord. It is my right and duty to secure the future of the Ruphiri nation of which you clearly know nothing."

Have I offended him? This Ruphiri swine who boasts his conquests to me? I open my mouth to parry his censure but realize I have walked wide of my purpose. "How did you come to be in Malesiir?"

"It should be obvious," he chastises then returns to his corner of the cell. He appears to make himself comfortable though there is no comfort to find in such a place. "I am done speaking. You may return tomorrow."

I stride forward to snarl in his face, but meet Valor's resistance. He does not allow me to get closer, however, his caution does not hamper my voice. "Your words offend, *Zar*."

"As does your ignorance, *Královna*."

Anger burns up my neck. I will *not* return tomorrow.

"In the meantime, you ought to tend to the commander's shoulder," the warlord lazily suggests. "He would not accept my offer to tend the injury I dealt him as he so kindly did the one he dealt me. I believe infection has begun to set in."

My eyes snap to Valor as the bottom falls out of my stomach. I search him for visible signs of injury that escaped my notice. I feel the intense curiosity in his gaze as I lead him from the filth of the jail.

CHAPTER TWENTY-SIX

ERIANNA

"What did he say to you?" Valor demands as I lead him across the bailey.

"You have a wound on your shoulder that you have neglected?" My question sounds like an accusation.

"I have neglected nothing, but why—" He interrupts himself to redirect his thoughts. "Did he tell you who he is?"

"A Ruphiri warlord." I shudder again. *It should be obvious how they arrived in Limba.* But *how*? We have been rigidly guarding the Ascent. There is no other way into Malesiir from the Continent. They would have had to come by ship, but no ships are sailing right now because of the winter storms and ice. Could they have arrived in Port Veritae as stow-aways from the Commonwealth? I push through the vestibule into the great hall. Question's stack upon questions. I need to get to my office to sort through—

"Are you listening to me?" Valor abruptly pulls me around then grimaces when I land against his chest, jarring him.

"You *are* injured!" My every concern is scattered like dust before this gale.

Valor is wounded. Badly. He is accustomed to lesser amounts of pain. The cuts and scrapes he gains while training at swords are a mere inconvenience. For him to involuntarily reveal pain...

Panic floods my veins. It coats the back of my throat and rushes into my limbs, causing me to tremble. I feel a gut deep instinct to fight or flee.

Valor is gravely injured.

I grab his hand and pull him in the direction of the newly completed bathing room near the kitchen.

"What are you doing? Erianna, you must calm down." He tries to reason with me, but I am so far beyond being reasonable that there is nothing he can do to change my mind or slow me down.

Not even the middle aged nobleman half undressed in the antechamber of the bathing room hinders me when I barge in.

"Your Majesty!" He stammers, reaching for a tunic to cover his sagging gut like a mortified maiden.

"Forgive me, Lord Fett, but I require the bathing room." I wait impatiently in the doorway, but he simply sputters.

"Leave!" I snap.

He scrambles to gather his belongings and darts down the hallway, pulling his tunic on backwards in his haste. My guard snickers at the sight while I shove Valor into the antechamber.

"Erianna!" Valor is dumbfounded.

"Not a word from you!" I bite out and drag a stool from the corner. "Sit down!"

Uncertain what to do with me in this state, he falls back on his foundational training as a soldier—obey the orders of one's liege—and drops onto the stool.

I poke my head into the hall. "Fetch me Physician Cervil straightaway."

Valor interjects, "He is tending the gravely injured soldiers, of which I am not one."

"Then get me Tirzah and tell her to bring her healer's things!" I slam the door closed before Valor's shout of astonishment can leave the room.

"Would you stop and think for a moment!" He jumps to his feet. "Consider how it will look for me, you, and Tirzah to be in here."

"You lost the grounds to contest my decisions when you went and got yourself maimed! To think you have the gall to criticize my poor judgment where my physical wellbeing is concerned! And I told you to sit!" I bark at him, pointing to the stool then march through the archway to the tub. It is full of clean, hot water prepared for Lord Fett's bath. Good. That is one less thing to do. I fill a basin with the heated water, grab a stack of wash cloths and bar of soap.

In the past two weeks I have come to know Tirzah partly out of necessity from our farce but mostly because we both felt badly for our behavior. What began as genuine apologies has become a fresh chance at friendship. Once I learned to accept her unabashed candor as honesty not criticism and she understood my reticence to stem from caution not superiority, we got along well. As it happens, we have a few common interests. She also shared that she is the assistant to the midwife in Parse Kítaran and is frequently called upon as a novice healer. She did not wish to speak of her past before she came to Parse or the circumstances that led her to the community three years prior, thus I did not press her. I sensed it was something that pained her to recall.

My agitated steps slosh the water in the basin over its rim. "Stupid, reckless fool," I mutter, placing the basin on another stool I drag opposite Valor's. "Give me your weapons belt."

"Take it," he taunts to make me abandon my pursuit but hastens to comply when I do not hesitate to reach for the buckle. While we wait for Tirzah, I divest Valor of his remaining weapons and armor. He resigns himself to my attentions but does not help the process along. With only his shirt remaining, I pause to touch the backs of my fingers to his brow.

Valor hums deep in his throat. "Your hands feel cool."

"Because you are fevered," I criticize, hearing my voice quake.

"No," he takes my hand in his, pressing a kiss to my fingers. "Because I haven't greeted you properly."

I jerk my hand away and swat the air between us. "And you will not until this is done! Can you lift your arms?"

With an eye roll, he reaches for the back of his shirt and pulls it over his head. "I am not an invalid, Erianna."

It is beyond me to blush at the sight of his bared chest, but it is well within my ability to gasp at the multitude of lacerations on his arms. Everywhere his armor did not protect is nicked. A thick bandage is wrapped around his left shoulder, concealing the worst of his injuries. "You did not mention anything about a battle!"

Grumbling, he admits, "The warlord did not go down easily."

This was all the work of that one man?

Gently, I unwind the bandage from his shoulder. The final layer of linen is saturated with blood and yellow liquid. More offensive than the rusty odor of blood is the overlaying sour scent of flesh begun to fester. I swallow and remove the last layer. It sticks fast to the bed of the wound, so I work a wet cloth over it until the linen lifts free. Swollen red flesh outlines the incursion of the blade through skin into the muscle beneath. It weeps watery blood with the linen bandage removed.

Stoically, I dip another cloth in the basin and lather it with soap. I shut out all other thoughts, saying not a word as I cleanse the infected wound. Again and again I wring the cloth in the sudsy water. I refresh the water in the basin when it is fouled then kneel at Valor's side once more. Consumed with my task, I do not hear the tentative knock on the door until Valor's fingertips graze my hairline, tucking an escaped strand behind my ear.

I shift my eyes to his face, noting the pain he tries to hide in the fine creases about his eyes and brow, the hard set of his jaw, the perspiration on his brow. But his eyes are unspeakably tender.

A tap on the door followed by, "Erianna?" brings me to my feet.

I crack the door. Tirzah stands with her basket clasped to her waist, looking uncertain. "You asked for my help? Are you well? Your guard found me with Leelah and will not say what is wrong."

All I can do is nod as I widen the gap to invite her in.

Perhaps I should have warned her, for upon seeing Valor bare to the waist she is flustered. "Well! You certainly don't have a paunch."

Valor barks a laugh but having heard her own words spoken aloud, she glances guiltily at me. I want to tease her back. Normally, I would have something witty to add to make us all laugh. But I don't feel like laughing.

Nothing about this day is funny.

"The wound on his shoulder is the worst. I cleansed it but perhaps not well enough? It is beginning to fester. Please…" I swallow the emotion threatening the integrity of my voice. "Can you help?"

"I am sure you did the job perfectly. I will check then see what else needs to be done."

Valor huffs. "I know what needs done. I simply did not have the supplies to do so. It needs to be packed and—"

"Valor!" Tirzah exclaims, looking at his shoulder. "No! You know better than to have let it get so bad! At this point you do not get to tell me what needs doing. You know the risks from not treating a muscle wound properly. It can cause permanent damage to the arm. It can poison your blood. Or you could…"

The ringing in my ears drowns out Tirzah's dire predictions. My body's defense may work against outside voices, but it cannot overcome the ones in my own head.

You are going to lose him.

You cannot save him either.

You will watch him die slowly.

So alone… Next to another grave.

Valor growls louder than the ringing. "None of that is not going to happen, is it? This is nowhere near so serious. You are being unnecessarily dramatic to prove your point."

I raise my eyes to Tirzah's. She smiles apologetically. "Yes, I was only being dramatic. Forgive me. A few days and this bit of infection will be resolved. A few more and it will only be a little scar. It is certainly not the worst place to be injured. These sort of injuries heal quickly because of the strength of the muscle."

"You see? There is nothing to worry about." Valor extends his hand, drawing me to his side. With a sly grin, he preens, "As my beloved has so often noted, I do maintain an impressive build. I have that to my advantage."

"Conceited," I mutter while Tirzah says, "To be sure."

I arch a brow at her, and she flushes. "Medically speaking, of course."

"Do not encourage him," I chide. "His confidence does not need bolstering." My voice sounds distant and tinny. A wave of nausea intensifies the trembling in my hands. My mouth fills with saliva.

Valor's fingertips slide into my hair then down my jaw. He snares my eyes while his thumb strokes a sensitive spot on the back of my neck, diverting my body's focus from the physical effects of fear toward him. He goads me with his half smile. "Are you claiming that I have never left you speechless?"

Despite the fear poking it, my heart skips, finding a faster rhythm. His thumb makes a teasing circle on my skin. "I have never been speechless. I simply choose not to express my thoughts."

Valor's voice deepens to a flirtatious rumble. "I dare you to voice them next time."

Tirzah whistles a jaunty tune while inspecting his shoulder then bends to her basket of supplies. We have embarrassed her.

"Can I help?" I volunteer.

"Certainly. The rest of his cuts need to be cleansed and treated with a salve. Will you do that while I pack this nonsense and make a poultice to draw out the infection?" She places a small jar of salve in my hands. "But first, more water."

I empty the basin I used while Tirzah dissolves a sachet of salt in a pitcher of warm water.

Valor groans when Tirzah instructs me to position the basin under his arm to catch the water she will flush through the wound.

"Hush!" She scolds. "You knew this was coming. It is your own fault."

With a practiced hand, Tirzah upends the pitcher in a continuous stream. The water trickles over his skin, pooling in the basin beneath, tinged pink with blood. Simultaneously, the color leaches from Valor's face as if she also washes it away.

He sways on the stool. "Unsympathetic sadistic woman."

We brace him between us until he steadies.

"There," Tirzah smiles brightly. "The hard part is over."

While Tirzah packs the wound with a single layer of clean linen, I work a fresh lathered cloth over his sword arm, washing the lesser injuries.

"What did the warlord say to you? He has not said so much in the past week."

I relate our exchange, puzzling over what he told me. "It was strange. He seemed to be taking my measure, like he wants something from me."

Valor's arm settles possessively around my waist. "He will get nothing from you."

I soothe his ire with my fingers as I apply the salve to the shallow cuts on his right shoulder. "I believe those taunts were a test, of my mettle or yours, perhaps. The rest of our exchange felt oddly like an introduction."

"With a barbarian?" Tirzah skeptically notes.

"A barbarian of the noble class," I say. "He seemed so controlled and cultured."

"You have described Zavaan similarly," Valor points out. "To me he is of the same ilk."

Is he like Zavaan? The careful control to conceal his depth… The intelligence… His eyes…

They were a muddy hazel. Perfectly unremarkable. Except…

"Zavaan uses his control to hide his darkness. Whatever is readable on his surface is an affectation. All the expressions and charisma he presents are not him. They are learned behaviors. He mimics emotion, but I have only ever felt three genuine emotions in him. Anger, fear, and pleasure. I do not think he is capable of anything beyond that. There is something deeply wrong with Zavaan."

Having sunk into that place where my thoughts reflect more impressions and emotion than logic can put words to, I am shaking from the recollections that support my conclusions.

Valor holds me tighter, his hands spread on my back. The heat of his skin breaches the fabric of my gown, chasing away the cold that pervades me whenever I remember…

Pungent herbal scents from the salve lay heavy in the air. They tickle my nose bringing me full circle to why I placed them on Valor's skin in the first place.

"The warlord, however, is a man of deep feeling. His control hides that. He is not of the *Vragh's* ilk. In fact, I am certain he disapproves of the way he uses women." I recall his hazel eyes in my memory as he spoke. "He is angered by what the *Vragh* did."

I weigh our exchanged words again. There was something more… Something he wanted from me? Wanted me to acknowledge? I am not certain.

Valor tilts his head back to catch my expression. "What are you thinking?"

My fingers tease the hair at his nape. "I am not sure yet. But this warlord is significant."

He hums his acknowledgement and slides his arms from around me.

Arms?

Where Tirzah stood packing his shoulder, she is no longer. She has stepped back with her gaze fixed on the ground to give us a moment's privacy.

I sweep Valor's hair back, pressing a kiss to his brow that is definitely too warm. When I resume my task, Tirzah returns to our side.

"That seems like an awful lot to extrapolate from the single exchange with the warlord," she muses.

"Erianna has the gift of discernment," Valor explains.

I have never heard him put it that way before. "Does that differ from how you hear lies?"

"Aye, it does. You will gain that with time."

Tirzah concurs. "I also can hear lies. When the Spirit of Truth lives inside you and you practice truthfulness, lies sound flat to your ears."

The part about "practicing truthfulness" is not lost on me. Perhaps I will not gain it after all.

"Discernment is one of the gifts of the Spirit," Valor continues. "Gifts of faith, wisdom, mercy, and service are some others."

"How many are there?"

"Many. They are a blessing freely given to the Creator's people, used to build each other up. While we all have a measure of many gifts, there is usually one that stands out strongest in each person."

"What is yours?"

Valor smiles at me. "Faith. Even when a thing does not seem possible."

For the thing in which I am weakest, the Creator saw fit to give me a man to balance my lack. Fear is certainly the opposite of faith. Just as my discernment would benefit him when his temper leads him to make a snap decision.

My other half.

He devours the words I put in my eyes.

"You are doing that thing again," Tirzah complains. "As sweet as it is, I am going to excuse myself to go make your poultice. But before I do, are there any other bruises, lacerations, or injuries of which I ought to know?"

Valor waves her off. "Go make your poultice. I am fine."

I grab his chin and make him meet my eyes. "Guess on which word you lost my confidence?"

"Shouldn't I be the one saying that?" He counters wryly.

"Where." I demand.

He relents in the face of my determination and, unable to reach his own, draws a dagger from my belt. I step back as he cuts through his pant's leg to expose another gash on his thigh. Tirzah takes one look at it then narrows her eyes on him. I echo her expression with a glare of my own.

"Go bathe the rest of you and put salve on that," she orders.

I follow her out of the room as Valor says, "So be it, but I do not have clean clothing to wear after my bath."

I round on him with my hand on the door. "I ought to make you walk across the castle bare as a babe as punishment for your stupidity!"

Valor rises to his feet, muscle undulating beneath skin. "Very well. But it will be your responsibility to fend off the flock of admiring women that follow me to my room."

Anger burns my cheeks. "Why you arrogant—" I slam the door closed for emphasis and hear his booming laugh.

"He is arrogant, isn't he?" Tirzah chuckles.

"The very definition of it. Tell me plainly. How serious are his injuries?"

Tirzah sobers. "If tended with diligence, I do not believe he will suffer permanent damage or serious complications. But you must keep him from exertion. He needs rest, food, and consistent applications of medicinals."

"I will ensure that he has it. For what should I be watchful?"

"Fever. An increase in pain. If the wounds look at all worse or more inflamed than they did today."

I take note of what she says then begin massaging my temples.

This day is relentless.

Silla's betrayal. Lord Hugler's collusion. Mercenaries. Ruphiri.

Valor…

Tirzah lays a hand on my arm. "Whatever I can do to help, I am at your disposal."

"Thank you."

She turns for the kitchen, and I set off toward Valor's room, until she calls out, "Majesty, there is something I wondered while listening to you talk about the Ruphiri warlord."

"What is that?"

"Why did the Ruphiri warlord tell you Valor was injured?"

I cock an eyebrow at her, realizing why she thought that was odd. "That is an excellent question."

CHAPTER TWENTY-SEVEN

ERIANNA

"I am sorry, Majesty," Physician Cervil tells me. "I have done all that I can."

What trite words for the reality before me. Cervil motions me into the room then strides down the hall as if what he just told me is inconsequential. Dread uncoils in my stomach when I cross into the room that smells of death. I can feel it hiding in the corners, waiting for me to look away so it may steal from me again. My mouth goes dry. I swallow compulsively. This horrible amalgam of grief and fear is a sensation with which I am all too familiar.

I make myself take each weighted step. I cannot move my limbs properly.

The covers on the bed are pulled up high to sweat out the fever. I disagreed with Cervil's opinion, but the illness is too advanced to make any difference.

The hand I grasp is cold, a sharp contrast to the fever raging in his body. I lace my fingers with his and squeeze gently. He hasn't the strength to return the gesture. I have never before seen him weakened.

"Is that my Winter Eyes?"

My heart stutters. "I am here."

A rattling breath moves through his chest. "Good."

"Can I do anything?" I ask, smoothing his hair off his brow. I push it aside to find the strands of silver at his temples. I would have liked to see all his hair grow grey and match his eyes.

"Be with me." Another breath whistles in and out.

I climb onto the bed, wrapping my arms around him.

"Always wanted you in my bed," he teases.

"Then you must get well," I plead.

"I am losing this fight, Belov—"

His words are cut off by chills that shake him violently. I soothe my hands over his chest, praying the infection releases him.

"I am so tired. Will you forgive me if I sleep awhile?"

"I will." But I will never forgive myself. "I will be here when you wake."

"Lies, Erianna?"

"I swear it. I won't leave you." My chest cracks open. I will keep my promise this time. Maybe it will make a difference.

But it does not. Each breath is shallower than the last. Then they stop altogether.

I lay my hand against his cheek. "Valor?"

He does not answer me. I rise over him. "Valor?!" I shake his shoulders. But he is gone. "Come back! Please come back!"

Please come back!

"Erianna! Erianna!"

I wake sobbing. The bed I lay in is mine not his.

Karris shakes my shoulders once more. "Erianna!"

"Karris?"

"You were having a nightmare."

Disoriented from the feelings that made the dream seem real, I struggle to resolve the night from the nightmare. "Is Valor ill?"

Karris's brow puckers. "No, he is merely injured. You sent him to bed after dinner. Do you recall?"

My mind brings forth a hazy memory that does not feel as real as the dream. "You are certain?"

She bobs her head. "Aye. You only had a nightmare."

How embarrassing that I must be reassured by a child! "Karris, I apologize for waking you again. If you wish, I can make different arrangements so that I do not disturb you—"

"Psh," she flops onto her pillow. "I much prefer sleeping next to you than my sisters. They have nightmares, too. And sometimes they wet the bed. As long as you do not do that, I would rather stay right here."

I chuckle in spite of the fear clinging to my heart. "Alright then. Thank you." Opening the bed curtains as little as possible to prevent cold air from slipping into the trapped warmth, I climb out to shake off my nightmare in my parlor. But my feet carry me into my dressing room. I tell myself I am only dressing in my training clothes and donning my fur lined cloak and scarf for warmth. The boots, too, are for warmth. I want to be comfortable while I pace my parlor.

But the only reason I set foot inside my parlor is to pocket the key hidden in the spine of a book about horses. My guard shadows me as I walk silently down the corridors until the scene from my nightmare rises up before me, except the door is closed and locked.

I fit the key into the lock and turn it. The bolt clicks loudly. I draw a deep breath, promising myself Valor is well, probably sleeping. He is not…

I close the door and lock it after entering the darkened room. The glowing brazier is the sole light, and that casts only enough light to know where the brazier is. I navigate the room by memory, stepping up to the edge of the bed. The deep, even breathing of a man that slumbers eases the tightness in my chest. But I must ensure he is not fevered.

My hands reach across the bed, feeling for him in the dark. I find his arm and move upward seeking his brow.

"I would know the touch of your hands even if all other senses failed me," Valor murmurs groggily.

Profound relief causes tears to well up. I settle on the edge of his bed. "I am sorry to wake you. I only meant to ensure you had not become fevered."

Valor moves my hand to his cheek.

Warm. But not hot.

I bow my head and feel a tear fall to the covers.

"You had a nightmare."

I do not answer him. Instead, I stroke my hand down his cheek, moving slowly on the flat plane of his face. His beard has grown long in the past two weeks. It scratches my palm. My thumb marks the ridge of his cheekbone. I spread my hand wider. My small finger curves under the hard line of his jaw, holding his face in my hand. "I will let you get back to sleep."

The bed shifts with his weight as he sits upright. "Why won't you let me keep you company after your nightmares? This is the first time you have woken me and that was largely unintentional."

"There is no need for me to rouse you. I am…" I stop myself from saying *I am fine*. "I have learned to cope on my own." Karris might argue with that statement.

"You are stronger than you were."

"Yes."

Valor captures my hand in his. "I hope you never become so strong that you do not need me."

With those few words, he breaks me. All the emotion I trapped within my impenetrable armor gushes out through the crack Valor opened in my defenses. His arm circles my waist, and he pulls me to his side. Tears pave the path for me to confide in him. It all comes out in no particular order. My nightmare. The pain of Silla's betrayal. The horrible things the court said to me—Lord Sigure's words especially. My heartache at surrendering my throne to Lorennt, knowing it means I am a redundant queen in Malesiir but vital to Limba's future. Through it all, Valor holds me to him, bearing my burdens with me.

When I have poured out all my inner turmoil, I curl into his side with my palm on his chest, feeling the steady rise and fall of his breaths. I feel less burdened, but more vulnerable. It frightens me to let him in. He could hurt me so badly with my heart exposed like this.

Ever sensitive to the currents of my emotions, Valor reassures me not by platitudes, but by making himself equally vulnerable to me. "Zavaan's choice of human shield was a young woman heavy with child."

My heart drops into my stomach.

"I could have put a dagger through his eye. Anders could have run him through. Ten archers could have riddled him with arrows. But I did not let them." Valor's voice is tight and guilt ridden. "I just watched. I watched him… grope at that poor woman, and I did nothing. Her husband fought the Ruphiri even with a blade at his throat. He was screaming, and she was crying, and I did nothing." Derision tenses his body. "Not *nothing*… I knocked her husband unconscious when he broke free and ran to defend his wife."

The scene he describes unfolds vividly. Zavaan's evil smile, the way he toyed with the woman because it amuses him to hurt women, particularly married women. Meditating on why that is does not bear consideration. He is vile. I do not want to know why he targets the ones that he does. But I know what he hoped to achieve in that moment. "He was taunting you."

"He humiliated and violated that poor woman because I was there. I did not stop him. I watched him do it."

"You could do nothing else," I console him. "If you reacted, Zavaan would have done worse to her. He might have killed her or used your reaction as an excuse to turn his men loose on the rest of the villagers. You made the right decision."

"Little comfort that is to her. She was as frightened of me as she was of Zavaan when I caught her after he threw her to the ground. She fought me, too, because I did not defend her." He drags a hand down his face. "I never got the chance to explain or seek their forgiveness. By the time I returned to the estate, she and her husband had gone home to the village."

I doubt even Zavaan could have predicted how deeply his taunt would affect Valor. "Your restraint defended her."

But it is not only her Valor feels guilt ridden for not being able to defend. "Since then, I have had a nightmare that it was you he used as a shield. You suffering beneath his vile touch. Only that is not just a nightmare. It happened." His arms tighten around me. "I should have been here. If I had been here, I would have known who he was and could have prevented all of it."

"What Zavaan did to me is not your fault."

"You are mine. I knew you were mine since the morning you woke in Grass Lake. But I was a coward. I am sorry, Erianna. I should have held onto you and never let you go."

The guilt I was unaware he bears shrouds us like a blanket in the darkness. "Valor, listen to me and believe my words. No blame rests on you. What happened this summer is the *Vragh's* fault. He is a murderer. He would have murdered that family if you had interfered at the estate just as he murdered Leer and Illyanna. You could not have prevented that." I crack open a lid I shut firmly on an old nightmare to tell him the rest of what he must believe so he too can move on. "If you or I had fought my betrothal more than we did, Leer would not have hesitated to kill you. For months, I lived in fear that he would rescind his mercy and punish you. It was a blessing that you were far removed in the North."

Valor sighs from the depths of his being. "You wrote as much in your journal."

Have I unintentionally added to his guilt all those times I pulled away from him or went on shouldering my burdens alone as if he could not be trusted with them? "My Love, the reason I have not woken you to be with me after my nightmares is that I want to be stronger. I want to conquer them. I want to conquer all of it—my fears, my past, even the gossip of the court. After all that I have survived, I should not be affected by such little things. I hate feeling weak and vulnerable."

"But that is not who you are," Valor argues. "Beneath your considerable strength is a soft, intuitive heart that cannot help but feel deeply. It is part of what makes you the woman I love. I admire the Warrior Queen. She is strong and capable because Erianna is underneath the armor. You love consumingly with a warrior's heart. It makes you vulnerable, aye, but it also makes you compassionate to others. If you lock up that part of yourself, you will not be you." He gives me time to let his words settle into my bones. "Taking care of your precious heart is not tedious or inconvenient for me. I want to do it, Beloved. Even if that means losing sleep."

His words soothe my battered heart. Mine lighten his guilt. "I trust you. And I will wake you next time. I promise."

Valor lays his head atop mine. "I am proud of you for giving up your throne. Making the calculated decisions of the High Queen felt contrary to your character. I believe it exacted more from you than you realize."

The weight of the winter season and all the responsibilities I have born press on my shoulders. "You may be right. Nevertheless, I feel at a loss."

"Have you considered the other benefits? You now have the freedom to move about the kingdom. You are not bound to Malsihra anymore."

"I had not considered that." Though I have ruled this kingdom for over a year, I am mostly acquainted with its cities on maps and production reports. I would love the chance to see all of it.

"Once we hang Zavaan, which I feel will be soon now that we have so many of his men, I will take you anywhere you want to go."

The promise of freedom refreshes me like a breeze on an oppressively hot day. I want to do all that I can to hasten it, which requires the demise of Zavaan. "We need to have a plan before we speak to the warlord."

"We do. But it is high time I bid you goodnight. For your sake, I do not want the court to see you leaving my room at dawn."

I snort. "That hardly seems important anymore. They all think I am tossing sheets with you."

He chuckles. "No need to fuel their suspicions. Besides," Valor draws his hand up my arm. "You gave me orders 'not to exert myself.' If you stay any longer, I warn you that is exactly what I am going to do."

I grin. "Was that supposed to encourage me to leave?" My fingers find their way from his neck into his hair, pulling him closer to me.

He groans and sets his brow to mine, denying us both the temptation of a kiss, though the labored breath expanding his lungs evidences his inner battle with that decision. My lips tingle with the anticipation of tipping the scales of his struggle.

"Don't," he pleads. "I know you think I have boundless self-control, but I swear I do not."

I cannot help teasing him just a bit. "I suppose there is some sense in what you say. After all, I am in your bed."

There is nothing teasing in his tone. "You have no idea what your presence is doing to me."

After the emotional intimacies we shared, it feels natural for it to lead to physical intimacy. "Oh, I think I have have some idea."

Valor's resolve quickly wanes. "Erianna," he pleads, touching his lips to mine, breathing hard. He needs me to leave.

But he is asking me to stay.

It is time for me to prove I understand boundaries. Especially since my own restraint is less practiced than his, and the temptation of spending the night in his arms is too great. "Soon," I kiss his cheek then slip away, heading for the door. "Soon, my Love."

CHAPTER TWENTY-EIGHT

VALOR

January 6th

I gave my word to Erianna that I would not exert myself. After finally admitting how frightened she is of losing me, I cannot go back on my word to her, and I will not. But Jakab Sigure is going to answer for the vile words he spoke. Then I shall ensure the court knows how wrong they were in their assumptions.

However, there is someone I must speak to before I make the pup regret biting my beloved. I knock on the closed door, praying the Spirit of Truth will grant me favor and tell me what to say. One of the noblewomen, Lady Artice, I recall, opens the door wide causing silence to fall in the solar.

"Commander Ironforge," Queen Celiea says with more astonishment than distaste. She sets aside her sewing and rises to her feet. "Is Erianna well?"

The tremor in her voice guides mine. "She will be, in time, but I am concerned for her. Would you grant me an audience, Majesty?"

"Yes, of course." She invites me in and dismisses her attendants whose rampant curiosity is displayed in their backward glances.

"Please be seated, Commander," Queen Celiea motions me to take the end of the plush brocade couch she occupies. "What ill has befallen my daughter?"

"News of what her people have suffered at the hands of the Ruphiri and the betrayal of Lady Silla has left my queen heartsick. It does not help that the news came at a time when she was already aching from the cruel gossip of the court."

She does not hesitate to condemn me. "Something that can be laid solely at your feet, Commander."

"Not solely, Majesty. I suspect that you played a part in the worst of what she recently suffered."

Queen Celiea's refined countenance becomes spiteful. Before she can have me thrown from her solar, I continue, "I will apologize if I am wrong, but if you permit me to explain, we can settle this presently."

"I do not pretend to like you Commander, nor will I support your suit of my daughter. However, if Erianna is hurting I would know of it." She does not relax her stiff posture, but she grants my request. "You may proceed."

"As I am sure you know, Erianna has closely guarded the secret that she is unlikely to bear any more children. To my knowledge, it was only known among family." Of whom I include the Tareths.

"We have discussed this before, Commander." She reminds me of our conversation when Erianna and I informed her parents that we were courting. Boldizar insisted upon hearing from my own lips that I knew what Erianna could not give me and that I would never fault her for it. It was no difficulty to tell him that I was aware of her injury and nothing could move me from her side. "Have you changed your mind then?"

"Not in the least, Majesty. But in my absence, one of the noblemen cornered Erianna. He spoke vulgarly toward her and mocked her for being barren. I cannot ignore such an attack against her."

Celiea is outraged. "Nor will I! Who has said such things to her? And how did he learn of her infirmity? As you said, only family knows. I cannot believe Physician Cervil would speak of it. He is perfectly circumspect. Has Erianna confided in any of her friends?"

I withhold the censure from my tone and state as evenly as possible, "The nobleman was Jakab Sigure. He berated Erianna for wasting his time on a suit when she is barren."

Color leaches from the queen's face. "Jakab?"

"Erianna has never encouraged his suit. Quite the opposite. The conclusion I have drawn is that perhaps the woman who did encourage him to pursue Erianna was the same one who trusted him with a confidence of which he proved unworthy."

Celiea wrings her hands in misery. "It was me. We were discussing his siblings. I told him how much Erianna would enjoy being an aunt to his siblings' children since she cannot... But he is so infatuated with her. I did not think he would reject her for it. She is a beautiful woman. Lively. Kind. Generous. She is a twice royal queen, a member of our family. It should be enough."

"For the one who loves her, it is. But Jakab does not love her. Please tell me you understand, Majesty."

She nods.

"I will not let her suffer his presence any longer. I intend to confront him and force him to leave the castle this day."

"So be it," she consents, though I am not here to seek her blessing.

"Erianna loves you, Celiea. She speaks of you as her mother. It breaks her heart that she does not have your approval."

Celiea frowns. "But she does. It is because I love her that I have opposed your suit and encouraged Jakab." The older woman appears thoroughly miserable. "You are going to take my daughter away from me. I cannot let you do that, Valor. I cannot lose another child. Please."

I take Celiea's hand, feeling compassion for her. "I am not in control of the future. But I promise to cherish your daughter. And I vow to bring her back to you as often as I can. The thought of leaving you is crushing her, too. Please do not waste any of the present time you are afforded."

She squeezes my hand and dries the few tears that escaped. "Thank you, Valor. I cannot ask more of you than that."

※※※

ERIANNA

I spent the remainder of my sleepless night mulling over the enigmatic Ruphiri warlord. My pride contests the decision I arrived at, having sworn I would not speak to the warlord on this day, but it must be. The other decision I arrived at concerning the warlord will certainly cause Valor to be put out with me, but again, it is necessary.

Seizing the opportunity after breakfast when Valor and I part ways, he needing to attend to his own unspecified duties, I slip off to the jail alone to attend to mine. I instruct the jailer to move the warlord to an interrogation room where he is to be shackled hands and feet. I saw what the warlord did to Valor. I am no idiot.

The jailer leads us through the maze of corridors to the interrogation room. When I move to follow him inside, my guard halts me.

"Majesty, ought we to wait for Commander Ironforge?"

"The commander is not coming, and I forbid you to inform him."

Suspicion places my guard between me and the door. "With respect,

Majesty, this seems dangerous. I am to use my best judgment to protect you. This goes against it."

Would he go so far as to hinder my plans? If so, the "head of my security" and I are going to have a disagreement later. "Your caution is noted. I trust you will be diligent in your watch."

His mouth disappears into a thin line of stifled disapproval, but he steps aside. "Aye, Majesty."

The two guards that brought the warlord from his cell stand to either side of him. Two more guards wait in the hall. My personal guard follows me into the room and before allowing me to sit in the chair opposite my prisoner, he personally verifies the integrity of the man's bonds.

The Ruphiri is pleased with this arrangement, but his smile is his only comment regarding my caution. "You must have been desperate to see me this day, *Královna*. I did not think your pride would allow it."

My opening parry is deliberate and thoughtful, as is my choice to speak in Limban to prevent our conversation from being known by any but us. "Pride is the downfall of many. I have succumbed to it before, but I am not its slave."

"Neither am I a slave to it. Thus, if your choice of temporarily removing me from my cell was in appeal to that friend and foe, I am afraid you will find me unmoved."

"I wish to speak with you, just you and I. That is why you are here."

"And why your commander is not," he notes.

I incline my head. "I can hardly title you '*zar*' for the entirety of our conversation. What is your name?"

His eyes narrow in consideration over sharp cheekbones. "My title does not offend me, nor does yours. I will make a bargain with you, *Královna*. If at the end of our conversation I am pleased with you, I will tell you my name."

I cock my scarred brow high. "Keep it to yourself if you wish. But do not think to make a queen grovel. I am not a slave to pride, but I do possess it."

"You are off to a good start, *Královna*." A genuine smile renders him more attractive than I estimated him to be. More surprising, I do not sense anything slithering behind his control. When Zavaan smiles, it is like the grin of an adder. Not so with this Ruphiri.

"*Hmm...*" I know what I want to know, but I am now uncertain I should begin with it. Will I be able to keep this question close without him realizing it? Timing is critical to negotiations. I must not waste any more dithering. "It was not desperation that prompted me to speak with you again. It was curiosity."

"Oh?"

"You intuited something that few have because of their own preconceived notions." I know that I am on the right track when a keen look moves about his face. "How did you arrive at the conclusion that unless told I would not know of Valor's injury?" I intentionally drop his title, not from lack of respect, but to emphasize the intimacy Valor and I share. "After all, would I not have seen it when I removed his clothing at day's end?"

The warlord is not swayed in his beliefs. "Would you have? No, I think not. A widow you are, but the commander's lover you are not yet. Nor will you be, I think, until an arrangement of permanence occurs."

"It is curious to me that you who know so little of me has correctly surmised the nature of our relationship when everyone else including my personal guards who shadow my every movement have presumed that the commander and I are bedmates. What was the foundation of your conclusion?"

"You seek to understand me..." This thought pleases him greatly. "Am I more intelligent than the rest, perceiving something that others did not, or have I received information from a source close to you?" He takes my measure again. "As it happens, the full truth is that I know things about you that even you do not. However, that is an outlandish claim. So let my answer be aye, *Královna*. I am more perceptive than the rest."

My brow finds its way upward in another show of skepticism. "I find that claim more outlandish than you having an informant."

The warlord does not argue, but neither does he change his explanation, he only expounds. "There is a subtle bond between a man and the woman he has known. When two move as one in the night, they begin to move as one during the day. You and the commander do not."

I blink. That almost sounded as if this lethal man who tried to kill Valor has a heart.

Correctly interpreting my response he says, "I told you *Královna*. I like women."

"Yet you serve Zavaan? And keep company with those who ravish women and steal them from their families?" I challenge.

"I am Ruphiri," he replies, as if that is all the explanation required.

Allegiance before conscience.

Tamping down the urge to call him a barbarian, I ask, "What does being Ruphiri mean?"

"You will admit to your ignorance?" He weighs me again.

It pleases me that I continue to defy the expectations he has of me. "I will agree to admit to my ignorance if you will agree to enlighten me."

He smiles, almost affectionately. Instantly, I am put off by him and stiffen my spine dropping all pretense of civility.

Chains clink with the raising of his palms in a gesture meant to soothe. "Apologies, *Královna*. For a moment I was reminded of my wife."

"Which one?" I deride.

"You cannot see past that, can you? I wonder if it would repulse you so, if not for—"

"It is a repulsive practice," I judge and condemn him.

"Your ignorance is showing again, *Královna*," he cautions.

I breathe deeply, putting aside my own feelings on the matter. "Then enlighten me. I know the Ruphiri chose to leave Limba some eighty years ago when the Vrock king's taxation became unbearable."

"Your great grand sire taxed the Limban people so heavily that it was all the people could do to feed themselves. The cities near the Spire Mountains were the primary source of ore for steel. It was a life so harsh that men did not live beyond the age of forty. The avaricious king demanded more and more. Then his soldiers came and forced our women and children into the mines to extract ore to forge the swords that terrorized our people. I assure you, *Královna*, the atrocities your sire levels at the Ruphiri were learned at the hands of Vrock soldiers."

"How can you be certain?" I do not know why I want to believe otherwise. Violence is synonymous with the Vrock name.

Chains rattle as he leans forward, stretching his bonds to make me understand. "Children were sent into the deepest parts of the mines. It was more efficient. Children could fit through smaller holes and chase the veins of ore deep into the roots of the mountains. Such small tunnels did not require bracing like fully excavated ones. The ventilation required for them was also less than for a grown man. When the tunnels inevitably collapsed and trapped sixty-four children in the mines, there was nothing that could be done. The soldiers held back fathers from the doomed endeavor of trying to rescue their children while mothers wailed from the deepest parts of the mine they could reach."

I want to clap my hands over my ears to protect myself from the horrible story. I stop myself shy of doing so when the warlord leans back in his chair. "My grandsire was one of the lucky children. He was ferrying a load of ore to the surface when the shafts collapsed. His three siblings were not so fortunate. His mother was never the same. It was after that final atrocity that our forebearers rebelled against the oppression of the Limban king. They fled into the mountains with as much as they could carry."

The dark events that led to their secession from our kingdom were justified, as I always feared. I stare transfixed at the man brought up with such hatred toward Limbans that he crossed the Continent to apprehend me, heir to the Limban throne.

Or am I?

"Reports from the Malesiirian stronghold at Farreach tell that Arcto Vrock has not yet named a successor. Can you confirm that?"

The warlord frowns. "You claim to want to know of the Ruphiri, yet your interest has already returned to yourself?"

"Hardly."

He glares at me for minutes. Is that the key to maneuvering this man? An interest in the well-being of the Ruphiri people? The same people that took more from me than I ever thought I could lose. Or was that all Zavaan and his cohorts? There is only one way to learn.

"My interest is in the future of Limba and the Ruphiri. To my mind, the Limban people have suffered extensively under the rule of the Vrock dynasty, the most obvious symptoms of which are widespread starvation, sickness, and poverty. Likewise, the Ruphiri are determined to escape the hardships of the Spires and to avenge old wrongs by seizing control of Limba. They make themselves odious to the King of Limba at the expense of the Limban people that are undeserving of their animosity." I lace my fingers together upon my lap then lay the foundation for gaining what I need from this warlord. "The situation in Limba is desperate. I am deeply concerned about the people that will be trampled, that have already been condemned to the grave, by the power struggle." That does not even touch upon the atrocities committed at Zavaan's behest.

The warlord chews on my words then swallows them. "You have given me much to think on *Královna*. I anticipate our next exchange will be even more enlightening."

Rather than press for more, I allow him to conclude what feels very much like negotiations between two rulers.

"You do not know this, *Zar*, but I, too, held something in reserve pending my estimation of you." I beckon to one of his guards who opens the door admitting Tirzah. She agreed to aid me with this scheme of mine when I presented it to her this morning. I could not trust another healer to be close lipped, nor did I think the warlord would be amenable to a man tending him.

"What is this, *Královna*?"

"It occurred to me that you were in the same state as Commander Ironforge but without the benefit of remedy. Thus, my healer."

The warlord looks between me, Tirzah, and the basin covered with cloth. He opens his mouth then closes it.

For Tirzah's benefit, I shift into the common tongue. "I trust you like women sufficiently that you will not harm this one who has consented to tend your injuries?"

Why? He blatantly wonders, but does not say it. Instead he posits, "You would not poison me, would you, *Královna*?"

The Warrior Queen delights in the calculated words I choose. "That is not my style, *Zar*. If I decide to kill you, I will do you the honor of informing you death is coming."

"I will not harm her," the warlord says softly then crosses his arms so that his empty hands rest palms up on his opposite knees. From that position, he will be unable to attack Tirzah faster than the guard at his back can put a sword through him.

A memory of Valor kneeling before me to render himself disadvantaged and less intimidating when I was frightened strikes a comparison to how this warlord presents himself. I cant my head to the side, surprised by the unexpected comparison between the two men. What does it say of the warlord's character that he would submit without being forced to do so? Other than Valor, the only man I know who can so intuitively calm a woman's fears is Kragorn. It takes a profound level of sympathy for a powerful man to see himself through a woman's eyes and humble himself to her.

The warlord remains unflinchingly still through Tirzah's ministrations, only answering the questions she asks to direct her healing hands to his concealed injuries. He tracks her movements with his eyes until Tirzah bows over his hand to examine the stump of his finger. He averts his eyes from the vantage point afforded him by the gape of her neckline. A quick glance around the room reveals that the guards standing nearby do not show her the same courtesy.

The Ruphiri's gaze wanders about the room until he realizes his mistake when my satisfied smile and arched eyebrow call attention to what I have noticed. Too late, he attempts to conceal his honor beneath a lascivious smile and fixes his eyes on Tirzah like the other men in the room. As I suspected when he gazed at me in the same manner yesterday, there is no real lust in how he looks at her. It is an affectation.

More certain than ever that this warlord is as different from Zavaan as water is from sand, I clear my throat to demonstrate my disapproval to the guards. They avert their gaze from Tirzah, and one prods the warlord in the back with his sword, demanding he do the same. He complies, shifting his feigned countenance to me. I merely chortle.

This Ruphiri does not simply "like women." He respects them.

When Tirzah concludes her work, I rise with her. "Until next time, *Zar*."

"*Královna*," he returns to our shared language. "My name is Torvarik."

A chill trickles down my spine. "*Torr var rik?*"

He slowly inclines his head in assent. "*Torr var rik.*"

I want to doubt him. I want him to be lying. But he speaks true. What an inopportune moment for me to begin hearing the ring of truth in a man's words!

I steady myself. "Named for the place of your birth or for your character?"

He smiles wide with all his crooked teeth. "Good day, *Královna*."

※ ※ ※

Torvarik. His name is *Torr var rik*.

I shiver as I follow Tirzah into the corridor. No sooner do I exit the room than a hand turns around my arm and hauls me to the side. I yelp and reach for a dagger, but another hand closes overtop mine before I can draw the blade.

"Valor," I breathe his name in relief. What a nice name "Valor" is. Trustworthy. Honorable. Courageous. Defender of the weak. Valor.

I hardly notice that I have surrendered to his guidance to pass through the connecting corridors.

Torvarik.

What a thing to name a person! I suppose it could be worse. He could be named *Devourer of Children* or something equally frightful.

But Torvarik? Not exactly what I would have chosen. I would much rather him be named *Ray of Hope* or *Answer to my Prayers*.

But no. The warlord's name is *Torr var rik*.

Place of Ruin.

His name is *Place of Ruin*!

Perhaps it is good that I not delude myself about whom I am dealing with. I quite nearly forgot after his unintentional display of chivalry. And what of it? He respects women. Surely that does not preclude him from being a murderous Ruphiri.

Valor's terse instructions to my guard return me to the present, making Valor my focus. "Escort Tirzah to the castle. My Queen and I will be in the gardens." His hand is still on my arm, marching me that direction. I let him do it, knowing that he does not do so to control me, but that he is reassuring himself that he has me and I am safe.

When we reach the gardens, I slide his hand to mine and lace our fingers together. I match my steps to Valor's anxious energy that will not allow him to sit still until he has stamped it out by pacing.

"You speak," Valor demands through clenched teeth, holding back a flood of chastisement that he does not want to release on me.

Understanding the reasons behind his behavior, however, does not mean I will set a precedent of tolerating it. "How was your morning? Did you accomplish all that you hoped?"

He grinds his teeth, gripping my hand tightly. I pretend as if we are having a conversation and rub my opposite hand up and down his arm. "I hope you followed orders and did nothing overly strenuous." Had I not been looking, I might have missed the satisfied gleam in his eyes, the momentary relaxing of his jaw. I do not trust that a bit. "What *did* you do this morning?"

He releases me to clasp his hands behind his back. "I met with Queen Celiea."

"Truly? What did she require of you?"

"A clarification of my intentions toward you, which pales in comparison to the morning you had. Why did you meet with the Ruphiri without me? And why did you involve Tirzah?"

"Do not change the subject!" I plant my feet in his path so that I may gaze fully upon his carefully controlled expression. I smell an evasion. "When did Celiea summon you?"

"I spoke with her after breakfast."

My eyebrow rises in challenge. "*Did* Celiea summon you?"

His eyebrow rises to match mine.

"What were you up to?" I ask softly, lethally.

His bored expression cracks into a grin. "You do that very well."

"Am I to conclude that you did something I would disapprove of just as I did something about which you are not pleased?"

Valor's anxiety falls away. "That seems to be the case. Shall we dispense with the mutual overreactions since we are both in one piece?"

I cannot know how irritated I will be with him for whatever he did, but if I can sidestep an argument over my own premeditated actions, then I am willing to make the bargain. With a wry smile, I consent. "That seems reasonable."

His eyes linger on my mouth a moment before he brushes his lips over mine. At the gasps of a party strolling a little ways off, his eyes turn roguish, and he steals another kiss. "Besides the way they treated you, do you know what really sticks like a bur in my backside?"

I shrug my eyebrows.

His fingertips outline the curve of my jaw. "I have been compelled to restrain my crowing that you are mine, and I have not done near enough strutting to satisfy myself. Having the privilege of you at my side makes me incorrigibly proud." He whispers the last in my ear making me titter and blush. With confident conviction, he meets my gaze. "We will learn to work together, Beloved. I promise."

I angle my head teasingly. "If I promise not to overreact, you will confess first?"

"Imp," he chuckles. "Just remember, you promised." He raises his right hand so that I may see his split, swollen knuckles. "Sigure and I had a little talk—with Celiea's blessing."

CHAPTER TWENTY-NINE

ERIANNA

January 7th

To keep Torvarik off balance, Tirzah attends to his injuries at the beginning of our meeting. He does not attempt to conceal his chivalry. Instead he goes so far as to thank Tirzah for her assistance and compliments her skill. The guards do not know what to make of his gratitude. I infer that his ruminating on our prior exchange has brought him to the same conclusion at which I have arrived—proceed cautiously to the next level of negotiations.

"Is your Hand unwell, *Královna*? I cannot believe he would allow you to speak with me unchaperoned a second day in a row."

I smile. "The commander and I share a deep mutual respect and faith in each other's decisions. He did not contest my choice to speak with you." Because he is standing in the corridor flipping a dagger. "First things first. You said that it should be obvious how you and the Ruphiri reinforcements came to be in Malesiir. Irked as I am to admit it, I am unable to deduce it. Enlighten me."

"A play at my vanity? *Tut tut, Královna*. Vanity is akin to pride. We have already decided that is not the way to gain cooperation from either of us."

My brow rises high. "My healer tended your wounds and I offered you a bit of blatant honesty. That is what I gave in exchange for your information."

Condescension drips from his tone. "You paid up-front. Incentives ought to be held in reserve until you have what you want."

"For most arrangements, that is true," I allow. "But you strike me as a man who does not like to be indebted to anyone. Now, I have placed you in mine."

Torvarik, gives me another appraising look then smiles. "You are enjoying this."

I am. Perhaps I should not in light of who he is, but I am.

"Very well, *Královna*. I do not like to be indebted. A clever deduction. Thus, I shall clear my debt straightaway." With no more prevarication he states, "We arrived by ship."

My mind's wheels whir. Ship? Port Veritae is our only deepwater port. Could they have smuggled aboard one of our vessels returned from the Commonwealth? I disregard that thought instantly. There are too many of them to hide. Though our ships do ferry passengers, some of the Ruphiri do not speak the common language, and their clothing would have given them away before securing passage, therefore they could not have boarded in disguise. They also brought their horses.

Could they have sailed on their own ship? Perhaps rowed in from off the coast? Or…

"You anchored in Halden," I realize. "In October when Zavaan was harrying the town. That was why he was there. Somehow, he distracted the town and allowed you to slip in through that harbor. It is our only other deepwater port."

Torvarik inclines his head.

We need to build the town up quickly and have a patrol stationed nearby to prevent such a weakness being exploited again. I chew on my lip, deeply concerned over the possibility of Zavaan launching a full invasion from the port. Thankfully, that could not happen until spring when the seas are more calm.

I push aside those troubling imaginings until later when I can share them with Lorennt and Valor. I am out of my depth when it comes to such military strategy. In the meantime, there is more groundwork to be laid where my knowledge of the Ruphiri is concerned. As long as Torvarik is willing to speak of them, I will take whatever strategic advantage can be gleaned. "When my history lesson ended yesterday, the Limban miners had been forced to flee into the Spires. What happened next?"

He settles into his story with a grimness that bodes ill for his forebearers. "The Spires were not welcoming. With only the provisions they managed to carry on their backs and no chance to return for more, starvation was the first enemy they faced. It claimed many lives. The Spires support little in the way of edible forages. Mountain goats and fish from the Sky Lakes sustained them but only just. Shelter was the second enemy they vied. The Spires are more stark than the plateau of Limba. There are no trees on the steep cliffs. Grass grows across the sheer faces in the summer and moss in crevices where snow cannot accumulate during winter."

"No lumber for houses," I conclude. "Did they hew stone for houses? Or," I hold up a finger, lighting upon the solution, "they took refuge in caves?"

"Frith," he rolls the short Limban word meaning "refuge" across his tongue. "No. There was no *frith* for my ancestors. Stone is labor intensive to hew, quite an endeavor with a full belly, impossible for men fighting starvation. The caves did shelter them at times, but within them they met their third foe. Wolves."

Dozens of pairs of eyes reflect firelight as my nightmare becomes darker still… I shudder.

Torvarik's sharp eyes do not miss it. "Packs of wolves inhabited the caves of the Spires. They hunted my ancestors, snapping up the men who stayed behind to defend their families. After months of such torment, the women and children with a token number of men pressed deeper into the Spires than any had before traversed. They went so far that the Eastern Ocean appeared beyond the cliffs. Hopeful the ocean would provide the sustenance the Spires denied them, they established a settlement upon the beach. During the remainder of the year, they learned to harvest what seemed like a bounty from the salt water. Their health was restored, and the swollen bellies of their children were filled. That is not to say, however, they were free of hardship. The winter storms that blew off the ocean drove them back into the shelter of the Spires. Because of the imbalanced numbers of women to men, each man took responsibility for a group of women and children, protecting and providing for them."

"The first harems," I interject quietly across the room that I have begun to pace.

Torvarik inclines his head. "At the outset the relationships were not of a marital nature. But as you can understand, they evolved into such."

It is not difficult to imagine women vying for the attention of the few men, nor is it a stretch to believe that most men would be willing to entertain more than one woman. But to abandon the institution of marriage so thoroughly seems a leap. "Coming from a culture that is monogamous—"

"Outwardly monogamous," Torvarik corrects. "Do not deny it, oh

Noblewoman."

I grudgingly acknowledge it with an eye roll that makes him chuckle. "*Outwardly monogamous* among the noble class, but *typically monogamous* among the lower classes."

"Do not disappoint me with prejudice now, *Královna*. Men and women are subject to the same sins whether noble or common. You know this."

"What did you say?" I startle back into the common tongue at his choice of word. *Sins*.

Torvarik smirks. "You apprehend my meaning perfectly. Noble or common, king or soldier, what man would not leap at the chance of possessing more than one woman?"

The sharpened words find their target in my chest. I retaliate, snarling into his face. "An honorable one, of which you will never be!"

My guards surge forward with a shout and the door bangs open. Fury leaves no room for fear though my wrists are manacled by long calloused fingers.

Torvarik's hazel eyes burn into mine as a smile curls up his face. "You have forgotten my name again, Erianna Rodiharian. Why is that, do you think?"

Valor's dagger kisses Torvarik's throat while the points of three swords tickle his back and sides.

His tone scolds me. "At least they take your safety seriously even if you do not. Maybe you will survive this year." With a taunt that is the height of foolishness, Torvarik then reproves Valor in the common tongue. "Your woman trespasses upon me, Commander. You must take her in hand if you hope to make a compliant wife of her."

My palm connects so forcefully against Torvarik's cheek that his head is knocked askew. "We are done here."

I stride from the room, not bothering to remind Valor we are keeping the warlord alive for the time being. Let him add to the injuries he already dealt the villain.

It is not until I have stomped partway down the corridor that I draw up short to gaze at my wrists beneath a sconce. They are not sore. Not bruised. Not even red. Had Torvarik been of a mind, he could have snapped them or at least pained me if he values his life too much to do me bodily harm. But he did not. Nor do I recall breaking his hold on me. He released me.

"What game does he play?" I mutter to myself.

※ ※ ※

* * *

VALOR

Erianna storms out of the interrogation room in a high temper, but there was nothing of fear about her. Torvarik watches her exit with something akin to resolve. My anger stutters as I read his complete lack of anger towards my queen for striking him with bruising force. Did he intentionally provoke her as she claims he did to me?

"What are you about, Torvarik?" I demand.

He does not deign to respond, merely fixes his gaze on the wall opposite him.

"Do you know who waits in the other interrogation room?" I ask, wondering if he will do what Zavaan did not and defend their informant. "Lady Silla Hugler has been granted an opportunity to defend herself before tomorrow's sentencing. Is there anything you wish to share on the matter?"

The warlord's voice is harsh for all its quietude. "Traitors are granted no mercy. Not for themselves. Not for their kin. Is it so different in Malesiir?"

I look long upon him, but he yields no more secrets. "Return the prisoner to his cell."

My queen stands in the bitter cold outside the jail. Wind tosses the midnight strands of her hair across her face like the wisps of cloud skittering across the winter sun in the sky above. "It was impulsive of me. You do not need to say so."

"I did not come to criticize." I draw alongside her, following her vacant observation of the lower bailey that bustles with the comings and goings of servants and soldiers. A pair of noblewomen escorted by a middle aged lord wave a greeting to Erianna as they venture into the capital. She acknowledges them with a nod of her head.

She remains quiet, becoming lost to the world for a time. Her mind is too active to notice her surroundings.

"That warlord gets beneath your skin. It was the same with Zavaan." Not that she told me so, but she described their exchanges with her hindsight commentary in her journal.

"But this is different, I think. At least, I hope I am not so daft as to be blind to danger when it is seated across from me."

"Beloved, I am afraid you are not the most objective at recognizing danger. You did not see the danger of Zavaan, you do not treat this Torvarik as lethal although we know he is, and, to be perfectly honest, you are not afraid of me even though I can still frighten Leelah."

"But you will not harm me. Not physically," she qualifies.

"And I shall endeavor to never harm you in any other way, but the point stands."

Erianna mulls on it. "But I am reserved around others, especially men. My initial impairment to reading Zavaan can be attributed to him, not me. He is the errant factor—a man without conscience or true emotion. And you…" Erianna looks across her shoulder at me, "Well, I think my heart knew its other half even if my mind was too naive to accept it."

I warm at her words and settle my hand beneath her hair on the back of her neck, squeezing gently. She hums in response.

"But why this warlord? He is not emotionless like Zavaan, nor am I drawn to him as I am to you. What is it I am missing?"

"I cannot say. But I can verify he is different from other Ruphiri." In the distance, I discern Lorennt, his guard, and Trent approaching. "It is time to put aside thoughts of this."

She sighs. "Aye."

After a distinct pause in which she wrestles with something, Erianna hesitantly requests, "Valor, when this is over would…" She hesitates, lacing her hands at her waist. "Would you stay with me and…" She groans then rushes to say, "Would you knead my shoulders?"

That she has made herself vulnerable to ask for my company *and* my touch is a step forward where her trust is concerned. Thus, I do not leave her in suspense and quickly agree, deciding I will do for her something better and find a nice quiet corner for us to while away an hour following this meeting.

Lorennt's dour expression makes Erianna tense as he comes even with us. "I do not know why I have agreed to an audience with this traitor. She cannot sway me from my belief in her duplicity."

I glance at Trent before I reply on behalf of my mute queen. "Silla's duplicity is unquestionable, but she may possess additional information we need. And I, for one, hope she can explain her actions in such a way that lessens the severity of her sentencing tomorrow."

"Do not hope for that," Lorennt bites out, striding into the jail.

The furrows between Trent's brows deepen while Erianna wraps her arms about herself defensively. I drape my arm across her shoulders, guiding her back inside the stone structure.

Silla's hands are shackled together. She bows low at the entrance of her king and queen, holding until Lorennt waves a hand at her to be seated.

"If you have anything compelling to tell us, now is the time," he launches into the hearing, though his tone conveys quite clearly that he has no inclination to hear what she would say.

"Perhaps you should begin at the beginning," Erianna suggests, not altogether unmoved by the sight of her bound and dirtied companion. "At what point did you engage in the plots against the kingdom?"

Silla seems prepared for such a question and holds her gaze on Erianna as if they are the only two in the room. "The night of King Lorennt's wedding after you departed. My father pulled me aside and forbid me from leaving the castle. He told that plans had been set in motion to give me a third chance at a crown."

"Third chance?" Erianna asks.

Silla clarifies, "Aye, Majesty. Third. The first being under the auspices of wedding King Grandileer when I took up residence at court. King Grandileer and Queen Celiea encouraged me to give my father false hopes so that I would be permitted to reside at the castle instead of beneath his…" Silla stumbles in her accounting and takes a moment to compose herself. "Beneath his heavy hand. Queen Celiea can verify my assertion that we told my father what he wished to hear and that there was no truth to it. However, Queen Celiea did entertain considerable hopes that an attachment would form between King Lorennt and I, though, it never did and I was content with that." Silla draws a deep breath and flicks at her skirts though it does nothing to remove the accumulated grime from the fabric. "I speak of this so that you will know, Majesties, that my father lusts for power. He has sought to expand his lands and increase his wealth for decades. Seating me on a throne became his means to achieve his ends, though I did not participate in his plots. That is, until he gave me no choice in the matter."

Silla's eyes dart to Trent, but he remains cold to her.

Lorennt pounces, sinking his fangs into her story. "You say you were without recourse, yet you had daily access to the Queen and Queen Abdicàt. Do tell—what sort of recourse could you have needed that you did not already possess?"

Silla winces. "I have given the matter considerable thought and realize now that I should have confided in Queen Erianna, but at the time, I was too afraid for my mother's life."

Trent snorts. It is not difficult for me to interpret his frustration. If what Silla led him to believe was, indeed, a genuine attachment between them, she should have confided in him. But, for whatever reason, she did not trust Trent with her problems either.

"Continue," Erianna nods.

"Knowing that my cooperation would not be forthcoming, my father removed my mother to our family estate. He vowed that if I resisted or made known his plots he would exact retribution not on me, but on her. He left me in an untenable position, Majesty."

Erianna nods her sympathy, but Lorennt folds his arms saying, "Hardly. You chose the life of one over the hundreds that have died at Zavaan's hands since then. You chose wrong."

Silla hardens at the words of the king. I watch her reevaluate her chances of escaping punishment and arrive at the same conclusion I have—Lorennt will not forgive her offenses. Rather than crumble, Silla draws herself up and presses forward. "My father did not confide in me what all of his plans were, nor did he tell me how the Wolves entered the city. I only knew that he was complicit. He often encouraged me to draw Queen Erianna into the city without her guards. I did not know at the time what he meant to do, but I knew he meant the queen harm. I presume that he intended to capture her and deliver her to Zavaan through the hidden passage."

"You never asked me to leave without a guard," Erianna points out for Lorennt's benefit. "When I suggested the idea to you, I always found myself hemmed in by guards. Even those days that I meant to slip out to the barracks without escort, my guards awaited me in the bailey."

Trent explains, "Silla relayed to me all of your plans so that I could ready an escort for you."

"You protected me," Erianna surmises.

"I never wished to see harm befall you," Silla concurs. "Thus, I told Trent of your plans while making excuses to my father that your guards would not hear of you leaving without an escort, and we were unable to slip away without their notice."

"Thank you," Erianna murmurs.

Silla inclines her head. "Neither did I wish harm to befall Lady Nev."

Lorennt snorts. "I doubt that."

Silla and Erianna do their best to ignore him. "Fearful that my father would find a way to slip a poison into her food, I made it my business to have my father watched. Twice he found a servant willing to do her harm."

"It would not have reached her," Lorennt argues. "All the food that goes to my wife and sister has first been sampled by a taste tester."

Erianna startles around. "I had no idea."

However, Silla knew. "Unfortunately, my father found a way around your tester, Majesty. He extorted two servants by taking captive the man servant's wife and a woman servant's child. I retrieved the captives from my father's house in the city and provided the servants with coin to flee."

Disbelieving her claim, Lorennt contests, "I thought you were fearful for your mother, that you would not do anything that saw retribution befall her."

This, I can answer definitely. "Harm did befall Lady Hugler for Silla's interference. She told me that twice Zavaan beat her and cut off locks of her hair."

Silla clasps her hands together in a white knuckled grip. "I received letters from Zavaan with bloody locks of my mother's hair pressed between the page. That was when I learned how desperate my mother's situation was. I did not know until then that the Ruphiri were at our estate."

Trent leans toward Silla as if to offer comfort but catches himself.

"I am sorry, Silla," Erianna whispers, feeling guilt that is not her due. She still feels responsible for Zavaan.

"When my father came to me and claimed that General Tareth was getting close to uncovering the truth of his involvement, he provided me with details about General Kannik to muddy the waters of the investigation. He said that if I did not cooperate in full, a beating would not be my mother's punishment this time."

I lay my hand on Erianna's shoulder when her face pales.

"My father does not care for my mother or me," Silla offers the paltry excuse for what Lord Hugler would have ordered done to his wife.

"So you delivered the anonymous letter incriminating Kannik," Lorennt clarifies.

Silla nods.

Recalling the timeline of events, I ask, "What was the latest scheme Hugler concocted, the one meant to kill Nev and Erianna?"

Silla shrugs one shoulder. "He did not tell me, only that I was to help him unconditionally when the time came. From his cryptic remarks, I gathered that he intended to help the Ruphiri invade the city again. I argued with him, asking if he wanted Malsihra to burn. He either did not care or the destruction of the capital was part of his plan."

A taut silence descends on the room. It is broken when Lorennt inquires, "Do you have anything else to tell, Lady Silla?"

"Your Majesty," Silla addresses Erianna, "I do not deny frustrating your investigation or hiding my father's involvement. However, I also endeavored to protect you and Lady Nev at great cost. I ask that you recall our arrangement, all of the favors I have accumulated by aiding you, ways which stretched beyond this business into dealing with the court and," Silla's eyes flit to me then back to Erianna, "other matters. In spite of my complicit deeds, you are indebted to me, Your Majesty."

Erianna slashes her hand through the air when Lorennt would have derided Silla's claim. "Go on."

"As such," Silla calmly continues, "I wish to claim all favors owed to me in exchange for my mother's freedom and a stipend for her after my father's death. You cannot object to her release as she played no part in my father's plots. She is innocent but by the unhappy association of being married to a villainous cur."

Erianna does not take long to consider Silla's bargain. "Granted."

Silla exhales, settling back into her chair.

"Do not look so relieved, Lady Silla," Lorennt ominously cautions. "You have not been granted clemency."

Silla smiles tightly. "This I know."

CHAPTER THIRTY

ERIANNA

January 8th

The charges are repeated at length with legal words attached to them. Malfeasance. Venality. Party to murder. Extortion. Harboring an enemy of the realm. Treason. Intent to commit Regicide.

Most are hanging offenses by themselves. Stacked atop each other, there is no escape for Lord Hugler.

Silla made certain of that.

Though Lorennt wants Silla to hang alongside her miserable sire, I am convinced that Lord Hugler left her few choices and believe that she never wanted harm to befall Nev or I. To that end, she *did* work as my spymaster and thwarted some of her father's plans.

"But not enough," Lorennt declared following Silla's private hearing. My pleas on her behalf fell upon deaf ears. Lorennt means to have justice.

"Lord Galderon Hugler," the king pronounces once all the witnesses have spoken and all the evidence has been presented to the court at the formal trial, "I find you guilty of all charges. You are sentenced to hang at dawn on the morrow. All your property and possessions are hereby confiscated by the crown excepting a stipend for your widow."

"Lady Felice Hugler. Step forward." The guard takes the lady by the arm and helps her toward the king. "I find you innocent of any involvement in these dealings with the Ruphiri and clear your name of all charges brought against you. You are free to go." The ugly clank of manacles contrasts sharply with Lady Hugler's sweet voice expressing her thanks.

Louder than her mother's gratitude and the murmurs of the masses is the silent peace expressed on Silla's face. Lorennt has granted her mother freedom from her tormentor as well as the gallows. Silla is content with that resolution.

"Lady Silla Hugler. Come forward."

I grip the arms of my chair as Silla approaches the dais with quiet dignity then bows before Lorennt. "Your Majesty. I thank you. I accept your judgment of me as just."

Lorennt arches a brow at the woman. "You have not yet heard my sentence."

"I do not need to," she replies. "Thank you for allowing me to call your court home these past years. It was a kindness I shall never be able to repay." Silla bows again then walks toward her father, knowing the death penalty also awaits her.

Lady Hugler begins to weep and dashes toward her daughter. The guard restrains her. Lady Hugler collapses in his arms, reaching for her little girl.

Run, Erianna! Run! Please, Arcto! Not our little girl! Spare her, please! My mother's own screams leap across time as my father's wickedness sentenced her to death. If I could have traded places with her, I would have. Silla found a way to do just that.

Hot tears fall fast from my eyes, staining the bodice of my gown. I bite my tongue till I taste blood. I must not interfere. This is the high king's decision, not mine. Behind me, Valor's hand settles on my shoulder, commiserating with me in the present and bracing me for what is yet to come. I grip it tightly.

It was not at all difficult for me to sentence the brigands to death. They earned it. But has Silla? According to the charges, yes, she has committed treason, aided in a plot to murder, lied to the queen, was complicit in the attack on the west side that led to a massacre by not speaking out when she should have. But in my heart, I know she never wanted any of that. She protected the one she loved, and it cost her everything. Justice should allow room for mercy.

"Lorennt," Nev whispers, taking her husband's hand. "Please."

Lorennt's temples pulse with anger. I do not move from my throne though the room shimmies through the veil of my tears. *This is Lorennt's decision. He is high king,* I remind myself once more. My shoulders shake with the force of my contained sobs as I fight the tide of my mother's final pleadings for my life that somehow sound the same as Lady Hugler's for her daughter.

Silla looks toward me and offers a sad smile. *Friend,* she mouths the word to me.

I remember her holding my hand a few months past when my grief following Leer's funeral capsized me. Silla also sat stalwartly with me after Lorennt's anger nearly killed Leer. And Silla was the one who washed my babe and wrapped her for burial in the blanket I sewed to welcome Illyanna into the world.

Friend, I reply to Silla. *Forever.*

She wipes tears from her eyes with manacled hands.

"Lorennt," Valor urgently mutters. "Do not let your anger set a course that cannot be undone. Leave room for mercy."

The king looses a slow breath and looks at the three of us, though he lingers on me. Quietly he mutters, "I owe you, Sister. Nor can I be the one to visit grief on you again. I told you that I regretted that day when my anger nearly killed Leer. I find myself presented with the chance to prove it to you.

"Lady Silla," he calls out. "I did not grant your leave. Return to the dais." After another long minute of expectant silence, Lorennt rises to his feet and descends to face Silla. "Lady Silla, I find you guilty on the counts of lying to the queen, abetting a criminal, and interfering with our investigations. However, I do not find you guilty of treason. Furthermore, I believe that you were extorted into committing them upon the verified mortal peril of your mother. It is my judgement that as such you will receive a lesser sentence. Effective immediately, I strip you of your title and all the privileges thereof. You shall be reduced to a penniless commoner and sentenced to work in the castle until such a time as we are satisfied with the recompense for your crimes."

The uproar in the great hall covers the sobs I can no longer contain while I watch Lorennt take the key from the guard to personally unlock the manacles on Silla's wrists. Whatever words they exchange are drowned by the clamor of hundreds of shocked exclamations. Silla lowers to her knees, bowing humbly before Lorennt as the guard releases Lady Hugler. Mother and daughter cry on the floor, clinging to each other as Lord Hugler is dragged off screaming profanities at all of us.

Part Three

Take Heart

CHAPTER THIRTY-ONE

VALOR

January 13th

"Tell me a story, Warlord." Erianna circles the small room, drifting through beams of moonlight.

"What sort of story, *Královna*?" The shackled prisoner sits at his ease, watching my queen move about the room. He does not comment on the oddity of being woken in the middle of night or that we are the only three in the room.

I, however, tried to reason Erianna out of her decision to speak with Torvarik immediately since it is half past two. But she was insistent.

"Where did the name 'Ruphiri' originate? It is not a Limban word, nor an ancient word. Neither is it a family name. How did our people come by it?"

"*Our* people?" He stresses in the common tongue they use for my benefit by unspoken agreement.

Erianna passes behind him while she grounds her assertion. "That is what you have been attempting to impress upon me with our little talks—that the Ruphiri are as much mine as is the native language we share. Zavaan also seeks to impress reminders of my Limban people upon me, though I suspect his motives vary from yours, Torvarik. But I am content to continue playing these verbal matches of hide and seek between us. Thus, do tell. Why 'Ruphiri'?"

Torvarik smiles, a sharp looking thing, until Erianna passes through another beam of moonlight. His expression shifts toward longing of such affectionate depth that I step forward, blocking her from his view.

The warlord blinks, clearing away the offensive expression. "As told, your *Královna* brings to mind my wife."

"And as she said, *which one*?" I repeat Erianna's words, embedding them with malice.

Torvarik considers us, holding close his thoughts until Erianna returns to his view. "My first wife. Annekeh." Her name is issued with reverence from a mouth that seems better fit for curses.

His expectation of a rejoinder hangs in the air, but he will be disappointed if he thinks Erianna or I would deride the love of a husband for his wife, even if it is surprising to glimpse it in this Ruphiri.

"A lovely name," Erianna responds. "I wonder that you consented to leave your harem for such an extent of time."

"It was not a decision made lightly. But you are skipping ahead in our game, *Královna*. Let us return to the matter at hand." He crosses his arms, setting the manacles to clinking. "The name 'Ruphiri' did not originate in Limba. It was brought to our people in the spring following their first winter in the Spires."

"Brought to them?" Erianna queries.

"Brought to them," he confirms, "by the barbaric Ruphiri tribe that sailed across the Eastern Sea to harvest from the rich waters off the Limban coast."

"Truly?"

Torvarik continues the history of his people. "The barbarians spied the smoke from our people's fires on the beach. Seeing the plentiful number of women, they struck out for the shore. Our people were startled but defended themselves well, beating back the Ruphiri while capturing some of the young men of the tribe. The barbarians fled, abandoning their own. It seemed like things could only get worse from there since some of the few Limban men were killed in the skirmish, but as it happened, the Limban women were most welcoming to the Ruphiri men. By the time the following spring came around, the Ruphiri men were one with the Limban people of the Spires. When the barbarians returned en masse, they were greeted warmly and invited to remain on the coast of the Spires. Eventually, the Limban people and Ruphiri became indistinguishable from one another. They intermarried and adopted many of the traditions of the Ruphiri including the name."

"Fascinating," Erianna comments, ceasing her pacing with her back to me. "Does that account for most of the differences between the Ruphiri and Limban people these days?"

Torvarik inclines his head. "Today, we Ruphiri have more in

common with our barbaric ancestors than our Limban ones."

Erianna leans her back against me. I wrap my arms around her shoulders before asking the most pertinent question in my mind. "How will that affect inviting the Ruphiri back into Limba?"

"I should think it is quite obvious," Torvarik states. "Zavaan has promised them the conquest of Limba. He intends to wield *Královna's* power to capture the Limban throne. Once he has Limba by the throat, he will bring the Ruphiri down from the Spires and turn us loose on Limba, dividing it into territories governed by warlords—*zars*."

Erianna shivers, though it is less from cold than trepidation. I bring my mantle forward so that it drapes her frame, covering us both.

"Why are you telling us this?" Erianna murmurs.

Torvarik's glower darkens the shadows in the hollows of his cheeks. "Because Reuel Zavaan will be the downfall of the Ruphiri Nation."

We should have anticipated this. Maybe Erianna did. But I have only seen the probability that Torvarik wishes to hand Erianna over to Zavaan.

"You want to replace him."

"I want what is best for the Ruphiri. That is not Zavaan."

"Then why not kill him before now?" I challenge.

"Because I have not been afforded the opportunity without risking the lives of those under my protection."

"Your harem," Erianna states.

"My wives. My children. The thralls that serve my family. I am responsible for a village of hundreds. If Zavaan heard even a hint of dissent from me, their lives are forfeit. The evil he would bring upon my wives would be unconscionable."

Erianna presses closer to me. "What do you want from me, Torvarik?"

The warlord measures the queen, but his gaze rises to meet mine. "Kill Reuel Zavaan and all the Ruphiri who serve him."

CHAPTER THIRTY-TWO

ERIANNA

February 1st

"Surely you do not mean to wear *that* dress for your outing?"

My chamber maid is a bit saucy, but I do not mind. She is preferable to a dullard.

"You do not think it pretty?" I stand before the full length mirror, turning this way and that. The rich plum velvet shines in the morning light, accentuating my figure, but her dissent makes me reconsider the third dress I have donned.

"It is a fine dress for an evening at table, but you are going out with your suitor. You need something more eye catching. Preferably with a lower neckline."

A blush stains my cheeks. "Silla!" I am glad Karris is not still sharing my room to hear that, sad as I was to see them go. Kragorn escorted his family home a few days after the trial and has just returned from settling them in.

Silla titters while rifling through my dresses. "Look askance all you want, but rumor has it that the two of you were seen climbing out of the hayloft in the stable when you were supposed to be training that cantankerous horse of yours."

A smile of chagrin tilts my lips. Playing hide and seek with Valor in the stable seemed like a fine idea at the time, but I really did not think through my plan to have him catch me in the hayloft until we were having far too much fun *dancing* in the hay.

"Our dallying did not go as far as the stablehands have purported." Though we did redefine the word *boundaries*.

"*Mmhm*. Then why did I comb hay out of your hair yesterday?" She teases, pulling a dress from the hanger. The white on white patterned dyaspin silk gown is a recent purchase. I look like a queen of winter in the elegant garment with a modest train.

"Set that one out for dinner." I explore the depths of my rainbow reminiscent dressing room.

"I am not your lady's maid," Silla retorts, though she returns the dress to the hanger to remove the wrinkles.

"No, you are my *chamber* maid," I tease. "You have to earn your way up to lady's maid."

She grumbles incoherently though she does not mean it. Silla felt the threads of her life sever one by one and was beyond grateful that Lorennt halted the fraying of the rope before there was nothing left.

I withdraw a samite gown in hues of pale pink shot through with gold. The neck sits off my shoulders in a straight line just beneath my collarbone with layers of sheer fabric softening the skirt.

"That is a spring dress, and it makes you look more youthful than a queen ought," Silla weighs in on my selection.

"*Ah*, but that is the point." It makes me look and feel youthful, like a first flower of spring. Like a young woman who has no cause for reservations regarding marriage.

Valor offered me a new beginning. I intend to look the part today when I ask him to give it to me. When I ask him to take me as his wife.

"Besides, Valor has never seen me wear it."

"When are you going to marry that man?" She taunts, oblivious to my intentions.

I finger the pink samite. My ribs feel like an inadequate cage for a score of sparrows. "I will let you know after today."

Silla halts mid step. "Today? You mean to ask him today?"

It amuses me that Silla knows me well enough to realize it would be me asking Valor, not he asking me.

My breath trembles with nervous anticipation. "Today."

Silla's broad smile lacks artifice of any kind. "That is wonderful. Congratulations, Erianna."

"Help me off with this," I set about the laces on the front of the velvet dress when a knock sounds on the door. "Come!" I call out. Nev promised to help with my hair this morning. Silla has not mastered that skill as of yet.

Valor appears in the doorway to my dressing room, his face ashen.

I drop the laces of the velvet gown leaving it parted over my chemise. "What is wrong?"

He extends a missive to me. "Leelah."

My heart lurches as I rush to take the missive shaking in his grasp. "Oh, no! The babe? She was doing so well." The babe has already quickened and Leelah is beginning to grow round.

"No." Valor's stilted reply is not sufficient warning. "Zavaan captured Leelah."

Trent's hurried writing leaps off the page.

January 29th

Leelah was taken captive by the Ruphiri at dusk yesterday. I was in Parse when she was taken and have followed their tracks toward the Ascent. General Kannik has denied my request for a company to pursue them. He plans to lead a contingent in pursuit later today, but it is a token gesture. He claims that the Ruphiri are using the capture of one woman to leave Chishelm and the new fort vulnerable to attack. He does not care that it is Leelah who was taken. In fact, I think he is glad of it.

I will track the Ruphiri and not rest until I have Leelah in my sights. If I can rescue her, I will. At the least, I will prevent them from harming her.

All the children are safe. Tirzah is watching over them.

Look for the trail I will mark for you.

Come quickly.

Trent

Silla gasps over my shoulder. "But they have had her for three days…"

I clap a hand over my mouth, swallowing bile.

"Zavaan means to trade you for her."

I am unsure which of them voiced it. Fear clouds my vision, forcing me to cast Leelah into my role.

Leelah being dragged into dark caves.

Leelah suffering Reuel's hands.

Leelah losing her babe when he…

"No!" I snarl. The room comes into sharp focus, every detail heightened. "We will get her back. I will not abandon Leelah to my fate."

I put the missive back in Valor's hand. "We leave in one hour."

My ferocity helps him find his. He must have received the missive while waiting for me at the bottom of the stairs. "Full armor," Valor orders before turning on his heel.

I rip the laces from my gown and throw the velvet garment to the floor followed by my chemise. Silla passes me layer after layer of clothing. Then come the boots, greaves, vambraces, and my cuirass.

"What was Trent still doing in Parse Kítaran?" Silla wonders aloud. "He was only supposed to help Kragorn escort them home before heading south to visit his family."

"Thank the Creator he was there. It buys us time to formulate a plan." I strap my dagger to my thigh.

"Under the best of conditions it could take you a week to reach the Ascent, and that is if you ride without rest."

"Then you best pray we do not have to go all the way to the Ascent." I take stock of my weapons after buckling the heavy belt around my hips. Leer's dagger. My twin dagger. Daisy.

I sling the baldric for Violet across my shoulder. Perhaps she will finally be christened with blood.

Nev appears in the doorway to my dressing room. "I just heard." She passes a fussy Laszlo to Silla and steps behind me, gathering the length of my hair. "Lorennt has gone to help Valor rally a company."

"Surely he does not mean to go, too?" Silla worries.

"No," Nev assures us. "He knows better than to leave Malsihra without a defender."

But the strain in Nev's tone conveys that it was she who had to remind her husband of this. Nev works my hair into a pair of tight braids then weaves them around my head so that no amount of tugging will pull them free.

"Thank you." She knows that I mean both for my hair and for making Lorennt see reason.

"Wait," Silla says and turns to my drawers of accessories. She pulls out the pair of stiletto-like hair pins she gifted me for my birthday the previous year. Nev accepts them from her and weaves them into my hair until only the decorative ends are visible. They present as a bit of vanity not the lethal weapons I could make of them.

"Kill him, Majesty." Silla fiercely commands with her vulpine smile.

I return it with a nod.

"We will pack your bag for you," Nev declares, taking my saddle bag from the shelf. "Go."

※ ※ ※

VALOR

Kragorn's wrath rumbles like a landslide. Nothing and no one can turn back the obliterating force. "Not. My. Wife."

If Zavaan ever made a tactical error it is this—Leelah Tareth was not meant to be a player in his game.

I plant my hands on the map of Malesiir, glaring down at the topography separating us from Leelah. "I estimate we have two day's advantage over the forthcoming demands from Zavaan."

"Not that Kannik is due any thanks for it," Anders grumbles.

"He will answer for that." Kragorn marks one more man for destruction for standing between him and his wife.

"We will deal with him later." I don the role of the voice of restraint that Kragorn normally fills. "Our goal at present must be to utilize the warning Trent bought us to lay a trap." My finger marks the paths that lead to the Ascent. "We know they passed by Chishelm. This route will take them directly to the Ascent, but not without drawing attention. It is more likely they went this way or this way." I tap the two locations.

Anders points to the southerly route. "This path is mostly open fields. It is less travelled, but there is not much cover. But this," he indicates the northerly trail, "cuts right through a canyon. If I were settin' up an ambush, this is the one I'd choose."

"Agreed," Kragorn says.

"We can assume that Zavaan means to trade Erianna for Leelah. He has been unable to draw her out of the capital any other way, so he has baited his hook with something she will not ignore." I stare through the map, envisioning how the exchange might go. "If we try to escape the exchange with both women, Zavaan will kill Leelah." The truth sounds colder than it did when I acknowledged it in my head, but there it is.

"You know what we must do," Kragorn warns me, on a parallel track to my own. "We need to give him what he wants."

I nod, giving outward acknowledgment of what seeks to shred me inside. "But only for long enough to extract Leelah." How I will give my beloved into that murderer's hands even for a short time I do not know. I attempt to shove my fears for Erianna aside at present.

"Once we have Leelah, we get our Majie back." Anders drags a finger across the map. "This is where we spring our own ambush and disembowel that gutless poltroon for cowering behind our women."

Growls of approval roll from Kragorn and I.

"We must assume Zavaan still has spies in Malsihra, if not the castle itself," I caution Anders. "That means you need to leave straightaway and collect your company from Old Fort. Go toward the Ascent from the southerly route then lay in wait here. You need to beat a path there if you are going to outpace us and Zavaan."

"I'll get there in time," Anders assures me.

"If Zavaan had a care for his own men, I would suggest trading our Ruphiri prisoners for Leelah," Kragorn points out, wishing that the cost of recovering his wife was not the endangerment of the woman who will be mine.

"But he does not."

Anders chomps at the bit. "If you're just gonna yammer, I'm heading out."

I give him my signet ring to grant him access to whatever troops he requires, then clasp his arm. "Good hunting."

"You also," Anders grips my shoulder. "Tell that little warrior of yours I'll be waiting for her at the Ascent with a sword and a smile."

My chest tightens to the point of pain as I nod.

Anders clasps Kragorn's arm next. "I've never met a woman with more fortitude than your wife. If anyone can make Zavaan regret the day he crossed paths with them, it's Leelah Tareth."

"Well I know it," Kragorn affirms. "Good hunting."

※※※

ERIANNA

I stalk the tiny room, glaring at the beautiful day outside for daring to shine brightly when my world is so grim.

The clank of chains turns me about. Two guards lead the warlord into the room toward his customary chair.

"Leave us," I order the guards.

"Majesty?" They pause in affixing his shackles to the chair.

"Leave!" I snarl, baring my teeth.

Whether from my bearing a shade away from violence or the real threat of the sword in my hand, the guards drop Torvarik's manacles and back out of the room, joining my royal guard in the corridor.

"What has he done?" Torvarik questions softly.

"He has taken my best friend hostage. I am awaiting his ransom note demanding me in exchange for her."

He sighs. "I am sorry, *Královna*."

"There is nothing for which to be sorry. I am going to get her back."

Torvarik is thunderstruck. "You cannot be serious."

"Do I look serious!" I retort extending my arms to the side, Daisy still clutched in my sword hand.

"You will not survive an encounter with Zavaan," he rebukes. "Your friend is lost to you. Accept it and move on."

"You lie!" My blade becomes acquainted with his neck. "I shall use you to increase my chances of success."

"He will not trade me for her. You know him better than that."

"I do."

Torvarik moves like a flash of lightning, wrapping his hands around my sword hand and slamming me into the door. "He will break you, Erianna! He will not stop until you are on your face before him, your crown on his head, his boot on your back! You cannot trade yourself for her!"

At the commotion, my guards try to breach the door but Torvarik bars it with the press of our bodies.

That is when I know for certain. Even with him this close, at his mercy, I am not afraid. And I tell him so. "I am not afraid of you, Torvarik. You will not harm me, though you have wanted me to think you will." I smile up at him. "You need me alive, too."

The warlord glares down at me. "You are reckless."

"This I have been told," I smirk. "Sit down in that chair so my guards do not interrupt Valor from his preparations."

"And then what?" He retorts.

I sheath my sword, trading it for the key that I fit to the locks of his manacles. His eyes open wide as, one by one, his bonds spring open then fall to the floor. "Then we will come to terms, Torvarik."

※※※

I know how far Valor and I have come when I stride into the lower bailey leading Torvarik by his loosely rope-bound hands and Valor does not react.

"We need him," I offer by way of explanation.

If Valor notes my twin dagger missing from its place alongside Leer's, he does not comment. "Tell me how you are going to recover me from Zavaan once we trade me for Leelah."

"I am glad you arrived at the same conclusion we did," he says though the tension rampant in every inch of the muscled warrior does not abate.

"Turn her aside from this fool's plan, Commander," Torvarik

mutters beneath his breath so none overhear.

Valor's eyebrows scale his worry lined brow. "What concern is it of yours, Warlord?"

Torvarik glowers. "Let them believe you will trade me for this Leelah if you must. But when it comes time, I pray you do not turn *Královna* over to the *Král Vragh*."

"Careful, Torvarik," I chide with a satisfied smile. "Your faith is showing again."

The Ruphiri glares at me with a look that falls short of loathing.

Valor gapes at me.

Ask him, I silently encourage.

With solemn quietude, Valor says, "Torvarik, were you redeemed by the Creator? Are you one of His own?"

Torvarik narrows his eyes on Valor and locks his jaw. But as Valor knows, it is unthinkable for anyone who has been redeemed by the Creator to deny Him.

Truth rings in the few words he utters. "I am His."

Valor is stunned, but I chuckle once. Then I begin to giggle. They both stare at me like I am mad.

"I found a sheep in *Wolf's* clothing!" I chuckle again at the absurdity of it all.

Torvarik shakes his head, deploring my bad joke. Valor rolls his eyes.

"Now what?" Kragorn demands, striding forward.

My mirth dries up. "I am bringing insurance with us."

Kragorn glares at Torvarik. "We decided he would not be useful for trade."

"I am aware," I concur. "But they," I shrug my brows in the direction of the onlookers, "do not know that. I think it best we keep everyone guessing about our intentions as long as possible."

Kragorn jerks his head. "Fine. But my sword is thirsty, Ruphiri."

Torvarik dips his chin ever so slightly before Kragorn and Valor break for the ranks of the cavalry.

"Leelah is his wife," Torvarik states.

"She is."

"I do not envy the man." Now that I have peeled back his mask, Torvarik deigns to reveal a bit more of his character to me. "I have spent the past eight years concealing my Annekeh from Zavaan's notice. It will not be a kindness to your friend to return to him what is left of his wife once Zavaan is finished with her."

Dread finds a home in my stomach. I take up Leelah's weapon of choice to fight it. "Pray, Torvarik. Pray and pray and pray."

CHAPTER THIRTY-THREE

VALOR

February 4th

Zavaan's ransom letter arrives shortly after dawn by an unexpected courier. General Kannik rides upon our company followed by a modest contingent of soldiers west of Chishelm. Kragorn is only too happy to greet the general with a fist to his face.

"You blethering imbecile!" Kragorn roars. "Why did you deny Trent the command of a company to rescue my wife?!"

At the promise of violence, Erianna's personal guards close ranks around her. Torvarik also stays at her side. Though Erianna asserts that we could release his bound hands without fear, I am not so trusting of the Ruphiri, even if he truthfully told he is one of the redeemed. Rather than press for his freedom, Torvarik argued that he must appear as a prisoner lest spies carry word back to Limba ahead of him that he is a betrayer and his family suffers the consequences. Nevertheless, my queen had her way in that he is bound so loosely he could free himself if needed, and I suspect the dagger bearing the inscription *Warrior Queen* is somewhere on his person as another bit of insurance.

"I followed procedure," Kannik argues, spitting blood to the ground. "A lone soldier arrived at my fort demanding the use of a company without a scrap of evidence to support his claims or note of writ from a superior officer."

I nudge Granite forward. "No evidence excepting his first hand account and your knowledge that Trent answers directly to me."

Kannik glares. "As I said, I followed procedure."

"Does your defense still have legs now that all Trent told proves true?"

Kannik holds his tongue, scanning the large company at our backs while Kragorn opens his fist to read Zavaan's letter then hands it over to me.

Dearest Wife,

Or do you prefer to be called Beloved these days? Happily, I will know soon enough.

It has taken me longer than I hoped to discover the means of securing our joyful reunion, but at last, I have it. Rather, I have her, though I cannot say for how long. Your friend has a barbed tongue that I would like to tame. Knowing how you feel about infidelity, I have kept myself for only you, my Little Queen. But I am quite taken with the remarkable shade of her hair and those wildcat eyes of hers.

I will await you in Aspen Canyon west of the town of Larkspur. Come prepared to greet me with open arms, and I will release your friend to her husband. You know how I hate breaking apart families, but I am determined to have my wife at my side when I return to Limba.

Do not tarry.

Ever Yours,

Reuel

Hope and despair war within me. I desperately hope that Leelah has not yet suffered at Ruphiri hands. I despair that I must surrender Erianna to that ravishing murderer.

"Well?" She calls out.

I fold the letter and tuck it into my pocket. "It is as we expected."

"Then we must hurry," she urges.

I jerk my head. "General Kannik, return to Chishelm straightaway with your patrol."

"If you are hunting Wolves, I will accompany you," he argues. "It is tactically foolish to not avail yourself of additional soldiers."

"You will return to Chishelm or receive disciplinary action!" I order, riding upon him.

The animosity he levels at me is nothing less than insubordination, but I do not challenge him for it. There is another he has more greatly wronged. That man sidles forward to issue his own challenge.

Kragorn's sword sings as he draws it from its scabbard. "Kannik. I call your honor as a man and a soldier of Malesiir to account. You have spat upon our vows of conduct by refusing to set aside your pride and aid my defenseless, hurting wife and see justice satisfied. After I have recovered my wife and spilled the blood of her captors, I will have my satisfaction from you. I demand a trial by sword."

Kannik draws his own sword and touches the flat of it against Kragorn's blade. "I accept your challenge and will defend my honor with my life."

If Kannik does value his life, he will tender his resignation immediately and shove off to start a new life in the Commonwealth far from Kragorn's reach.

Our company parts to let Kannik's through. I track his every step, not trusting him to go without stirring up more trouble. My vigilance pays in dividends when that fool of a man draws even with my queen. He smirks at her and mutters something I cannot hear. But Torvarik does.

In a blur of motion, the warlord launches from his saddle, tackling Kannik to the ground. Horses prance around the men brawling in the snow churned road. Erianna shouts commands in Limban that Torvarik chooses to ignore as he hammers his bound fists downward upon Kannik's prone body. Soldiers rush forward to separate the men, dragging the warlord off the general.

I jump to the ground to take control of Torvarik before he forgets himself and directs his punches toward the soldiers hauling him back.

"Enough!" I bark, shaking him hard.

Frenzied eyes meet mine while his crooked teeth part in a growl. "He deserves death!"

"He will get it," I assure him though the warlord is not appeased.

"Get off me!" Kannik bellows, shoving away the help of his men and stumbling to his feet.

The general is a bloody mess but a quick perusal reveals the warlord is merely muddied.

"I will kill you!" Kannik shouts then spits in Torvarik's face.

Torvarik roars back, "Repeat what you said to *Královna* for the commander to hear and it will be you who dies!"

Kannik sneers at us then mounts his horse.

"We do not have time for this," Erianna reasons. "Mount up." She taps her heels to Reaper's flanks, taking away my option to square with Kannik as our company follows her lead.

When we are alone, I bow my head to Torvarik. "Much obliged, Warlord. I am only allowed to settle so many disagreements with fists."

His lip curls in disgust. "Malesiirian rules. We Ruphiri have no use for them."

Though loath to admit it, I prefer the Ruphiri way of solving arguments.

※※※

Dusk slashes a pink line across the indigo sky as if the painter's brush got away from him. The open field dotted with fires and tents affords us a magnificent view of the heavens. But my eyes stray toward the earth searching for a different depiction of winter's radiance.

Despite being the very heart of our company two hundred strong, our queen has slipped quietly to the fringes. Apart from the men gathered around warm fires, she sits huddled beneath a fur lined mantle, attempting to blend into the shadows of evening. I cross the distance between us that has been taut since she insisted on reading Zavaan's letter.

Wanting to respect her desire for space if she needs it, I sit alongside her, leaving room for the evening breeze to wend between us. But Erianna slides closer to me, laying her head on my shoulder. My heart convulses as I press a lingering kiss to the top of her head.

"Can you do it, Valor?"

I grimace. "Let you be brave and face him alone, even if only for a short while?" I rub my gloved hands down the rough wool of my pants then clasp them together between my knees, fidgeting.

"You have not thought about it, have you? Not truly."

"No. I cannot."

Her hand settles overtop mine, stilling my anxious motion. "It must be."

"Must it?" I argue, turning my gaze upon her and unsettling her from my shoulder. "Almighty help me, Erianna, but if it was not Leelah, if it was anyone else, I would not let you do it. Even now, even for Leelah with the life of her and her babe in the balance, I keep praying for another way."

My selfish honesty does not make Erianna run. She only comes closer, stepping over my legs to sit between my thighs and reclines her back against my chest. It is where I need her. I need to wrap her safely in my arms, sheltering her from the harsh world.

"This will be over soon," she vows.

"It will." I am terrified of how it will end.

The Voice of Truth braces me from deep within. *Take heart! Be of good courage! For I have overcome the world.*

The promise carries me from this moment to the next, and the one after, and will remain true even on the day that I will watch her walk into the camp of the enemy.

"I have been thinking about after. About the future." Erianna fiddles with the buckle of my vambrace. We have not dared to remove our armor even while we sleep, necessity demanding we remain in a state of readiness at all times.

"Oh?"

"I am sorry I cannot give this occasion the holiness it is due. I had planned on it being so special."

I frown at her strange apology, drawn fully into this moment with her distracted from my fears of the future. "What occasion?"

"I suppose this might be better though, with all my plans delineated down to what truly matters. Just you and I." Erianna angles her body to gaze up into my face. "Valor Ironforge. You are my heart's love. You are my other half, and I will never be whole without you. It is my greatest desire to share all of my days with you. Will you spread your mantle over me, giving me your name and the protection of your love evermore, and redeem me from widowhood? I wish to be your wife."

Within those beautiful winter eyes is surety. She is convinced of my love for her, certain that she can trust me, and confident that our lives are meant to be united.

I pull my mantle around to cover Erianna. Just as Boaz once covered Ruth, the widowed foreigner in his land, I do as she asks, granting the humble request made by a heart far braver than mine.

I do not know how I manage to speak past my throat choked with emotion, but I fit words to the action. "My beloved Erianna. I will redeem you. I will give you my name. I will protect you and shelter you." Tears glimmer in her eyes like so many stars. I wipe them away, cupping her elegant face. "I will love you with my whole being and cherish you every day of my life. Not a day will pass that you do not know you are loved." I remove my glove and open the palm of my left hand to her, revealing the scar where my blood mingled with hers, binding our lives together though neither of us could know what that would look like at the time. "Nothing can move me from this vow."

Erianna's tears course faster as she touches her radiant smile to my palm, kissing the scar. The feel of her breath and soft lips twists and flips my insides. "I love you. As soon as we have returned from this, I want to become your wife."

Her determination makes me smile. "You know I will not oppose that plan."

She laughs, tucking her head beneath my chin.

I gather her to me, holding her through the night and into the uncertain light of dawn. No matter what may come, she is mine. Just as I have ever been hers.

CHAPTER THIRTY-FOUR

ERIANNA

February 6th

The Creator is merciful to us. The distance we cover could not have been achieved without His speeding our way. We pass Larkspur at midday six days after leaving Malsihra. With only a few miles remaining between us and the canyon, Valor arrests our ground eating pace.

He and Kragorn call all the captains forward for a final review of our plans. Truthfully, the action is unnecessary since we all know what is supposed to happen today, all of which hinges upon Anders awaiting in ambush at the Ascent. This little stop is just to make Zavaan, who is surely watching for our approach, think we are scheming to attack the second we have Leelah. But therein lies the diversion. Presuming the Ruphiri ride like hellhounds out of this canyon, something Valor will ensure happens by pursing them with two hundred soldiers, I will be safely returned to Malesiirian hands by nightfall.

Just a few hours in the company of my enemy. I have survived longer. It is the smallest price I could possibly pay to free Leelah. I only hope Zavaan spoke true, a daft hope if ever there was one, and Leelah has not suffered beneath the Ruphiri.

I lean in the saddle to pat Reaper's neck. He licks at the bit in his mouth and prances beneath me. My frayed nerves are doing nothing to reassure him. I glance around our company. All the horses are flicking their ears to and fro. I wonder what they hear? Can they smell the predators nearby?

I straighten and adjust the baldric slung across my shoulders securing Violet. From my periphery, I note Torvarik's ambling approach.

"Come to talk me out of this?" I query.

His bound hands draw back on the reins. Reaper does not like the other horse crowding his space and nips the palfrey to show his displeasure. Torvarik pushes his mount forward rather than allowing him to retreat. Reaper tosses his mane, flinging slobber in annoyance.

"I come to prepare you for battle, *Královna,* in the way of your people." He loops his reins around the pommel then from a pocket withdraws a small piece of charred wood. The warlord raises the coal tipped wood and touches it to my cheek, drawing a straight line down. "Two lines," he illustrates his words by drawing a parallel line to the first. "The first denotes the worthiness of the bearer as a warrior of great honor. The second marks him as a warrior of courage, fearless in combat against his enemy." He draws the two vertical lines on my opposite cheek. "The last lines," the wood touches near the corner of my eyes and smudges a black line across each of my temples, "mark you as a warlord, a *zar* among your people. One capable of commanding others and delivering your enemies to the grave."

I hold my chin high as Torvarik makes the same marks on his face. In spite of the danger to his family and his own life, he has claimed me as an equal in a way that the Ruphiri will recognize.

"There is loyalty and blood between us, Erianna. We are kin. We are of Limba." Torvarik faces forward, staring balefully down the road that will bring him into a battle against his own men.

I jerk my chin in agreement, certain that any words I offer will be redundant.

The captains disperse into the ranks of soldiers. My heart thunders in my chest.

Take heart! Be of good courage! For I have overcome the world. The verse Valor impressed upon my mind sends deep roots in every direction. I repeat it to myself over and over. Storm cloud eyes meet mine across a sea of faces.

It is time.

I let Reaper's reins out ever so slightly, giving him permission to carry me onward. Valor's gaze moves over my war marked face then past me to Torvarik. He nods his approval. I imagine Torvarik does the same. The language of warriors transcends borders and needs no words.

Valor takes my gloved hand in his and kisses the back of it. Within his eyes is the consuming declaration of his love.

The miles between us and Aspen Canyon fall away with each jarring beat of our destriers' hooves as I ride between Kragorn and Valor.

For Leelah. I tell myself. *For an end to Zavaan's reign of terror over my Ruphiri people. For justice for Malesiir. For Leer. For Illyanna.*

The trees shrouding the sharp sides of the canyon tower before me.

Take heart... Be of good courage...

Take heart...

Take heart...

Take heart!

We slow to a walk, pressed close on our sides by the canyon. No more than four can ride abreast. Our soldiers will not be able to rush to our aid.

Concealed within the trees I sense the weight of dozens upon dozens of eyes. Not all of our men will come out of this alive.

The unfairness of it all strikes me afresh. Why should my life cost more than theirs? Why can none of them see that there ought to be a way forward that is not paved with death?

But the time for reasoning and wondering is over. At the opposite end of the canyon are the mounted ranks of the Ruphiri. Zavaan waits on foot at the fore. Leelah stands at his side positively livid. Bruises mar her face as though she has been repeatedly backhanded.

I am enraged.

"That is far enough, Commander," Zavaan calls.

Valor and Kragorn draw to a stop, but I am tempted to unleash Reaper on the scourge. My anger carries me several lengths past the men at my side.

Zavaan's burning gaze warns me not to be foolish. "Anxious to greet me, Wife?"

I stop Reaper and slide to the ground not needing to be told how this will play out.

"You do not need your weapons," Zavaan instructs. "After all, you are among family." The hate in his voice cannot be missed nor the way he scans the long line of men behind me for the one who marked me as a Ruphiri warlord.

I lift Violet over my head and hang the baldric from the pommel of the saddle followed by my weapons belt and the dagger from my thigh. When I leave the small throwing daggers in my vambraces and step away from Reaper, Zavaan shakes Leelah, making her hiss in pain. Apparently, my faculty with weapons is not something he will risk. I stow the two daggers in my saddlebag and take a step forward, grateful for Silla's foresight with my hairpins.

Valor orders, "Send Leelah to us then Erianna will come to you."

Zavaan smiles. "I think not. They will proceed simultaneously."

He does not warn us that if we cross him Leelah will die. We already know that is his intention.

It is up to me now.

For each step that I take forward, Zavaan takes a step forward with Leelah. I hold tight to my anger, fixing my eyes on her face, not his. But it becomes more difficult as the distance narrows. I glimpse Zavaan slavering at my approach.

You are mine, Little Queen.

I shiver and reach a hand to my hip to grip the hilt of a weapon that is not there. Instead I return my gaze to Leelah's then slide my eyes down to her waist that is beginning to swell with her babe.

Worth it.

I hold my head high and march on.

Zavaan stops and releases Leelah. I keep walking until I draw even with her. Leelah wraps me in a hug. I hug her back tightly.

"It is going to be alright, Majie," she whispers to me when I should be the one reassuring her.

"I know," I whisper back. "Do not worry. Go to your husband."

"Touching," Zavaan drawls. "Had I only known that the life of one means more to you than the lives of hundreds…"

My gut knots as I step out of Leelah's embrace. "Go."

She hesitates, looking at me then back at Zavaan before continuing.

There is nothing left but to fix my eyes on the *Král Vragh*. Defiantly, I meet his gaze.

I am not afraid.

His lustful eyes move over me, voracious for the power of my royal blood. His hand reaches for me.

I will not be afraid.

His anticipation gets the better of him, bringing him toward me. "Greetings, Wife."

I lock my jaw, pouring all the hate I feel for him into my expression. It amuses him.

I will not be afraid.

Reuel Zavaan's hand closes around my arm.

Instinct overtakes reason. I jerk back, trying to break his grip on me, but as with a dog, resisting only makes the situation worse. His fingers bite into my arm, easily pulling me off balance since I had not intended to fight him. My body collides with his. Again and again I tell myself to be still, to stop fighting, but I cannot. My ingrained responses are in control.

Almighty, help me, I am afraid!

"No!" I scream, battering him with fists and feet until he spins me around and bends my arms behind my back, knotting a length of rope around my wrists.

"This is not 'open arms,' wife. I see I must remind you of your place." Then Zavaan's face is buried in my neck, forcing his repulsive attentions on me. His tongue laps my throat. "Your fear tastes like wine."

I buck in his grasp, turning my pleading gaze to Valor as I rail against Zavaan.

"Leelah, move!" Valor shouts.

I hold the face of my betrothed in my sight, wordlessly begging him to *do something*.

"Leelah!" Kragorn demands.

I do not understand! What are they waiting for? This was not supposed to happen! The exchange should have been so fast that Zavaan did not have time to shame me.

"Leelah, hurry!" They urge her.

Halfway between them and Zavaan, Leelah has come to a standstill, watching Zavaan and me.

"Run!" I scream at her. Valor cannot charge Zavaan until Leelah is safely hidden from the arrows trained upon her.

With determination, she looks to her husband. "It is like we always say, Kragorn. If only we had been there…"

"No!" He bellows. "Do not! Leelah!"

But Leelah turns on her heel and runs *toward* me. Zavaan lifts his head, bemused by the turn of events.

"Where Erianna goes, I go," Leelah declares overtop the background of Valor and Kragorn's roared dissent.

Zavaan laughs loud and long. "Far be it from me to force a woman to do what she does not want to do."

"Leelah!" I plead with my friend, touched by her loyalty and furious with her stupidity.

"Sorry, Majie. This is not going to go your way today." She walks confidently into the waiting ranks of the Ruphiri. Zavaan propels me after her with a firm grip. A rider leading Zavaan's horse breaks away from the pack.

I fumble over what to do now that Leelah has utterly ruined our plan. Do I continue resisting and risk Zavaan punishing Leelah as a means to hurt me? Rescuing both Leelah and I will be more than twice as difficult for Anders, especially since he is not prepared to do so.

I dare a look over my shoulder at Valor hoping he knows what to do. It snaps something fundamental in him, because he damns all our plans and digs his heels into Granite's flanks. Kragorn follows. The hissing of loosed arrows fills the air. I am unable to see what happens next because Zavaan hoists me to the fore of his saddle and swings up behind me. Leelah has been scooped up by a cowled Ruphiri.

At a full gallop, Zavaan aims for the ranks of Ruphiri who part before him then close the gap to protect his escape. A portion of the Ruphiri wheel their mounts around to follow us. The sounds of battle recede rapidly as we depart the canyon, pounding over the road toward the Ascent.

But then the unthinkable happens.

Zavaan turns his horse off the road and takes a game path deeper into the heart of Malesiir.

Far away from Anders's waiting ambush.

CHAPTER THIRTY-FIVE

VALOR

Arrows fall like hail as the Ruphiri spur out of the canyon, leaving a remnant to bar our path, while our own archers attempt to shoot the enemies out of the trees. "Advance!" I bellow, dismounting and rushing up the incline to contend with the resistance before running Zavaan to ground. Our soldiers cannot move into the valley until we make room for them in the tight funnel.

Kragorn is climbing the hill alongside me when an eager archer looses a volley in our direction. We take cover behind the thick trunks of the aspens for which the canyon was named.

"There is something wrong with your wife! Very wrong!" I yell at Kragorn. "The worst I would have called her before today is eccentric, but now—"

A steel tipped missile cuts off my words as I peer around the trunk. Since it nearly cut open my throat, I can hardly complain at the interruption. "What did she mean by 'If only you were there?'"

Kragorn scowls so deeply that I think not even Leelah will be able to remove its permanent mark from his skin. "It is what we say about our daughters. If only we had been there the ills that we help them recover from would never have taken place." Kragorn draws a dagger, gripping it by the blade, and nods that I do the same. "She thinks she can protect Erianna from what Zavaan will do to her."

"That courageous lackwit!" I do not know whether I will throttle Leelah or kiss her on the face when next I see her. That woman inspires the most extreme of emotions in me. "And curse us as fools for loving such indomitable women!"

Kragorn leans around the tree then ducks behind cover when

another arrow whistles through the air stabbing into the grooved bark. "In the crotch of the tree forty feet out. Don't miss."

The dagger fits between my fingers with a familiar weight. A smile curves my mouth that is nothing short of bloodthirsty. With savage delight, Erianna has told me this smile is the last warning she has to stop me from bloodletting. In this mood, there is little that could turn me from the edge I leap over save her small hands. But they do not hold me back now. If she were here, she would lead me over the edge and plummet gleefully at my side.

Kragorn leaps from behind the trunk, ducking low to present a smaller target as he throws his dagger. It resounds off the trunk of the tree with a disappointing clang. But it is of little consequence since he was just the distraction to provide me the extra seconds to line up my throw that fells the Ruphiri from the tree like a partridge.

There is no time to exult with the sounds of battle echoing over and again off the hillsides of the canyon. If Torvarik did not stray from the truth, the reinforcements that arrived before winter numbered near a hundred. Presuming Zavaan left half of his number here to impede our pursuit, we could be locked in combat for some time.

I pray fervently that Anders is prepared when Zavaan reaches the Ascent. Because if he is not…

※※※

The shroud of night makes one man appear much the same as another. Though it is something rarely done owing to the dangers of racing headlong with little visibility, we lope over the road to the Ascent. It worries me that we have come so far without encountering Anders. He was to take this route to meet us after recovering Erianna and now Leelah.

We are nearly upon the Ascent when all around us men roar, leaping into the road. I have my sword to hand and nearly bring it down upon the head of a man wearing the colors of my kingdom.

"Hold! Hold for Malesiir!" I command louder than the battle cries.

"Hold!" Anders echoes the order.

I push Granite toward the hulking giant that appeared in the midst of my cavalry. "Anders! What in the blazing depths is going on?"

"You tell me!" He barks back. "Been waiting here a full day for you to push the Ruphiri into us."

The earth opens at my feet, threatening to swallow me whole.

"What do you mean? We made the trade this afternoon at Aspen Canyon. They came this way!"

"That's what I'm telling you!" Anders reiterates. "They never showed!"

Panic races in white capped rivers through my veins. "Zavaan has Erianna."

With a profane shout, Anders drives the point of his sword deep into the earth.

Kragorn makes his way toward us from the back of the pack, echoing my words exactly. "What in the blazing depths is going on!"

"They are not here," I repeat while casting my gaze around the darkened forest, hoping with a bit more searching I might find the hole Zavaan has crawled in to wait out the night.

With my betrothed.

"But you have Leelah," Anders says. "Is she—"

Kragorn roars, his fury made poignant with fear for his wife. "She is with Erianna and the Ruphiri! Leelah would not leave her!"

"What!" Anders's voice climbs an octave.

I scramble for something to grasp to stop this madness. To turn back time. To return Erianna to my arms.

But she is with Zavaan.

My beloved Erianna is passing the night in Zavaan's depraved hands.

A guttural sound of rage erupts from my chest silencing the confusion of the company around me.

CHAPTER THIRTY-SIX

ERIANNA

February 7th

The night is old, well into the next day when Zavaan finally brings us to a stop. I feel as numb as my hands that long ago lost sensation. I slump to the ground in a heap where Zavaan drops me.

I close my eyes praying darkness claims me quickly. The thick Ruphiri dialect of Limban rumbles incoherently around me. I press my ear into the ground, trying to block the noise. Maybe if I don't hear and don't see, this will be only one more nightmare.

"Cut her hands loose, you barbarian!" A strident voice crashes upon my mind.

"As you are once more a recipient of my hospitality, I will do you the courtesy of reminding you what you seem to have so quickly forgotten," Zavaan's patronizing voice precedes the sound of flesh violently meeting flesh. "You do not give me orders, Leelah Tareth!"

There is barely a pause in Leelah's demands. "She needs water! You will have a very dead queen on your hands if you do not allow me to attend to her. That would make you a greater fool than I know you to be!"

A strangled sound makes me fight. "Stop!" I roll about, struggling to sit with my hands bound behind my back. "Zavaan!"

With a gasping breath Leelah falls into me. She inhales sharply, regaining her breath only to loose it again in a creative litany of nearly profane phrases. At her vehement utterance of "horse apples," I double over, cackling. This is the most absurd situation in which I have ever found myself. Me, Reuel Zavaan, and Leelah Tareth who is audaciously making demands of a mass murderer but is too scrupulous to utter real profanity.

I laugh harder until hysteria turns the sound brittle. A sharp slap cracks across my face, snapping my head to the ground. I catch a mouthful of gritty snow. I spew it out between bouts of hysterical laughter.

Valor has no idea where I am.

But Leelah is here to care for me.

Leelah—whom I am risking my all to rescue.

But she seems determined to rescue me.

I laugh harder, gasping as knives of pain stab between my ribs. "Cannot… breathe…"

My hands spring apart behind me, but it does me no good as I cannot feel my arms from my shoulders down.

Cruel fingers dig into my cheeks pulling me upright. "Stop this!" Zavaan snarls.

My eyes widen in fright at his fury, but I am not in control of my response, which is gasping hysteria.

"Give her over to me and pass me a water skin?" Leelah says sternly, but it sounds like a request not a demand.

With a shove, Zavaan releases me. My face connects with her knee causing me to bite the inside of my cheek. Blood pools in my mouth, gagging me with its metallic taste.

The spout of a water skin touches my lips. I sputter on the first mouthful of water. The cool liquid serves the dual purpose of cleansing my mouth and being a shock to my overwhelmed body.

"There, there." Leelah whispers, stroking my back. "I am here. Everything will be well."

Tears gather along my lashes, but she quickly brushes them away.

"No weakness. Do not give them anything to wield against you. It is time to be brave, Erianna. Be stronger than them. Takes the hits and the cruel words without showing fear. They feed on fear—Zavaan especially. Deny him what he wants."

I grip her hand around the water skin. "Did he… He… hurt you?"

"No," Leelah utters. "And he will not hurt you in that way either."

But the fear of the night presses down, crushing me. "He will."

"Listen to me," she hisses urgently. "You must not show him your fear. You must take it captive and submit it to the Almighty. He has not given you a spirit of fear but one of power and sound mind. Cling tightly to that truth. Trust me, Erianna, you are stronger than this. Show your enemy the Warrior Queen." She looks pointedly at the black cloaked men stalking through the shadows. "They are weak. They need to incite fear in others to make themselves feel powerful. Deny them that feeling. Do not give them what they want."

"Alright." I struggle to hold myself upright.

Leelah takes my gloved hand and presses it to her belly. Beneath the palm of my hand, I feel the fluttering kicks of her babe, so innocent and utterly unaware of how fragile its life is. "We are going to get through this. I would not risk my babe if I did not believe that with absolute certainty. Do you hear?"

Not for myself, but I will do anything, absolutely anything, if it helps protect Leelah and spares the life of her babe. I grit my teeth and jerk my head, remembering to run to my Fortress. "Almighty, give us Your strength. Make us strong for the fight. See us through these shadows. Lead us out of the camp of the enemy into the light of day."

"We are not alone." Leelah smiles like a mountain lion. "Within us is the most dangerous force to fight the darkness. They have no idea the foolish thing they have done by taking up arms against the Almighty."

※ ※ ※

VALOR

I am not sure who makes me see reason and convinces me to give the order to set up camp, but I am going to break his ribs. It is unconscionable to be pouring over a map while Erianna and Leelah are at the mercy of the Ruphiri.

"I told you!" Torvarik accuses from across the tent. He has already said this twice. His reproving glare has not wavered from me for the last hour as we collected reports from all the soldiers who had the best vantage of the Ruphiri fleeing our onslaught.

Torvarik still wears the blood of his countrymen that splattered him when he made good use of the Warrior Queen's dagger. It now hangs on a weapons belt he relieved from a fallen Ruphiri along with an assortment of other gear. His armed state makes our soldiers nervous, but he earned it. Besides, we have far greater concerns.

"Why did Zavaan not go to the Ascent? What could he gain in waiting?" I ask him.

"Zavaan never does what he ought to do. He always does the unanticipated. That is why I have not been able to bleed him dry. I tried to tell you, but you would not listen. I have been trying to kill

Zavaan for years, to undermine his reign, but he is too slippery. Now, because of your arrogance, Limba's brightest hope, our *Královna,* is in Zavaan's camp being torn apart—"

"You think I do not know that! That it is not all I can think about?" I bellow into his face.

"You let this happen!" Torvarik yells back, bristling for a fight.

Anders pushes us apart before our shouting match becomes bloody. "Enough! You must have some idea where he went."

"None that is logical," Torvarik counters. "He has what he wants. His goal will be to get her out of Malesiir as quickly as possible. That was always his plan, and we all knew it. Get *Královna* and get out of Malesiir. He cannot afford any more delays. The Ruphiri warlords have grown restless. If he remains in Malesiir much longer, he risks insurrection."

"Then he may still go toward the Ascent." Kragorn stares down at the map. "Would he suspect our ambush and have gone into hiding to wait for us to clear off?"

"It is possible," Torvarik allows.

"What else might he have done?" Kragorn asks while I pace. "You said that you and the other reinforcements arrived by ship anchored in the harbor at Halden."

Torvarik confirms it. "We sailed on one of the Malesiirian ships we captured off the coast of the Commonwealth. We weighed anchor in Halden under cover of darkness in the month of October."

"So that was what you lot were doing in the North!" Anders exclaims.

"Zavaan kept the townsfolk so busy fending him off that they did not notice the ship that sailed in and out of their harbor." Torvarik's explanation does not endear him to any of us, but, again, we have greater concerns.

I ask, "Where is the ship now? Could the ship dock at Port Veritae and receive the Ruphiri?"

"It sailed back to the Commonwealth," Torvarik says. "And no. Zavaan would never take *Královna* through Port Veritae. The risk of discovery is too great."

I feel something go still inside me as I ask my next question. "What if the ship returned to Halden? Would he cross Malesiir with her?"

Torvarik weighs his answer. "He would. But to what end? He cannot sail at this time of year. The winter storms off the coast of Limba would topple the ship. Even sailing as far as the

Commonwealth would be unwise."

"But if pressed to choose," I continue, feeling this is significant, "would he chance fighting his way out of Malesiir or being at the mercy of the weather?"

Torvarik's expression draws tighter, considering.

Kragorn adds another thought. "What if he did not mean to sail far, only far enough to find a place to set ashore within the Commonwealth. Halden is much nearer the Commonwealth than Port Veritae, after all."

Anders scratches his bearded chin, "Escape open conflict with us and chance the weather only a little. Two days with good wind would see him out of Malesiir."

The warlord's expression resolves into a nasty smile. "He would choose the ship. And," he adds with a look bespeaking consolation, "Zavaan would be moving fast. So fast that breaking *Královna* might not be his first priority."

I seize on that wild hope. "Do you know the path he would take to Halden?"

Torvarik approaches the map spread on the ground. "I am afraid that he will try to counter whatever information I might give you by taking a path I do not know. But that does not mean we would be foolish for choosing the fastest route to Halden."

Kragorn recommends, "We break the company into three units and block all the exits. One group remains here to guard the Ascent. Another small contingent goes to Port Veritae and places the city on alert. We take the bulk of the cavalry to Halden."

"There is also the possibility that Trent managed to stay on the Ruphiri," I point out. "I have a strong suspicion that he made himself into a contingency plan by remaining out of sight. He might have been able to follow Zavaan though we failed. If that is the case, then he may be marking the trail for us."

"We can hope," Kragorn agrees.

CHAPTER THIRTY-SEVEN

ERIANNA

February 12th

Zavaan's frenetic northerly pace is the greatest evil he visits on us for five days besides the token blows to our faces to remind us we are captives. He even ensures we are regularly fed and watered, though not for our own sakes. He will not permit us to become weakened and slow them down. Because Zavaan is so determined to ride with all haste, I feel the need to make it difficult for him. But there is little I can do. To maintain the speed Zavaan demands, Leelah and I are bound to our own mounts. It is no small mercy that I do not have to ride on the fore of his saddle.

As if I have bandied my unspoken rejoicing too loudly, Zavaan makes a point of slowly unbinding my hands from the pommel and brushing his fingers over my arms and legs as he pulls me from the saddle when we pause to rest at midday. I do not allow myself to recoil but hold my head high pretending he is not worth my notice.

"Do you wish to play games with me, Little Queen?" Zavaan asks.

"I wish you to die," I retort.

He grins maliciously. "I really hope you try to kill me. I have always appreciated your spirit."

"Give me half a chance," I snarl. "I made a vow to put a dagger through your heart," I slap my hand against his chest, "or whatever this black thing is."

He seems surprised that I have dared touch him without being forced. As such, he tries to return us to the unequal footing he prefers by subjugating me. "What of your own heart, Erianna Zavaan?" His hand settles over it. "Does your heart beat with vengeance? Or does it beat for your husband?" He slides his hand downward to my breast.

But I cannot feel it. My hardened leather cuirass acts as a protective shell. Lest he realize this, I spear him with all the loathing I feel for him. "You repulse, *Vragh.*"

My response is not what he expects. Like a predator sniffing out a weakness to exploit, he assesses me. Then his lip curls. "I think we can dispense with the traces of your infidelity, Wife." A dagger materializes in his hand. I fight him for control of it, but there is no contest. The steel slices through the cuirass's leather laces beneath my arms. He rips it over my head, wresting it from my grasp.

For every piece of armor he removes from me, I struggle, not surrendering anything easily. Let it serve as a glimpse of the battle he will endure every day that he tries to hold a warrior queen captive. By the time my gloves, greaves, and vambraces are cast into the bushes alongside my cuirass, Zavaan and I are both bloodied.

I smile with feral satisfaction at the trickles of blood from his nose and mouth, the scratches on his hands, and the swelling knot hidden beneath his pants leg where my elbow connected with muscle. Actually, he might be more bloodied than me. I laugh in his face. To balance the scales, Zavaan throws one more punch that knocks me into darkness.

When I come to, Leelah kneels protectively at my side, her fists clenched. Zavaan and Brynjar, Leelah's keeper, have kept us separated these past days. I want to hug her and ask her how she is faring, but my slightest movement makes me moan. I feel the beating my body took in every inch of me, not the least of which is my pounding head.

"Be still. Keep your eyes closed," she whispers. "Pretend to be asleep."

I do as she asks rather than asking questions.

"What are they saying?" She murmurs.

I tune my ears to the heated conversation spoken in Limban then repeat it. "They are arguing about… a ship?" One of the men is quite upset about something. "The lord of the sea will not forgive a trespass in winter… Too dangerous…"

I have wondered where Zavaan is taking us, but he has not revealed anything nor have the other Ruphiri. Could this be a clue?

The dissenter's voice drops. "…Not all the way," I repeat. "Just far enough to be rid of the dogs on our trail."

"Kragorn," Leelah whispers his name like a prayer.

"…Traitor knows of Halden. Too great a risk… No other way…"

"What is in Halden?" Leelah asks.

My aching mind fumbles backward, aided by mention of the traitor. "The Ruphiri came by ship to Halden. That must be where they are taking us."

"And why we are going there so fast," she says. "Our men are close."

I open my eyes heavenward, but it is not Leelah's gaze that claims mine. Standing above us with a gleaming sword is Leelah's keeper. Brynjar's eyes are fixed on me, watching my recovery, but they are not the unfamiliar eyes of the enemy. They are the warm brown eyes of a dear friend.

"Trent," I mouth.

He winks though his menacing posture doesn't shift. A wash of relief flows through my aching body. We are not alone. Leelah is being cared for by Trent. He kept his promise.

Leelah says, "He found me within days of my capture and infiltrated their ranks."

I want to leap into the safety of his arms, but I hold myself still, protecting his identity. Trent's Ruphiri blade catches the sunlight, reflecting it and throwing it across the camp toward our enemies. If Zavaan or any of the others attempt to compromise or kill us, Trent will bring them down.

His attention shifts as a shadow crawls over me.

Zavaan's face blocks the sunlight. "We ride."

"To Halden?" I dare, hoping to help Trent plan our escape. "You are daft to sail at this time of year!" I do not know that for certain, but I know ships do not sail during the winter and the Ruphiri did not seem pleased about it.

Zavaan's eyes darken ominously. "You test my patience, Wife."

The things he names me have lost their power over me. Nothing Zavaan says will change what I know to be true. I know who I am.

That bolsters my confidence to foolish heights. Or, perhaps, I have been hit about the head too many times. "Try harder, little *Zar.* You are no *král* that can make me kneel."

Murderous light enters Zavaan's eyes as he bends over my prone form and whispers in my ear. "Do hold on to that reckless spirit until we reach the ship. I want you at your best when I lock you in my cabin and take a week to bring you to your knees before me. Again."

"Never again," I fiercely declare though a chill runs down my spine.

His hand closes around my neck. Slowly, his fingers spread, moving like snakes as they reach beneath the collar of my tunic. "It has been so long since I have had such a spirited woman as my wife. Thayas, my first wife, also possessed such spirit. Not surprising since she was the younger sister of Torvarik."

My eyes fly wide. No wonder Torvarik was so quick to join my side.

Zavaan chuckles. "Torvarik likes his secrets." But the thought of the man who betrayed him must leave a repugnant taste in his mouth, for Zavaan's hand once more clamps around my neck. He lifts me by my throat till my toes just brush the earth. "She broke quickly in my house. Too quickly. I cast her body upon the Spires for my wolves. But I have learned since then. I will not use you up so quickly, little queen. I will take much pleasure in making your days of torment stretch into years. Then, when you are unrecognizable, once I have all of the Continent at my feet, what is left of you will fill the bellies of my wolves."

Darkness blankets my eyes as he speaks, drowning out all save for his insidious voice. To prove his control, just before I lose awareness from his strangling grip, Zavaan drops me to the ground in a heap.

Lights burst in painful colors as I gasp for air. Leelah's arms come around me. I think I hear her growl.

Zavaan hums his approval at her. "You, however, I will not be so deliberate with. I will feast on you. And once I have had my fill, I will give you to my men. You, Leelah Tareth, will not last a single night."

Leelah pulls me to my feet alongside her. She looks into the face of evil and boldly declares, *"Make your plans, but they will come to nothing. Speak your words, but they will not stand. For the Almighty is with us."*

Zavaan's certainty trips over her proclamation lifted from the Holy Texts. But he collects himself and barks a laugh. "Is He?" Zavaan glances left then right. "I do not see Him. No, you are quite at my disposal, Leelah." He advances on her, but she holds her ground looking him straight in the eye. "Make no mistake. I will dispose of you. Far sooner than the woman for whom you relinquished your freedom." His eyes move down to the modest swell of her belly. "Very foolish." He shifts his focus to me. "How many have died for you, Erianna? Even I do not know the number."

I glare at him, though I am shaken to my bones.

"Mount up," he orders.

But Leelah will not let the enemy have the last word.

"In the Almighty, whose words I praise, in the Almighty I trust. I shall not be afraid. For what can mortal man do to me? Though all his thoughts against me are for evil, though he watches my steps and seeks to steal my life… in the

Almighty I trust. I shall not be afraid. For the Almighty has delivered my soul from death and has kept my feet from falling that I may walk before Him in the light of life."

To my astonishment, the *Král Vragh* takes a step back. Confusion and —dare I say—a touch of fear moves like a shadow over his face. He turns away from Leelah's fire and seeks his horse, ordering his men to bind us and make us ready to ride.

Leelah clasps my trembling hand. "You see, Erianna. The lies of the enemy crumble against the power of the Almighty."

I regret the dearth between the amount of Text I have committed to memory and the amount she has. "If only I knew more. I cannot recall the words of Truth to fight him like you do."

"Of course, you can! Even my little girls could. You need only sing. Our songs of praise are verses taken directly from the Holy Texts. It is why we teach them to our children. Those songs are the first verses from the Texts that they learn." Leelah hugs me tightly until the Ruphiri pull me away from her. As Trent leads her to her horse, she urges me once more, "Sing! Sing to fight the darkness, Erianna! Sing through the night!"

They bind my hands together then lift me to the saddle, tying the ends of the rope around the pommel. The horse's reins are placed in Zavaan's grasp.

He avoids Leelah's victorious countenance and fires his attack on me instead. "You look afraid, Little Queen. What has put a dagger through your heart? Surely not memories of what we shared in those caves?"

I see him murder Leer once more. I taste the revulsion on my tongue when he set his hands on me. The falsity of my bravado is leveled just as Zavaan desired. But what rises up in its place is not forced.

It is a song Ivy taught me atop the wall surrounding her home. She pointed out to the valley and the hills swathed in green and dotted with white sheep. I hear her sweet voice sing the verses that became written upon my heart. I match mine to it.

"I lift up my eyes to the hills, from where comes my help?" The first notes of the song quaver, but then they grow stronger and certain as Truth makes itself known. *"My help comes from the Creator, the Maker of heaven and earth. He will not allow my feet to be moved. He who keeps me neither slumbers nor sleeps… The Almighty will keep me from all evil. It is He who holds my life."*

The words echo off the trees of the forest. They vibrate on the air.

They shine with light that pierces shadows.
And Reuel Zavaan is shaken.

※ ※ ※

VALOR

February 13th

Malesiir passes beneath us in what feels one long unbroken ride. Doubts pile upon us as mile after mile falls away without evidence of the Ruphiri. I look for the signs Trent would have left if we are on the right track. There are none.

If we have made the wrong decision, if this gambit proves fruitless, we will be so far removed from the last known location of Erianna and Leelah that there will be nothing we can do for them. Still, we press on.

My prayers that were once composed of many words have become a groaning refrain. *Almighty, please. Please, protect them.*

Kragorn has ceased speaking. He only doles out orders when necessary. But I know my brother. The less he expresses himself outwardly, the greater the number of his inward thoughts.

I am wrecked for him. What consolation can I offer? I can be assured that Erianna is alive, though Zavaan is surely destroying her. But Leelah is expendable. There is nothing compelling Zavaan to keep her alive and whole, nor to afford her any consideration for her delicate condition with child.

My gut roils again recalling Erianna's stricken expression, her eyes that pleaded with me to *do something* when Zavaan set his filthy hands on her. Will she ever recover from this?

Torvarik rides at the fore of our company that has dwindled in numbers with each day. Not all of the men or horses are equipped for the grueling pace we demand. Torvarik burned through three palfreys before I placed him on Reaper. That horse makes up for what he lacks in condition with sheer obstinacy. Granite is managing quite well, emphasizing Erianna's argument that the magnificent blue roan be the foundation stock for our someday stud farm. I happened to agree with her completely, but I pretended I did not so that she would persuasively argue me around to her point of view. Truly, I just wanted to see her speak passionately. My betrothed is vivacious.

Or she was.

Almighty, please. Please, protect them.

"Commander," Torvarik rides back from where he turned into the forest to search for tracks. He and I have shared the responsibility these past few days when he proved himself adept. "You will want to see this." He tosses a leather object to me. It is one of Erianna's vambraces.

My heart attempts to pound a hole through my chest as I ride ahead with him, Kragorn close behind. Torvarik veers into the bushes, dismounting and pointing out what he discovered. Erianna's cuirass is propped at the base of a gnarled tree. Her other vambrace, gloves and greaves sit neatly next to it. I take the cuirass between my hands noting the cut laces on either side and the blood flecking it.

"See here," Kragorn opens a rolled note that was stuck into the sheath of the vambrace then reads aloud,

"E drew first blood from Z. L and E are whole. Their singing scares the R.
Fly to Halden. They sail.
February 12th"

I cheer, seizing Trent's hastily dashed note and reading it for myself.

Kragorn's face splits into a smile that I feared was forever gone. "My wife knows how to fight!"

Torvarik reads the note over my shoulder and grins with all those crooked teeth. "I think I shall like serving *Královna*."

CHAPTER THIRTY-EIGHT

ERIANNA

February 19th

The brine of the sea awakens me during the night. For one fantastical moment, I think, I hope, I pray that it is Valor come to take me home. But the salt on the air is borne from the dull thrumming of the breakers crashing on the cliffs, not the scent of his skin. Nor is the detestable voice forcing itself upon me his soothing rumble.

"Do not think you will escape me as you did last time, Wife," Zavaan whispers in my ear.

I strain against the length of rope that binds my wrists together and my arms to my sides. My feet are likewise bound at the ankles. Zavaan made the mistake of waking me two nights past while attempting to wrap around me and steal my warmth. The flesh I gouged from him made him reconsider my limited freedoms.

So when he pushes me to my back and spreads himself atop me there is little I can do. Though he means only to scare me this night, my body still responds as it always has when a man I do not trust is too near. Bile rises in my throat giving me a way to fight I had not considered. I indulge my feelings of revulsion then expel my stomach upon him while my hands ball into useless fists at my waist. He shoves away, cursing me with every foul name, and prepares to take recompense for the insult out on my body. Even so, I am supremely satisfied—though I, too, am sullied with some of the refuse—until we seem to remember at the same moment that Zavaan has a more effective way of punishing me.

"No!"

He drags Leelah upright and promptly strikes her face with his fist while I scrabble uselessly on the ground. She doubles over, shielding her babe from the next blow aimed at her belly, and the one after that. The thuds of the Vragh's fists on Leelah's flesh are unbearable.

"Do not! Zavaan!" I kick to move myself across the frozen forest floor. My screams drown out the twang and whiz as rapidly fired arrows sink up to the fletching in the necks of the Ruphiri nearest Leelah. Zavaan is too near Leelah for Trent to risk slaying him in the dark of night. I must put distance between them.

"They have found us!" I exult, though I know it to only be Trent firing from the dark edges of the camp. "Here! Here!"

As I hoped, Zavaan abandons Leelah sprinting for me instead. He shouts orders in Limban, commanding his men to seize Leelah and defend the camp. Trent's arrows fell a few more Ruphiri who attempt to lay hold of Leelah. Zavaan lifts me off the ground, carrying me backward like a shield. Another Ruphiri who starts toward Leelah crumples.

"Run, Leelah!" I scream at my friend. "Run!"

This time, she obeys. She staggers with her first steps, but gains momentum until she is hidden by the cloak of night, arrows still covering her escape.

Zavaan hauls me away using me as both captive and shield while several Ruphiri peel away into the shadows to hunt the enemy and pursue Leelah.

"Here! Here!" I keep up the ruse that an army of Malesiirian soldiers is nearby until Zavaan shoves a wadded rag into my mouth. He seats me on his horse, and we vanish into the darkness, pushing onward to the coast.

Almighty, hide them. Help them, please!

※※※

The Ruphiri return empty handed to camp and report that there is no evidence of soldiers in the vicinity. With quietude, they tell of seeing Brynjar capture Leelah and ride after us, but Brynjar and Leelah are nowhere to be found. Then they hand Zavaan the bloodied arrows they pulled from their fallen—Ruphiri arrows.

In response, Zavaan does not yell or fume. He does not threaten or beat me. But my life is poised on the edge of his eroding self-possession. Death stares out from his burning eyes.

Men like King Boldizar who have devoted the better portion of their long lives in submission to the Creator exude His love. In an antithetical way, the manifestation of Reuel Zavaan's lifelong pursuit of darkness is the evil emanating from him. He has fully given himself over to the Deceiver.

It is not only me who senses the utter depravity of the man advancing on me. The other Ruphiri retreat, glancing about as if planning their escape. They have seen this side of him before and dare not be present when he comes unfettered. I tell myself not to cower, but I shrink back in fear as the veneers flake off and Reuel Zavaan's truest self is exposed.

He is wickedness itself.

Zavaan reaches out to stroke my face. His eyes crawl over my features that cannot be called attractive with weeks of grime caked on my bruised skin. Nevertheless, he looks at me with desire. I tremble when I understand what he sees when he looks upon me.

He is indulging in imaginings of how he will murder me.

His fingers stroke my cheek. Slowly, they spread to cover my mouth.

I restrain my screams behind clamped teeth. My fear is an invitation to use me for his every depraved whim. My suffering is the choicest of delicacies to him.

His thumb becomes enamored of my thrumming pulse. He presses into it. Ponders stopping it.

I want to look away.

But I am terrified to shut my eyes.

Zavaan's hands close around my throat, testing its fit between his hands.

"She is *Královna,*" someone speaks up. "Do we not need her alive *Kyzar* Zavaan?"

Calling upon him as their overlord is a ploy meant to preserve what he has insisted they need. I am under no delusions that they care whether I live or die—or in what manner either happen. Zavaan has convinced them that they need my twice-royal blood to claim Limba. That is what they want. In this moment with his layers stripped away, I finally see what it is Zavaan wants.

He craves the power to destroy. To hold death in his hands. To watch the Continent burn to ashes on the wind.

His hands close tighter around my throat at the same time the grip on his control goes slack.

Madness is the only thing remaining in his fevered expression.

Reuel Zavaan is insane.

"*Kyzar* Zavaan!"

His hands fall from my neck to his daggers. I scream, ducking my head behind my shoulder in a futile effort to protect myself.

Zavaan whirls around, unleashing himself upon his own men.

Blood sprays like ink across the forest. Ruphiri crumple to the ground. The smart ones flee like I try to do, heedless of my bonds. Landing hard, I twist my body to and fro gaining mere inches for all my struggle. Not that it matters. Some foolishly loyal soul picks me up thrashing and screaming.

It is all over in less than a minute.

Bodies lay in the snow. The metallic scent of blood is oppressive on the night air.

Zavaan stands in the midst of his murdered men. He turns in a circle searching for any others marked for death. Through heaving breaths he snarls, "You betrayed me and lost me one of my prisoners. Do not lose the other." He departs, stalking out of the camp alone.

We all hold our breath until the night swallows him up then wait in painful silence for another full minute, ensuring he is gone.

The air quivers with the shrillness of my voice. "Why serve a *kyzar* such as that? Why follow one who cares naught for you, who kills you without remorse?"

They have no answer for me, most will not even look at me. I suspect that they have a certain appreciation for his murderous tendency—until it is turned on them.

But a few Ruphiri toss guilty glances my direction.

They leave me bound wrist to wrist, arms to my sides, feet together. They do not give me water, though I ask, nor do they allow me to relieve myself, for which I also ask. I surmise that although they are convinced my presence here is for the good of the Ruphiri, it is to Zavaan whom I belong. They will not interfere with his possession. For interminable hours they leave me helpless on the ground. *Physically helpless only,* Leelah would say. My spirit, however, can fight. So I go to war.

I pray for Leelah and her babe's safety and that Zavaan will not find them. I pray that Valor will find me before Zavaan tries to break me aboard his ship. I pray that I would be given the chance to end Zavaan. I pray for an end to all of this.

A touch on my face rouses me from the sleep that claimed me against my wishes.

The metallic odor permeating my conscious thoughts makes me

long for this to be a nightmare from which I can wake and run into Valor's arms.

But it is not a nightmare conjured by my mind. No, this nightmare was conjured within the wasteland of someone else's imaginings.

"It seems only right that I should mark you as my wife since Torvarik marked you as one of my warlords."

Zavaan's hand imparts a bloody smear on my skin.

I jerk my head down, wiping my cheeks on the damp earth, on my tunic, anything to remove the stain of what he has done.

He laughs then spreads himself out alongside me on the ground. His arm snares my waist, dragging me nearer and imparting Ruphiri blood to my tunic. "Sleep well tonight, Wife. There will be no rest for you tomorrow."

A horrified scream climbs its way up my throat. I stifle it, cramming all my emotions behind the walls only Valor knows how to breach. Cold logic takes over, demanding that I search for a way to end this. Even if the chance is slim, I must try.

Zavaan cannot be allowed to live one more day.

CHAPTER THIRTY-NINE

ERIANNA

February 20th

Halden Harbor appears forbidding in the grungy dawn light. The sea is not of a mood to be trifled with. But that does not prevent the ship from advancing over its turbulent waters.

My eyes drift to the city of Halden that does not stir to life in the chill new day. Though I desperately long to see friendly faces, it is for the best. I do not want more of my people to die beneath Zavaan's hands. Instead, I take in the details of the structures. The framework of the city that will one day rival the vast expanse of Port Veritae seems stark and insignificant seated upon the hillside sloping toward the harbor. This place Leer named to honor me might very well be the last I ever see of Malesiir. Zavaan certainly means for it to be so.

"Look at it," Zavaan says, standing behind me upon the precipice and turning my chin toward the encroaching ship. "Does it look familiar to you?"

His presence at my back causes prickles of fear to rise over my skin. I can tolerate him at my back the least of all. He has me at such a disadvantage. But I will not cower. I breathe through the panic, tamping it down with the rest of my feelings so that I may evenly reply, "Should it?"

"Perhaps you need a closer look," he says then propels me to the edge of the cliff.

Heights have never bothered me. I rather like being perched atop the ramparts, sitting in treetops, or viewing the world below me from the prospect of a mountain. But Zavaan threatens my sanguineness in such things with the toes of my boots poised over the sheer face of the cliff. Far below, the ocean beats angry white fists against the rocks that bar its path.

Zavaan wraps his arm around my waist and pushes me another step that I cannot take. The heels of my boots scrape the promontory, kicking dirt into the air. My heart hammers louder in my ears than the violent ocean attacking the base of the cliff. I can either lean into Zavaan or lean into open space.

For one frightful moment, with the ship that will be my floating prison bearing down on us, I consider my chances of surviving the fall.

There are none.

Could that be the answer to my prayers? Surely, I could struggle sufficiently to drag him over the edge of the cliff with me. It would be a mercifully quick end to my life. Like the snuffing of a candle. Relatively painless, I imagine, especially weighed against what Zavaan has planned for me.

"You have gone so still that you no longer tremble," Zavaan notes, speaking into my ear above the onslaught of the wind. "Perhaps I should ease your turmoil and present you with the conclusion I drew last eve." A dagger appears in his hand, slicing through the rope that binds my arms to my sides. Were he not so well balanced on his feet, the motion of my arms springing free would have made my choice to fall or not moot. As it is, we remain atop the precipice, though for how long, I cannot yet say.

"What I learned," Zavaan continues, "Is that my future and yours are bound. You cannot disentangle our lives. If you kill me at this moment, your future vanishes with mine. If I kill you, my future is imperiled. The warlords will turn on me, and my surety of ruling them is no more. Within both scenarios, the Ruphiri and Limban people continue to suffer. We need each other, Erianna. There is no future without a partnership between us."

His words meant to persuade me do everything but that. Open air becomes more tempting than the embrace of the murderer. If I take him down, Valor can aid Torvarik's return to the Spires. Torvarik can take control of the Ruphiri. And wouldn't it be better for all the kingdoms if Zavaan was no more?

I fix my eyes on the horizon, accepting the action I must take, though I want there to be another way. I do not want to give up my life. But for my people, I will stop the slaughter.

A blast of sea air hits me full in the face.

Borne on it is a charge: *Take heart!*

I inhale the biting cold wind laden with salt and freedom.

Be of good courage!

The refrain seems to come from without, wrapping around me with the sort of embrace for which my heart longs. Then clearer still…

I have overcome the world. The Voice of Truth whispers within, pervading my every fiber. *Fear no evil, Daughter. I am with you. I am your deliverance and theirs.*

In the Almighty I place my trust, I say inwardly. Then I lean back into Zavaan's grasp.

And feel the force of Valor's gaze land upon me.

※※※

VALOR

The might of the ocean cannot compare to the powerful rage that thrashes within me. I watch from afar as the enemy holds my beloved over the edge of a cliff, toying with her life. One wrong movement could see them both plummeting to their deaths. It was what she wished for months past. She wanted to be the one to deliver them both to the grave.

Almighty, grant her courage! Overwhelm her fears and her guilt! Deliver her from evil!

Tantalizing moments pass. Finally, Zavaan steps back, carrying Erianna away from death and bringing her closer to me.

"Kill him slowly, Valor," Torvarik murmurs.

"You will not argue that the right is mine?"

"I have right aplenty," Torvarik asserts. "But the *Královna* gives you greater claim. I will content myself with cutting a path for you to the *Vragh*."

A path will be needed for the vast number of enemy soldiers that brazenly descend the cliffs in an arrogant line. By riding through the nights, we secured our position the day previous. A narrow margin but one that permitted us time to safeguard the shore of the bay and alert the inhabitants of the town to stay within their homes until the danger of clashing armies has passed.

On the opposite side of the beach, Kragorn is poised with half our soldiers to slam the Ruphiri between us. I count the enemy's numbers again and again to ensure we will not be surprised by reinforcements.

"They are all accounted for," Torvarik concurs. "Arrogant. His feet are surely stepping into his own snares this time."

Anticipation lengthens the time that cannot be more than a half hour from the moment I spied them upon the cliff to the moment Ruphiri begin alighting on the shore. I descry Erianna gripped in Zavaan's arms atop his horse, but Leelah is not at once apparent. Where is she? Her vibrant red hair should stand out like a beacon.

"Do you see Leelah?" I ask Torvarik.

He takes a moment to sort through the milling group. "I see only Ruphiri and *Královna*."

The knots in my gut twist tighter.

"She was—"

I sever his thought. "Keep searching for her."

The ship is within the harbor now, drawing nearer to the single pier projecting from the shore at which a vessel can dock. We watch and wait. My head aches from the restraint needed to keep me hidden while the Ruphiri congregate on the beach and dismount from their horses, preparing to embark.

Timing is quintessential to our plan that aspires to reclaim more than just our queen and Leelah this day—wherever she is. Unfortunately, Erianna does not know this or she certainly would not threaten the fabric of our scheme. I feel the fight growing within her even from this distance. I wordlessly plead with her to hold off just a bit longer. As Zavaan propels her over the distance between us, the filth on them both that I originally attributed to mud is not that innocuous substance.

It is blood. Dried blood streaked over her swollen bruised face and much of her torso.

"Where in the cursed depths is Leelah!"

Torvarik adjusts his grip on his sword, not voicing the conclusion that explains the excess of blood on them both as well as Leelah's absence.

Erianna docilely carries herself at Zavaan's side. It is the calm before the storm.

"Do not do it, Beloved," I urge.

She takes no heed of my quiet pleas. For what she has endured, I cannot blame her for wanting her pound of flesh from Zavaan, though it could impede our plans. Before the ship docks, my brave, bruised queen makes her stand. With bound hands, she launches herself at the murderer. I laud her fortitude and the range of maneuvers she executes with her hobbled hands, but it is for naught. Zavaan's fist comes up underneath her jaw, sending her into oblivion.

Torvarik restrains me when my beloved collapses in a heap at Zavaan's feet. "Not yet!" Torvarik hisses.

Zavaan hoists Erianna over his shoulder. She flops helplessly as he strides toward the dock that the ship—our stolen Malesiirian ship—draws alongside. Finally, with a reverberating thud, the ship docks and the gangplank is lowered.

My breath rushes into my chest in gusts. Urgency collides with opportunity. Bloodlust heats me like the scorching air from a furnace. Righteous violence erupts as I lead the charge against the Ruphiri.

On foot, we thrust into the line of Ruphiri queued on the shore, dividing their force in two halves. Behind me are the most accomplished soldiers, those capable of withstanding the intense fighting demanded by our battering ram strategy. The concentrated force of our attack is a risky gambit necessary to secure our ambitious ends. Torvarik stays my side, cutting down his countrymen with a ferocity that matches mine. In that prescient sense that comes in the heat of battle, at once intensely focused and dispassionately aware, I know the moment that Kragorn brings his cavalry to bear against the flank of Ruphiri. He cuts off their escape and forces the enemy to fight from two fronts without the benefit of organized command. Nevertheless, they rally quickly, calling on archers to pick off our cavalry while forming ranks to counter our attack.

It will be a bloody day all around. Both sides are travel worn and sleep deprived. But we do have the advantage of numbers. Slightly. Nearly fifty of the cavalry could not match the grueling pace that delivered us across the length of Malesiir. I estimate we outnumber the Ruphiri by a mere quarter.

I tear through my opponents, not attempting to fully incapacitate them as I plow into their ranks. My goal is to reach the other side of the fray, not necessarily aid in the battle. The boiling depths of my fury will be poured out on one man. And he is escaping.

Zavaan strides along the dock, Erianna limp over his shoulder.

"He leaves!" Torvarik bellows then momentarily slips into the Limban tongue to yell something before translating, "Zavaan abandons them! He abandons his own!" A moment of confusion hobbles the Ruphiri. They begin to shout what sound like curses.

I grin in spite of myself, liking this warlord more by the second. Torvarik is seeding doubt in Zavaan's leadership. It takes hold with the vigor of wildfire.

"Coward!" I bellow, bolstering his ruse.

Torvarik shouts in Limban, stirring up strife in his people. Some of them turn in disbelief to watch as Zavaan's boots trod up the gangplank. It makes it all the easier to rend their souls from their bodies, delivering them to the judgment of the Almighty. But a very real fear sets its hand upon my shoulder, as I watch Zavaan carry Erianna further away from me. What if he *does* abandon his own men now that he has claimed his prize? "She cannot board that ship!" I shout the words to Torvarik, but it seems to be another who reacts to them.

Suddenly reanimated, Erianna touches her hair then twists upward, violently pounding Zavaan's neck with both fists. He drops her instantly, sending her rolling down the steep gangplank while Zavaan roars. He twists, grappling at his neck, but for what I do not know.

"Faster!" Torvarik demands, seeing what I did not, so focused was I on Erianna. Ruphiri descend the gangplank to aid Zavaan while others rush to recapture my queen.

Swinging our swords before us, we press to the other side of the battle, closing the distance to Erianna while she finds her feet and sprints madly toward me. At my back is the resounding clash of steel where Torvarik has turned back to defend our flank. We made it to the dock on the other side of the battle, but we have isolated ourselves from our reinforcements. It was a necessary risk.

Though my eyes are hungry for Erianna, I move them past her, training them on the enemy. Blood runs in a stream down Zavaan's neck. Erianna did that! The *how* of it eludes me, but the *why* I grasp. My heart swells with pride. That magnificent woman planned her own escape and, by the looks of things, very nearly killed her tormentor.

I battle the last two Ruphiri that turned back to guard Zavaan's retreat. There is no mercy within my being for the men standing between my woman and me. One villain stumbles into the water clutching his arms across his belly, his insides protruding through the line I drew across his middle. I feel the bite of steel on my leg, I let the pain fuel the reciprocal stab into my second opponent's chest. Bone grabs the edges of my sword. With a kick and a jerk, I dislodge my weapon and shove the slain into the icy harbor.

Zavaan watches the scene unfold with preternatural stillness. His eyes hollow into unfeeling things that home in on Erianna as she escapes. Dread transforms to horror so quickly that I struggle to push the word of warning past my lips. Then he draws a dagger.

"Drop!"

In a show of blind faith, Erianna flings herself to the hard planks of the dock, choosing instant obedience over a gentle landing. That choice spares her life. Zavaan's dagger flips end over end through midair and clatters to the dock rather than severing her spine.

Lost to a predatory instinct that defies reason, Zavaan draws his sword and sprints across the dock. He means to kill her. No matter the cost. If she is not his, then she will be no one's. He is completely mad!

The glaive I kept safe these two weeks bangs against my shoulder as if to remind me of my duty to return her to her mistress. I drop Violet alongside Erianna's prone form as I race past her to engage Zavaan.

CHAPTER FORTY

ERIANNA

"*Královna*, rise!"

My disorientation ebbs, bracketing definition around individual sounds.

The ring of steel on steel.

Screams of pain.

Shouts of battle.

Horses' whinnies.

The pounding of boots that shakes the dock beneath me.

Wind and waves drone all around.

"*Královna*! Take up your weapon and fight!"

My weapon?

I open my eyes.

The most welcome sight greets me. Dark, ornamented wood tipped at one end with a mace and the other with eighteen inches of gleaming, curved steel. My eager hands reach for Violet but are restrained by the rope that binds my wrists. I groan as I crawl to the cutting end of the glaive. All of me hurts though I cannot give consequence to the pain. Cautious of the lethal steel, I squeeze it between my legs positioning the cutting tip against the rope. Intentionality rather than speed is needed to break the strands of coarse rope. Each thread of captivity that frays beneath my determination emboldens me and chases the layers of pain from the forefront of my mind. With a drawing motion, I pull the rope against the honed edge.

Calm.

Steady.

"*Královna*!"

Impatience threatens my control as the warlord calls to me, urging me to join the fight.

Steady.

My eyes stray from their task. A deeper set of emotions do more than threaten my control as the man that I would bind my life to wields his blade against that of my greatest enemy.

I nick my skin on the honed blade. It angers me. Why must my blood be the first to ever touch Violet? I attend to my task with renewed fervor.

Another cord of my bondage is rendered impotent. One remains.

My hands shake. I pull the rope taught, dragging it against the steel.

It snaps, falling away in a useless, frayed mass. My chafed wrists sting in the cool briny air. I welcome it, finding unparalleled pleasure in having been the one to remove my bonds.

Liberty now reclaimed that was willingly sacrificed, I spring to my feet, bringing Violet with me. I plant my feet apart, the right slightly behind to ready me for action as I assess the raging battle.

Ahead, Valor stands between me and the crazed fury of Reuel Zavaan, trading blow for blow. Both of them have already let blood from each other, but no mortal wounds have been dealt. I cannot help Valor without engaging Zavaan from behind, which I cannot do without jumping into the sea to circumvent their savage battle that occupies all of the limited dock. Zavaan's Ruphiri that came down from the ship face the same predicament as they wait at Zavaan's back for a victor to be decided.

"*Královna*!" Torvarik calls my attention away from the blood-fevered men.

I turn to face the coast where Torvarik holds back the onslaught of Ruphiri advancing from the shore.

"Here, *Královna*!" He struggles to bring the men down as they fight two abreast. Each man that he fells is replaced by another. Torvarik loses a stride of ground while I watch. If they break past him, Valor's back will be exposed.

Torvarik makes room for me to fight at his side by shortening the arc of his sword and adjusting his stance. I step into the gap, holding the line. Without restraint, I bring the mace end of Violet down on a Ruphiri. The blunt force kills him instantly. He slumps to the side, falling into the bay. There is no time to ponder his death, the first man that I have killed. A man whose name I will never know. Another steps forward to take his place. I shove him back, parrying his swings on the inflexible pole of my glaive. A rap on the head with the mace kills my opponent. Then he falls into the bay. That makes two.

"What is the plan?" I ask the warlord, trying to assess the battle being fought on the shore without splitting my focus. Because I do not do a good job of it, a sword grazes my forearm. How I miss my vambraces!

Torvarik covers my blunder, crossing his sword before me and cutting open the great vein in the neck of my opponent, spraying us with his blood. I position my glaive to shove his body aside, but Torvarik stops me. "No! We need a barrier to slow them."

He means to make a wall of bodies.

It is good that I have already distanced myself from my emotions. I spin Violet around and drench her blade with Ruphiri blood. The space in which we must fight is perfect for the lengthened reach of my glaive. I parry, thrust, and slay with impunity, doing all while protecting my vitals from the swords that cannot reach me.

"Where are our reinforcements?" I ask. Skilled as the warlord is, I would rather be fighting at the side of Anders or someone else whose moves I can anticipate.

"Attend, *Královna*!" He hurls a dagger into the chest of a Ruphiri before the enemy can make use of his drawn bow. "We hold the dock until your soldiers cut off the enemy tide. We cannot lose the dock! All is dependent upon it."

I commit myself fully to the battle, looking no farther than my next opponent. Then the next. Then the next. I force myself to stop counting when it becomes a distraction.

The sea churns red with the blood of the fallen.

※ ※ ※

VALOR

Zavaan attacks with the ferocity of an army condensed into a single man. His sword is an extension of his body, not a mere weapon. Every swing is perfectly timed, perfectly powered from his core. The length of the arc of his blade is trimmed to the optimal length from beginning to end, lending advantage to his transition from one move to the next. There is no room to strike with a thrust to undermine the path of his sword at the beginning of its arc. There is no time at the end of its arc to force him into a defensive maneuver. He is, in my weighty estimation, the most accomplished swordsman on the Continent. And I have entered our battle on the defensive.

The warnings that Erianna gave regarding the unpredictability of Zavaan's movements prove more than true. It is as if he is fighting three moves ahead of me at any given moment. Every strategy I lay out he has already seen to its conclusion before I can enact it.

I draw upon the hours of tactics I discussed with Torvarik, attempting to apply what he conveyed of Zavaan's fighting style to my advantage. The most I am able to do is hold my ground and prevent him from gaining an advantage over me, which is, in itself, a disadvantage.

I need more.

Zavaan smiles, cracking lines into the dried blood on his face. "You will not fall as quickly as the dead king, but you will fall."

I hope for an opening while he goads me as he did Grandileer, but Zavaan is still too many moves ahead of me.

"Do you know whose blood I wear?"

Parry. Parry. Thrust. Parry.

"Some of it is my wife's."

I grit my teeth. Parry.

"Most belonged to that other woman. What was her name?"

Leelah. I cut downward then adjust my sword's arc, rapidly changing the trajectory to cut diagonally. Zavaan leaps back, parrying.

"Was her name Leelah? Ah, yes. I recall my little wife crying it while I—"

A guttural yell erupts from my throat while I cut upward. Zavaan's blade bites into my arm as payment for my negligence. I twist, pushing away the edge of his sword on my vambrace.

Listen, the Spirit of Truth calms the frantic grappling of my thoughts.

"Where is Leelah?" I demand.

Zavaan's smile is satisfied by having provoked my question, ready to wield his answer like a knife hidden behind his back. "I killed her."

Liar.

Though Zavaan is coated in blood, I very much doubt if any of it belongs to Leelah. He has proved once again that he is a deceiver. Lies are his native tongue. I will hear nothing else. Nothing he says can change the course of what must happen this day.

His eyes flick past me but return to our battle. The Ruphiri shift anxiously at his back, gazing past me. Zavaan's eyes dart to my injured left arm planning to strike there. I ready my defensive parry, but remember at the last moment that he has not once conveyed a single intention with his body language. He strikes for my legs in one of the most subtle feints I have ever witnessed. I catch his blade on mine and shove into him with my shoulder. Not off-balanced, but made wary of my skill, we exchange cursory hews.

Again his eyes move behind me, wetting my curiosity, but I dare not lose focus again. Zavaan snarls. A knife sails through the air sinking into a Ruphiri behind Zavaan. Another follows, passing through a throat. Zavaan barks out an order in Limban that sends the men at his back scurrying for the safety of the ship.

"You are not leaving my kingdom alive, Coward!" The fury of Malesiir's Warrior Queen lashes across the brine. My sword echoes her edict, drawing a stream of scarlet from our enemy.

Torvarik's commanding voice slows some of the retreating Ruphiri. What he says in their language, I cannot know, but they take stock of their position between Zavaan and the ship that is being made ready to sail. Erianna adds her words to the warlord's, bargaining by the tone.

Zavaan interrupts my queen with a blatant threat while parrying my attack. The Ruphiri look between each other. Erianna's authoritative voice bites out a final time. It is the needed catalyst. Then chaos reigns.

Ruphiri turn on each other. Zavaan cannot see the mutiny at his back, but he hears it. And he rages. "I will take Valor from you for this! You will watch him die like Grandileer!"

It is not a hollow threat. Zavaan believes what he says, filling his declaration with truth.

I meet his fury, strike for strike, neither one of us gaining the upper hand. The puncture wound on his neck dealt by Erianna bleeds freely. The cut on my arm pains like a shard of glass that not even battle fever can entirely dull, likewise the one on my leg pulses with each flex of that muscle. Still, I press Zavaan hard, intent on being the one to avenge all of Malesiir against him. No matter the cost.

So much of what my beloved has suffered is because of this vile man. I will not be satisfied until I have bathed my sword in his life's blood. He owes that much and more.

"Together," Erianna says, asking me to enact a plan to bring an immediate end to this.

"No!" I vociferate. "He is mine!" My rage against Zavaan is consuming. Again and again I beat my sword against his, drawing blood and losing more in return.

I feed the flames of my rage with memories of what Zavaan has wrought till it becomes a pyre of vengeful hate.

The deaths of innocent people caught in his path of destruction…

The murder of my king…

The way he toyed with Erianna's life on the edge of the cliff…

The look on my beloved's face as he forced his vile touch on her… My impotence to stop him… To stop whatever came next…

As if sensing the bent of my thoughts, Zavaan feeds me poisoned images. "Erianna is mine. She will never forget my touch! Never forget how she whored herself to me!"

The pyre of hate threatens to consume me as well as my enemy, burning up righteous anger in place of vengeful wrath.

"Valor." The pleading voice of my beloved is like quenching rivers of water to the flames within. "Be righteous."

Her gentle plea does not attempt to deny or erase the evil that transpired, but it calls me to return to a higher standard, to take hold of holiness and give over wrath and vengeance to the just hands of the Almighty Creator.

I lose a step of ground against Zavaan. He takes it eagerly, feeding on the weakness in my defense. Countering his swings one after another, I wait until the time is ripe. His sword arcs toward me. With a shout, I throw my whole body into parrying his sword, shoving it down and pinning it to the side, following it to ground so that I am exposed to the dagger Zavaan draws.

Grinning up at him past the dagger poised to deliver my death blow, I witness shock eclipse the murderer's triumph.

Violet arcs through air in a hewing cut as my Warrior Queen satisfies justice. Steel severs flesh. Blood sprays. Erianna beheads Reuel Zavaan.

※ ※ ※

ERIANNA

Horror supplants disbelief in the hateful gaze that meets mine. The moment lasts an eternity in which I feel everything—the weight of my glaive, the momentum that pulls my arms and tugs my body round as I make the fatal cut, the resistance of his flesh then the release as it gives way against steel. Zavaan's head thuds on the wooden dock and rolls toward the churning sea. Torvarik shoves me to the side, and I stumble. He lunges for the head of the *Král Vragh*. Seizing it by the hair, he holds it aloft, screaming at the Ruphiri who still fight to the death for their unworthy ruler. My ears ring with the thousand sounds that assail me at once, unable to pick out a single one amidst the cacophony.

I thought I would feel immediate relief, yet I can only stare at the slumped headless body of Reuel Zavaan. The blood soaks the dock and streams into the sea, making the churning waters all the more violent for the clouds of crimson spreading outward from the slaughter.

Violet becomes a leaden weight in my hands, too heavy to continue holding upright let alone wield. The steel gouges the dock, reverberating through the pole of the weapon into my bones, but my ears do not let in the sound.

I pull my eyes away from Zavaan's body to look behind me, suddenly fearful that I will find the enemy advancing on my exposed back.

But there is only the carnage wrought by my and Torvarik's hands. Countless men who are now only piles of bodies and limbs. How many lives did I end this day? I stopped counting after the first few.

Appalled, I tell my hands to let go of my glaive that I desperately wished to grasp for weeks. I try to cast it from me, this weapon of destruction, but my hands will not obey. I lower my gaze to their white knuckled grip around the pole.

So much blood…

I flinch away from the gloved hands drenched in blood that wrap around mine, easing the death grip of my fingers till the glaive clatters to the dock. Those same hands hold mine, so large that a single one can clasp both of mine. The other gently guides my chin upward. My eyes follow.

Through blurred vision, I look into concerned storm cloud grey eyes. I stare into those stormy eyes for several moments trying to lose myself or center myself, I am not sure which. Nothing around me makes sense. I feel adrift. The steady touch beneath my chin holds my gaze in place, dropping an anchor into me. I recognize the other half of myself behind those eyes. Everything will be alright.

I am safe.

I am home.

"Valor?" His name is a whispered question that asks a hundred things at once. "Valor?"

He touches his brow to mine, not letting go of my gaze as his arm slips around my back. My knees weaken beneath me. He takes some of my weight off them. Slowly, his words find their way into my ears, displacing the ringing. "You are safe. It is over, Beloved. I have you. You are free."

My repetitions of his name are broken by uncontrollable trembling that chatters my teeth.

What is wrong with me?

"It is shock, Erianna. You are going through shock. It will pass," he assures me. "Unless you are injured?"

I start to shake my head, then wonder, *Am I?*

He sees the uncertainty in my eyes and efficiently searches my body for life threatening injuries but finds none. His query, however, raises one of my own that is answered far less satisfactorily when I discover numerous lacerations on his limbs, several that have not fully clotted.

My brow lowers in reproach. He laughs, though it holds an unusual brokenness. "You scold me for wearing the marks of battle when you wear them too?" He fingertips skim my face, though it is pressure enough to remind me of the bruises that surely march like colorful banners across my skin.

I bow my head to conceal them, embarrassed that, once again, I could not defend myself.

"Stop," his head dips to catch my gaze once more. "You do not have to hide from me. Not any of your wounds. Do you understand?"

I do, and I mean to tell him straightaway that I am not so wounded as he fears, but loud shouts go up from the far end of the dock. Valor does not hesitate to draw his sword before turning us that direction. Tucked safely into his side, I gaze upon my would-be prison. My skin prickles with fear that I refuse to acknowledge, though my arms lock around Valor's waist.

Torvarik strides across the deck of the ship while holding Zavaan's head high. The comparatively few Ruphiri that allied with us at the end stand around him, brandishing their gore slicked weapons and punctuating his speech with shouts of assent.

"What is he saying?" Valor asks.

I listen to the words blown toward us on the steady wind. "Torvarik says, 'Here is the traitor to all Ruphiri. Here is our enemy. No more is his sword on the back of our necks. No more are our clans in peril from this murderer without honor. We have ended his torment of our people."

Valor considers the men who have perpetrated crimes against our Malesiirian people. "What did you promise them? To make them turn on Zavaan." Tension limns his words equal to that within the muscles flexing their grip on his sword.

My answer will not please him. "I swore to allow them to return to the Spires if they repented and turned against the true traitor of their people."

"After what they have done? What they watched Zavaan do to you? No! I will not allow them to escape unscathed!" Valor's fury feels unquenchable, a violent tempest within him. And he does not yet know that the bruises upon my flesh are not solely from Zavaan, but also from the men I am pardoning.

However, I have my reasons for making the decision I did. "Valor, they were just as captive to the *Vragh* as Torvarik was. It was what made it an easy choice for them to turn on him. I watched him murder his own men last night."

He shakes his head, struggling to accept it. I make one more attempt to convince him using his own words from Silla's trial. "We leave room for mercy."

Finally, the tempest within him yields to the Spirit of Truth that extended mercy to us when we were also undeserving. His sword determinedly lowers to his side.

I set my left hand over his heart. His arm tightens around me in response.

The silent communion between us is broken by a thought that bursts from him. "Leelah! Where is Leelah?"

I wince, jarred by the remembrance of the last time I saw her. *Zavaan's fist striking her face... The horrid sound of his fist thudding against her abdomen...* Was the babe injured? Worse?

"Erianna," Valor demands, now on a level with my face and gripping my shoulders. "Where is Leelah?"

"Last night when Zavaan—" I retreat from illustrating what transpired in the moments before Leelah's escape. "She ran. Trent covered her escape. They could not find either of them."

Valor's eyes search mine, trying to make sense of what he sees there.

But Leelah has never been one to allow another steal her glory.

A strident whistle trills across the battlefield. Vibrant hair the color of red wine whips in the wind, drawing our gaze to the source of the sound. High upon the road that leads down to the bay, seated atop a Ruphiri horse, and safe in the arms of Trent, is Leelah. As they amble forward, an answering shout goes up from the shore. Kragorn climbs upon the nearest horse and spurs it toward his wife. He covers the distance separating them at a gallop. Leelah's smile flashes white, urging her husband onward. Kragorn leaps to the ground and reaches for her, returning her to the safety of his arms.

Tears sting my cheeks. "She chose to walk through the shadows with me. She protected me. She lent me her faith to stand on when mine was inadequate." A choked laugh steams the winter air. "Zavaan was afraid of her."

Valor's probing gaze meets mine. The unspoken fear that has plagued him these weeks, I can finally put to death.

"No. We were not defiled. What you see," I gesture to my face, "is what we endured, though Zavaan threatened much. Trent watched over us, ready to intervene if—" I shudder. My words dry up before I can explain last night, but my succinct explanation suffices for now, because the underlying torment in Valor's expression dissipates.

He lowers his mouth to my brow and presses a gentle kiss there, holding me fast in his arms.

CHAPTER FORTY-ONE

VALOR

February 25th

We remained in Halden for two days following the battle to oversee the burning of our dead and that of the Ruphiri. After much debate concerning the inherent risk of the seas at this time of year, it was decided that we would be best served by sailing for Port Veritae upon the stolen Malesiirian ship to sooner deliver our wounded to the hands of physicians and return us to our families. The merchant ship had room aplenty for all our men, horses, and was already provisioned with supplies by the Ruphiri.

When we made to embark the day prior, it was not surprising that Erianna and even Leelah balked upon the gangplank. The women and Trent relayed the story of their capture to Kragorn and I the evening following the battle; thus, I was prepared to bolster Erianna when she set foot aboard what was to have been her prison and refused to take a room belowdeck. Instead, I wrapped her in blankets and held her beneath the wondrous expanse of the night sky. Though she was not made to suffer the worst of what Zavaan could have done her, it is painfully apparent that she did suffer. I sense it in the distance she has placed between herself and her emotions. She has not fully come out from hiding behind her walls yet. I intend to give her all the time and love she needs to do so, even if that means extending the length of our betrothal for a few months, contrary to her original declaration of wedding as soon as we returned.

As I make my way down to the lower deck, I pass Kragorn following Leelah up the stairs for fresh air after her midmorning nap. Kragorn has attended to his martial responsibilities while making good on his vow to never allow Leelah to leave his side again. For once, the fiercely independent woman has not resented his involvement in every aspect of her day. Although none but her husband will ever be allowed to see it, I suspect that she did not come away from her abduction unscathed. In light of this, I could not find the words to express my thanks to Leelah for choosing to be with Erianna and see her safely to the other side of her living nightmare. She understood my faltering words and assured me, "*A sister is born for adversity.* I could not allow Erianna to face that darkness alone." Praise the Almighty, one of the wounds Leelah was dealt was not the loss of her babe. Trent's timely intervention prevented that.

I remain deeply grateful to Trent for his steadfast watch over Leelah and Erianna. Without Trent's aid, I doubt Leelah would have survived. I also doubt that we would have reached Halden in time had he not urged us onward. Over the past several days whenever I must leave her side, Trent immediately steps in to guard Erianna. Their friendship has only deepened following her capture. It gladdens me. However, something about Trent is different. I often find him standing apart, deep in silent contemplation. I suspected that it must be owing to the rift between he and Silla that drove him from Malsihra following her trial. Erianna intimated that she believes there is more to it, perhaps something that has to do with why he was still in Parse Kítaran when we all expected him to be visiting his family after escorting the Tareths and Tirzah home following their stay at the castle. Time will tell, I suppose.

Torvarik wasted no time bringing the Ruphiri that switched sides during the battle to heel. He knew most of the men personally and could vouch for their character. Many found themselves in the same untenable position he did beneath Zavaan's rule of the Ruphiri. Given the opportunity, they welcomed the change in leadership. However, Torvarik informed Erianna that there are those among the renegade Ruphiri that he believes are opportunistic vultures and are not worthy of trust. Rather than allowing him to execute them promptly, Erianna requested that he keep a close watch on all of the renegades and keep secret which men he did not trust.

Today, her reason for doing so will be made apparent.

I find the warlord belowdeck overseeing the Ruphiri while they tend the horses. He sits reclined with his feet propped on the box containing Zavaan's head. Though Erianna finds it unsettling, I grin at his intentional disrespect of our enemy in death. It has become commonplace to find Torvarik with a boot propped on that particular box. He rarely lets it out of his sight and our soldiers have reportedly found him sleeping propped against it, though that is an exaggeration. I think.

"Commander." Torvarik offers me an insouciant greeting.

"Have the Malesiirian soldiers given your Ruphiri any more trouble?"

"Nothing in which I have needed to intervene," he replies off-handedly.

After the bloody brawl of the day prior, his remark lacks reassuring details. But I do not expect the tensions between our two people to be resolved in a matter of days.

"Our impromptu captain," an ancient sailor that resides in Halden who we persuaded to captain the vessel, "believes if the weather holds we will reach Port Veritae in three days."

"So I have heard."

Likely from the experienced and able-bodied Ruphiri Torvarik recommended as a first-mate. Had our queen not insisted upon it because knowledgable sailors were in short supply, we never would have given the Ruphiri the position. Our soldiers declared they would rather drown at sea than take orders from a barbaric Ruphiri. With Ruphiri-dealt bruises still coloring her cheeks, Erianna stalked into the Malesiirian ranks and declared that if *she* could tolerate him as first mate, then we could as well. And that was that.

"My queen would like to speak to the Ruphiri this afternoon, assuming the weather is fair. She would like to interview them one at a time in the captain's cabin."

Torvarik's eyes flash. "Why in there?"

Not wanting to vent my unspent rage upon Erianna when my compassion better serves her, I found myself confiding in Torvarik what Zavaan had planned to do to my beloved. The warlord's rage nearly equalled mine. He knows the particular cruelties Zavaan threatened to inflict upon Erianna were not simply hollow threats. In turn Torvarik confided in me that he has lived in fear for the last decade that Zavaan would turn his perverse gaze upon his own wives. Though the threat from other warlords persists, the terrible evil of Zavaan has ended. We toasted that victory, and I joined him in putting a boot upon Zavaan's head while we did so. In that moment, it became quite clear to me that Torvarik needs the visceral reminder that the ones he loves are forever beyond the reach of Zavaan. I cannot fault him for that.

"My queen says that it is time she personally becomes acquainted with the renegades. She means to discern their character."

Torvarik hums his understanding. "*Královna* is wise. Does she wish me to be present for her interviews?"

"No. She wishes to speak to them alone. Maintain your guard over the rest."

"Very well." Torvarik barks at a Ruphiri who stopped to listen to our conversation. The man returns to shoveling manure. "Why did *Královna* not deliver this message herself?"

I hide a grin. Erianna's nausea should not amuse me, yet somehow she makes seasickness comical. "She is on deck staring at the horizon."

Torvarik chuckles. "Give her my regards."

※ ※ ※

ERIANNA

I occupy the simple chair in the captain's cabin, waiting for the first of the Ruphiri renegades. The room has lost much of its power to cow me since my audacious best friend took up residence here with her husband as a way of mocking the threats the *Vragh* spat at us. My own defiance lacks the brazenness of hers. It has taken the form of me resuming leadership of my people as their conquering Warrior Queen and presenting myself as undaunted as ever. Because of this, the blood I shed in the battle, and beheading the *Vragh*, my soldiers and the Ruphiri renegades view me as an indomitable—almost mythic—warrior.

But Valor sees through my sham. He has seen me startle at the least things. He has caught me looking over my shoulder for the enemy that is no more. And during the night, he muffles my cries within the safety of his arms.

No, I am not yet healed from the terror I endured, but the Almighty delivered me from the hands of my enemy, and I know that His peace will overwhelm the open wounds of fear lingering on my soul.

Valor squeezes my shoulder when a knock sounds upon the cabin door. With a steadying breath, I bid, "Enter."

Torvarik precedes the first of the Ruphiri. "*Královna*. Your renegades, as requested." He backs out of the room and closes the door, leaving Valor and I alone with one who was to be my captor but was perhaps a captive himself. That is what I mean to discover.

Our gaze shifts to the door as it again opens admitting Trent. Without a word he takes up a defensive position along the wall. The Ruphiri glares at him. Trent glares back. Though we found and offered him alternative clothes, he continues to wear the garb of the Ruphiri man he slew absent the cowl. It has cost him in blood, though he has not said so.

I return my focus to the presumed renegade before me. A young man of perhaps eighteen, he is unfamiliar to me, thus he must have arrived on the ship to facilitate the Ruphiri escape. "What is your name?" I ask in the Limban tongue.

"Gren, *Královna*."

"Gren." I lace my fingers together and set them upon my lap. "Tell me about yourself and how you came to be in Malesiir."

Gren glances at Trent then Valor then back at Trent before replying in Limban, "I am a thrall in the house of *Zar* Kinlor. I work on the Bordu coast. When *Kyzar* Zav—"

A growl from Trent makes Gren rapidly shift his response. "When the *Vragh* called upon the clans to supply sailors for his—*umm*... *your* stolen vessels, *Královna*, *Zar* Kinlor sent me and seven other men."

"Why seven?"

He glances behind me where Violet is fastened to the wall. He pales, recognizing my glaive. "*Královna*?"

"Why did *Zar* Kinlor send the eight of you? Why not five or ten?"

Gren shifts on his feet. "Because of clan law. *Zar* Kinlor has a small clan of three hundred and fifty. He sent as many men as needed to pay his debt—one man for ever fifty members of his clan."

There have been no less than two hundred Ruphiri in Malesiir this year. If Gren speaks true, does that mean that there are *ten thousand* Ruphiri in the Spires? Such a number seems unfathomable. I keep my tone unaffected as I ask, "Were all of the Ruphiri that came to Malesiir here because of the clan debt?"

"Oh, *uh*..." Gren looks at the floor, his brows knotted.

"Gren," I insist, "answer my question."

"Are you *Král* Arcto's daughter?"

The question surprises me. "I am. Why do you ask?"

"*Zar* Torvarik says that *Král* Arcto being your father doesn't make you wicked the same as him being *Zar* Orjek's brother doesn't make him a cullion." He winces at his base choice of words. "Sorry. It's just that, I'm worried what you'll do knowing how many Ruphiri live in the Spires."

A smile tweaks my mouth. "*Zar* Torvarik is correct, and you are bright. I do wish to know how many Ruphiri live in the Spires. If you do not wish to tell me, you need not."

He frowns, at war with himself. "*Zar* Torvarik said I must answer you honestly."

Torvarik gave me an easy Ruphiri to read. I sense Gren is as good as he is loyal to his people.

Gren's eyes move over my face, studying the bruises. "They should not have done that to you, *Królovna*. *Zar* Kinlor and *Zar* Torvarik would never have done that. The Ruphiri do not hurt women. They especially don't assault them." His eyes move to the bed bolted to the floor and the trunk beneath it. A fire lights his eyes as they return to me. "I am not at all sorry that Zavaan is dead. The Ruphiri that came with him were mostly from his clan and the rest were from the clan debt. Only the *kyzar* knows exactly how many Ruphiri live in the Spires, but I can tell you there are seventeen clans. It takes at least a hundred and fifty people to make a clan, and the largest clans belong to the *kyzar*, *Zar* Orjek, *Zar* Travor, *Zar* Lyek, and some say *Zar* Torvarik, though no one's ever seen or proved he has more than three hundred people in his clan."

I try to absorb the flood of information, but Gren blasts me with one more figure. "*Zar* Kinlor thinks there are about nine thousand Ruphiri in the Spires."

A breath whooshes out of me. Valor and Trent shift, ready to bring Gren down for an ill spoken word. "Let him out, Trent. He will not harm us," I say in the common language then switch back to Limban. "Thank you, Gren. You may go."

Valor takes a knee at my side, overly protective and anxious for me. "He surprised you. With what?"

"There are seventeen clans and possibly nine thousand Ruphiri in the Spires," I repeat.

"Impossible," Trent interjects.

Torvarik pokes his head into the room. "Ready for the next renegade?"

I quirk a brow at him. "My lessons in Ruphiri continue, I see."

He smiles—half taunt, half approval.

"Don't look at her like that," Trent snarls, causing Valor's eyes to widen.

Torvarik tames his expression. "Calm yourself, Brynjar."

Trent's lips pull back in a feral threat.

"Send the next man," I order.

Torvarik obeys without another glance at Trent.

Five more men, including the current first mate, come through the door to answer my questions. I judge them all to be trustworthy, though none so much as Gren. After the interviews, I will confer with Torvarik to ensure my assessments match his. I hope that with our contrasting angles, we can avoid being duped.

"Do you have a family, Drogh?" I ask my current renegade. A few of the men, him included, have had difficulty looking me in the eye after watching Zavaan harass me and doing nothing to lend me aid.

"*Deh, Královna,*" he says to his boots.

"Do you have more than one wife?"

He shakes his head. "I am not a *zar*."

Are *zars* the only Ruphiri permitted to take multiple wives and *hetaeraz*? I must ask Torvarik. "But you do have a wife?"

"*Deh.*"

"Any daughters?"

"*Deh.*" His head hangs lower.

"Would they be proud of you, Drogh?"

His jaw pulses as he grinds his teeth. "*Na, Královna.* My wife would be ashamed." His countenance turns suddenly fierce, and he leans toward me. "But I promised to return to her. Zavaan would have, well, you saw what he did to those who opposed him. I could not help you."

"What would happen to your family if you died?" I wonder.

"*Zar* Bryvek would assign them a new protector, maybe make my Kynna one of his *hetaeraz*. Marry off my daughter to another clan." The corners of his mouth pull down. "She's of age, but fifteen is too young to become a wife."

"You were forced to choose between protecting the women in front of you—Mistress Tareth and I—or keeping your promise and returning to protect your women. Your family."

"*Deh, deh.*" His palms turned up in supplication, he takes a step closer to me. Trent sees only Drogh's advance and lunges between us, raising his fists. The Ruphiri backs against the door.

Hate exudes from Trent like heat from a fire. His gaze condemns Drogh as he has done them all, though he cannot understand the words exchanged between us. I rise and go to him, a deep worry etching my heart.

Drogh sneers, "The spy judges me though he, too, watched Zavaan beat you?"

I clasp Trent's left hand between both of mine, leaving his right free to reach for his sword should he need to defend. "This man, Drogh, is a warrior and friend. He is riddled with guilt for what happened to Leelah and I. He would have protected us with his life, but he had to wait for the opportune time to free us which meant watching us be mistreated. You changed sides not because it was the right thing to do, but because Zavaan's defeat was imminent. You never intended to intervene. What he did and what you did are not the same."

Drogh's head droops between his shoulders. "Forgive me, *Královna*. I cannot say I would not make the same choice again, though I hate what was done to you. A true Ruphiri would never do that."

I incline my head to Drogh and dismiss him while pondering this repeated assertion that true Ruphiri do not abuse women. It harkens back to the stories Torvarik told me of the Ruphiri origins, forming harems to better protect the women from the dangers of the Spires. However, it contradicts the Limban stories of Ruphiri raiding villages and abducting women and children. I heard of those firsthand in my rare visits to Vortigern, Limba's capital. Where is the truth?

The ship lurches, dropping into a trough then riding up the wave. My stomach matches its movements. Trent braces me when I sway.

"Time to go above deck?" Valor asks, setting his hand between my shoulder blades.

Torvarik enters in time to hear his query. "Indeed. *Královna* looks pale." The warlord's steps do not falter despite the pitching of the ship.

"It seems everyone has their sea legs but I." Proving my point, the ship jolts, seeming to bounce on the water. I stumble, but the three men are all there to keep me from landing on my face. Though their intention was kind, the press of their bodies near mine and the scent of toil embedded in their clothes does me no good. Prickles of fear run down my neck then shoot through my arms, coiling my hands into fists.

I push between Valor and Trent to sit on the edge of the bed, warding them off with my outstretched hand. "Thank you, but stay over there."

Perceiving what I do not say, Valor crouches to the floor. Torvarik takes the seat I vacated, and Trent leans against the door.

I sip the stuffy air, filling my lungs then slowly exhaling. No one moves while I wrangle my anxiety into submission.

"Better?" Valor asks after some moments.

I force a weary smile. "Aye."

Though Valor and Torvarik wear expressions of concern, a deep anguish smudges Trent's countenance. I catch his gaze. "It is not your fault, Trent. You were there when I needed you, when Leelah needed you. I am so grateful to you."

"Don't," he argues. "I should have rescued you."

"It was impossible to free us both. You acted as Leelah's protector and cared for her—"

"Stop, Erianna." He tramples my gratitude with his guilt. "Stop."

Valor attempts to bring Trent around with reason. "She speaks true. You were precisely where the Creator wanted you to be. Had you not been in Parse and available to track the Ruphiri and infiltrate their ranks…"

Trent advances on Valor, stiff-armed and bristling for a fight, though Valor does not rise to give it to him. "You have no idea of what you speak, so don't blame that on the Creator."

Somehow, even more regret floods Trent's tone. It reminds me of what Silla said, wondering why he was in Parse Kítaran when he should have been in Gistin visiting his family. "Trent, why did your plans change? What kept you in Parse?"

He cannot meet my eyes when he says, "I'm going below to check on the prisoners."

When the door clicks behind him, Torvarik relaxes into his chair. He moved with such stealth that I did not realize he had made ready to fight. "He wears a cloak of shame."

"Not only for his impotence to defend our women," Valor agrees.

My fingers worry the coverlet on the bed. "I wish he would hear me. There is naught he could have done."

Torvarik dips his head in agreement but contends, "Knowing that will not erase his guilt."

Valor extends his hand to me. I lace my fingers with his, grateful that I do not have to fear being separated from him again. "His absolution cannot come from you, Beloved. It must come from the Almighty, then he must forgive himself."

CHAPTER FORTY-TWO

VALOR

March 6th

"You asked for it to be a happy time, the next time we arrived at Malsihra." I wave behind us to the friends, soldiers, renegade Ruphiri, prisoners, and the box containing Reuel Zavaan's head packed in snow.

Erianna's gaze sweeps the royal retinue riding toward us. Despite looking worn through, a peace settles upon her shoulders. "It is over, Valor. I am free of him. We have won."

I interpret that as her hearty agreement. Today is a day of rejoicing.

The standard bearers part and come to a halt, allowing King Lorennt to ride into our midst. He draws alongside Erianna, ignoring Reaper's complaints, and pulls her across his saddle into his arms. "Days and nights, Sister. So many days and nights I spent on my knees in prayer." Another stiff-necked king brought to the feet of the Almighty because of Erianna. Malesiir and the Rodiharian line are forever changed because of her.

Erianna clings to him, allowing another of the walls around her emotions to topple. "Your prayers were answered. I am whole, and the *Král Vragh* is dead."

"And Mistress Tareth is safe as well!" Lorennt lowers Erianna to the ground then nudges his mount through the ranks to greet Leelah riding on the fore of Kragorn's saddle. "Nev has had many letters from Tirzah. Your children are well. We sent a courier to inform them of your safe return as soon as we had word of your arrival in Port Veritae."

Leelah turns her face into Kragorn's shoulder, undone by the news.

Kragorn clasps the king's arm. "Thank you, Majesty. We are anxious to be with them."

Our triumphal return to Malsihra draws every man, woman, and child into the streets. They parade with us to the castle, following behind our soldiers. The children throw snowballs at the Ruphiri prisoners though we do not encourage it. Once they are deposited in the city prison—excepting Torvarik who is disguised beneath a Malesiirian cloak—our parade advances upon the castle.

When the iron door of the jail locks into its frame with a resounding clank, I feel it in the marrow of my bones, dissolving burs of tension.

Erianna's thoughts prove apace with mine. "I can finally take a full breath. There is more room in my body without that burden." She tilts her face to the sun and inhales, serenity softening her features. "I wonder if I have ever breathed so freely."

Trumpets blast the report of our victory in volleys of sound that are nearly drowned by the clamor of the castles inhabitants. Shining ribbons wave in the breeze held aloft by jubilant women—noblewomen and servants alike. Men of all social classes clap each other on the back while shouting, "Huzzah!" As we dismount, the people come round us, clasping our arms and celebrating the end of the plague of fear.

A slight serving woman weaves through the dancing mass, shoving to the fore. I glimpse Silla launching herself into Trent's arms and kissing him soundly before they are lost in the crowd. It seems they will sort themselves out after all.

Erianna is latched to my side, overwhelmed by the throng that presses upon her. Caught in the fullness of the moment, I drop to my knees and boost Erianna to my shoulders, lifting her high above the chaos. She wobbles and laughs, finding her balance. Women pass streamers to her hands that are better acquainted with weapons. I spin with her to the thrumming tune of the revelry. Erianna throws her arms to the sky relishing the novelty of freedom.

※※※

March 7th

"You expect me to pardon the Ruphiri prisoners!" Lorennt thrusts to his feet and stomps across the office, reinforcing my distaste for the volatile nature of this sibling relationship. "Did they strike the sense from your head?"

"Careful, Lorennt," I warn in a lethal undertone, unwilling to make light of the bruises liberally smattered on my queen.

He ignores both my tone and the absent honorific. "Answer me, Erianna. How do you see this happening? Do you want me to stand before our people and announce that despite the death and destruction the Ruphiri have caused, I have granted them a pardon because they switched sides in the last fevered moments of a battle? Our people would revolt!"

Erianna casts a sidelong glance at Torvarik who is eyeing the distance between the king and her. Before she can draw breath to answer, Lorennt wields his words again. "Or should I say *my* people? Is that what has caused this insanity? A few men swear fealty to you in your native tongue and you forget the kingdom that rescued you?"

Erianna is simultaneously stricken and affronted by the accusation. Lending credence to Lorennt's fear, Torvarik growls a terse sentence in Limban that forces Erianna to respond in kind.

Speaking over her again, Lorennt says, "Why is that villain in my office? He ought to be imprisoned with the rest of the vile, murderous —"

"Enough!" I surge to my feet. "My queen did not endure capture and torture twice for you to disrespect her and question her loyalties! If you do not begin behaving the king, then I will call you out as a cur."

Lorennt's chest heaves, and his hands twitch toward his sword, but Erianna finally slides her words between his posturing.

"Are we finished, Your Majesty? May we discuss the business of our kingdom like learned men and women or must I get my glaive?"

"Get your glaive," Torvarik taunts, propping his chin in his hand.

"*Jziit*!" Erianna snaps at Torvarik. He curls his long fingers around his mouth, ill concealing the crooked teeth bared in a grin.

"Will you sit, Majesty, and listen to your queen?" None would mistake my words as a request.

Lorennt glares at me but lowers into a chair. He glances about the room. "I see I am outnumbered. Perhaps it is time I choose a Hand to even the odds."

Though spoken in jest to lighten the tone, I treat his request as pertinent. "I agree and have a man in mind."

He considers me then nods. "We shall speak."

"I do not make my recommendation lightly," Erianna begins. "While I was held captive by Zavaan, I witnessed the fear he wielded over his men and realized that many were as captive as I."

Lorennt crosses his arms but does not interrupt.

"When I gave them the opportunity to join our cause and fight against Zavaan, it took very little for them to turn against him."

"What did it take?" Lorennt asks.

"I am coming to that," Erianna stalls. "While aboard the ship, I personally interviewed each renegade, as we have named them, and learned why and how they came to serve Zavaan. What I discovered was that the Ruphiri who turned against him were not in Malesiir voluntarily. They were conscripted."

"Being conscripted does not give them the right to pillage and ravish," Lorennt rebuts, barely restraining a full tirade.

"True," Erianna agrees, pretending he is not a breath from storming about the room in a rage. "Which is why I interviewed the men and have sifted the renegades from Zavaan's loyalists."

"There is a difference?" Lorennt queries.

"Aye. *Zar* Torvarik is here to give an account of his and the renegades time in Malesiir."

"*Zar*?"

"Warlord," Erianna translates. "He is a clan leader among the Ruphiri."

"Very well," Lorennt shifts his attention to Torvarik.

"*Královna* was wise in her discernment of the Ruphiri. She first deduced that I was not the loyal *zar* I portrayed then guessed rightly that I am one of the Almighty's redeemed. It also came to her notice that I did not mistreat or disrespect her or the healer Tirzah as others did." Torvarik speaks in the unhurried, thoughtful manner I have come to expect. It does not garner him favor with Lorennt who prefers his information delivered concisely.

"Had you mistreated either woman you would have been quartered. Erianna, I see no reason—"

"Hush, Lorennt!" Erianna snaps. "I have lost patience with your insolence. Please continue, Torvarik."

Anger sets sparks dancing in her eyes and color high in her cheeks. Though Torvarik is speaking, Erianna has snared my attention. Woe's sakes, she is a sight! My gaze draws her notice. She meets my eyes, a slow flirtatious light displacing the ire in her eyes. Her lips curve in a smile that could make me drag her from this room if the fate of kingdoms were not at stake. I have not kissed her, not how I want to, since she was stolen. She has been skittish, and I would rather cut off my arm than frighten her by taking more than she is ready to give.

Though the way she is looking at me…

After this? She invites with her winter eyes, reviving our wordless conversations that have also been dormant.

A storm crackles in my veins, every muscle going taught with the need to hold her, taste the honey of her kiss. *Or now,* I counter her offer.

She grins but shifts her gaze back to Torvarik. Perhaps she thought I was jesting.

"Which is why Zavaan's rule was repugnant to us true Ruphiri. *Královna* discovered that for herself during her interviews," Torvarik looks to Erianna for confirmation, which she gives with a nod. "Most of us who were conscripted did not condone or participate in the abuse of Malesiirian women. I know those who did and will gladly mark them for death."

"How can I trust you when the death of Zavaan is an opportunity for you?" Lorennt probes. "Or does being the new *kyzar* not appeal to you?"

Erianna enters here, speaking to the plan that sits dark and heavy on the horizon. "Lorennt. You and I both know that with you as the high king, I have become superfluous."

I expect a contradiction from him, but he does not issue it. Interesting.

"The plans that Leer made for you have circled around to land upon me, perhaps where they should have been all along." She takes a fortifying breath and raises her chin. "King Arcto must die, and a new ruler must take the Limban throne."

Lorennt looks between Erianna and Torvarik. "I suppose that leaves me with but one question. Which of you will it be?"

※ ※ ※

March 13th

Wind whips through the largest city square alongside the prison. The nooses hanging from the gallows dance without the weight of a body. Erianna's grip strangles my hand, though none of her subjects would realize the Warrior Queen clad in her full, repaired armor has dreaded this moment.

She vowed never to look upon the face of her tormentor again, but that frozen crate is pried open on Lorennt's order. His newly christened Hand of the King reaches inside and holds it aloft. "Here is King Grandileer's murderer, fought and beheaded by your Warrior

Queen!" The crowd roars their praise at his declaration.

Erianna shifts closer to me while Lorennt's Hand fixes Zavaan's head to a pike next to the gallows. "Well, that steals your glory. It may have been Violet who dealt the cut, but it was you who did all the fighting."

I stroke my thumb across the back of her hand. "Discussing the particulars of a battle is tavern conversation. It doesn't fit within a speech because one must reenact bits of it."

She chuckles.

"Besides, I'll let you steal my glory any day. I have plenty to spare."

Erianna's eye-roll is so pronounced her whole head rolls with it.

"Today, I shall deliver justice to the rest of the Ruphiri, but let us remember," Lorennt says over their renewed cheers. "Let us remember that there is a difference between revenge and justice." That quiets the crowd to a murmur. "Revenge takes our pain and forces it back upon the wrongdoers—and not in equal measure. Justice holds men accountable for their crimes, yes. But justice leaves room for mercy."

The crowd shifts, attempting to sort how the king plans to show mercy to the Ruphiri who have wronged them. In recent memory is the lessened punishment of Silla, which they would not accept as just for these Ruphiri, but the people are mollified from outright protest by Zavaan's head upon a pike. A king who would do that would not completely ignore justice, would he?

Erianna makes a disgruntled noise in her throat. "I suppose I can see why he insisted upon this gruesome display." She nods toward Zavaan's head. "For all the griping you lot make about my bloodthirsty nature, you ought to take a long look at yourselves."

I grin and resist the urge to pinch her side. How long will it take to shake off the sobriety of these hangings and return her to my arms?

"Thus, I have evidence to present to you before we dispense with the judgement." Lorennt unrolls a parchment for effect and begins to read the words inscribed by Torvarik. "According to the clan law of the Ruphiri, any man who has compromised a woman becomes responsible for that woman. He is to wed her and provide for her. If he refuses to do so, he is to be held accountable for his crimes by his clan's warlord and put to death. If the aggression was committed against a child, the punishment is death. According to the clan law of the Ruphiri, the punishment for murder is death. In the case of an unprovoked attack, the one who was attacked or his family may avenge himself upon the attacker without causing intentional death.

The punishment for the unprovoked, willful destruction of property is repayment in full plus a fifty percent interest. The punishment for theft of any kind is repayment in full plus a fifty percent interest."

Lorennt rolls the scroll and passes it to his Hand. "I could continue reading, but as you can see, the laws of the Ruphiri are just and harsher than our own Malesiirian laws." Lorennt paces along the platform and comes to a stop beside Erianna. "Over and again, Queen Erianna and I heard from several of the Ruphiri that no true Ruphiri would ever harm a woman. They found the abuse of her contemptible and offensive. Then why do stories abound in the kingdom of theft, murder, and ravishment at the hands of the Ruphiri? Because those men willingly served the murderer Reuel Zavaan, the former Chief of the Ruphiri." Lorennt gestures to that obscene sight. "But what of the several Ruphiri who detested Zavaan and his treatment of Malesiir's people?"

Lorennt's Hand extends the parchment to him once more. "According to the clan law of the Ruphiri, every clan must remit one man for every fifty clan members to serve at the behest of the *kyzar* in whatever way he requires." He lowers the parchment. "Conscription. That is why some of the Ruphiri are in Malesiir against their conscience and against their honor. *Zar* Torvarik, step forward." Out of the shadows beyond the platform, Torvarik joins Lorennt in his full battle armor. "Here is the first of several Ruphiri to fight at our side, to turn against the corruption of Zavaan that polluted his people, and aid us in routing the enemy from our kingdom." Lorennt claps Torvarik on the shoulder. "He led the charge on that day of battle in Halden Harbor alongside Commander Ironforge and convinced many of his fellow Ruphiri to renounce Zavaan and fight on the side of Malesiir. This man is honorable. This man is just. This man—"

"Nearly severed my arm," I mutter to Erianna. Her fingernails bite my palm.

"Is the man that Malesiir recognizes as the next *Kyzar* of the Ruphiri. *Kyzar* Torvarik."

Torvarik scans the crowd. "Malesiir has suffered at the hands of Reuel Zavaan. The Ruphiri have as well. But no more!" He shouts, pointing to the pike and inciting a resounding cheer from the people. "To honor the Ruphiri law and the laws of the great kingdom of Malesiir, I shall ensure that Malesiir is recompensed for all that was stolen plus fifty percent interest. Until my true Ruphiri and I return to the Spire Mountains, we shall begin working to pay our nation's debt to Malesiir. This day, I swear it to you. The Ruphiri will no longer be a threat to Malesiir. We shall be allies, working together for our mutual good. But first, the wicked must be brought to justice!" The answering shout pounds in my bones.

"He has the qualities of a great leader," Erianna whispers. "I am impressed."

"So impressed that you aspire to become his third wife?" I taunt.

Her gaze slowly finds mine, promising dismemberment. "Do not cross me today, Churlish Oaf."

King Lorennt gives the order that the crowd has been awaiting. "Bring forth the prisoners!"

Erianna grips my hand and fixes her gaze past the justice of today toward the hope of tomorrow.

CHAPTER FORTY-THREE

ERIANNA

April 29th

A spring breeze tickles my face. I sigh into it, watching the sun dance over verdant fields. White clouds billow high over the valley in spectacular plumes.

"What do you see, my Love?" I lower my gaze to my lap where Valor's head rests. But his contented eyes are not on the grandeur spread out around us.

"Only you, Beloved."

I bend to kiss his brow, threading my fingers in the tawny locks that Leelah cut in preparation of our wedding tomorrow. His smile as I pull back dazzles me.

"Will you tell me a story, Valor?"

"What story?"

"Tell me what it was like, what you felt, when you dreamed of my eyes." I was too frightened of the future in light of my past to receive what he wanted me to know when he first spoke of his dreams to me. But now, I want to know.

He looks through me straight into my heart. "That first night, I went to bed discouraged. I felt alone. Miserable. I watched the soldiers I commanded find company in the arms of tavern women—perfect strangers that they would never see again. I knew I did not want that for myself, that it would not provide me with what I truly wanted."

"What did you want?"

"A friend. Someone with whom I could share my life. I lost so many people when I was young that I ached for my other half, the one that would stay by my side no matter what came. So that is what I asked for. I prayed that if the Creator had formed a woman for me, He would bring her to me. I wanted to find her so badly."

I remember that loneliness. Until Valor came into my life, I did not realize how deep my longing for companionship went.

"As He sometimes does, He revealed what I asked for in a dream." Valor smiles, stretching out his hand to touch my face, his thumb tracing the soft skin beneath my eye, perhaps assuring himself that the intangible has been made tangible. "I saw the most captivating clear blue eyes ringed with sapphire. There was such love in them. And understanding. When I woke, I knew. I knew He had made my other half, I only needed to find her, to find you, Beloved.

"I chased you across Malesiir every single day. When my search proved fruitless during the day, I longed to lay down on my bed each night so that I could find you in my dreams. Though I never saw your face, I saw your eyes express a thousand things. I saw them dance with laughter. I saw them spark with irritation. I saw your playfulness," he grins, and I laugh. He continues softer, "I even saw your eyes shine like stars in the night sky, as if we had just made love. I learned that you were compassionate before I ever met you. That you would pursue justice with me even though it was hard. I admired your character, because I had seen all of it in your eyes.

"Then you were no longer a dream. You were real. But how we met was all wrong, to my way of thinking. None of what happened in that first month made sense to me. I could not accept that you were my Winter-eyes."

"Because of my past?" I ask.

"No, Beloved. Because you were mine, but you were not mine. I could not see a clear path to a life with you, and I was frightened that if I did accept who you were to me, I would lose you, that I would be powerless to hold on to you. But none of it mattered in the end. Because I fell in love with you. With all of you. I saw your beauty and your flaws, your character and your heart. I knew that one day, somehow, you would be mine. Because you were my other half."

Valor's brow furrows. "It undid me to think I had lost you. But that brokenness was necessary. It made me realize that I had put my hope in you, in a future with you. I could not make sense of anything then. Thankfully, the Spirit of Truth guided me through that darkness. He restored my hope to where it should have been all along—in Him."

I twine my fingers with Valor's. "Even our brokenness had meaning."

"It was part of His plan all along," Valor agrees. "Just as bringing us together was part of His plan, too."

"That is a good story, my Love."

"Stories of redemption are the best ones, my winter-eyed Girl."

※ ※ ※

April 30th

"Leelah, what is taking so long? It is as if you have never laced up a gown before," I complain as my friend takes her sweet time adjusting the laces of my wedding gown until they are perfect.

"Nearly done." Leelah forms the loops for the bow then tucks the ends beneath the fabric. "Mercy, it seems someone is anxious for her wedding day." She arches an eyebrow at Nev who giggles.

"Didn't you predict just that happening?" Nev taps her lips. "Yes, I recall you saying that she would be marrying Valor before you had your babe because she would be so anxious to be his wife."

"Actually, what I said was—"

"That will do!" I interrupt Leelah.

Mother Celiea joins in the laughter at my blushing expense. How Valor and Lorennt managed it I will never know, but they made it possible for all the people I love to be here to celebrate this day with us. What a stir our royal entourage made entering Parse Kítaran the day before last! Leelah opened her home to everyone as only she could, orchestrating the thing so that everyone had a place to sleep and meals to eat. She has thrived amid the domestic chaos, happily playing general of her domain. Kragorn has been as good as his word and has not left her side since they were reunited two months past. Well, excepting those two days when he and Trent rode into Chishelm to have a word with General Kannik. They were despicably stingy with the details of their "discussion," but the result was that the new fort at Chishelm required a new resident general. Lorennt accepted Kragorn's request that he be given the post to keep him near home.

"All set?" Tirzah pops her head into Leelah's bedroom. "Oh, Erianna! You look lovely! Valor will be beside himself."

"Aye, he will," Leelah agrees, linking her hands on top of her rounded belly. "And so will you."

I give her a pointed look. "What did you do?"

She gives me that mountain lion smile of hers. "I worked what amounts to magic and made Parse Kítaran the location of your wedding. You are welcome."

I grin. "You did, at that."

Lorennt and Kragorn bustle us out the door and load us into the carts that carry our large party through the valley toward the split log chapel overlooking the river.

"Leelah!" I exclaim looking at the tables covered with homespun cloths and overflowing with sprays of wildflowers. Exactly like the fellowship meal, the people of Parse Kítaran have all contributed to my wedding feast. It looks as if every person in the valley has turned out to celebrate my wedding. To ensure that everyone who wanted to attend could, blankets dot the hillside while children play amid it all. An arch of tree boughs adorned with ribbons in a riot of colors forms the centerpiece at the top of the steps leading into the chapel. The doors are opened wide at our approach.

My heart bursts into flight as my groom steps forth to claim me.

The next moments pass in a brilliant haze as Lorennt and Mother Celiea kiss my cheeks. Nev hugs me tightly with happy tears in her eyes. Father takes my arm and walks with me toward the chapel. He kisses my brow, and places my hand in Valor's.

Atop a verdant hill beneath the clearest sky, Valor pledges himself to me and I to him. In a beautiful symbol of all that he vows to give me, Valor unfastens his mantle and drapes it over my shoulders, covering me with his love.

"My beloved Erianna. This day, I give you all that is mine. I give you my name. My protection. My love. For the rest of my days. My life bound to yours evermore."

In a like manner, I take my blue scarf from my waist and tie it around his sword arm. I wind the length of the scarf slowly around. "*I am my lover's, and he is mine… Place me like a seal over your heart. Wear my love like a seal around your arm.*" I tie the scarf and tuck the ends under itself. "All that I am is yours. My love, respect, and devotion. My life bound to yours evermore."

Then he kisses me. Valor Ironforge. My warrior. My love. My husband. I twine my arms around his neck as he lifts me off my feet, holding me to him.

While our friends and family clap and cheer, Valor whispers his love in my ear. "My bride. My sweetest friend. My beautiful idiot."

I giggle.

He kisses me again. "You are mine, Erianna Ironforge."

※ ※ ※

* * *

The wedding stretches into a glorious celebration with dancing and laughter. Anders whirls each of Kragorn's daughters about the hillside and declares them the best partners he has ever danced with. In spite of everything, a smitten Trent is doing his very best to convince a particular woman of his attachment. Their match seems almost certain at this point.

Of my groom's own interest, there can be no question. He is besotted with his bride. He tells me so every other minute, keeping color in my face for most of the day.

"Valor!" I exclaim after a particularly blush eliciting murmur.

His troublesome half smile makes an appearance. "Wife?" He draws out my fresh title, savoring the single syllable as it falls from his lips.

I arch a brow, resisting the way only a word from him can dissolve my pique.

He draws me closer as we dance, his voice rumbling through me. "You are my wife now, and I swear that you will never question my attraction to you."

My heart races at his nearness. "Which I should interpret to mean you will share every thought that passes between your ears?"

"That's right, Beloved. I have kept so many to myself for so long."

I give him a playfully appraising look then declare, "Well, I suppose that is only fair. Share as you will, Husband."

He twirls me over the spring grass, dancing with me for as long as I wish.

Later in the day, I catch Anders and Trent casting glances our direction and see money change hands. Curious, I leave Valor speaking with my family to investigate.

"What are you two about?" I ask, slipping up behind them.

They startle, trading guilty looks.

"Nothin' at all, Queen Ironforge," Anders says cheekily. "Just go on back to your new husband."

"There's no hurry," Trent argues. "Stay and talk with us a while."

"What is this about?"

"Nothing," they chime.

"Let me make this simple." I step between them and point across the gathering. "Do you see that devastatingly handsome warrior standing right there? Well, he is my husband and if you two do not confess straightaway, then I am going to start crying and tell him that you have ruined my wedding day."

Anders is downright terrified. "It was all Trent's idea."

"It was not," he argues.

"Last chance," I offer as Valor looks my way with a tender smile.

Anders crosses his arms. "We were simply speculating on how long you and Valor intended to stay and celebrate before, *uh,* leaving."

I gasp. "You were betting on when we would *leave*?"

Trent looks chagrined. "Something like that."

I am tempted to tell Valor what they were wagering about, but a better thought comes to mind. "Let me tell you what is going to happen since you have been found out." My tone allows no room for argument. "As it happens, I have no interest in preparing meals for the next few days. Thus, you will deliver the noon meal and evening meal to my home for the next three days as recompense for gambling at my wedding. Are we clear?"

"Aye, Majesty," they mumble like penitent children.

"Carry on then," I say and saunter toward Valor.

I brush off his unasked question with a wink. "I will tell you later."

My heart is filled by having all the people I love gathered in one place. Here. In this special valley where my life began anew.

Valor draws me aside in the golden hours of late afternoon. With his arms about me, he whispers in my ear, "Come away with me, my Beloved, my Bride."

"It is not yet night," I point out.

"Exactly." His lips brush my ear. My neck. "I mean to know my bride for the first time in the light of day without a shadow in sight."

Valor's considerate declaration washes over me like a wave of joy.

Everything is new.

This day is ours alone.

We slip away quietly without the traditional send-off. Just he and I. Walking hand in hand along the river, the silence between us neither empty nor unbroken, we cherish the companionship we have found. All our winding paths have brought us here, though I could not have plotted the journey even given a map. It took the foresight of One far mightier than Valor or I to bring us to this moment, this union of our lives at which everyone marvels. Though for us, we knew long, long ago that it was not by happenstance that a broken princess and a lonely warrior found the other holding the missing half of themself.

We follow a stream along a gravel road and cross over a little bridge. At the fence, we pause to pat Granite and Sacha. With Valor's arm around my waist, we ascend the steps into our home.

This past month he spent a few days here without me, making his home ours, though I do not know what that means beyond moving some of my belongings here. "I am curious to see what you have changed," I say as he unlocks the door.

He pauses, gripping the door handle. "I cannot take credit for all that was done. Leelah and her merry band appeared on my doorstep yesterday to give the place a thorough cleaning and stock the pantry. My improvements were less… I wanted to make our home comfortable for you so I spoke with Queen Celiea and…" He shrugs. "Why don't I show you?"

"If I did not know you better, I might think you are nervous," I tease.

He huffs a laugh. "Then it is good you know me better."

Valor leads me over the threshold into the pine cabin. From the first, this place felt like a haven. I think it felt that way because it was decidedly his. Like stepping into the safety of his arms, his home felt like an extension of himself. Safe. Tucked away from the weight of the world. Warm and wonderful.

Walking into it now though, it feels like it belongs to me, too. "Oh, Valor." The simply furnished cabin has been softened with my favorite sorts of belongings. So attentive was he to the details that it could have been me who arranged them. Before the riverstone hearth is a plush rug with the pair of arm chairs set to either side of it. A table sits beside one of the chairs boasting a stack of new books tied with a ribbon. Nearby, a basket overflows with soft blankets. There are flowers on the hewn table and beautiful dishes stacked neatly on a shelf in the cupboard. The other shelf holds jars of tea, loaves of fresh bread, and, if I am not much mistaken, a box of cookies. But something else is different besides the obvious. The whole place is brighter than usual, even without the lanterns being lit. I turn in a circle trying to understand how he achieved that, then I look up.

Past the rafters, the planked roof above has been whitewashed. It lends the cabin a feeling of being open and airy despite its modest size.

I wander across the main room into the single bedroom still looking up. The whitewashing carries into here as do the added comforts. A new wardrobe containing my belongings stands against the wall opposite his along with a pile of pillows and new linens on the bed.

I turn to my husband who leans against the doorframe watching me. "Valor, it is perfect. The whitewashing must have taken you ages to do."

"I never wanted our home to feel dark to you."

His overly simplistic explanation reveals how well he knows me. There are no lengths to which he will not go to care for my heart. For the rest of my days beginning with this one, I dedicate myself to giving my all to Valor so that I can love him as well as he loves me.

I gaze upon my husband, admiring his steadfast character, the consideration he unwaveringly shows to others, his unshakeable faith. His smile grows wide, and his eyes shift toward silver as he watches me watching him. A flash of nervous energy makes me look around the room once more. He does not rush my second perusal, letting me adjust to the changes between us at my own pace. The sun has dipped lower in the sky, slanting into the room through the glass window. It gilds the air we breathe in a golden light. The plush, white linens on the bed are a soft butter yellow, warm and inviting. Our bedroom seems transplanted inside a sunbeam. My gaze returns to Valor, noting how the light makes his eyes shine and the grey at his temples glitter. He eases away from the threshold, leaving the door ajar, when my eyes beckon him closer.

I open my arms to him wanting us to become one in every way.

Valor's lips meet mine taking all the love I feel for him. His unreserved passion steals my breath, but that hardly matters because I have his breath. The taste of him is on my tongue, overwhelming my senses. All I know is Valor. His fingers sink into my hair, sending warmth spiraling through me. I feel the breadth of his shoulders then frame the hard line of his jaw while his touch kindles my ardor.

When my hands find their way beneath his shirt, he breaks our kiss long enough to seize the linen collar and lift it over his head, dropping it to the floor. I run my hand from the hollow of his throat downward, tracing hard lines of muscle and scarred skin. My fingers stop shy of the waistband of his pants, returning to his shoulder.

"Take your time, Beloved," he encourages with a kiss that begins on my lips, moves to my cheek, my jaw, my neck, then lingers on my exposed collar bone.

I reach for the laces of my wedding gown needing less between Valor and I, but my trembling fingers will not cooperate. I turn my back to Valor, putting the task to him. "Help me with the laces. I cannot do it. My fingers are shaking."

"You think mine are not?" His wry laugh blows across the base of my neck as he sweeps the curtain of my hair aside then places a kiss on my nape that makes me shiver with anticipation. His admission of nervousness takes the edge off mine. He frees the knot hidden at my lower back then meticulously loosens the laces until my dress slides from my shoulders, pooling at my feet. Before I can reconsider, I remove my undergarments also. Valor's whooshed exhale tickles my skin. His calloused hands trace feather soft lines on my bare shoulders, my back, and hips.

I take a deep breath. In a smooth motion, I turn to face my husband and reveal every imperfect inch of me, hoping that he is not overly disappointed. After all, he has waited for me for a decade. If ever there was a moment for him to regret that decision, it might be this one.

When I find the courage to meet his gaze, for once, I cannot interpret the emotions raging there.

"You are…" His throat bobs. His voice shakes. "Are you mine? Truly?" For the first time, he seems uncertain of the claim he laid on me long ago. His eyes caress me then return to mine. "You are my wife."

My chin wobbles as I nod, not because he is displeased, but because of the undeniable awestruck wonder filling his tone.

His palm holds my cheek while his thumb caresses my lower lip. With a conviction that unravels my critical perspective of myself, Valor asserts, "You are the most beautiful sight my eyes have ever beheld."

I smile into his palm before stepping into his waiting arms. Mine wind about his neck. I tilt my head back to see his eyes. "Promise me something?"

"Anything," he fervently whispers.

"Hold me, my Love. Hold me and do not let me go."

The silver of his eyes turns molten. "I swear it."

CHAPTER FORTY-FOUR

VALOR

June 1st

I reread the missives then compare them to the map, ensuring everything is in order for our journey tomorrow. After a glorious month spent in Parse Kítaran, Erianna and I, along with King Lorennt's new Hand and his wife, will set out across Malesiir in a lengthy tour of the kingdom. I will be formally introducing him to my contacts in all the provinces to ease the transition as I step down from my role serving Malesiir. This tour will also give Erianna one final chance to see all of the kingdom that embraced her as its queen before we sail for Limba at the end of the summer.

As Boldizar predicted, our future has roots in Limba. Malesiir cannot ignore the threat of that treacherous kingdom and the equal threat of the Ruphiri Nation. Torvarik must return to the Spires to unite the Ruphiri under his rule, though with sixteen other *zars* vying for the title of *kyzar* and Torvarik's year long absence, it may be impossible. Plans have also been made to overthrow King Arcto and, at least temporarily, seat Erianna upon the Limban throne with the aid of Malesiir. There is much uncertainty in Limba's future. Since Erianna is unlikely to bear children, the Vrock line will end with her. What then will become of Limba?

When I hear the bedroom door open I set aside the responsibilities that weigh heavy on us for a few more hours. Erianna crosses the room, rubbing the sleep from her eyes. "You did not wake me this morning."

"I wanted to let you sleep. You will not have the opportunity again for sometime."

"Then I thank you." She climbs into my lap, taking her time to fully awaken. With a sigh, she snuggles into my chest.

I pull her legs across my lap, smoothing the fabric of my shirt that she has taken to wearing when we are at home. Seeing her in it has not ceased to affect me. *My wife.* She is mine.

"A letter arrived for us that I thought you would like to open." I pass her the thick, sealed pages.

She reads the direction then squeals, "Tis from Hellah!" And precedes to tear into it like a gift. Her eyes dart across the page reading to the end before she winces and says, "She wanted to attend our wedding. She said she will be 'terribly disappointed' if we are wed without her bearing witness."

I wince too. My adoptive mother makes showing her 'disappointment' an art form. "I will never hear the end of this. She is going to require a lengthy apology, gifts, and a visit from us when we pass through on our way to… What has put that calculating gleam in your eyes?"

Erianna meticulously lines up the pages along their creases then folds the letter and sets it aside. "Hellah mentions that she is looking for an assistant to help her with the apothecary shop and to treat the patients with lesser illnesses."

"Are you thinking of changing occupations, my Warrior Queen? We do have a looming campaign, you know."

She does not offer the expected rejoinder. Whatever she is considering must be quite serious. "Actually, I was wondering if Tirzah would be interested in apprenticing to Hellah. The arrangement would surely be beneficial to both of them."

Her sobriety is justified. "Do you think proposing this to Tirzah is for the best or that she would even accept given what has happened? Perhaps before, it would have been the perfect arrangement, but now…"

"I think it is not for us to decide. However, I suspect she would want to know of this opportunity. The timing may be providential."

Trusting my wife's instincts in this more than my own, I advise, "Then you ought to present the idea to Tirzah tomorrow and write to Hellah before we leave."

Erianna agrees then curls into me. When I kiss her hair, she angles her head requesting a kiss on her cheek too. She smiles contentedly when I oblige.

Even knowing her as well as I did before we wed, it surprised me how much she yearns for physical affection. She wants me to hold her and kiss her and simply be near her, constantly. When I commented on it, she was embarrassed, but I assured her it was no hardship for me. It makes me realize how wretched the years following her mother's death were, when the only familial touch she received came in the form of a fist. I wonder if that is why she is so hungry for affection. Daily, I make a conscious effort to show her my love through these small, affectionate touches that mean much to her. In the past month, I have had the pleasure of witnessing her confidence grow as a result of our marriage.

Erianna reciprocates my kisses, placing hers on my shoulder. "This is what I have longed for the most."

"What have you most longed for, Beloved?"

She settles her hand over my heart. "Being known by you."

"I thought that was what you were most afraid of."

"It was," she affirms.

"Then?"

Erianna shrugs. "I am a contrary woman."

I chuckle, wrapping my arms around her where she fits perfectly. "Aye, you are. Beautifully contrary."

My wintry-eyed wife smiles into me then sets her lips to mine. I relish the taste of her, the intimacy that goes much deeper than what is physical. That thought makes me smile.

"What?" She asks, arching that scarred brow of hers.

"Should I be offended that it is not the lovemaking you most longed for?"

She pinches my side. "Do not be a churl when I am being sweet."

"You are right. I apologize."

She hums her acceptance.

"You being sweet is such a rare occurrence that I had best savor it." I laugh at her outrage and catch her punitive fingers as they aim for my side. But the peace has been disturbed and is not restored until I wrestle her to the rug before the hearth, winning our playful scuffle.

"Now then," I spread myself atop her while she giggles. "Yield, you bloodthirsty little imp."

My wife smiles up at me. "I yield."

I am astonished. "You do?"

She threads her fingers into my hair, pulling my mouth down to hers. "To you, Valor, I yield my life, my body, and my heart for the rest of my days. But only to you, Valor. I shall only yield to you."

Epilogue

TORVARIK

August 20th

The sea cooperates this morning, but that does not mean it will be accommodating for the month-long journey to the Commonwealth. But I pray that it does.

I cannot know how dire the situation in the Spires will be by the time I reach the foothills. It was a year ago that I sailed away from the stone strewn beach leaving all that I loved behind in a desperate attempt to free them from Zavaan's oppressive rule. With our *kyzar* rotting in a shallow grave, the *zars* are undoubtedly in the throes of a power struggle.

My only hope is that Annekeh has managed to defend our mountain from assault. She is capable and well versed in its defenses, but if the *zars* mounted a systematic attack…

The rock of the ship sprays brine in my face. I white-knuckle the railing on the forecastle, praying away the miles that separate me from my family. *Be their fortress, Almighty Warrior. Be their defender. Guard their earthly bodies as surely as you guard their eternal souls.*

I pull open my eyes when my honed senses alert me to the presence of someone at my side. It chafes that the commander possesses such preternatural stealth that I did not become aware of him until he was upon me.

"How fares your wife?" I ask the question that I long to be able to answer of my own.

He braces his feet wider as the swells of the sea lift the boat then drop it into a trough. "She is rueing the day we decided to go by sea rather than land."

I smirk, imagining the curses spewing from the diminutive woman. "Peeling the paint from the walls, is she?"

"Tirzah has threatened to scour her mouth with soap if she does not sanitize her language."

"And?"

Valor grins at the expanse of sea. "Erianna opted to curse in Limban. Tirzah opted to prepare a sleeping draught for her."

I find myself amused in spite of my worries for my family. "Then *Královna's* mouth will certainly need scouring. Limban curses are worse than the common ones."

"Regarding that," the commander turns to me, "I have a request to make of you."

I meet his gaze across my shoulder.

"Would you help Erianna teach me the Limban language? I would like to be passably conversant by the time we reach the kingdom."

He already knows that the language is a challenging one, thus I do not bother cautioning him. "If you wish."

"Good. Let's begin immediately. There is something I would like to tell my wife later."

The phrase he wants translated makes me chuckle. "When she turns her nasty little glaive on me for teaching you such things, I cannot be held accountable if I toss it overboard."

"Just climb the mast," he points upward. "She will never follow you up there with the ship swaying."

"Already made contingency plans for yourself?"

"You live in the Spires where being house bound must be common during winter. You cannot tell me you don't have a few places to hide from your wives."

I wryly admit, "There are places in my mountain where not even Annekeh can find me."

That perceptive look appears in his eyes, the sort that makes me take a step back lest he learn something I cannot allow him to deduce. He lands precariously close. "Annekeh is the only wife of whom you speak."

Because she is the only one that matters. "Because she is my favorite."

I sense the questions he ponders and ready my answers.

"Do you not feel conviction for having more than one wife?"

My answer is practiced and bored. "The ancient King David of the Holy Texts—a man after the heart of the Creator—had many wives and concubines. Why should I also not avail myself of the benefits of being *zar*?"

Valor disapproves of my response, but he is not sharp as Erianna would be. "It was not the Creator's intent for King David to take many wives. His lust for women led him so far astray that he committed murder."

This I know. Annekeh made the same argument when I began building my harem all those years ago. "It is not my lust for women that led me to take additional wives and *haeteraz*. I built my harem to fulfill my obligation to protect my clan and increase my strength as a *zar*."

He shakes his head. "I will not let this be a point of contention between us, Torvarik, but I will tell you that I disagree with you."

All this talk does nothing to turn my thoughts away from Annekeh. I caress my hand over the wind smoothed railing, imagining it is the creamy skin of my first wife. Thoughts of her inevitably lead me to memories of the round faces of our children and of our third child whom Annekeh was not yet delivered of when I departed. Fear works my guts into knots. *She survived the birthing. I would know if she did not. I am certain I would feel it.*

My vision resolves upon the stern of the ship ahead of us bearing a portion of the horses that will carry us across Limba including the noble beast I appropriated from Zavaan. Besides the political maneuver of taking the *kyzar's* horse as my own, the stallion is of exceptional stock.

Off the stern of our ship is the rest of our fleet ferrying an excess of a three thousand Malesiirian soldiers and half as many horses along the trade route to the Commonwealth where we will make port to resupply before continuing on to Limba. The size of *Královna's* army and need for secrecy were the deciding factors that saw us traveling by sea rather than land.

Though the Malesiirian king was generous with the resources he devoted, launching an attack against a kingdom with an army of a three thousand is more of a strategic endeavor than full scale war, yet that is the task before us. The conquest of Limba has begun. Thus, it is time I reveal what I have kept secret these many months.

"Commander, there is sensitive topic I must discuss with *Královna*. I hope you can advise me how best to begin the conversation."

Valor lends me his full attention, perhaps thinking it has to do with our discussion of my harem. In a circuitous way, it does. "It was not paranoia or happenstance that caused King Arcto to become suspicious of Queen Illyanna."

The wind claws at us as the ship bounces on the white peaks of successive waves. "Erianna's mother?" Deep grooves bracket Valor's squinted eyes. "We know that she was one of the redeemed, a judge during the time of the purge. Arcto named her a witch to excuse murdering her."

I map the trajectory of each word before I speak it. The fate of Limba and the Ruphiri rests upon what *Královna* and her commander do with this information. They must not destroy what was begun long ago. "Aye, Queen Illyanna was one of the redeemed, but that is not why Arcto lost faith in her."

With his wife's heart at risk, Valor abandons the camaraderie that has developed between us and becomes solely her protector, squaring off against me. "Speak plainly, Torvarik."

"I know why Illyanna was murdered."

A Note from the Author

Dear Readers, thank you for spending time with me in the world of the Redemption Saga. I hope you were pleased with the conclusion of Erianna and Valor's tale. What a journey it has been getting to their happily ever after! What began in my mind as a trilogy has become an entire saga with multiple stories springing up from this fictional realm. I cannot wait to share them all with you! Though the epilogue concluded with the perspective of the mysterious, somewhat antihero Torvarik, before we can approach his story, we must travel back a little ways and discover what precisely Trent has been up to. We will see him in the next novel cast alongside his heroine. If you are sad to bid farewell to Erianna and Valor, I can tell you that we've not seen the last of them. They have much work to do in the Kingdom of Limba with Torvarik. If you'd like to be the first to know about teasers, bonus chapters, and books I recommend, subscribe to my website at www.elcrossbooks.com.

If you enjoyed this story, would you please consider leaving a review? It is the best way you can support me as an author and help fellow readers find their next great read.

Thank you!

About the Author

Erin L. Cross is a wife, homeschooling mother, author, and part-time landscaper. A native to Florida, she divides her time between reading, writing, and turning her suburban backyard into a homestead. Being a life-long learner, she is not satisfied until she has exhaustively researched a subject of interest.

This habit proved fruitful in fully developing the fictitious yet historically inspired medieval world and characters in her first novel *Redemption's Pursuit*, a story that was ten-years in the making. On that solid foundation, she dove into writing The Redemption Saga, a six book story arc that will conclude in 2023.

Erin's deepest desire is that in whatever she does, she will do it to the the best of her ability, to the glory of God.

www.ingramcontent.com/pod-product-compliance
Lightning Source LLC
LaVergne TN
LVHW041105080826
845145LV00007B/1690